Song of Destiny

Song of Destiny

Paul Legler

To Julie, who always had faith in me.

First edition: September 1, 2013

Printed in the United States of America

Printed by
North Star Press of St. Cloud, Inc.
P.O. Box 451
St. Cloud, MN 56302

www.northstarpress.com North Star Press – Facebook North Star Press – Twitter

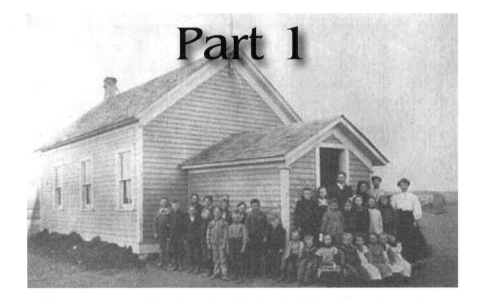

Part 1

1

November 2001

M Y GRANDFATHER USED TO SAY that the dust of the plains settles into your flesh and bones and stays with you the rest of
your life. Sometimes that can be a blessing and sometimes
it can be a curse. On this morning, the dust weighed me down. I had
slept fitfully and my mind was clouded. For a moment I struggled to
recall why. Then I remembered what I faced that day.

It was 5:30 a.m. and still dark outside, but I could hear the foot-
falls of my fellow monks bustling down the hallway past my door. The
monks rose early at St. John's Abbey. They were emerging from their cells
to prepare the communal breakfast before morning prayers. I was not
going to attend, but I stopped by Brother Michael's cell to say goodbye.
His door was open, as usual, and he was sitting peacefully in his chair
by the window reading the Bible. I was almost hesitant to interrupt him.

He smiled when he saw me and offered me a chair. I declined
with a shake of my head.

"So you're off then," he said.

"I have a lot of matters to attend to. I may be gone for a week
or so."

"How are you feeling?"

"Terrible," I replied. Stunned first by love and now by death,
what else could I say?

Brother Michael rose and crossed the floor. "Just remember that
you are not alone. I'll pray for you and Jake," he said and he lightly
touched my shoulder as I left. "May peace be with you."

I felt a brisk cold wind coming off Lake Sagatagan, the air felt
damp, and leaves scattered across the monastery garden as I walked out-

side to the common garage. Before I left, I checked to make sure there was a shovel in the trunk of the car. Snowstorms can strike suddenly in this part of the country. I hoped I wouldn't need it, but you never know.

It was still dark when I hit Interstate 94 and headed west. I had a two-and-a-half-hour drive to the North Dakota border and then three hours more to reach the ranch. As the day began to break and the first light appeared, the Minnesota countryside slowly began to reveal itself—rolling hills dotted with lakes and ponds, groves of trees, and scattered farms. Just past Sauk Centre, I counted twenty-four silos, rising up from the horizon as if trying to bridge the gap between heaven and earth. A few miles farther, I passed a turkey farm. A semi-truck was backed-up to the door of the barn, and I saw two men tossing turkeys into the rear, wings flapping in a fruitless attempt to escape their fate.

This area is picturesque much of the year, but on this late fall day with the sun hidden by a low ceiling of clouds, it was simply bleak and brown. I stopped in Alexandria for coffee at the Holiday Store and impulsively grabbed a pre-packaged bologna sandwich to eat later in the day. My mother used to make them for me as a child, with thick slices of German bologna on home-baked bread and a large smear of soft butter.

I was soon back on the highway. Just past Fergus Falls the hills began to diminish, and by the time I was twenty-five miles east of Fargo, they disappeared altogether. The highway here crosses the Red River Valley, formed by the ancient glacial Lake Agassiz, and it is numbingly flat. Once I got fifty miles or so further west into North Dakota, a few hills appeared on the horizon, and I entered the true Great Plains. The amount of annual rainfall the land receives declines with each mile west, the landscape is less green, the crops become thinner, the hay is poorer, the grass more meager, and the farming and ranching become more and more precarious.

Twenty miles west of Valley City I passed the exit to Eckelson. There is nothing distinctive about it, no signs other than the green highway sign marking the exit and a smaller blue sign indicating "No Services."

Few people take this exit, only an occasional farmer going to Jamestown or Valley City, or a truck filled with grain heading to the elevator. Yet, for me, there are memories attached to this area so strong that whenever I pass here it is like tumbling into a vertiginous pit.

Just north of this exit, old U.S. Highway 10, which was once a major highway running from east to west across the country, parallels Interstate 94. A few miles west on that highway a coulee runs north to south, and if you are traveling west on Highway 10 the road climbs over a small rise before descending to the coulee. At that spot twenty-three years ago, my brother Jake—a former high school honor student and star athlete, 4-H Club President, Vietnam Veteran, and a winner of the Bronze Star for valor—driving his blue 1969 Ford LTD, with his friend Spencer in the passenger seat, high, laughing, and counting some $8,000 in cash, came over that rise and slammed on his brakes, tires screeching to a halt before two Barnes County Sheriff Department cars and three North Dakota Highway Patrol cars blocking the highway. They were immediately surrounded by four officers, one on each side, and two in front of the car, pointing short-barrel shotguns at their heads.

Before the date of Jake's trial, the sparse details of that day were revealed. Jake and Spencer had risen at noon, found that they only had half a pack of Marlboros, a pint of vodka, two cans of beer, and a jar of my mother's pickled beets in the refrigerator. Jake poured the beer into glasses and added the beets, making a magenta-red concoction that they sometimes drank in the morning to cure hangovers. That put them in a better mood, so they drank the vodka too, took a few hits of speed (amphetamine tablets they called white crosses) and smoked three joints of home-grown marijuana. They fired up my brother's car and drove north and then east on Interstate 94, taking a few more hits of speed for the road. Their original intention was simply to drive to Jamestown and get some breakfast at Big Jim's Restaurant, but perhaps feeling the rush and euphoria that speed provides, pursued a mad scheme instead.

They drove past Jamestown, where they might have been recognized, and took the second exit into Valley City, thirty miles east. They turned up the hill to the Winter Show building and next to it they found a red Chevrolet Impala, which Jake hotwired. They transferred an old single-shot twenty-gauge shotgun, which had once belonged to my grandfather, from the trunk of their car to the front seat of the Impala. They drove that car down the hill and north several blocks to the drive-up window of the First National Bank of Valley City. My brother pointed the shotgun at the teller, Mrs. Rita Johnson, and demanded all the money she had. She put $8,342 dollars, everything in her drawer, into the tube and slid it out to my brother. Mrs. Johnson later told the sheriff that she didn't know the glass at the teller window was bullet proof and she did not press the alarm button for approximately two minutes after they fled. "My hands were shaking so hard I could hardly pick up the money," she said, "I was just praying that they wouldn't shoot me dead."

Jake and Spencer drove back to the Winter Show building and changed cars, wiping down the Chevrolet Impala of any fingerprints, and then drove north to old Highway 10, thinking they would avoid the main highway, and headed back west.

But for an incredible occurrence, they likely would have escaped clean with the cash. It turned out that Robert Backes, a sixty-six-year-old retired school teacher, heard about the robbery on his police band radio. Driving by the Winter Show building on his way to take his dog for a walk, he saw them get out of the Impala and into the Ford LTD with the shotgun. Now, the chance of someone listening to a police band radio, hearing about a bank robbery, and then seeing the robbers switch cars in Valley City, a town of less than ten thousand people, is obviously infinitesimal. Call it a wild coincidence, call it incredibly bad luck, or call it an act of God, but it happened.

Backes tailed Jake's Ford far enough to see that they had headed west on Highway 10 before he called the sheriff's office, who immediately called the Highway Patrol, and together they set up the roadblock.

When Jake and Spencer came over that rise and stopped at the road block, they both raised their hands in the air. As Spencer did so, he dropped a bundle of cash he was counting and, without thinking, reached down to toss it under the seat, more of a reflex action than anything. There was a deafening noise as one of the officers, thinking Spencer was reaching for a gun, fired his shotgun, and the blast from close range nearly took Spencer's head clean off and sprayed Jake with shattered glass, bits of flesh and skull, and a fine mist of dark-red blood.

My brother was pulled out of the car as he stared in shock at what was left of Spencer. They threw him to the ground and handcuffed him with his arms behind his back. One of the deputies kicked him as he lay there. "Goddamned hippie," he said.

As I drove west past that exit and this memory all came back to me, I thought about my brother and his long journey in life, and I realized that we did not turn out so differently after all. I knew that in God's eyes, what I did, which also left a man dead, was just as damning, if not worse.

2

I CONTINUED DRIVING, and west of the exit I saw a flock of snow geese high in the sky, heading south with the wind, white specks against an immense gray backdrop. For three or four months of the year this country has intense colors, emerald green fields of wheat stretching from horizon to horizon in the early summer, golden barley and yellow stands of sunflowers in the fall, and, of course, the never ending blue sky. Pure white cumulous clouds float across the sky, casting purple-shaded shadows onto the fields below. But for the rest of the year, the colors are limited, especially in the daylight, the blue sky set against the brown stubble of grain fields cut and harvested, or the blue sky set against the snow. And if it is cloudy, like that day was, there is only one color, a lifeless concrete-gray of sky and snow cover and blowing dirt that stretches across the field of vision, interrupted occasionally by a shelter-belt of trees, a farm surrounded by dull-gray grain bins, a weathered barn, or a steel Quonset.

Thirty miles west I turned south on State Highway 56. The land is mostly tabletop flat here, scarred with occasional gullies, sloughs, and scattered rocks left behind by the retreating glaciers. A few low-lying hills rise up here and there, but they are mere remnants of what they had once been. The land is empty, harsh, and desolate much of the year, although it still manages to support wheat and corn and soybeans during the brief summer. Agricultural production is marginal. If it rains sufficiently, the crops can be good, but in other years, they wilt in the dry heat. One cutting of hay is all you can expect, and the ranchers pray that it will feed their cattle through the winter. There are scattered herds of cattle, almost all Black Angus now, but the ranchers herd them with ATVs, not horses.

As I continued south I began to recognize farms and ranches I once knew, although many are also remnants now, the farmers and ranchers of my parents' generation having passed away and their children abandoning rural life to move to bigger cities where they have jobs as software designers, sales associates, and Walmart managers. I passed the Kurtz Ranch, but the home was abandoned years ago and the red barn, although still standing, bowed in the center. Next to it stood a bladeless windmill, a fallen-down corral, and a crumbled stock tank.

South of the Kurtz Ranch, I turned onto a sparsely graveled road and a half-mile farther took another turn onto a rutted track that was once the driveway of our home. There used to be a sign at the entrance, "Penner Ranch," and below that, "Registered Angus Cattle," but it must have blown down. The house still stood, its windows boarded up and the paint blistered with age, still all in one piece, though the porch had buckled on the west side. I had not seen the ranch since the auction after my father passed away, but I was not surprised the barn had been torn down, probably to salvage the old wood. A few out buildings still stood—a chicken coop, two granaries, and a pump house. Grandfather made those buildings to last—the old Germans built things right.

I picked up an old white plastic pail that once contained chemical herbicide, brought it up on the porch, turned it over and sat down, out of the direct wind, facing northwest towards the old swing set. I had two hours before I was scheduled to meet the sheriff, and I needed some time to sort in my head what happened to Jake over those many years. I sat there undisturbed, letting the memories tumble over me, one leading to another and then another, but chaotic, not chronological, like chaffs of straw blowing in the wind.

The earliest memory I had of my brother was of him coming in from the field at lunch time or in the evening. I must have been about four years old, and he was fourteen and already driving the tractor out in the field. He came in with his face caked with black dirt and his eyes red from the dust the tractor kicked up. He washed the dirt off in the sink by the back door and sauntered into the kitchen smiling and patted me on the head. "How's the buckaroo?" he asked. He got down on the linoleum floor on all fours, and I climbed on his back and pretended he was a horse. He neighed and bucked, and I hung onto his flannel shirt, gripping with all my might as I giggled and laughed. Mother and Father watched and laughed, too.

On the far side of the yard stood an old swing made by my grandfather, with heavy tall posts and a thick wooden seat, still hanging by its chains. I had been swinging the day my brother told me he had volunteered for the Army and was going to Vietnam.

I looked up at him excitedly. "Are you going to be a Green Beret?"

He laughed, "Well, I have to go to basic training and get some experience first, but then I can test for the Green Berets."

In my mind the Green Berets were something special. Jake had bought the record, "The Ballad of the Green Berets," by Barry Sadler, the year before and played it over and over on our sisters' Zenith hi-fi. I listened to it too, lying on the living room rug and dreaming of green berets and silver wings on America's best soldiers. I remember how proud I was of my brother at the time just thinking about it. *A Green Beret!* The thought sent shivers up my spine.

My parents had been more than proud. After all, this was Jake, their first son, their golden boy. Jake could throw one-hundred-pound alfalfa bales around like a full-grown man and shovel grain like there was no tomorrow. Jake was a natural athlete and pitched and played first base on the Gackle baseball team and in basketball, although somewhat short at five-foot-nine, he was good enough to start on the high school team, and he scored twenty-two points, including the winning basket, in the District Eighteen championship game against Medina. Besides that, he had raw good looks, with thick dark hair that he inherited from my mother's side of the family, and dark brooding eyes with thick lashes. At Jake's high school graduation in 1968, he was recognized, along with four other classmates, for his enlistment in the military service. Everyone in the auditorium stood up and applauded and they sang "America the Beautiful." I remember that I looked up at my mother, and she had tears in her eyes and she took my father's hand and squeezed it. Jake also received the Scholar Athlete Award, and as he went up to the podium to receive it, my mother whispered to my father, "I never dreamed that one of my children would win the Scholar Athlete Award." And then to me she said, "Look at what you can accomplish if you are good and work hard."

Jake reveled in being the All-American boy, and he thrived in the clarity of the black-and-white world in which he grew up. The rules were clear, and if you worked hard and played by the rules, you succeeded. If you didn't, you failed, and you deserved the consequences, no matter how harsh. My brother bought into that ethic one hundred percent. He worked hard at basketball and practiced his jump shot every day after school in front of the garage, and he could see his success on the basketball court. He went up to his room and studied his chemistry after he finished his chores in the evening and he received an A in chemistry. And he woke up at 5:30 a.m. and fed and watered his steers and received a blue ribbon at the county fair. Doing the right thing led to success, and this thinking was reinforced at home, in school, and in the community.

Jake had volunteered for the Army; he hadn't waited for a draft notice. It was before the riots at the Democratic Convention in Chicago, but already the young people elsewhere in the country were turning against the war. Robert Kennedy was killed a week after his graduation and Eugene McCarthy, a graduate of St. John's University in Minnesota, was already gaining popularity for talking about making peace. There were growing demonstrations against the war on college campuses across the country. The thing is, the growing opposition to the war hadn't reached our little corner of the world yet. Hippies and peaceniks and war protesters were something we only heard about on TV. Jake faced no moral dilemma about the war, no decision about seeking a deferment, or going to Canada, which would have been only a few hours drive away. People in that rural area believed that America was a great country and if its leaders decided to go to war, then joining the military was viewed as the right thing—the American thing—to do. And God was on our side, of course.

3

SOMEWHERE IN THE DISTANCE I heard a cow bellow. I got up off the pail and walked around to the back yard. The clothesline still stood, but one pole was tilted and the wires now sagged. I walked out past the two rows of Russian Olive trees bordering the north side of the out buildings, where the land sloped away gradually for a half mile or so to Seven Mile Coulee. The land here was cut into swells and hollows, but the bottom of the coulee was flat, and marshy sloughs were scattered along its floor.

I remember the morning my brother took me muskrat trapping there for the first time. I had been pestering him to let me go for some weeks, as I was prone to do. "Can I go too? Can I go too? Please Jake. Pleeeeease."

He pulled a sled with the traps, an axe for chopping into the reed muskrat huts, and a wooden stick to knock the trapped muskrats on the head. Still, he made room for me on the sled and bundled an old blanket around me. I must have been about six years old at the time, so I was small, and Jake was already a strong teenager, and he pulled me easily. We had gotten up at 5:00 a.m. so Jake could get the trapping done before he did his chores and still catch the seven-thirty bus to school. It was very cold, and the sun wouldn't rise for nearly three more hours, so Jake used a flashlight to see where he was going, quietly pulling me along, clouds of breath rising as he exhaled into the icy cold air. It was dead still out, without a sign of life, and the only sound was the runners of the sled against the frozen crust of snow. I was looking straight ahead, holding on to the sides of the sled, when, at one point, Jake turned the flashlight off and whispered to me, "Just look at the stars, Pete." I arched my back and looked up, and the sky seemed immense. There were dazzling stars all around, and it seemed like such an enormous universe and just the two of us alone in it. We sat there for maybe ten minutes, not saying a word, our breath seeming to rise up to meet those very stars.

"How many stars are there?" I finally asked.

"I don't know. Millions or billions maybe."

"Do you think people will ever travel there?"

"Someday," he said. "People can do about anything when they decide they want to."

"I want to be the first person to land on one."

"You can't do that. They are like the sun. You would burn up."

"Oh, right . . . I knew that."

"Maybe people will land on the moon someday, though."

I looked at my brother. "Do you think they have muskrats on the moon?" I asked.

"I doubt it, but you never know. They have craters up there and some of them could have water in them, so maybe there could be muskrats up there."

"If there are, maybe we could go there together someday and trap them all."

"Sure. We'll do lots of things together, Pete."

Jake pulled me the rest of the way down the coulee bank to the slough, and we checked a dozen or so traps, finding three trapped muskrats. He dragged the muskrats out of their huts by the small chain attached to the trap. They clawed and struggled desperately to escape, but the jaws of the trap and the chain always held tight, and he dispatched them with a single blow to the head from the stick. When we got back to the ranch, he took pieces of wire and wrapped them around the muskrats' legs and hung them on the side of the barn. They would quickly freeze solid and hang there until he had enough to take to town to sell at the Hide and Fur Company. They were worth ninety cents each, not bad money for kids at the time, and Jake would later give me half the money from those muskrats.

We walked in the back door of the house, and I could smell the fried sausage as soon as we opened the door. My mother was standing at the stove, stirring a pan of oatmeal. The toast was already made and set out with honey and jam.

"Get any?" she asked.

"Three," my brother said.

"Oh, my," she said. She walked over to the stairs and yelled up to my father, "Albert!"

"What?"

"Jake got three muskrats this morning."

"Good," he yelled.

Then she turned to me, "You need to eat your oatmeal if you want to grow up and be a trapper like your brother."

I didn't like to hear that. I hated oatmeal with a passion. It didn't help that I often dawdled and got to the table late and by then the oatmeal was cold and lumpy. So I never ate oatmeal unless my father made me, as he sometimes did, forcing my mouth open in a fury and shoving the oatmeal into it. I would try desperately not to gag and just sit there, tears streaming down my cheeks, while he yelled at me to eat it. My strategy was to outwait him, so I would pretend to chew, and then as soon as he left the room I would go to the bathroom and spit it out in the toilet. Luckily, he never caught me doing that. My brother would eat a big bowl of oatmeal and then request seconds. Mom would add raisins or brown sugar to it if he asked.

My favorite breakfast was a thick slice of bread, spread with butter and my mother's homemade jam. On winter mornings, like the day I went trapping with Jake, I would take it and huddle next to the hutch, where the only heat register in the kitchen was located, to warm up. There was just enough room for me to sit cross-legged and eat. If my feet were cold, and they usually were, I took off my socks and pressed my toes up against the metal of the heat register until I could no longer stand the heat. I liked to sit there and listen to my mother and father talk at the kitchen table.

My father would usually have breakfast at six in the morning and then go out to do chores. Around nine he would often come in from his work for a mid-morning break and have a cup of strong black coffee and some toast or a cinnamon roll. My mother would sit across from him at the table and they would listen to the farm market report on the radio coming out of Bismarck. This would set off a conversation between the two of them, and this is where I first began to learn about the world.

The weather was always the first topic of conversation, and it was always something to be worried about. In the winter they would be anxious about the severe cold or brutal blizzards, which were hard on the cattle. If it was a nice winter day, it was just a sign that a high pressure system was on its way, waiting up there in Canada someplace, ready to sweep down sneakily and bury the calves in a late winter storm. Summers were worse because, listening to them, it seemed like every year was a bad drought. So they talked about the need for rain endlessly. If it did rain, it didn't rain enough, or it rained too much and the wheat would get rust or they wouldn't be able to combine. If it was hot, it was too hot; it was killing the oats or barley. If it was cool, there was some reason why that was bad too. And then in the late summer before the harvest, there was the daily fear of a thunderstorm that would bring hail. A hailstorm could wipe out the crops and be financially devastating, so mother would often look out the kitchen window, scanning the sky for the heavy dark clouds that could mean hail, and fingering her rosary beads every time there was a deep rumble of thunder. Who can say that her prayers were not answered, because somehow we were always spared the worst of the hailstorms that hit our neighbors.

After they had talked about the weather, they talked about the grain and feeder cattle prices, which were reported on the radio at 9:10 a.m. every morning. The grain and cattle prices were always too low; that was a given, but were they going up or down? Was it better to sell the cattle or wheat now or wait until next week or next month? And, according to my parents, the big grain companies and railroads and food processors were always conspiring to keep the grain and cattle prices low. Any fool could see that because you sold your cattle for twenty-five cents a pound, and that same beef sold for a dollar fifty a pound in the supermarket in Bismarck or Jamestown.

After that subject of conversation had been exhausted, they always turned to talking about the neighbors. Sometimes it was their daily coming and goings. "I saw Victor Klouberdanz hauling cattle to the stockyard," father would report, and this would lead to mother talking about Alice Klouberdanz and, "Did you notice the purple pansies by the wishing well in her front yard?" This in turn might lead to a discussion of their ranch and their cattle and their children and relatives and so on, lasting until my father had been revived by his coffee and carbohydrates and headed back out to work some more.

4

FTER I WALKED AROUND to the north of the house, I circled the shelterbelt to where the corral and the feedlot had once been. The area was now overgrown with Canada thistle and rag weed, but at one time we wintered all the cattle there, along with a dozen horses. My father used to haul the hay stacks in from the fields with a big hay stack mover in the fall and line them up, perfectly straight in a row. When I was small, my brother built snow forts for me there by digging a cave into the snow banks where the snow had drifted against the back of the stacks of hay.

Between the shelter belt and the hay stacks the cattle could get out of the worst of the wind and they were fed by using the tractor with a farmhand loader, tearing off enormous fork loads of hay, and dropping them in piles. This would be supplemented by oats or corn, which in those days had to be hauled out by hand in buckets across the feedlot and poured into the feed bunks. The cows would crowd together to get at the feed and when you brought another bucket out you had to push the cows' rumps aside to get to the trough. When it rained, the feedlot would turn into a mucky swamp so that every step you took you had to pull your overshoes up and they made a slurping, sucking sound. If you were unlucky, an overshoe would stick in the mud and your foot would come out and you would be hopping around trying to get that overshoe back on without your foot touching the muck and manure.

I remember the morning when I was following my brother around while he did his chores, and we found a heifer near the barn that had recently calved. The calf hadn't stood up yet and it was sitting on its hip with its front two legs straight out. The heifer was lying in the manure next to it and couldn't seem to get up at all. I saw a shiny bluish-gray pile near her rump.

"Jake, are those her guts lying there?" I asked.

He looked at her for a minute. "No. I think her womb must have come out."

"Shit, Jake. Dad's gone. What are we going to do? She'll probably die."

"No, don't worry. We can fix her up."

"How are we going to do that?"

"We just have to push it back in. I've seen Dad do it before."

Jake got some rope and tied the heifer's legs so she couldn't get up and then he went to the house and got some soapy warm water in a bucket and washed the womb off. He had me sit on her neck so she wouldn't struggle too much and he pushed the womb back through her vagina with his bare hands all the way in, so that his arms were inside her past his elbows, and as he pulled his hands back out I remember that they were colored crimson red with blood. He got up and went to the barn to get my father's veterinary kit—a wooden box filled with syringes, antibiotics, iodine, tranquillizers, hemodust, and a myriad of pill bottles for every equine and cattle sickness known—and gave the heifer a shot of penicillin.

The two of us watched the heifer for thirty minutes until she finally got up slowly and licked the slick film off her calf. The calf blinked and bleated and stood up on all fours.

"It looks like they'll be all right," he said, wiping his hands off on his jeans.

I had to take a deep breath and steady myself. I looked at my brother and wondered if I would ever be like him. He always seemed so strong and self-assured. At that time, I would never have imagined that ten years later, after he came back from Vietnam, he would steal the horse tranquilizer out of that same veterinary kit and lace marijuana with it to make "angel's dust" and go on a wild high and end up leaving his own blood spattered across the floor of the bowling alley in town.

* * *

JAKE WAS THE FOURTH in our family after three girls. Annette and Eva were about a year apart, then two years later Marie was born, followed by Jake another two years after that. Then there was a long break. A fourth daughter, Donna, was born premature nine years later. My mother never talked about Donna, but my sisters told me about her. They said she had the tiniest hands and feet you could possibly imagine when she was born, just like a doll. She was sickly from the day she came home, and my mother had to care for her constantly. When she was eight months old she began to develop bouts of pneumonia. The first bout passed, but two weeks later she got a reoccurrence and the doctor had my mother put a sheet over the crib with a vaporizer underneath in an attempt to relieve the congestion. My mother would sit by that crib all day long, just listening to make sure Donna was breathing, but after three days Donna's breathing grew increasingly labored. My mother and father rushed her to the hospital. As they were driving, each breath seemed to be farther and farther apart, and they were about three miles from town when the next breath did not come. My father stepped on the gas and drove straight through every stop sign, but it was too late by the time they got to the hospital door, and there was nothing that could be done.

I was a year younger than Donna and born only four months after she passed away. My sister Marie told me later that mother was in so much sorrow and depressed from the loss of Donna that she could not care for me for the first year. Marie fed me and changed my diapers. I have no memory of that, obviously, but I can see Marie doing that. She was responsible and capable, even from an early age.

I still have a family photo of all of us kids that my mother must have taken when I was about two years old. In the photo my three sisters are lined up wearing baby-blue chiffon dresses that extend to well beyond their knees. Their hair is fixed almost identically, shoulder length, and flipped in with a Doris Day look, and the bangs are cut straight across in front. Marie is holding me up in the crook of her arm and I am wearing a white shirt with suspenders, and my eyes are on Marie's face and not the camera. My brother stands in front of all of us, chest out, with a proud, confident smile, and he has a red-and-black embroidered cowboy shirt on and what looks to be new cowboy boots.

When I look at that photo I realize that I hardly even knew my two oldest sisters growing up. By the time I was old enough to have any memory, they were already away at college and then they got married and moved out of state. Marie was the only sister I knew well and was close with, since she was the youngest and still lives in North Dakota. She became a nurse and served in the Peace Corps in the Congo. She nearly died there after contracting Chikungunya Fever, but she eventually fully recovered and later married a family practice physician in Grand Forks, North Dakota. They have four children and when I was growing up the whole family came to visit every other Thanksgiving, Christmas, and Easter, and Marie and the children came for a week or more in the summer.

* * *

BEFORE HE JOINED THE ARMY, my brother used to love working on the ranch, and he did so like a man from the time he was twelve years old—driving the farm machinery in the fields, hauling grain, herding cattle—whatever needed to be done. He worked horses with an easy confidence and had an eye for both horses and cattle. When he was in his teens, he was the president of the township 4-H Club and exhibited steers at county fairs and once at the North Dakota State Fair in Minot.

Jake liked a good cow pony, and he had a girlfriend in high school who rode horses and competed in barrel races in local rodeos. Her name was Patty Schoot and they were pretty steady his last two years of high school. Besides barrel racing, she was a cheerleader for the basketball team, active in the girls 4-H club (called the Peppy Pals), named the "Gackle High School Betty Crocker Homemaker of Tomorrow" her senior year, and she attended the same Catholic Church as we did, St. Anne's. My mother adored Patty and sometimes Patty would help her with the cooking or sit and sew with her.

Jake used to invite her over on Sundays to go riding, and she would come over after church with her dad's pickup and stock trailer and have Sunday dinner with us. After dinner she might join Jake on the davenport as he watched the football game. She didn't know anything about football, but she would sit there next to Jake, just glad to be with him, and he would put his arm around her. If my parents left the room, they might kiss, but that was about it as far as I saw. She was very attractive, I do remember that, with thick dark hair she wore flipped up, a constant mouthy smile, and long shapely legs. My brother always fancied beautiful women and beautiful horses.

I was about seven at the time they were dating and at the age where I saw no use for girls. I guess it would be fair to say I resented her somewhat, because if she wasn't there, maybe Jake would help me with my train set or go outside with me and build me a fort in the hay bales.

Later in the afternoon, after the football game, Jake would saddle up the horses. Jake always wore his good black Stetson hat and brown leather riding jacket, and Patty had a white hat and a blue riding outfit, with white fringe and silver embroidery, that she had sewn herself. Jake rode a speckled gray at that time, named Rowdy, and Patty rode a black-and-white pinto, Spokane, who she spoiled by constantly giving him sugar cubes. The two of them were quite a pair, and I remember my mother yelling to my father, "Albert, run and get your camera. They look just like Roy Rogers and Dale Evans all dressed up like that. Hurry up . . . I hope you have film in the camera."

The two of them would go riding for hours, over to the coulee and up through the hills. They would come back, putting their horses to a gallop the last half mile, and then wipe down the lathered horses and give them a healthy ration of oats. My mother would be watching out the window for them to emerge from the barn so she could invite them in for more cake or cookies and see if she could get them interested in a game of Whisk. When Jake left for the Army, I think there was this unspoken expectation on the part of my parents that Jake and Patty might marry when he returned.

I was the only child left on the ranch after Jake left and expected to take his place. Unlike my brother, however, I was a big disappointment to my parents, and especially my father, when it came to ranching. I was always doing something wrong, like when I accidentally backed the tractor into the grain auger and wrecked it, or when I accidentally left the gate open and the cattle got out and it took a whole day and help from the neighbors to round them up again. I was a bit of a dreamer, and I hated the eternal chores: shoveling grain, feeding hay to the cattle, picking rocks off the field, cleaning manure out of the barn. Never ending dirt and dust and shit.

One time when I was about eleven, my father sent me out to walk the fence line where I was to look for any posts where the staples had fallen out and the barbed wire was loose, and tighten the wire with a fence stretcher if necessary. I was about two miles from home when I saw a glistening rock that attracted my attention and I picked it up. I had started a rock collection, and I was always on the look-out for new rock specimens. It was just a piece of white quartz with a few black specks, but any kind of distinct rock was a rarity in that country and something to be treasured, in my mind. Pretty soon I was bent over, peering at the ground, occasionally reaching down and putting a rock that interested me in my pocket.

I heard the faint rattle of a pickup and I looked up. My father drove up in the old International pickup, but it was too late to pretend I was working as I was a hundred or so yards from the fence line. He jumped out, stomped over to where I was standing, and yelled, "What the hell are you doing?"

"I found these rocks," I said, and I took them out of my pocket and showed them to him. He looked at them for one second before tossing them far away.

"Rocks . . . shit . . . we don't have time for that. Quit dawdling and get back to work. Now!"

He swatted me on the back of the head. If he had a stick he probably would have used it, he was that mad. He was never one to use corporal punishment to the extreme, but he wasn't averse to walloping us with his belt or a stick if he thought we really deserved it. I was fortunate, I guess, that he never used a buggy whip or a rope dipped in water like some of my friends' German fathers did. I still remember my friend Wesley telling me about his father beating him with a rope dipped in water until it raised red welts on his backside, all because he had missed the school bus and was late doing his chores. He had been talking to a girl he liked after school and didn't even notice the bus leaving.

I rode horses when I needed to, but I don't ever remember riding, even once, for pleasure. It was always work-related, cutting cattle or moving them to pasture, and I remember that it was often hot, and I would spend the time in the saddle wiping the sweat from my brow and swatting horse flies that bit me when I least expected it. The one exception to my general dislike of work was that if the weather was good (a big if), I did not mind sitting on the tractor and doing the field work, like cultivating. I liked the smell of the freshly turned earth and the work was mindless, driving back and forth across the field. I could daydream the day away.

I would rather read books than work, and I read incessantly when I was young. We had few books at home, other than an old set of the World Book Encyclopedia, and while our school had its own library, it was small, really just two bookshelves, and I had read all of the good books by the time I was ten. What I lived for was the county bookmobile, which came to our school once a week. Up until I was about fourteen, I never missed it, and I always took out the maximum number of books you could have at a time, which was five. I read everything, but what still remains in my memory are the You Were There series, *Robinson Crusoe*, *Gulliver's Travels*, *The Yearling*, *Black Beauty*, *Tom Sawyer*, and *The Call of the Wild*. Books gave me the gift of imagining another life. My mother encouraged me to read and when I was little I would often perch on her lap in the evening and read to her, but my father thought there was little to be learned from books, especially fiction. Besides, too much reading interfered with work. "Get your nose out of that book and get to your chores."

South of our house in the pasture was a grassy butte, the highest point around, and I would climb up there and imagine that the Plains Indians probably used that point to scout for bison on the prairie. The Dakota and Sioux Indians had roamed all over this area before the military and cattle ranchers chased them out, and even before them this area was roamed by Paleo-Indian tribes pursuing the bison and living off the land for at least 10,000 years. You can imagine the fear and confusion they must have experienced when they saw lightning and thunder and tornadoes rolling towards them across the treeless prairie. There was absolutely no place to hide and they must have felt powerless. Archeologists believe that even those earliest Paleo-Indians had shamans who helped the people make sense of the natural world, including the weather, which was indistinguishable to them from the spirit world.

Uncle Herbert and my father found a number of Indian hammer heads in the pasture north of there when they were kids. They were of a granite-type stone, oval-shaped, as big as softballs, with rings chiseled out of the middle in order to tie on a bone or wooden handle with a piece of rawhide. My father gave me his hammer heads when I was ten, and they were objects of marvel to me. I spent hours imagining the people who left them there and wondering how this landscape shaped their existence.

As I got older and entered junior high school and then high school, I loved to wander off on my own, especially in the fall and winter. I could just head out on foot away from the ranch in any direction. It was all open space. Sometimes I would be looking for hammer heads or rocks for my collection; at other times, I would just be daydreaming and thinking. In the fall, I would hear geese and cranes flying south and look up to see them pass overhead in great V-shaped formations, the geese sounding like a chorus of melodic voices, the cranes sounding as if they were terribly out of key.

In the winter, the land was as bare as a desert landscape and almost entirely devoid of wildlife. Very few animals could survive the fierce winters of North Dakota when the wind whipped out of the north and swept the snow and the dirt off the fields and into dirty gray drifts against the road ditches and shelterbelts. Occasionally you would see a jack rabbit or small flock of Hungarian partridges and rarely a coyote loping across the pastures looking for an afterbirth or a dead cow, but that was about it. Still, the winters held their own attraction and often I would stop and lie on my back out of the wind and just look at the sky. No one watching, no one listening, like I was the only person in the world. I found that I treasured solitude and later in life that was one thing that attracted me to the monastic existence—the prospect of finding something sacred in silence and solitude.

5

I WALKED OVER TO WHERE the old barn used to stand. A small bush, maybe eighteen inches high, with red berries, was striving to root next to the crumbled foundation and for a moment I was struck by this small bit of beauty in an otherwise bleak spot. Other than that stone foundation, a pile of old shingles and a few shattered boards were all that was left of the barn that was once one of the largest in the county.

My grandfather Josef built that barn in 1919, when cattle and grain prices were high after World War I and many farmers and ranchers built new barns with the money they had accumulated for the first time in their lives. It stood over seventy years and witnessed two generations come and go. Seeing that old foundation made me think about our family history and wonder about how the past shapes the future.

Grandfather Josef moved from Ontario in 1907 and bought the land, 320 acres, from the original homesteader. He came from a farm family of nine children, seven of whom were boys, so there was not enough land near their home in Ontario to support all of them. Being the youngest, Josef struck out on his own. He chose this spot in North Dakota because many Germans had settled in the area, and he was able to buy the land cheap. Much of the land here was rocky and hilly, less than half was tillable, so the settlers adapted and raised grain where they could and ran cattle on the rest.

The ranch is about eight miles southwest of the town of Gackle. When Grandfather first came to the area, Gackle was less than ten years old but already considered a thriving town, with a post office, cafe, lumber company, real estate office, dry goods store, harness shop, livery and feed stable, hotel, creamery, bank, and elevator. There was no bar, although there was a "Blind Pig" where you could purchase liquor about three miles outside of town.

Both Grandfather and Grandmother spoke German at home and in town their entire lives. My grandfather Josef was the grandson of John Penner, who had migrated from Sinsheim, Germany, in 1853. Grandfather used to tell stories about his grandfather John who farmed and was known all throughout Ontario for the Percheron draft horses he bred and sold. The story goes that when John and his brother Otto migrated from Germany they only had enough funds and a passport for one passenger on the ship, so they decided to take turns hiding in a shipping barrel during the passage across the Atlantic. As brothers they looked similar, and they grew identical beards for the passage; all they had to do was avoid close scrutiny by the crew. At night, they changed places so that the one who had been inside the barrel could swap places with the one who had been outside on the deck.

The arrangement worked well until about halfway across the Atlantic when Otto met a fellow who was selling bottles of schnapps. Now Otto was nursing an inner wound from a lost love that had married another, so he was susceptible, and the idea of a drink began to play on his mind. He resisted buying any for days, as they had very limited funds, but one especially cold day, his resistance weakened, and he told himself that it wouldn't hurt to have a nip to keep the cold at bay. One nip led to another, and by nightfall he was dead drunk and fell asleep about the time he was to relieve John in the barrel. John wondered if something was wrong when his brother didn't come at the appointed time, but he didn't dare get out of the barrel for fear that they would be discovered. He had some bread and pickled herring and enough water with him, but he had to relieve himself in a small tin pail and the smell grew rather rank over time. His legs had to remain bent in that barrel, of course, and by the second day they caused him excruciating pain. When Otto finally woke up from his drunken stupor and regained his senses, he asked a fellow passenger what day it was. When he found out that he had missed relieving his brother by a day, he was fearfully shaken, and he rushed to the barrel and pulled his brother John out and apologized profusely. John could hardly walk at first, but he soon recovered and he didn't hold it against his brother. Otto, on the other hand, swore off alcohol and never took another drink in his life—a lesson some of their descendants could have benefitted from.

No one on board the ship ever found out about the ruse and both went on to homestead next to each other in Ontario. Otto married and had eight children before he died in 1867 after being kicked in the head by one of the Percheron horses. John built a large stone house and took in and cared for Otto's wife and their eight children, in addition to the nine children he would have with his own wife.

Josef was a hard worker. He started out with only that small acreage of land and when he arrived in North Dakota his sole possessions were a span of horses, a plow, a disc, and two milk cows. He lived in a two-room wooden shanty the original homesteader had erected on the property, which was heated with a claw-footed iron stove where he cooked his fried beef and dough biscuits.

Grandfather preferred to raise wheat, but he was immediately hit by some lean years, like 1911, when there was a severe drought, and his wheat crop burned up in the hot July sun. He was smart enough to realize that he had to raise cattle as well as wheat. They could always find something to eat in the draws leading down to the coulee, so he began raising beef cattle, Herefords, as well as horses.

When World War I came, the German immigrants in that part of North Dakota faced a real dilemma. They loved Germany, the land of their birth, and they couldn't see themselves killing their own kind, so they searched their souls for where their loyalties lay, and more than a few opposed the war. Grandfather was against the war, but like most of his neighbors, he was not politically minded. They just wanted to be left alone to raise their wheat and tend their cattle. That type of attitude would change, of course, in no small degree, by the time my brother Jake enlisted in the Army.

By 1917, anti-German hysteria began to sweep the country. The teaching of German was prohibited in high schools and German books were withdrawn from libraries. In some parts of the country, the speaking of German in public was forbidden and symphonies no longer played German composers. Some North Dakota residents proposed changing the state capitol's name from Bismarck to something more American sounding. The hysteria sometimes bordered on the ridiculous, as hamburgers were renamed "liberty sandwiches" and sauerkraut became "liberty cabbage."

This anti-German sentiment hit home for Grandfather when he went into Jamestown one Saturday to buy fencing wire. He was walking past the drugstore when a couple of Norwegian farm boys spit on his shoes and called him a "dirty kraut." He kept his dignity, as he wasn't about to fight with mere teens, but he always said that it "stuck in my craw" and he never forgot it.

Many of the men in that area around Gackle were drafted into the army in 1917 and 1918, even though they were against the war. Fortunately for Grandfather he was thirty-two years old by then and he was married so he was never called up.

6

GRANDFATHER MARRIED a German Russian girl, Rosina, in 1916. Her parents, Gottlieb and Trinka Oschner, had arrived with thousands of other German Russians migrating to North Dakota in the late 1800s, reaching this desolate prairie following a circuitous route. It started when Catherine the Great decided that Russia needed to populate the lower Volga River and Black Sea Region in southern Russia as a buffer against the Turks. She issued a manifesto in 1763 offering free land to settlers from Germany, along with exemption from service in the Russian Army, self-government, and religious freedom. As a result of the manifesto, Germans migrated en masse and prospered in this fertile region of Russia.

In 1874, Tsar Alexander II ended the exemption from service in the Russian Army and self-government because he wanted to assimilate ethnic groups throughout Russia and "modernize" the country. He required that the Russian language be taught in school, instead of German, and that all records be kept in Russian. Cossack soldiers came riding through the country on their horses, trampling wheat fields, and conscripting young men into the military service. This was too much for these Germans to bear. It was a betrayal of the promises made to them and they weren't about to die serving in the Russian Army, so they looked to the United States as the new land of opportunity. North Dakota offered free land, not dissimilar to where they had come from in Russia, which could be homesteaded by those with the courage to settle on the empty prairie.

In our day and age I don't think we can begin to imagine the hardship and suffering the early German Russian immigrants faced. It is summed up in the Black Sea German proverb that Grandmother's ancestors brought with them: "For the first generation, there is death. For the second, there is want. Only for the third, is there bread."

Rosina's parents were from the village of Denovitz and arrived in Eureka, Dakota Territory, in 1887 after a twelve-day passage on a steamer, the *Vera*, and a three-day journey on the Chicago, Milwaukee & St. Paul Railroad. They had three children when they migrated and five more followed in the next ten years. As they departed the train in Eureka, they looked out at an endless prairie of waving grass stretching from horizon to horizon. It was a place where the wind faced no obstacles, not even a single tree, and immigrants guided themselves by taking bearings on large stones or piles of buffalo bones. The distant howling of wolves could sometimes be heard at night, reminding the immigrants of the stories they heard as children about the packs of wolves in Russia that preyed on travelers crossing Siberia.

Gottlieb and Trinka had only thirty-five dollars and a few meager possessions carried by hand in bundles when they arrived, but they trusted in their own strength and their God when their strength was not enough. They were fortunate enough to know a family that had come ahead of them, so they got directions at the train station from someone who spoke German and walked seventeen miles, carrying their bundles and the youngest child, who was only two, across the prairie until they reached that family's home, which was really nothing more than a small "claim shack" made out of tarpaper and boards. They arrived so dirty and tired they could barely put one foot in front of the other, but they were joyful of their safe deliverance, and they fell down on their knees, kissed the earth, and gave thanks to God.

They stayed with that family in their small shack that first summer until they could build a sixteen-by-twenty-two-foot sod house, made with sod strips dug by a steel plow attached to a wooden beam and pulled by a team of oxen. The inside of the house was plastered with clay. It only had two windows, so it was often dark inside, and it was lit by a single kerosene lantern on the cold, dark North Dakota nights. A stove was made out of stone, cemented with clay, as was the floor. Fuel for the stove was buffalo chips and twisted slough grass.

The new immigrants were unprepared for the severely cold winters of North Dakota. We think of Russia as cold, but the winters in the Black Sea Region were relatively mild in comparison to the North Dakota winters. Winter arrived early that first year, with a blizzard on October 28, burying their sod house in snow except for the chimney. It seemed to Trinka that the wind never stopped blowing that entire winter. It was so loud and ceaseless that she would sometimes cover her ears and moan to drown out the sound, or she would sing the *Schicksalslied* (Song of Destiny) at the very top of her voice:

Das Schicksal wird keinen verschonen,	(Destiny will spare nobody.)
der Tod verfolgt Zepter und Kronen.	(Death pursues scepters and crowns.)
Eitel, eitel ist zeitliches Glück,	(Temporary bliss is vane, vane.)
alles, alles fällt wieder zurück . . .	(Everything, everything returns . . .)
Die Tränen sind Zeichen der Liebe,	(Tears are signs of love,)
doch sind sie nur irdische Triebe.	(But they are only earthly urges.)
Nur um eines, um eines bitt ich:	(I ask only one thing, only one.)
Betet täglich, ach betet für mich!	(Pray daily, pray for me!)

Gottlieb was fortunate that he had purchased a buffalo robe on the advice of a neighbor. This was a godsend because they could bundle up the children underneath it on the coldest winter nights, when the wind whistled through the cracks by the door, and the floor would be covered in a frost by morning, and they could still stay warm. Many of the immigrants lost babies in those early years because their houses were so cold and had very poor ventilation.

Besides the cold of winter, food was a problem those first few years, and the children often cried because they were hungry. They would eat a thin soup called "rival soup," made out of flour and water, or bread three times a day, and during the toughest times the bread would be made out of barley, because it was cheaper than wheat. The children thought it was a great treat to get an onion with their lunch. Seeing his children hungry tore at Gottlieb's soul. In hopes of easing their suffering he labored from dark to dark, sometimes crying out to God in his despair, "*O Gott, du muscht helfa!*" (Oh God, you must help!)

They arrived too late that first year to plant a crop, but Gottlieb hired out on a threshing crew for a dollar a day, leaving Trinka home alone with the children for weeks at a time. They made a little additional income from picking up the sun-bleached buffalo bones scattered across the prairie, which were hauled to the railroad and sold for seven dollars per ton to be ground up and used for fertilizer. They had no choice because they needed money, and eventually they acquired a team of oxen, a breaking plow, a disc, a wagon, and a few cows. Gottlieb broke forty acres the second year, feeling joyous as he turned those first prairie furrows and the black earth was revealed. He planted flax and wheat, and the rains came. Trinka planted a garden, too, and they milked a cow, so the children now had vegetables and more food to eat. They were thankful God had provided.

Gottlieb and Trinka lived in the sod house for nine years until they built their first wooden house in 1896. It was built in the tradition that they had used in Russia for generations and before that in Germany, using "puddle clay," built up in layers between wooden studs.

Grandmother Rosina and her twin sister, Esther, were born in that house a year after it was completed. The twin girls were the youngest in the family, and life was better for them. When they were six, they were able to attend a one-room school house and learned to speak English, quite an accomplishment in an area where everyone spoke only German at home and in town. The country school only went up to the eighth grade and very few of the German children would go further with their education, some only finishing a year or two of school. It was thought that learning to read and do simple arithmetic were enough. Working with one's hands was God's work. Sadly, they had not come from a tradition that valued education, because the only educated people they knew in Russia were lawyers and judges, who often took advantage of the poor.

None of Rosina's and Esther's brothers or sisters had gone past eighth grade, but both twins decided they wanted to continue. They wanted go to high school and become teachers. Gottlieb and Trinka were not so sure. The nearest high school was too far away to travel every day, so the girls would have to move away from home in order to attend. But Rosina and Esther begged and begged, so one Sunday, after the church service, Trinka stayed to ask the priest what they should do. The priest, Father Kinzler, was young in years, but with a long beard, and already harsh in judgment. He said to Trinka, "The church does not prohibit girls from attending high school, but it is no use. They will just marry and have children anyhow. It would be like pouring good milk into the ground. It is better that they learn to cook, and sew, and keep house."

Trinka thought about this for a moment and said, "If they become teachers they can teach boys to read the Bible. Then the boys could become priests when they grow up."

Father Kinzler could not argue with that, so he took another tact. "You have been blessed with five healthy girls," he said. "God has a purpose in that. He expects that at least one should become a nun. A good Catholic should know that. I will give my blessing for one of the twins to attend high school, but only if the other becomes a nun."

Trinka went home and told the two girls what the priest had decreed. Both of them wanted to be teachers, rather than nuns, but they could see that since the priest had spoken, they must abide by his judgment. Gottlieb said it was best to leave it in God's hands and the two girls drew straws to determine their fate and Esther got the short straw.

Esther entered Blessed Virgin Mary of Sacred Heart Convent in Fargo. She later taught as a nun at Shanley High School, the Catholic high school in Fargo, for forty-four years, so she did become a teacher after all.

Rosina moved to Bismarck and boarded with a family in exchange for helping take care of their children. She went to high school during the day and graduated in three years. After that, she attended Valley City State Teacher's College, where in those days you could receive a teacher's certificate after three months of training. After graduation, and not yet quite eighteen years of age, she was hired as a teacher in a country school house ten miles from grandfather's ranch, teaching twenty-six students, all with foreign accents, in grades one to eight.

Soon after she started teaching, she met Grandfather. He'd heard there was a pretty new teacher at the schoolhouse and being very lonely on the ranch by himself, and with a dearth of marriageable women in the county, he decided to ride over to meet her. He put on his best clothes, shined his boots with tallow, dusted off his cowboy hat, and rode his finest roan stallion right up to the schoolhouse and introduced himself. He must have received encouragement, because he bought a new buggy, a smart-looking surrey with a fringed top, so he could court her properly, and he was soon traveling those ten miles every week to see her. He took her to neighborhood parties and barn dances, where they would do two-steps, polkas, and waltzes. Rosina insisted that she have a chaperone whenever they went anywhere. She did not want her students' parents to think she behaved improperly. Her teachers' contract strictly forbade being in the company of men unchaperoned. She also couldn't drink beer, wine, or whiskey, smoke cigarettes, or "wear face powder or paint her lips."

When they were older, Grandfather used to tease Rosina by telling stories about their courting days. According to him, he had been seeing her about six months and one day he summoned up all his courage and said, "Rosina, you sure are a sweet girl. How about one kiss?"

Rosina looked at him crossly and replied very indignantly, "I do not indulge in promiscuous kissing."

Years later, that saying became somewhat of a family joke with my sisters. I heard them repeat it many times, but the time I remember the most was when I was about seven years old and my sisters were all home from college for Christmas. I heard them talking in their room, and I crept slowly down the hallway, so as not to cause the floor boards to creak, and listened at their doorway. Eva was talking about her boyfriend and what a great kisser he was. "He has these dreamy lips and he kisses me all over, and I get so I can hardly stand it." I could hear them all giggling.

"How about you, Marie? Eva asked. "I bet you've met some cute guys at UND. Have you kissed any yet?"

Marie said, "Of course not. I do not indulge in promiscuous kissing."

My sisters squealed with laughter.

Then Marie said, "Actually, I've been seeing one guy quite a bit."

"And?" Annette asked.

Marie lowered her voice to almost a whisper that I could barely hear. "We did the dirty deed three times."

My sisters squealed again when they heard that.

"It was wonderful," Marie added.

I had no inkling at the time what "the dirty deed" might be, but even at that age, hearing this titillated me because I knew it must be something naughty.

* * *

GRANDMOTHER ROSINA AND JOSEF were married after her first year of teaching. The ceremony was held in Napoleon, North Dakota, and Rosina wore a white dress she sewed herself and trimmed with crocheted rings. Afterwards they served sandwiches, baked beans, cake, and cookies and celebrated with a wedding dance called the "*Hochzeit*," "High Time," which was a tradition with the German Catholics. Music was provided by a violin and an accordion, and Josef danced every dance with his young bride.

Nine months after their wedding, their first son was born. In the evening Rosina had noticed a small flow of bloody mucus and the pains and cramps began to wrack her body. Josef hitched up the buggy and fetched the community midwife, called *die Geburtshilferin*, the birth helper. In those days midwives were highly respected and thought to be "angels of mercy." Late that night the baby was born, pulled out by the midwife as wet and slippery as a flopping fish, and he let out a cry that shattered the stillness of their tiny home. Josef and Rosina named their beloved child Jacob—my brother Jake was his namesake.

Grandmother Rosina worked side-by-side with Josef on the ranch in those early days. Besides tending the baby and doing the housework, sewing, and cooking, she mowed hay, shocked grain, raised a garden, helped clean the barn, milked two cows, and raised chickens, selling the extra eggs in town for six cents a dozen. Cattle and grain prices rose during the war years, but times were still tough and any little money they made went back into the ranch. The winters were especially long and harsh for Rosina. She had come from a large family with lots of children, so she often got lonely with just the three of them in the house, and she would sometimes become depressed when it was too cold to go outside for more than a short trip to the barn for weeks at a time. If she did not have little Jacob she would not have known what to do. Many evenings their sole joy was to play patty-cake and peek-a-boo with him or watch him play on the bed with the wooden toys Josef carved for him. He was a cheerful baby, rarely cried after the first few weeks, and giggled and laughed easily.

During the winter of 1917-1918, the terrible flu epidemic struck and many of the neighbors lost husbands, wives, and children. There were no vaccines or medicines in those days that did any good. When there was a death, people would say that it was God's will. That was the only way that they could cope. Grandfather was one of the few men not to get it and he helped neighbors with watering and feeding their cattle. When neighbors died, he dug graves. The old cemeteries in the southern part of North Dakota still show lines of gravestones where whole families lie buried with 1918 as the year of death.

Josef and Rosina thought they had escaped the deadly flu and gave thanks to God for sparing them. Then in May of that year, when the worst of the flu seemed to be over, little Jacob came down with a fever. Rosina refused to believe that it could be the flu. He was such a happy and healthy baby, surely God would not take him away. She fed him *rahm* soup, a cream soup that cured almost any ailment, applied mustard plasters, and rocked him constantly. But within two days little Jacob was dead, passing away in the night as she held him in her arms. Grandmother Rosina was so grief-stricken that she used to go out into the wheat field to hide herself in the high grain and lie there and scream out her anguish.

7

GRANDFATHER KEPT AT RANCHING through the bad times and saved what he could and then bought more land as other neighbors gave up and sold out, or passed away. By 1920, Grandfather was known for the fine horses he bred, both the large Percheron draft horses to pull the machinery in the fields and smaller cow ponies for herding and roping cattle. Grandfather was one of the better ranchers at training and breaking horses, and he not only broke his own horses, but many of his neighbors' as well. People said, "For every man, there is a horse he can't ride," but Grandfather had never met his yet. He had a way of working slowly with horses. He might work with a difficult horse for weeks, a few hours a day, and start by just petting it and rubbing its nose so it would get used to humans before he even tried to mount it. He would spur a horse only if necessary, and then only lightly in the hindquarters, or he would twist its ear to get its attention, but he didn't believe that raking a horse excessively made for a good riding or roping horse. He always contended that even the most devilish horse, like a man, needed to retain something pure in his heart that remained unbroken.

Many of the old ranchers in our area still remember the story of Grandfather and the Texan cowboys, and we heard the story many times. The way they told it, a neighbor rancher that Grandfather knew, Konrad Schweinhart, hired Grandfather to break a young stallion, named Blackjack, he had recently purchased. Blackjack was one of a half-dozen horses Konrad had purchased from a ranch in Montana. The horses were decent cow ponies with the exception of Blackjack, who must have been thrown into the lot using a little deception or as a bad joke. Blackjack was a blaze-faced black with white stockings, wide in the shoulders and high in the hips. You could put a saddle on Blackjack, and even a bridle and bit, but woe to anyone who tried to mount him.

Grandfather had been working with Blackjack in his sure, slow-handed way for a week, but Konrad, never a patient man, was starting to question his progress. One day when Grandfather was working in Konrad's corral, getting Blackjack used to a little weight, in the form of a sandbag on the saddle, he heard the pounding of horses' hooves and three riders rode up on large bay horses with tooled Mexican saddles. The leader of the bunch, Charlie Dunn, was an unpleasant-looking fellow with a bristly mustache grown long at the corners of his mouth. Charlie explained that they had met Konrad at the bar in town and he had bet them five dollars that they couldn't break his black horse. They were Texans, they said, as if that made them experts, and they had just finished up some roping and branding work at the YO Ranch, located about twenty miles due west, and were looking for more cowboy work before heading back south. Grandfather explained to them that he had already been hired to break the horse, but the three of them were insistent, so Grandfather stood aside and watched.

One of the men, named Morris, a short, wiry fellow, put on some spurs that looked like they had been recently sharpened like razors, and quickly mounted the stallion. The horse laid back its ears, lowered his head, snorted, and then broke into some hard pitching. Morris was evidently a seasoned bronco buster because he somehow dug in his heels and hung on. Blackjack tried every trick in the book, twisting and bucking in every direction, but eventually he began to tire. Even then, Morris kept spurring and raking him good and plenty to break his spirit and whenever Blackjack got close to the fence Charlie would hit him with a heavy quirt across the face and laugh as the horse snorted and pitched even higher and higher. Blackjack began to bleed profusely from the heavy spurring near his shoulders, the blood spattering the dust in that corral. Most Dakota cowboys wouldn't spur in front of the saddle like that, as it was considered just too cruel. Grandfather yelled, "Ya, dat's enough, no more," but the men ignored him.

After a time, Blackjack was about wore out, still snorting and bucking some, but breathing heavily, his ribs heaving, and foaming at the mouth. Morris was trying to make him turn around in the corral and he must have let up on his guard because Blackjack suddenly pitched and twisted and threw Morris. Morris jumped right up, furious, and he said he would mount the horse again and this time, "teach that son-of-a-bitch a lesson." He went over to his saddlebag and pulled out a "bear trap" bit. This was a vicious bit that had a three-inch spade running back above the horse's tongue that could cause a horse to slobber and bleed at the mouth.

Grandfather had heard of the bit being used in south Texas but no one in the Dakotas would employ something so brutal. It was too much for Grandfather. He had seen enough, and even though he was outnumbered three to one, he said, "You ain't puttin that bit on. I won't let you."

Charlie cussed him and told him, "Mind your own damn business." He and Morris were approaching Blackjack with the bit when Grandfather punched Charlie hard in the jaw, and he went down. Grandfather was immediately jumped by Morris and the other man and Charlie got up too and the three of them proceeded to beat Grandfather to within an inch of his life, kicking him viciously with their cowboy boots even when he was down.

Rosina went looking for him later that evening when he didn't show up for supper and found him lying unconscious in the corral, dried blood caked about his nose and mouth. She was able to haul him in to the doctor with the wagon but it took many weeks for him to recover from a broken jaw and four cracked ribs, and he pissed blood for weeks. When Grandfather told the story he always said, "Sometimes you gotta do what's right and take your beating." So that became a family saying that my father often repeated.

* * *

BY THE TIME THE "DIRTY THIRTIES" came along with the Depression and the dust bowl that broke the souls and spirits of so many farmers in North Dakota, Grandfather owned over 1,600 acres of land, and somehow he coped and held on to it all through those mean, lean years. He accomplished that through ceaseless work and sweat, aided by the fact that he did not trust bankers, so he kept his money hidden in a crock jar and buried in dirt under the floorboards, and he did not lose it when the banks failed, like many of his neighbors did.

Those were the hardest of times for the farmers and ranchers of the Dakotas. Cattle sold for twenty dollars a head, when you could sell them. Grain wilted in the drought as the soil drifted. On May 9, 1934, a day known as "Black Sunday," a dust storm struck the plains like the fury of a vengeful god. The daytime sky turned as black as night and the cattle stumbled blindly across the fields, their hides and digestive tracts filling with dirt. Grandfather lost a dozen head of cattle and many of his calves that day. At one point, Grandfather was down to forty head of beef cattle, three milk cows, and two bulls, and it was so dry there sometimes wasn't any feed for them except thistle, which he mixed with a little molasses to keep his herd alive.

My grandfather passed away before I was born, so everything I know about him came from stories I heard from family and neighbors, but he is real to me even today, and sometimes when I think about him it seems like I could reach out and shake his hand. There are few photographs of him, but the one that sticks in my mind is of him sitting on a tall spotted horse. He looks rather scrawny and small on that horse and the photo was obviously taken in his old age, but he is looking into the camera almost defiantly, with his jaw set, as if he was still ready to take on the world.

Grandfather's favorite saying was "*Arbeit macht das Leben suss,*" meaning roughly, "Work makes life sweet." His life was centered on working dawn to dusk to build up the ranch. His work ethic not only equated work with goodness, but went beyond that: work was the joy of life. And I can understand that, for him, maybe it really was a joy. He started with nothing and built a house, barn, and granaries, and he could see his cattle, horses, and fields of grain increase, and he fed and raised a fine family. He was the epitome of self-reliance. His philosophy was that what you did with your life was either your doing or God's, and you didn't question God, so that left yourself.

My father, Albert, worked alongside my grandfather after he graduated from the North Dakota Agricultural College in 1941, until Grandfather deeded him the ranch in 1947 and moved to town. Even then, Grandfather drove out almost every day and continued to help my father on the ranch. He was fortunate, I guess, that he could ride horses and work cattle until the day he died. He taught my brother Jake how to ride horses when Jake was just four years old. Maybe that is why Jake was always so good with horses.

My grandfather's one concession to "retirement" was that he took up restoring old grain threshing machines and showing them at "Threshers Reunions" throughout the Dakotas and Minnesota. He loved this chance to get together with other old timers and swap stories about the early days. He did that until 1956, when he passed away from a heart attack while pitching bundles of grain into his prize Advance Rumley Threshing Machine at the Steam Threshers Reunion in Rollag, Minnesota. His last words, as he lay there clutching his chest, were reportedly, "Ya boys, don't stop, keep pitchin dem bundles into that son-of-a-bitch."

Grandmother Rosina lived until 1967, passing away when I was nine years old. I hold a distinct image of her though, with white hair, deeply wrinkled skin, scoured from her years outdoors in the sun and wind, and twinkling eyes. She smiled and laughed easily, even though she had severely arthritic hands and moved about slowly. Despite all the hardships she had lived through, she was always cheerful and full of life. She used to say in a combination of German and broken English, "*Vee must lookink to da heller seit*," meaning, "We must look to the brighter side of life." She was a devout Catholic and never ever missed the Sunday Mass where she always sat next to us in the same pew.

Grandmother remained active to the end, despite her arthritis, with her cooking and baking and tending a big garden. To her, the earth was a Garden of Eden if you were willing to work it hard enough. She raised cabbages, corn, squash, tomatoes, green beans, peas, carrots, parsnips, potatoes, radishes, and rutabagas, and what she couldn't eat or give to the neighbors, she canned or put in her root cellar. We often visited her in town, and she liked to come out to see us on the ranch where she spent so many years of her own life.

My fondest memory of my grandmother is when I would go to her house. My mother would drop me off and go do her shopping. Grandmother would greet me at the door, pinch my cheek, and say, "I wonder if there are some cookies in the cookie jar. Why don't you go look and see?" Then she would sit me down at the dining room table to do picture puzzles together. Her home was always neat and tidy and she had an embroidered white lace table runner on the table, but she would remove it so we had lots of room to do the puzzle. If we didn't finish the puzzle that day, she would just leave it there until I could come back. I remember too that she always pressed a bag of hard candies into my hand before I left.

Grandmother was taking a walk in Gackle in June of 1967, as she liked to do whenever the sun was out, and was just crossing the street in the crosswalk, when she was hit by a cattle truck with faulty brakes. The sheriff said that as far as he knew, she was the first pedestrian killed by a motor vehicle in the history of Logan County. Before that accident, the only motor vehicle deaths in the county were from roll-overs on rural country roads, usually when the driver had been drinking.

I think her funeral was the saddest one I have ever been to. I keep her in my memory and evoke her when I need to pull my mind out of a dark place.

8

FTER I LOOKED AT THE OLD BARNYARD I came back to the house. Being out in the wind had chilled me, and my teeth were chattering. I sat back down on my pail on the porch and pulled my collar up to stay warm. I still had almost an hour before I met the sheriff and considered seeking the warmth of my car, but it was tolerable out of the wind, and I prefered the outdoors, so I stayed. I took the bologna sandwich out of my coat pocket and took a bite. It tasted incredibly stale, so I tossed it in the weeds. Maybe the skunks that evidently lived under the porch would enjoy it. I looked to the northeast just as a flock of crows rose out of the shelterbelt, and my thoughts turned back to my brother.

When Jake joined the Army, he was shipped to Fort Lewis for basic training. He never made the Green Berets, however. He didn't even make the preliminary Army Ranger status because he failed to complete the fifty-meter swim test, which had to be completed in uniform and boots, on time. He hadn't ever learned to swim on the ranch and all he could do was dog-paddle. Still, he entered infantry training, and he was excited about his upcoming tour of duty in Vietnam.

Jake's absence left a hole in my life and in my parents' lives too, I guess. My father started coming in earlier in the evening so that he could shower before the Channel 4 News with Walter Cronkite came on. My parents would watch faithfully to hear about the fighting in Vietnam, and my father had a map of Vietnam that he had gotten with the National Geographic magazine, and he would lay it out on the dining room table and locate the places they talked about on television.

I tried to imagine what Jake was going through. The main thing I had to draw on, besides the news, were television shows that I had seen about World War II, like *Combat*, *The Rat Patrol*, and *Twelve O'Clock High*. I knew this war was different, but I didn't know how. I wrote my brother letters almost every week, but I only received a few letters from him the whole time he was gone. I kept those in a shoe box under my bed, along with the postcards sent by my sister Marie from the Congo, and I still have them. I received the first letter when Jake was still in training camp:

> *January 13, 1969*
> *Dear Buckaroo,*
> *Thank you for the letters. I don't get much time to write here. We are busy every day. I took first place in a test we had for M-16 accuracy. I placed six of six shots on target from 300 yards. I also did 200 pushups. I guess I got strong from lifting all the alfalfa bales. When we go to Vietnam I will show those commies what we ranchers from North Dakota can do!*
> *The food is pretty good here and we can eat all we want. We have good apples almost every day that are grown here in Washington. The roast beef is tough and stringy though, not like we have at home.*
> *Study hard in school and good luck with basketball.*
> *Sincerely,*
> *Jake*

Not much information there, but enough so that I could imagine him shooting a rifle at some Communist soldier in the future with deadly accuracy.

I was living a pretty secure and sheltered life the years he was gone in the Army. I wasn't old enough to drive yet, so my entire life revolved around the ranch and school. Nine months of the year I would get on the school bus about seven-thirty in the morning and it took nearly an hour for the bus to pick everyone up on the route and drive to town. After school I would get back on the bus and I wouldn't get home until four-thirty or five o'clock. Then I would have to do my chores, eat supper, and do my homework. It didn't leave much time for fun. In the summers I had to depend on my parents to get around, so I rarely went into town unless it was with my mother when she went grocery shopping, and she didn't do that often because between the livestock we raised and the garden, we didn't need much in the way of "store boughten" food.

The school I attended in Gackle had a little over two hundred students in grades seven through twelve. We thought that was pretty large. Most of the teachers were competent, with a few exceptions, one being Mr. Kirveda, who taught English in grades seven, eight, and nine, and took a sadistic interest in paddling male students with a large wooden paddle drilled with holes through it. He was eventually let go, but only after paddling some kid to the point where he could not sit on a tractor seat.

In those days I always considered it a treat to go into town because the main street was lined with pickups and cars and I would always run into kids from school I knew. There was a bowling alley back then and the Krieger Theater and the Tastee Freez and the baseball field and the tennis courts (although only the town kids played tennis), so we thought that the town was loads of fun. In the summer there was always a demolition derby and a parade on the Fourth of July. What we didn't know then was that the town was already on a downhill slide towards a slow death. Its heart was still beating, but that was about it.

The second letter I received from Jake was about two months after he had arrived in Vietnam.

> *September 18, 1969.*
> *Dear Pete,*
> *Thank you for all the letters. I hope you get this one. It is hard to believe that it has to travel all around the world to North Dakota.*
> *Right now I'm lying on my own cot with a tent roof over my head. I am fine but it is God-awful hot here, much worse than*

even the hottest summer days on the ranch because of the humidity. I am always sweating, even at night. The air field is close to us and the Phantoms and Skyhawks fly out of here twenty-four hours a day so that makes it hard to sleep.

When we got here we had some more training and we got to throw hand grenades. Wow, was that ever fun! Now we are doing some patrols but we have not seen any Viet Cong yet. They must have heard I was coming! We expect to go out in the field soon and then we will give them hell!

The food is good here. We get regular American food like hamburgers, chicken, ham, and steaks. We went into the city once and ate chicken cooked on a stick and pastries wrapped in some kind of weird rice papers. It was pretty good, too.

The country is beautiful here except for the barbed wire and bunkers everywhere. The people are nice so far, but dirty, and we are told not to trust them.

I have made some good friends. One of them is from North Dakota and grew up on a farm near Rugby. We knew some of the same basketball players from the towns we played. Another guy is from Minnesota. There are lots of black guys here. I get along fine with them.

I hope you can trap some muskrats this winter. Don't worry too much about me here. I will take care of myself. Be good.

Love,

Your brother Jake

It might seem strange to others for Jake to mention black guys, but where we grew up there were no blacks whatsoever. In fact, there were no Hispanics (we called them Mexicans then), no Asians (we called them Orientals then), no other races at all. The only blacks in the whole state were in the military at the Air Force bases in Minot and Grand Forks or a handful of students who had scholarships to play basketball at some of the state colleges and universities. We saw American Indians, but only rarely, in Bismarck. Mostly they were confined to the reservations. Migrant farm workers from Texas and Mexico came to the state in the summer, but that was only for hoeing sugar beets in the Red River Valley and we never saw them in our part of the state. We never saw any Italians for that matter, or Greeks, or Spanish, or anyone foreign other than Germans, Norwegians, Swedes, and a few Scottish and English. There were occasional Irish or Italian men who worked for the railroad, although none of them lived in our town. We heard about Gypsies who traveled through the state occasionally in caravans of cars, but all we knew about them was that we were supposed to watch out that they didn't steal our chickens.

Since we never met any blacks growing up, I don't ever remember any prejudicial comments made about them. They just weren't part of our world. When the Civil Rights movement started, we watched on television as blacks marching in the South had police dogs and fire hoses turned on them and they showed water fountains labeled "Whites Only." Anyone could see that was just plain wrong, and as far as I knew, everyone supported civil rights. If there was prejudice at all, it was against Southern whites who were viewed as a somewhat backward and ignorant people (our frame of reference was Jethro in *The Beverly Hillbillies*) and who had fought against us in the Civil War and were therefore forever suspect. Racial prejudice would come later to North Dakota, but not until the 1980s and 1990s, when television and politicians and talk radio began to raise fears of crime and welfare cheats and immigrants who didn't speak English streaming across our borders.

We maybe had a little prejudice against Norwegians. I'm not sure why, but I remember we told a lot of dumb Norwegian jokes as a kid of the "How many Norwegians does it take to screw in a light bulb" variety. I guess they had some prejudice against us, too, and especially the German Russians in the southern part of the state, who they called, "stupid Rooschians."

The third letter I received from Jake was when he was just starting to see some real action.

March 14, 1970.

Hi, Pete,

Yesterday the choppers brought in our mail and hot chow for us. We had steak, potatoes, gravy, two kinds of vegetables, bread, cherry pie, and chocolate milk. It was our first hot chow since Christmas. When we were on patrol all we would eat was C rations and I am so sick of them I can hardly stand it. I also got the food package that mom sent. Tell her thank you. That was a real treat, especially the malted milk balls and SweeTarts.

I have a new friend in the platoon. He grew up in southern California and we call him Wavy Davy. He is small and skinny and he reminds me of you. I feel sorry for him because he grew up without a dad. I'm trying to set a good example for him. I gave him half the malted milk balls.

I got all your letters. Usually they come in a bunch so I read them all but I haven't written more because we have been out in the field. We have taken some sniper shots. It is scary but we hit the ground and no one has been killed yet. I will tell you more about it when I get home.

How is the basketball team doing?

I have really bad athletes feet but other than that I am okay. I can't think of much more to say except don't worry, I'll be fine.

Jake

Setting a "good example" was something our parents preached to us constantly and they were quick to point out the individuals and families who were not good examples. Our neighbors, the McCormicks, were always held up by my father, in particular, as an example of what we should not be. The McCormicks lived on a small ranch just three miles north of us. The ranch was one of the most rundown, or perhaps the most rundown, in the county. Lilacs and hollyhocks had grown up around the house and had never been trimmed so we could only see the roof of the house, missing some shingles, from the road. The barn needed painting, the lawn was left unmowed, and their machinery was always broken down and scattered in the yard, never parked in straight rows like those of the German farmers and ranchers. They had maybe forty head of cattle, but they were a sad, skinny lot, stuck on a small overgrazed pasture in the summer and often with little hay in the winter. Worst of all, they also raised a few goats. No serious rancher raised goats!

Mr. McCormick was known as a drunkard, and his pickup could be seen outside Dani's Bar almost every night of the week. He was the last rancher to put up hay in the summer and the first to put the cattle out to pasture when the snow was still melting and the new grass just peeking out. His cattle were always getting out of his poorly maintained fences and into the fields of the neighbors. One time his cattle got out, and my father discovered them in our hay field eating one of our hay stacks. My father chased the cattle back to the McCormicks with his pickup and charged Mr. McCormick ten dollars for the hay they had eaten. He paid it, too, but not very happily. Another time, McCormick's mare broke through their fence and wandered over towards our pasture. The mare was in heat, and we had a coal black stallion at that time who went berserk trying to get to her and finally jumped our fence, badly cutting its hindquarter on the barbed wire. The vet charged my father fifty dollars to sew him up and my father wanted to charge Mr. McCormick for that and a stud fee to boot, but mother told him, "You need to build your fences higher," and he knew she had a point there.

The McCormicks had six children. When we were in grade school, I remember that they were teased mercilessly on the school bus for their worn and out-of-style clothing. Kids can be mean, and many times the McCormick children stepped off the bus in tears. Mrs. McCormick was a cheerful, chesty woman, and the women in the community thought she wore too much makeup. My mother was nice to her though and would sometimes stop at their house with a jar of preserves or some sweet corn and stay and talk. She said that Mrs. McCormick was often left alone in the house with the children and had no relatives in the area and was dying for someone to talk to. Once I heard my mother tell my father, "That woman needs to develop more backbone. Why, if I had a husband who sat in the bar all day, I'd walk right in there and yank him out by the ear."

* * *

I DIDN'T GET ANOTHER LETTER of my own from Jake for almost a year, although he wrote Mom and Dad once in a while and always put in a word or two to me. The last letter I received from him was in March, 1971. A late March blizzard had just subsided and we'd had no mail for two days. My mother was anxious to get the mail and asked me to watch for the rural mail carrier who would put our mail in our big silver mailbox at the end of the driveway. When I saw him drive up, I jumped into my boots and, without even putting a coat on, ran out to the mailbox. I looked through the mail, and there it was, addressed directly to me. I ran back to the house and ripped it open.

> *March 3, 1971*
> *Dear Peter,*
> *Well it's another rainy day in Vietnam. I need a shower bad. I haven't had one for weeks.*
> *I can't wait to come home. The war here is not going well and it is not what we expected or what we were told. I have seen many people killed and it is not like on TV. Two of our men lost their lives last week and many others have been wounded. One of the men killed was Wavy Davy.*
> *Don't ever join the army like I did. Do something good with your life.*
> *I should be coming home in a few months if I stay alive. Maybe we can go to the rodeo or the fair. I would like to eat some good hot dogs and ice cream.*
> *Love,*
> *Jake*

I didn't show that letter to my parents because I didn't want them to worry, but instead immediately hid it in that shoebox under my bed. That evening I went outside by myself and climbed the butte south of our house. It was about eleven o'clock at night and completely still. The only thing I could hear was the crunch of the snow with each of my steps. The blizzard wind had carved the snow into eerie snowbanks that sometimes pitched into sharp peaks that looked like mountains and other times rippled across the landscape like sand dunes in the desert. Where the snow was hard I could walk on top of these snow banks, but in other places I would sink down to my knees with every step. It took me awhile, but I walked to the very highest point of the butte and I lay down on my back and stared up at the stars dazzling all around. I listened intently, but there was not a breath of air, not a single sound, as if the world had taken a deep breath and was holding it in before it exhaled.

9

WHEN JAKE ARRIVED FROM VIETNAM at the airport in Bismarck my parents and I went to pick him up. We arrived an hour early and waited, scanning the sky for his plane. There is nothing more emotional than a son coming home from war and it was everything I'd seen on TV: the "Welcome Home Jake" sign that my mother had made, the waiting by the gate, the excitement as we first glimpsed him coming through the door. Mother cried out and gave him a long hug and kiss. Even my father hugged him. Then Jake turned to me. "It looks like the little buckaroo has grown up," he said. He tousled my hair and gave me a hug and awkwardly tried to lift me up, but I was now too heavy.

Later we went to the Country Kitchen Restaurant near the interstate. My parents liked the comfort of familiarity—nothing "spicy" like Mexican or Chinese. The waitress came over with the shiny menus and she stood there for a moment, smiling with her hand on her hip and looking at Jake. He still had his military fatigues on and she said, "Honey, are you in the service?"

"Army. But I'm out now."

"Were you in Vietnam?"

"Yeah."

"Well, welcome back. You boys are doing a good thing for the country over there."

My mother and father looked at Jake with big smiles on their faces.

Later the waitress came back to take our orders and she said to my brother, "I just talked to the manager. He said your meal is on the house. Whatever you want."

Jake thanked her and ordered two breakfast specials, both with eggs and pancakes and hash browns, one with ham and one with bacon, and the waitress didn't bat an eye. She brought out the orders all at once, balancing three of the plates on one arm. After she walked away, Mother said, "Isn't that nice? People can be so nice."

"Not like those long-haired hippies in Chicago," my father said. He had been angry about the war protesters, not because he was such a huge supporter of the war, but because he somehow saw their actions as an affront to his son's service. In his mind, hippies and war protesters were one and the same, and he never missed a chance to say how he felt about them.

Jake wolfed down his meal and didn't say much. I noticed dark semi-circles under his eyes and thought he looked tired and worn out. Mother tried to make conversation. She hated a lull in the conversation. "Do you want some more syrup, Jake? Look, they have two kinds of syrup."

"Sure, but it's not as good as your homemade," he replied. She beamed again, and then a moment later she said, "I thought we would have your Bronze Star framed and hang it in the living room."

He stopped chewing. He paused for a second and then looked up. "I threw it out," he said.

"Oh, you did not!" Mother said. There was a moment of silence. "Why would you throw out your medal?"

"Because it's bullshit, total bullshit."

He looked down again and took a hard stab at his bacon.

"What do you mean?" Father said, "They don't give those out for nothing."

Jake jerked his head up. "What do you know about it . . . you get home and they give you these medals and a citation and people who write it up weren't even there. They don't know what happened. Just a bunch of lying crap."

Jake reached into his shirt pocket, took out a pack of cigarettes, tapped one out and lit it with a brass lighter. He blew a long thin stream of smoke up in the air. Jake had never smoked before and no one had ever smoked in our family. My mother and father exchanged glances, and my mother bit her lower lip ever so slightly and she said, "Did you have enough to eat, Jake? Want anything else?"

10

WE DROVE HOME AFTER WE LEFT the Country Kitchen, and my father talked the entire way home about the ranch. He told Jake about the new 4020 John Deere tractor that had an eighty-three horsepower engine, and the expansion of the cattle herd, and the rotation of the crops. I am sure he just assumed that this was information Jake was just dying to hear about.

Work and the ranch were everything to my father and the essence of his being. He was the oldest son of Josef and Rosina's seven children and the only one to stay on the ranch. Five of their children were girls and three of them became teachers and moved elsewhere in the state, and two married local ranchers. My father's younger brother, Herbert, got his arm torn off by a steam engine belt when he was just sixteen years of age and decided that ranching was not for him and later moved to California. As a consequence of being the only son left to ranch, my father ended up with the 1,600 acres of land from Grandfather Josef and bought another 640 acres in 1958, and 480 acres in 1970. He had what was considered a fairly large ranch and feedlot operation for that period of time and we were running up to 400 head of cattle.

My father inherited the same work ethic as my grandfather, and his was magnified because of what he went through growing up during the Great Depression when he was in his formative youthful years. He used to tell stories about the years when they were so poor they never saw fresh fruit except when they would get an orange in their stocking at Christmas. Some of the neighbor families lost their ranches to the banks and had to move out to Washington or Oregon to pick apples. That prospect struck fear into him. Between the drought, dust storms, and grasshoppers, he observed that only the farmers and ranchers who worked ceaselessly survived. As a consequence, his work ethic seemed to be driven by the fear of failure, rather than the joy of work.

The image I have of my father is of him dressed in blue jeans, cowboy boots, and a long sleeved work shirt (no matter how hot it was), wearing a sweat-stained cowboy hat all year round, possibly pulling up his collar in the winter as his one concession to the cold. He smells of hay and manure and he is striding in from the barn or the field for a quick cup of coffee or to listen to the cattle and grain prices report on the radio before he heads out again. He worked until supper at six o'clock (mother was expected to have it ready on the dot) and then would go outdoors for a few more hours of work until he came in at nine or ten, had another bite to eat, and showered and went to bed. He very rarely watched television and never had any hobbies. The one exception was that he and mother never missed the Lawrence Welk Show every Saturday night. (Lawrence Welk, the accordion player band leader, had grown up just southwest of our ranch, in Strasburg, North Dakota.) He and my mother would play cards occasionally with friends, Whist and Pinochle, but not more than a few times a year. The only vacations I ever remember him taking were when he and my mother took the train to Seattle to see my sister Eva or drove down to Arizona to see Annette.

When World War II started brewing in Europe, my father was of draft age, but Grandmother Rosina was opposed to her son going off to war and discouraged it. Like families of other German Russian immigrants, she had not forgotten that one of the reasons their parents had come to this country was to avoid conscription into the Russian Army. In their view, wars were begun by aristocrats and the rich and the common people were sent to fight them. They did not want to be drawn into wars that they felt had nothing to do with their ordinary lives. As a consequence, many people in that part of North Dakota were isolationists and opposed the Selective Service draft. This isolationism changed considerably, of course, when Japan bombed Pearl Harbor. Still, many young farmers and ranchers sought deferments from service in the military from local draft boards who were allowed to grant deferments to agricultural workers, "essential to the war effort," to prevent a farm labor shortage. My father sought and received a deferment, so he never served in World War II.

* * *

DESPITE THE INCIDENT at the Country Kitchen Restaurant, I think my parents believed that Jake was basically fine when he came home from Vietnam. They assumed he would eventually go to college or start ranching, or go to college and then ranch, or get married and ranch, but maybe he just needed a little time to "sort things out."

Jake never talked about the war, not even once, and Mother and Father did not press him on it. It was understood that war was a difficult thing to talk about. Even though my father had never seen war up close, they had known many friends and neighbors who had been in war. It was common knowledge that many of them had come back damaged deep inside by the killing and the dying they had seen, but they just held it in. It was like they were afraid of what would happen if they let it out, and silence was a glue inside them that kept the pieces together. One of my father's best friends from town, John Kaupp, had seen a lot of action in the D-Day invasion, but he refused to talk about it, even though his wife said that he would wake up screaming in his sleep from nightmares about it some thirty years later. Most people thought that if people didn't want to talk about something, they probably had a good reason, and it was not polite to ask. Privacy is one of the highest values on the plains, and asking someone about almost anything other than weather, livestock, or crops was considered, "prying into other people's business."

Jake slept a lot the first weeks home, but that was to be expected, too. He would get up about eleven o'clock or noon and Mother would fix him a huge breakfast of waffles and sausages. He loved waffles as much as oatmeal and could eat a pile smothered in butter and mom's homemade chokecherry syrup. Then he would wander around the ranch or out to the pasture to look at the cattle. He would be gone for a few hours and then come back and sleep some more on the couch, always using the same old smelly pillow that he had since he was a small child. He drank a few beers and watched TV late into the evening, long after the rest of us had gone to bed.

Mother kept asking him when he was going to see his high school girlfriend, Patty. Patty was in her final year at North Dakota State University, majoring in home economics, and when she came back home one weekend soon after Jake's arrival, I think my mother was more excited than Jake. Jake was going to go pick her up at her folks and take her out for the evening, but when he came downstairs ready to leave in a worn army jacket and blue jeans, Mother was obviously irked and asked, "You wearing that?" When he answered yes, she made him head right back upstairs and put on some nicer clothes.

I don't know what Jake and Patty did that night. They probably just drove around or maybe went to a movie in Bismarck or Jamestown, but the next morning Mother waited for Jake to wake up and come downstairs so that she could quiz him. When he finally came down, she was all smiles.

"Did you have fun last night?"

"Sort of."

"Well . . . what did you do?"

"You don't want to know."

Mother was silent for a minute, and I knew she was thinking that over, wondering what that might imply, and whether she should pursue it. Finally, she asked, "When are you going to see her again?"

"Probably never."

"Jake, for heaven's sake, you can't expect to start up where you left off. Give it time. Patty is such a nice girl and the two of you are just like two peas in a pod."

"Mom, things are different now. I've changed and she's changed, too. Just drop it."

She wasn't ready to drop it. "You could go horseback riding. You always liked to do that."

"Yeah, right. That would be a lot of fun."

Mother stood up quickly from the table, "Well, get your own breakfast. I don't fix breakfast this late in the day."

Jake had been home about two weeks when my father thought that he should start doing something on the ranch. It would be good for him, help him get back into civilian life. After all, two weeks was long enough for anyone to rest up, and it was not healthy for people to sit around and do nothing all day. Father woke him up early in the morning and sent him out on the tractor with the cultivator to dig the summer fallow. I was helping my father vaccinate some of the calves. My job was to chase them into the chute, one by one, waving my arms in the air. Once they entered the chute and got to the far end, my father would shove a bar in behind them, so they couldn't back up, and he vaccinated them and attached a clip to their ears. It was hot work because those damn calves never wanted to go in that chute, and the sweat was dripping down my face and off my nose. So when Mother came out with some lunch for me to bring out to Jake in the field—a Thermos of coffee, bologna sandwiches wrapped in wax paper with rubber bands, an apple, and a cupcake—I was glad to take a break and get away from the cattle.

I knew he was on the north quarter, so I drove out there in the pickup and scanned the field for the dust kicked up by the cultivator. I didn't see any dust, and for a moment I thought he must have moved to a different field when I saw the tractor on the east side next to the pasture line. The tractor was not moving, which was usually a sign that it was stuck in the mud or something had broken down, but it was a dry summer and I knew he couldn't be stuck, and so when I drove up I expected to see Jake under the cultivator fixing a point that had broken off or making some repair, but he wasn't near the tractor and cultivator. I got out. It was windy, and dust was coming off the field with the gusts, so I shielded my eyes with my hand as I peered around. Where the hell was he?

Finally, I noticed something in the grass near the fence line two hundred yards away and I walked over. When I got closer I could see Jake lying on his back looking at the sky. He couldn't hear me because of the wind, so he didn't move until I was almost over him, and he jerked up when he saw me.

"What are you doing?" I asked.

He scanned the horizon for a minute, let out a deep breath, and then looked at me. "Nothing . . . I'm just wondering why I'm out here doing this. That's all."

"We have to kill the weeds before they go to seed. You know that."

"That's not what I mean. I mean what does it really matter . . . in the big scheme of things. Why are we out here, working our butts off, trying to scratch a living, when we all end up in the same fucking hellhole anyhow?"

He stared at me a moment, and I didn't know how to answer. He stood up and started walking slowly back to the ranch. When I started to follow him he said, "Just go."

I went back to the pickup, and then I saw the lunch lying on the seat so I drove up to him and rolled down the window and yelled, "Do you want your lunch?"

He just shook his head and waved me by and kept walking.

A few weeks later my brother fell off that swing in the back yard. I had gotten up to pee in the middle of the night and I walked by my brother's room and noticed that he was not there. I looked outside the front to see if his car was there and it was, so I knew he was home, and then I looked out the back and there was just enough light in the yard to make out something on the ground by the swing. I must have been afraid to go outside, but I went anyhow, and I walked out in the dewy wet grass with my bare feet, and found him lying face down under the swing in a pool of vomit. There must have been nearly a case of crushed beer cans lying around him. I was not sure what to do, but I went and woke up my father—quietly so as not to wake up my mother—and he came out, picked Jake up and wiped the vomit off his face with the sleeve of his robe, and hoisted him up with Jake's arm over his shoulder and carried him into the house. The next day Jake drove to Minneapolis to see his Army buddy, Nate Swenson, and we didn't see him again for more than two years.

11

WHEN MY BROTHER LEFT for Minneapolis, my mother and father assumed that he just needed some time and would be back soon. But when a few weeks had gone by, and they had not heard anything, mother began to worry. She tried calling Nate Swenson, but he was living with his parents and she didn't know their first names, so she called dozens of Swenson residences in vain, never finding the right one. Then she tried some of his local friends. Most of them had not been in touch with Jake since he had gone off to Vietnam, but she finally reached someone whose brother had also served in Vietnam and by some process, unbeknownst to me, Mother finally reached Jake in Minneapolis. To her consternation, he was not coming home. Instead he was driving out to the West Coast.

The next we heard of him was in November 1971. He was living in San Francisco. He called Mother briefly from there, but that made her worry even more. My mother had heard about San Francisco on television and in *Life* magazine and in her mind it was associated with Haight-Ashbury, psychedelic drugs, and free love. For someone on a ranch in North Dakota, San Francisco seemed like a very foreign and dangerous place.

After that Jake moved around a lot, but his whereabouts and what he was doing was always a sort of mystery to us. He rarely left a telephone number where he could be reached, so Mother would often be reluctant to leave the house for fear he would call and she might not be there. Besides San Francisco, he called from Venice and Chico in California at different times, and each time my mother and father would get out the road atlas and find the cities on the map. Often he would just tell us he was staying with friends he'd met. It was unclear how he supported himself, although he once reported that he had some type of "delivery job" when he was in Chico. When my mother heard that she said to my father, "Well, delivery can be a good career. People always need things delivered." Jake never came home during that period of time, even at Christmas, when he said he was going to Mexico where it was warm, and that broke my mother's heart.

My mother became much quieter during that absence, rarely singing or laughing like she used to. She also became more fervent in her religious beliefs. She had always been a devout Catholic, but growing up on a ranch that usually meant attending Mass on Sundays only. Now she became fastidious about observing all the rituals—every holy day, every rule and observance, and regular confession—although what she had to confess was totally beyond me. I thought that sinning was something young people did and it usually involved sex or thinking about sex. I couldn't even begin to imagine my mother confessing some kind of tawdry sinfulness through the wire mesh into the priest's listening ear.

I don't think my father ever became overly religious in the way Mother did, although he went to Holy Mass and observed the Sabbath. Almost all farm and ranch families are religious to some extent because living on the plains where a hail storm or drought can make or break you, you realize that you're struggling against forces you can't control. Believing in God gives you a sense that whatever you cannot control by sheer work and determination must be in the hands of a higher spirit.

Religion for my father was also a way to bring an order to his understanding of the world, as it made clear distinctions between right and wrong, good and bad, so that you always knew exactly where you stood with God. But he didn't believe in taking the rites and rituals around religion too far. He used to tell us how when he was young he saw them perform the *Taufe*, or Baptism, at Green Lake in Macintosh County, south of Wishek. In those days the baptisms were a huge community get-together and people would bring picnic lunches and sit in the grass on the hillside and watch, even the non-Baptists. The baptism was by immersion, and one preacher used to hold the people being baptized under the water for so long that they would come up sputtering and blue. As a child my father thought they were drowning. Ever since then, he was always wary of overt religious demonstrations. Consequently, he had a real distaste for the religious fundamentalists on TV who wore their religion on their sleeve. For him, religion was something between you and God and maybe the priest in the confessional.

Growing up, religion for me was just a part of our everyday life. There was not much made of the doctrine of separation of church and state in our little part of the world. Every year before Christmas, our public school had its annual Christmas pageant and the whole community would come, not an empty seat, and we always had a play or skit about the birth of the Christ child. I hardly knew a person growing up who wasn't a Christian. Besides us Catholics, there were Lutherans, Baptists, Presbyterians, and Congregationalists in our community. They got along fine with us, although the older folks did not think you should marry one. We knew only one Jewish person, Mr. Spindler, who owned the Hide and Fur Company in Jamestown, and who I was fond of as a child because he always gave me a Tootsie-Pop from a gallon jar he kept in his office when we brought our muskrats in to sell. We did not know any Hindus or Buddhists or Muslims, who we only read about in our geography books at school when studying foreign countries, and even then it would only be a paragraph or two about their religion.

I had learned my catechism in grade school as expected, although I really only became interested in religion in a more than obligatory way when I became fifteen and Father Ryan started a youth group which met on Wednesday nights at the church. Mother thought this would be a good activity for me. When I was young, I was known as the naughty one of us kids in the family, mostly because I got in trouble at school from time to time. It was mostly innocent enough stuff— throwing wads of paper, passing notes in class, and talking in line, but it got me called down to the principal's office a few times. The only time I got into any serious trouble was when we were having a snow ball fight at noon hour when I was in the seventh grade and I accidentally hit a third grader, Christy

63

Schwartz, on the side of the face, leaving a big red mark. I got paddled for that by the assistant principal, and Mother and Father got a call. In Mother's eyes, getting into trouble at school was a warning sign that you would end up in trouble as an adult, so she thought that the church youth group might help set me on the right path.

Mother had to make me go to that youth group the first few times, but I found that I actually enjoyed it and after that I went voluntarily. Youth group gave me a group of kids to hang out with, and I needed that because I did not fit in with the jocks at school. I was taller than my brother at five-foot-eleven, but I had little of his athletic ability, so it was clear I would not be an athletic star in high school like he had been.

Father Ryan was a charismatic figure, tall and good looking, with an imposing nose, and a booming voice. He wore a neatly trimmed stylish beard, smiled often, and did not have the dour, serious look of the priests we were used to. He came into our community like a whirlwind and brought some immediate changes to the church. At that time we still sang at least one hymn during every service in the original German language. All the older folks knew German and many would have continued to sing in German to this day if they had their way, but Father Ryan knew that this did not have an appeal to the younger people whose German was less strong or non-existent, so he ended the practice. He also was the first priest in our parish who was not of German heritage, and the older Germans thought he was snobbish because he did not speak with the German accent, like "Press the Lort" for "Praise the Lord" and "fate" for "faith." Some of the older parishioners grumbled too about his lack of humility, *Er Ist Bros*, because he sprinkled his sermons with anecdotes about his travels in Italy and Vatican City as a seminary student and occasionally made an anti-war inference. Pride was considered a dangerous thing in our community. Better to be unassuming and humble.

Father Ryan was one of the multitudes of priests who had flocked to seminaries with the fresh air that arrived with Pope John XXIII. Pope John and the Second Vatican Council renewed the church and in so doing attracted thousands of bright young ambitious men to the priesthood in the heyday of American Catholicism, the late 1950s and early 1960s. To top it off, the American president was a Catholic who exemplified the Catholics of that era. Oh, what vitality and energy there was in the church at that time! It would all fade, of course, when the Catholic Church retrenched after the death of Pope John, but for one short moment in time, that confluence of events produced priests like Father Ryan.

If he was not the kind of priest the older generation favored, Father Ryan was right for the times and the young people. He did not preach sin and guilt as a way to draw people to the church and then instill fear in them as the means of salvation, like most of the priests did at that time. He believed in the rituals of the church as a transformative power in people's lives and that they were the chief means to salvation, not guilt. And he wanted these rituals to be relevant to our lives, so English was always preferred over Latin.

Father Ryan was also a strong proponent of social justice. Whether he got that from his Jesuit training or not, I don't know, but he thought the church had a role to play in politics and social issues. In youth group he often talked to us about issues like poverty and civil rights and his former work on an Indian reservation in South Dakota. He even made a favorable reference to Father David Berrigan, the peace activist, on one occasion, which would not have set well with the older parishioners, had they found out. When Father Ryan talked to us, he often sat facing backwards in a chair, his legs straddling the sides, smoking cigarettes, and cracking jokes from time to time. He spoke to us like we were adults, not in the condescending manner we were used to, and made us feel like what we thought and said and did was important. All of us kids in the youth group looked up to Father Ryan with something that came close to adoration.

At the youth group meetings, we often sang hymns, and Father Ryan would sing along in his booming voice. One of the kids, Kurt Schneider, played the acoustic guitar, and he would accompany us. Father Ryan would let us sing the contemporary songs like "Here I Am Lord" and "Morning Has Broken." We would belt out those songs loudly, our eager young faces shining with happiness. Being in the youth group and the singing were the greatest joys of my teenage years.

The most important thing Father Ryan taught me was how to pray: "Prayer should not be asking for things for ourselves, but asking God to help us change in ways that conform to how Christ would want us to live." Each week one of the youth was asked to prepare a special prayer, and when the week came for me to give it, I was nervous, so I worked on it all week and memorized what I wanted to say. I prayed for an end to hunger and poverty and for God to grant us world peace and the strength to be a good Christians. At the end, I mentioned my brother Jake and asked God to protect him until he safely returned. As I gave that prayer, I felt like a different person. A confidence grew in me, and I felt at that time that God was close and I was really speaking to Him.

Afterwards, Father Ryan requested I come into his office. He lit a cigarette and motioned for me to sit down in an upholstered chair. For a moment I was worried I had done something wrong. The only time our former priest, Father Klundt, talked to us kids was when he wanted to admonish us, like he might tell a girl with a short skirt, "I don't want to see that in church. Only loose girls wear skirts like that," and give her a disdainful look, or one time when he saw me goofing around with another kid, he said, "It's good your grandmother is not here to see that."

But Father Ryan smiled at me, which put me at ease. "Peter, have you thought about what you might do after high school?"

"I don't know. I guess I'll go to college and then decide."

"You gave a wonderful prayer tonight. God has given you a special gift. You don't say much in group normally, but I can tell that you have God's spirit inside of you."

"I don't know."

"No, really, I mean it. It shines through you when you let it. You should think about the church as a vocation, possibly the priesthood. God may be calling you."

I felt terribly pleased he had singled me out, as I think he knew I would be. He had planted a seed, it just wasn't clear the soil was fertile.

12

ANOTHER REASON I LIKED the youth group was that Lori Bender was in it. Lori was the same age I was and I knew her from school. She was a town girl, however, not a farm girl, and she hung out with the town kids who had their own little world. They always wore clothes that were in style, they had straighter teeth, the girls were thinner and prettier, the boys cocky and sure of themselves. They didn't have to board the yellow school buses for long rides home after school and they spent their summers riding bikes around town, going to the swimming pool, hanging out at the Tastee Freez, and flirting with other boys and girls in a seemingly endless summer of fun, while the kids from the farms and ranches toiled on tractors, chased cattle, pitched hay, cleaned barns, and got their boots covered in manure that stuck and dried and marked them for who they were. She would have been out of my world, if not for the youth group.

Lori had a radiant complexion, unlike many of the German girls at that age, dark shiny hair, and deep-brown eyes. She was often quiet and serious. She wore glasses like I did, but she would take them off when she wasn't in school or reading, and her eyes sparkled and came alive if she was in the right mood. Unlike many of the kids who attended youth group because their parents made them, she enjoyed the Bible readings and discussion, and she took her Catholicism so seriously that many kids thought she might become a nun. Of course, being a nun then did not have the connotation that it does now for young people. "The Flying Nun" was a popular television show and everyone knew the music of the "Singing Nun." In the original Woodstock movie, three nuns attending Woodstock walk by, and one of them glances at the camera, and she is young and pretty, and she flashes the peace sign. It was thought that you could be a nun and still be cool.

The first year of youth group I rarely talked to Lori directly but I often turned furtively and look at her to see her reaction to what was going on and our eyes frequently met. When we bowed our heads in prayer, I would open my eyes ever so slightly, glance up, and study her countenance. I thought that no one could look more becoming in prayer, and I wanted terribly to kiss her slender white neck.

By the beginning of my junior year of high school, Lori and I were sitting next to each other, and when I took her to the school Halloween Dance, we became a couple. Being a couple meant that we sat together at football and basketball games or high school assemblies and often went out Friday and Saturday nights.

That summer I bought my first car, a used Monte Carlo, with money I got from selling some steers that father had let me raise on my own. The Monte Carlo was gold with a jet black interior and an eight-track music player. I loved that car and I washed it every week with a sponge and hose in front of the house. Eventually I saved up money and bought chrome wheels and jacked up the back end with spacers in the rear springs like all the cool guys did.

When you are sixteen years of age and you live on a ranch, and you get your first car, it changes everything for you. Suddenly you have the freedom to go where you want, when you want, and you don't have to depend on borrowing your dad's pick-up or your mom's old Buick. And it opens up the possibility of sex. It would probably be hard for most teenagers today who have both parents working outside the home to understand, but in those days, without a car, there was almost zero opportunity to be alone with a girl. And the backseats of those cars were big, a king size bed as far as we were concerned, and most of them did not have bucket seats so your girlfriend would ride right beside you in the front when you drove. There is nothing in a man's life that will ever compare to the feeling of being sixteen or seventeen years old and driving around with your girlfriend, and she is pretty and ripe as can be, and she is sitting right next to you and so close that your shoulders are touching and you can smell the Prell in her hair. Many times I have thought that if I could recapture that feeling, I would give up being a monk, and hold on to it and never, ever, let it go.

Once I got that Monte Carlo, Lori and I often spent weekend nights like every other kid, driving up and down our tiny Main Street, stopping at the Tastee Freez, or driving to another nearby small town where kids were doing the exact same thing, driving up and down Main Street and going to the Dairy Queen/Tastee Freez/King Kone. Besides my home town of Gackle, we frequently drove to neighboring towns: Alfred, Streeter, Jud, and Napoleon. Napoleon was a little further, but it had a recreation hall, called "the Rec," where kids would go to play pool and smoke cigarettes. If we were feeling ambitious we might drive to Jamestown (population 15,000), which was about forty miles away, or Bismarck (population 40,000) which was about 100 miles away. We considered them big cities, but they were quite a drive, so we didn't go often.

Most of the high school kids would drink alcohol almost every weekend—beer or wine or some exotic drink, like lime vodka. There were kids that were exceptions, but they were considered weird, the "good kids." When we started dating, Lori and I bordered on being in that weird, good kid category. Her parents were very stern, and though they liked me because I was active in the youth group, I don't think they trusted any boys (with good reason), and Lori had a strict 11:00 p.m. curfew, and her parents met her at the door when I dropped her off. Lori said her mom always came up close to her to smell her breath and see if she had been drinking. Towards the end of our junior year in high school this changed, however, and her curfew was extended to one o'clock on weekends. We started drinking occasionally like everyone else and Lori would suck on Sen-Sens to cover the alcohol on her breath. We also began "making out" like other kids our age. It was pretty innocent stuff to begin with, and even then we secretly gave it up that year for six weeks for the Lenten season. That was my idea, believe it or not. I guess it was my first bout of something like celibacy.

Lori was my first love, the one you never forget. Maybe it wasn't the kind of love that could last, but at the time I would rather be with her than anyone else in the world. I know I was infatuated with her femininity and putting my arm around her and the smell of her perfume and the taste of her lips when we kissed. Plus, she was the only one who I could really talk to. Mostly we talked about youth group and school, but I could tell her about my family and the ranch and how I hated the ranch work, and she would listen as if it was fascinating. Then she would tell me about her younger brothers and sisters and how she hated her father who owned Bender's Cafe in town and who was gone at work all the time and yelled at her mother when he was at home. We told each other things that we had never told anyone else before.

13

OTHER THAN WITH LORI, I had no sexual experiences before I graduated from high school, unless the time Betsy Schaller kissed me at a birthday party in the sixth grade or the time Sherry and Kathy McCormick kissed me are counted. I can barely remember Betsy now, but the McCormick sisters fueled my imagination for the next twenty years.

Sherry and Kathy were from the McCormick family, our neighbors my mother and father thought were bad examples. They were a year apart, Sherry was two grades ahead of me and Kathy was one grade ahead of me. By the time we entered high school they had grown up a lot, and they had reached "full bloom," with thick brown hair and curvaceous figures. They had beautiful long legs, which were tan in the summer and svelte year round so if one of them walked by, boys would comment and say things like, "Her legs run right up to her ass," or "I would give my right arm if she would wrap those legs around me."

Once they became teenagers, the McCormick sisters began to wear their skirts very short and this brought them a lot of attention, especially from the boys. It wasn't a secret that they would leave the house with their skirts at their knees, but once they got out around the corner of the driveway and out of sight of their mother, they would roll in the waistband to shorten the skirts while waiting for the school bus. You could see that the waistband was rolled, but they didn't seem to care about that.

The short skirts made Sherry and Kathy the center of speculation, which in a small town, eventually reaches the parents. My mother was willing to cut some slack for Mrs. McCormick's behavior, but she did not abide what she considered promiscuous or inappropriate behavior on the part of young women. According to my mother, the McCormick girls would, "end up like Joan Otegard," if they continued on the road they were on. Joan Otegard was a classmate of mother's from thirty-five years ago who got pregnant in high school. Whoever the father was never married her and she ended up raising a daughter on her own working for the local phone company, which in those days was rock bottom wages. Thirty-five years later she was still shunned by half the town.

As far as I knew, however, it was purely speculation on my mother's part where Sherry and Kathy were concerned. They were not "sluts." If they had been free with sex it would have gotten around and all the boys in high school would have known about it.

My memorable encounter with the McCormick sisters started one winter evening when I was sixteen and was on the way to town for the Friday night basketball game. It had been snowing and blustery all afternoon and there is nothing in this country to stop the wind so the roads were beginning to get finger drifts. That didn't bother me. I had been driving long enough to know how to hit the drifts at just the right speed so as to ram through them, but not hit them too fast so as to lose control and skid into the ditch. But a few miles west of the McCormick ranch I saw the McCormick's beat up Ford Torino on the side of the road with the front end halfway into the ditch. They had apparently hit a big drift too fast, lost control, and spun out, getting stuck. Both girls were outside the car in their heels, with their short skirts and fishnet stockings, trying to use a rubber car mat to scoop the snow away from the front wheel that had slid partly into the ditch. I drove up and rolled down the window and asked, "Are you stuck?" and immediately realized it was a stupid thing to ask. I recovered and asked, "Would you like some help?"

They both smiled. Sherry said, "Oh, God, we're so glad you came along. Thank you so so much."

I told the girls to get back in the car to get warm, and I would pull them out. The temperature was about ten degrees, but the wind was blowing hard, so it was cold, and I was not dressed too warm either, with just my short leather jacket and gloves and no hat. I retrieved the length of tow chain my father made me keep in the trunk and backed my car up to theirs. I didn't want to jerk their bumper off so I got down on my back in the snow and shimmied under the car to attach the chain to the axle.

By the time I pulled them out, my ears were so cold they burned like fire, and the girls could see me reaching down to pull out chunks of snow that had gotten up under my shirt against my bare back. They thanked me, but I was freezing, so I quickly jumped back into my car and left.

Two days later, on Sunday, I got a call from Sherry. She said that she and Kathy had made some homemade chocolate fudge and wanted to give me some as a thank-you present. She said they could drop it off, but I wasn't sure what my mother would think if they stopped over, so I said I would stop by their house and pick it up. When I drove up to the house I noticed that their cars were not in the yard—both their mother and father must have been out. They came to the door in their short skirts and with mascara and make-up on, and I knew they must have dressed up just because I was coming over. They invited me in. "You have to see our new stereo record player," Kathy said. It was a cheap thing of black plastic and fake chrome that they had bought at J.C. Penneys with money they had earned babysitting, but they were proud of it, so I made a big deal about how cool it was. I remember that they only had three LPs—Linda Ronstadt, the Eagles, and Abba—but they wanted me to hear all three of them, so we sat on the davenport and listened to them and ate the fudge.

As I sat there, I looked around and couldn't help but notice how poor the family was. The davenport was covered with a green throw, but I could see that it was threadbare at the arms. Besides the davenport, there was a battered La-Z-Boy and two blue chairs, also badly worn. The wallpaper on the outside wall had water stains, like giant dried salty tears, running its entire length, floor to ceiling. But if they knew how shabby their house looked, they didn't act embarrassed, and it was clean. I could see the tracks where they had recently run the vacuum over the worn brown carpeting.

There was a small V-shaped shelf in the corner of the room with a figurine of the Virgin Mary and an eight-by-ten sepia-toned photograph of three men. I walked over to the photo to take a closer look and I realized that one of the men was their father, taken some time ago, with two other men I guessed could be his brothers. The men looked very young, with the soft fresh faces and the innocent smiles of youth before life gets hard. "Who are these two people?" I asked.

Kathy said, "Those are our uncles, our dad's brothers. They were both killed in the war. Uncle Mike was killed in the South Pacific, and Uncle Roger was killed in Italy."

"I'm sorry," I said. This was news to me. The McCormicks had moved here and bought the ranch after the war, and I doubted that even my parents knew about the brothers.

I didn't know what else to say so we went back to listening to the records, and I insisted they have some more of the fudge. The three of us ended up eating the whole plate of fudge as I sat between the two of them on the davenport and they told school stories and giggled and laughed. Then they started loudly singing along to Linda Ronstadt's "You're No Good."

They already knew the words to the song, and they were moving and bouncing in time to the music. I couldn't help notice that Sherry's skirt had ridden up—way up—and she didn't have her legs crossed, as I am sure she had been taught to, and I could see that she had pink panties on with a pattern of tiny red roses, and she didn't pull her skirt down. I felt my breath shorten and my face redden as the blood drummed through my body. I'm not sure if she didn't know or didn't care, but I think she knew she was having an effect on me. Kathy's legs were showing plenty too and I tried my best not to make my glances obvious, but my eyes kept sliding downwards as I sat there, looking at one and then the other. *Breathe in, breathe out. Breathe in, breathe out.* Then they both got up and pretended they had microphones and started dancing and singing as if they were in the band and performing for me. They did that for that whole side of the Linda Ronstadt album and most of Abba, laughing their heads off whenever they messed up the words.

I sat on the davenport and watched them. I thought they were the most beautiful creatures on earth right then.

Eventually they said that their mom would be coming home soon, and I got up to leave. They both thanked me again and they simultaneously gave me kisses on my cheeks, one on each side. That's not much, but when you are sixteen, that kind of thing sticks in your memory and stays there forever. Sherry and Kathy were thereafter my fantasies number one and two.

Neither of the McCormick sisters dated in high school much that I recall, although I am sure they must have gone to the prom, since all the high school girls went. I might have been tempted to ask one of them out myself, but for my mother's likely disapproval. Plus they were both older, so I'm not sure if I would have had the guts to do that anyhow. After they graduated from high school, they both went to the University of North Dakota and studied nursing, and got married, and they did not "end up like Joan Otegard."

Years later I would wake up in my cell at the monastery, aroused as I would often get in my sleep, and try to think about other things. I tried to imagine something that did not involve women, though that was sometimes difficult at night in bed, but I would keep trying and I forced myself to think about cleaning the barn to distract myself. I could almost smell the manure and the trampled straw and I could see the Angus cows shitting and pissing in their pens and the manure spreader parked in the driveway of the barn. I could feel the pitchfork in my hands as I forked the manure into the spreader, and then I was thinking about Sherry or Kathy McCormick, sometimes both, but usually Sherry, and how she looked in that mini-skirt and her long legs. In my mind she was in the barn with me and was slowly lifting up her skirt, and I could see her pink panties. Then the barn was no longer full of cow piss and shit but instead it was a bed of clean golden straw and my hands wandered in that monastery bed. I would make one last effort to avoid these thoughts and I thought about putting a bag of ice on my privates, as the abbot had advised us to do when we were tempted to commit the sin of self-pleasure, but the thought quickly left me for Sherry.

14

IN THE SPRING OF 1974, when I was fifteen, Jake finally showed up, driving up to our house on a Friday evening, just as my mother was finishing cleaning up the dishes. My father looked out the front window when he heard the dog barking and didn't even recognize him at first. "Someone's here," he said, peering out to get a better look.

"Who is it?" Mother asked.

"Can't tell, but he has long hair and the car has California license plates."

"Well, for heaven's sake, lock the door."

A man got out of the car. Besides long hair to his shoulders, he had a mustache, torn jeans, and a worn brown leather jacket. He was almost to the door before Father recognized him.

"Oh, my God, Lois, it's Jake. Jake's come home!"

My mother screamed and ran to the door, flung it open, and hugged him like a little girl with a Christmas doll. "Oh, Jake, thank God you're home safe," she said. "You hungry?" She immediately sat him down and started taking food out of the refrigerator. "You should have called. I would have fixed something special for you to eat."

"A sandwich is fine," he said. "I'm pretty tired. I drove straight through all the way."

"That doesn't sound too safe. I thought you had more sense than that," my father said.

Jake didn't respond and he didn't say much at all that evening, just ate his sandwich and went to bed. He never did explain why he came back to North Dakota and it was a bit of a mystery. It was two years later before I found out that there was a Yuba County, California, warrant out on him for dealing marijuana. That was why he left.

Jake had only been home a few days when I began to sense some tension. It started when my father put a five dollar bill on the table one evening and told Jake to get a haircut. To his credit, he tried to be as diplomatic as he knew how. "I know the styles are different now, so get it cut the way you want, but you'll feel better once you get that hair off your neck. Think how sweaty you'll get when you are working."

My brother didn't say anything, but he didn't pick up the money either, and it was left there for days sitting on the end of the table. Then my mother offered to patch his jeans, but Jake told her not to bother, he liked them the way they were.

Jake sat up in his room a lot and played albums he had brought home from California on the old hi-fi: Deep Purple, the Moody Blues, Robin Trower, and Neil Young were the bands I remember. He turned up the volume until it was blaring, and the sound seemed to go right through the thin walls of that house. My mother and father wouldn't say anything, but they would look at each other with a worried look, and I could see a growing pain in their faces. I knew what the reason was without even asking. Their former good son had been replaced in their eyes with someone quite different, someone who looked a lot like a "hippie."

Now, by 1974, the country had changed dramatically from the 1950s, and even North Dakota had changed with it. Sex, drugs, and rock & roll had reached the smallest towns on the plains. But the change was a generational thing, probably even more so in the urban areas. My parents' generation still listened to their hero, Lawrence Welk, they supported Nixon and believed that somehow the liberals had unfairly chased him out of office, they thought that anyone with long hair was suspicious, they considered marijuana a dangerous drug, and they came from a generation that believed in waiting until marriage, even if that wasn't always followed in practice.

Jake usually left in the evening, fishtailing out of the yard in his 1969 Ford LTD. He would stumble in at two or three in the morning and at first my mother would get up and offer to fix him a fried bologna sandwich or eggs, but he was often drunk, so she quit doing that. It was too hard on her to see him in that condition and better not to know so that she could retain some hope. When he was home for a meal, it was uncomfortable, and my parents and Jake would usually end up in an argument about his lack of work. He refused to help my father with the ranch work, or to do any other work for that matter, and to both Mother and Father that was a terrible sin.

"You need to stop tomcatting around all the time and start working," my father said to him one day at supper.

"Your father's right," my mother added.

Jake didn't respond, he just kept chewing his food.

"You used to have gumption, Jake. What happened to your gumption?" Mother asked. (Gumption was my mother's favorite word.) "If you don't want to ranch, there are lots of other jobs around here if you just look for them. You could get a job at the grain elevator or the county road department. Just do something."

"Work is not that important to me," he replied quietly.

I could see the veins swell in my father's forehead and he sat there for a minute fuming before he exploded. "For Christ's sake, Jake!" he yelled, "your great-great grandfather came over from Germany with nothing. Nothing! They had to carve farms out of the Canadian wilderness. And then your grandfather worked from morning 'til night to build up this ranch. Work is not that important? What kind of talk is that? Hell, work is what separates us from wild animals."

Jake jumped up. His chair crashed to the floor. He picked up the salt shaker and hurled it across the room, shattering it to pieces against the stove. "It may be important to you, but it's not to me!" he shouted, "You don't know about anything except this damn ranch. Well, the rest of the world isn't like this ranch. It's fucked and you might as well have fun because everyone dies in the end anyhow . . . even good people. Your problem is you've never gotten off this ranch and don't know shit about what happens in the rest of the world." He ran out of the house, slamming the door.

The room fell silent until my mother couldn't stand it any longer and had to say something, so she turned to me and said forcefully. "I do not want swearing in this house."

"I didn't swear."

"I didn't say you did. What I said was, I don't want swearing in this house . . . like your father and Jake just did," and she gave my father a scornful look.

The next few weeks were a tense time. Jake stayed out late, God knows where, often came home drunk, slept late, and didn't even show up at mealtime. When he was home he was argumentative, and he and my father often ended up in yelling matches. My mother tried to be cheerful when Jake was around, and was constantly offering to cook him something, and he was polite to her, but he would just take off without saying a word about where he was going.

When he wasn't around, Mother spent more and more time on the davenport. She would have her eyes closed, not sleeping, but simply lying there motionless and sometimes weeping softly.

One day I tried to comfort her. "Mom, are you okay?"

"I'm fine, just a little tired," she replied, almost in a whisper, and she took a Kleenex out of her sleeve and blew her nose.

"Are you worried about Jake?" I asked.

"Just a little, Peter. It's hard when you see your children hurting and you can't do anything about it."

"He'll be fine, Mom."

"I hope so . . . I'm not so sure. Come here."

I sat next to her on the davenport and she reached out and took my hand. "I need you to be good, Peter. I can't worry about two kids. Promise me you will be good."

"I promise, Mom. Don't worry. Please don't worry. I'll be good and Jake will turn out fine, Mom."

Sometimes I think that the only thing that kept her going was her faith and attending Mass on Sundays. That gave her something to cling to—maybe God would answer her prayers. My father's way of dealing with it was the opposite of mother's. He would just go out to the barn to tend the cattle or start up the tractor and head out to the field. He needed to keep it all inside where he could control it.

15

SOON AFTER THE SALT SHAKER THROWING incident, Jake moved out of the house to the "Chicken Ranch." The Chicken Ranch wasn't really a ranch, just an old ranch house with a few surrounding acres that Jake and his friend, Spencer, rented about eight miles from where we lived. When they moved in, there were still a few old Leghorn chickens living there, so they nicknamed it the Chicken Ranch as a joke. It was only later they found out that there was a famous brothel in Nevada called the Chicken Ranch, but by then the name had stuck, so they left it at that.

Spencer was a friend of Jake's from high school. He quit college after his first year, came home and worked occasionally, driving a gravel or milk truck when he needed some cash. He usually wore a paisley red bandana tied around his forehead, a faded denim jacket with patches of an American flag and a marijuana leaf sewn on it, and Red Wing work boots. Spencer liked to play pool and he could often be seen with his customized pool cue at the Rec in Napoleon or he would drive to "the Ditch," the pool hall in Jamestown, if he wanted more competition. He was also a big Grateful Dead fan and liked nothing better than getting stoned, sitting back with a beer, and cranking up the stereo. Most of the young people thought he was pretty cool, and he would always be the first to roll a joint and pass it around. They were always fat ones and he never cared if they came back to him, either. He would just roll another.

The Chicken Ranch had a big old house and a barn at that time. The house was weathered white, with two stories, a slanted stone-sided cellar entry on the side, and a half porch off the back. There was a small shelter belt on the north side, although half the trees had been killed by some herbicide that had drifted over from field spraying, giving the trees a skeletal look and the place a rundown appearance. They paid $150 per month in rent, which the owner was glad to get. Houses left empty in the country had their windows broken in or worse, so it wasn't uncommon for people to rent abandoned houses for next to nothing just to keep them occupied. Jake and Spencer hauled in an old couch and some chairs which they set in a circle in the living room. The only thing that was not old and worn out was Spencer's stereo that he was so proud of and which had a Marantz receiver, a Kenwood turntable, and two huge speakers with twelve-inch woofers.

The Chicken Ranch soon became the weekend place to host keggers. Jake and Spencer would buy some kegs of beer and sell plastic cups for a few dollars at the door. The plastic cup entitled you to as much beer as you could consume. It didn't matter how old you were, kids my age, who had to get a ride because they didn't even have a drivers' license yet, all the way up to Jake's age, ten years older. Anyone was welcome to imbibe and get blasted. "Come on in."

Word spread quickly among the kids in the small neighboring towns whenever a kegger was held. Jake and Spencer seemed to know a lot of young people from Jamestown, too, which was about thirty miles away from the Chicken Ranch, and they invited them out as well. It wouldn't take very long and the yard would be full of cars, and kids would be milling about—drinking beer, talking, laughing, and having a good time. Most of the keggers were in the spring or summer, and there would usually be a big bonfire in the yard. Spencer would open the windows on the house and face his stereo speakers out, and there would always be music: Pink Floyd, Led Zeppelin, the Who, Foghat, Black Sabbath, Lynyrd Skynyrd, and, without fail, Iron Butterfly (the full seventeen minutes of "In-A-Gadda-Da-Vida," cranked up as loud as that stereo could go and not blow the speakers) and finally a little Mahavishnu Orchestra at the end of the evening if they wanted to mellow the mood out.

I went to a few of the keggers at the Chicken Ranch like everyone else my age. Some of the keggers got pretty wild, and kids would be talking about them for weeks afterwards, mostly about how drunk they or somebody else got. Drinking until you passed out was a rite of passage, and the only thing that some kids had to brag about. There was one particular kegger, however, that everyone talked about for years afterwards. It was our little town's equivalent of Woodstock. Even if you weren't there, you said you were, just to appear cool.

It was held shortly after Jake and Spencer had moved in and they hired a rock band from Jamestown, Buffalo Alice, who we all thought were amazingly talented. Jake and Spencer constructed a stage of sorts in the barn using barn doors set on cinderblocks, tore down the spider webs, and cleared out the old wagons and harnesses. Then they had some posters printed in Jamestown and put them on telephone poles in all the surrounding towns and rented a portable generator to handle the electrical load of all the equipment.

There must have been four hundred kids there that night, with twenty or more kegs of beer, and plenty of people passing around joints. The band played Zeppelin, Steppenwolf, Doobie Brothers, that sort of thing, and the music was cranked up so loud you could hear it a mile away on the prairie. I remember that the band had a tall, thin guitar player who played a black Les Paul guitar and his left hand scuttled up and down the fret board like it was possessed by the devil. We thought he was as good as any guitar player we heard on the radio. That was our standard of excellence, "as good as on the radio."

I walked around that evening and felt as if I had stepped into another world. The barn was packed, and people were also wandering around the yard and into the house. The atmosphere seemed electric and the air full of the sound of laughter and shouting. I was one of the younger people there and had only seen a couple of live rock bands in my life and never anything like a rock concert (I would see my first and only rock concert, ZZ Top, at the Bismarck Civic Center that next winter).

About 11:00 p.m. the band took a break, and I wandered outside and noticed flashing red lights coming down the road, the lights disappearing for a minute and then reappearing as the car crested a hill.

The car was traveling fast. After a few minutes, two sheriff deputies drove up and left the flashing red lights on, so that got everyone's attention. A crowd began to gather around the car. We could see one of the deputies through the window talking on the two-way radio. The other deputy stepped out of the car, thrusting his chest out and adjusting his belt. It was Allen Nordstrom. In a small community like Gackle everyone knew who the deputies were. Nordstrom was about the same age as my brother, a big, beefy guy with a military haircut. He came from a farm up by the Canadian border and had served as an MP in the Army.

My brother must have known him personally from previous encounters, because he stepped forward and said, "Hey, hi, Allen. What's up?"

I moved in closer to hear what was going on.

"You tell me," Nordstrom said.

"Just having a little party. We hired a band. They're really good. They're on break now, but you should hear them."

"I don't think I need to go in the barn." He loudly sniffed the air, which reeked of marijuana. "I might see something you don't want me to."

"Oh, yeah, that," my brother said. "It's all cool. Nothing hard here."

"Just make sure you keep it that way."

"Will do."

"And, one more thing, I don't want someone calling me in the middle of the night with a report that there is a car rolled over in the ditch. If anyone is falling-down drunk, have them stay overnight."

"Yeah, I gotcha."

That was it. Nordstrom got back in the car, turned the lights off, and they drove away.

Jake took a big fat joint out of his shirt pocket, very slowly and deliberately lit it, and took a deep drag. He knew everyone was watching him, and he held the smoke in his lungs for the longest time, before he blew a long thin trail of smoke into the cool night air. "Rock on, Gackle!" he yelled, and he threw his fist in the air. Everyone cheered.

Soon the band retook the stage and launched into the classic Doobie Brothers' song, "Jesus Is Just All Right." The band must have played until two in the morning. Everyone had an amazing time, and Jake seemed about as happy as I can remember. Some kids camped in the yard in tents while others slept on the ground in sleeping bags, and Spencer and Jake let anyone who wanted to crash in the house. That night seems special to me even now. It sounds corny, but it really did seem like a tiny moment in time when there was an innocence that we have never regained, the Age of Aquarius on the prairie.

16

ORTH DAKOTA MIGHT AS WELL be a million miles away from California in the winter. In fact, I am not sure if anyone in their right mind has ever made the trip from California to North Dakota in the dead of winter, so when a former girlfriend of Jake's from California showed up in late January of 1975, it was quite a surprise to everyone, including Jake. Her name was Cathy Danielson, and she drove up at the Chicken Ranch driving a yellow Volkswagen beetle. Those old Volkswagens had pathetic heaters, and it must have been ten degrees below zero that day, so Cathy had every piece of clothing she owned on and was still shivering, and she'd had to scrape the ice off the inside of the windshield with a piece of stiff cardboard every few minutes as she drove.

Cathy knocked on the door at ten o'clock in the morning. When Spencer answered it, she just said, "Brrr, I'm freezing. Let me in." She told him she was a friend of Jake's, so Spencer woke Jake up. He came down the stairs and when he saw her he let out a whoop and threw his arms around her. Cathy and Jake had met in Venice, California, two years earlier when Jake was crashing with a friend he met in the Army, and they'd had a party. She had showed up, and they did a little coke together and hit it off immediately. They apparently had a short, but steamy relationship, before Jake moved up to Chico, California. Cathy was a curvaceous little blonde, in her early twenties, with peach-fresh skin and full red lips. Within fifteen minutes of her arrival she and Jake jumped into bed. Spencer crudely commented later, "She was like a heifer in heat," and "She had a body crying out for breeding."

I met Cathy when I stopped by on a Saturday to bring a chicken divan casserole that mother had made just for Jake. Jake introduced me to her and I liked her fine. She was talkative, with a nervous laugh, maybe a tad overfriendly. When she commented that it was so windy here, I told her that our parents used to put rocks in our pockets when we were little so we didn't blow away—an old North Dakota joke—but she didn't get it, and just said, "Really. Wow!"

I couldn't figure out why she came to North Dakota in the dead of winter. When I asked she said, "It was pretty spur of the moment. I was feeling lonely, and I thought about Jake—something came over me, I'm not sure what—I wanted to be with him in the worst way. The phone was disconnected when I tried to call, but I knew he lived near Gackle, North Dakota, so I said what the hell, dusted my nose a little, and just started driving. He told me he grew up on a big ranch, and I thought it would be fun to see that too, and we could ride horses together and stuff."

I looked out the window at the heavy snow on the ground and knew no one was going horseback riding in this weather, but I didn't say anything. Later I found out that she had two little children, a girl and a boy, who she had before she met Jake, and I asked her about them and she said, "I love the little rug rats, but they're a lot to handle." She said she had left them in California with her mother when she took off. I thought it was strange to leave your kids like that and go driving halfway across the country, but what did I know? When you are a teenager you know there is a lot to life under the surface, but it's like looking down into a lake on a cloudy day: all you see is reflection.

Cathy stayed for almost five weeks and those five weeks were some of the coldest on record. For one ten-day stretch the temperature never rose above zero, and it dropped to thirty-one below one night. That old house on the Chicken Ranch had a fuel oil furnace that could put out enough heat to warm the downstairs pretty well, but the upstairs had never been insulated properly, if at all, and never got much above fifty degrees when it was that cold. The wind blew through the cracks around the joints of the windows, making a shrill whistling sound. Sometimes those windows had a quarter inch of frost on them. As a consequence, Cathy was always complaining about the cold. Spencer said that for the first few days, Cathy and Jake never left the couch, where they would sit, watching the television, with a dingy old quilt wrapped around them. More than once during the day, Jake would give Spencer a signal and he would trod upstairs so that the two could make love in private, although Spencer said that Cathy moaned so loudly that he could hear it all the way upstairs.

Apparently the love making wore thin pretty quickly, however, because Cathy soon got bored with staying indoors. She spent part of one day drawing faces in the frosted windows with her fingertip, but when she saw the designs frosted over again, she gave up. She told Jake, "I can't stand this place anymore, it's too fucking cold. I'll go crazy here." Jake wasn't insensitive to her needs. He could see that she needed more than the Chicken Ranch could provide in the way of entertainment, but there wasn't much to do around Gackle in the winter. By the time he finally decided to take her into Bismarck to see a movie and go to a bar and maybe do some dancing, a three-day blizzard struck and there was no way they could drive. They were stuck there until the blizzard let up and the county snow plow cleared the roads.

For those unused to them, blizzards often start with awe but end in arguments. After the initial wonder wore off, Cathy was crawling up the walls, wanting to get out of there so bad. She couldn't take being trapped inside all the time, unlike Jake and Spencer, who could have a good time as long as their pot didn't run out. They were fine just getting stoned and listening to music or watching their re-runs on TV, *The Mod Squad, Gilligan's Island, Hogan's Heroes*, and *F Troop*.

On the third morning of the blizzard Jake fried up some eggs and sausage patties and brought a plate over to Cathy on the couch. Cathy had had enough by then. Maybe it was what doctors now call "Seasonal Affective Disorder," producing chemical changes in the body from a lack of sunlight. In any event, she was melancholic and irritable at the same time. "I'm not eating this shit again," she exclaimed. "This is the third goddamn day we've had eggs." She slammed the plate down on the coffee table. It slid off, and the food spilled all over the floor.

"What do you think you're doing?" Jake yelled.

"I want some Coco Puffs or Fruit Loops or Pop Tarts. Not this crap."

"This is all we have. Eat it or starve."

"Fuck you. I need some decent food. I'm going to town to get something to eat."

"Like hell you are. Number one, the store is probably closed, and number two, you can't drive anywhere until the roads are plowed."

"Watch me," she said and she stormed upstairs and came back a little later with all of her clothes on and headed outside.

Jake couldn't let her do that. She would have never made it any-place in that Volkswagen, and she would probably have ended up stuck some place and froze to death. He doffed his parka and ran outside and grabbed her as she was brushing the snow off the car. She was still in-sisting on going, and she got in and started up the engine, but he jumped in the passenger side and talked to her for a long time. Even-tually he convinced her to stay, either that or she just got too cold sitting in that Volkswagen waiting for it to warm up and the windows to de-frost. Anyhow, she ran back in the house, tears of frustration frozen on her cheeks. Jake and Cathy didn't say anything to each other the rest of the day. Spencer said he heard her moans again that night, so they must have made up enough to resume love-making, although that doesn't take much sometimes. Once the roads were cleared off by the snow plow about three o'clock the next afternoon, Cathy said she had to leave and go where there was some sun. They watched out the window as that yellow Volkswagen disappeared down the road against the immense backdrop of pure white, the back end swerving back and forth, trying to gain some traction on the road.

17

THE NEXT YEAR, when I was almost seventeen, there was another kegger I would never forget. It was raining hard, so everyone was crowded into the house when I arrived. Spencer was selling cups at the door. He said that everyone had to pay, although he only charged me half price. One person was already passed out in the front hall, which was covered in mud people had tracked in, but I stepped over him like everyone else. The hot, sweet, thick smell of marijuana hung in the air. The house was so packed I could only inch myself through the crowd by weaving in and out. I found Jake sitting in a big recliner against the back wall with a beer in one hand and a joint in a roach clip in the other. He looked half out of it and was tapping his foot with a nervous energy. "Hey, it's my little brother," he shouted when he saw me.

I went over to him and asked him how he was doing, but the noise from the stereo and the crowd was so loud that we couldn't hear each other very well. I just shook my head like I could hear him for a minute and then I went and got a cup of beer from the keg. There must have been sixty or seventy people crowded in the house. I found a corner and sipped my beer and watched.

It was a crazy night with two fist fights and broken furniture, but about two in the morning people began to leave. I had been drinking for a few hours, slowly, but it was beginning to make me pretty drunk. I had told mom I was staying overnight at a friend's house, so I wasn't worried about having to go home, but I wasn't sure where I would find a place to sleep. I asked Jake if I could crash upstairs, and he said sure and led me up the steep narrow stairway to the second floor where there were four bedrooms. The two bedrooms overlooking the front yard belonged to Jake and Spencer but he pushed open a door of one of the bedrooms in the back. There was no furniture in the room, but five or six people lay in sleeping bags and blankets on the floor, either sleeping or passed out.

"It looks like this one's occupied," Jake said. He led me to the bedroom across the hall and turned on the light. There was no furniture in this room either, only an old musty mattress on the floor, with a girl sleeping on it. Clothes lay strewn about the floor with a pile of old *Penthouse* magazines in the corner. The girl was out of it and did not stir. I didn't know her, but Jake obviously did. "Connie," he said, "wake up." She just moaned and turned her head. She was partially covered with an old blanket and Jake pulled it off. She was naked underneath except for her brassiere, which was pushed up around her neck, and I couldn't help seeing a little bit of her bush and her heavy breasts.

"Oh, shit," Jake said.

I turned my head and took a step back towards the door.

"Hey, where you going?" he said. "You can still sleep here. It's a big mattress. Heck, you can even screw her if you want to. She's not a bad piece of ass, really. She won't care. She'll screw anyone. She's into free love and all that."

I thought he was just kidding, but I looked at his face, and he had a weird faraway look in his eyes I had never seen before, and I wondered if he was on something. Then I looked at Connie, and I had a sick feeling. The mattress she lay on smelled like piss and was covered with brownish stains and I noticed a bloody tampon lying on the floor by the foot of the mattress. I knew nothing about sex at the time, but I knew that this was not what I wanted.

"She's gross," I said. "Besides, she's passed out. Don't be a stupid moron."

He looked at me. "Don't call me a stupid moron. Don't you ever call me that, you hear!"

I had never heard this tone in his voice before—an ugly, mean tone that sounded as if it came from somewhere hidden deep inside.

He grabbed me and pushed me down on top of her, gripping me on the back of my neck and pushing my face into hers. Her breath smelled like puke, and I turned my head to the side and struggled to move away. She didn't even wake up, just moaned a kind of deep guttural moan.

"Let me up," I yelled. "I don't want to do this."

He finally released me, and I rolled off to the side.

"You think you're so damn good," he mumbled. "You don't know shit."

And then, after a pause, he said in a louder voice, "Dumb ass," and he kicked me in my side. "I was just like you once you know . . . but I found out that there's no point in trying to do the right thing all the time. You might as well learn that before it's too late." He walked out of the room and slammed the door.

I laid there for a minute wondering what the hell set him off, and then I covered Connie with the blanket, pushed her over to one side as gently as I could, and lay down next to her. She came to just enough to mumble, "Jakey, Jakey, I love you, Jakey."

"I'm not Jakey," I said.

The next morning I woke up and sunlight was coming through the eastern window. I had a dry taste in my mouth, and my side hurt. I lay there for a moment watching the columns of dust floating in the air through the filtering light. *Was there a pattern or was it simply chaotic?* After a while, I glanced over at Connie. She was sleeping, and there was a slight bit of dried drool on the side of her mouth. I felt sorry for her at that moment and I thought I should do something for her, but I didn't know what, so I got up quietly and walked down the stairs. I went to the kitchen and got a glass of cold water from the tap and drank it in great swallows. I was still thirsty, so I drank a second, and then I got an idea and poured a third glass and took it upstairs to Connie and shook her gingerly. She sat up halfway and drank the water. She whispered in a hoarse voice, "Thanks," and lay back down. I went back downstairs. A few people were sleeping on the couch and floor in the living room. The same person was still passed out in the mud in the front hallway. I stepped over him and drove home.

18

I SAW MY BROTHER AGAIN about a week later when my mother asked me to bring some caramel rolls over to his house. She had only been at the Chicken Ranch one time to see him. She had walked right in without knocking, and it was the morning after a party. The house was littered with cups, the floors were filthy, and there were several people she didn't know sleeping on the floor in the living room. So she never went back because she didn't want to know what kind of "shenanigans" went on over there. She often invited Jake over to our house for dinner, although he rarely showed up, except for Thanksgiving and Christmas. The only thing she knew to do was to send food over with me—rolls, pies, cakes, cookies, and hotdishes. On Fridays she often sent over a fish stick casserole to remind him that he was Catholic and keep his soul safe.

This particular day it was late morning, and my brother was sitting out on the front steps in the sunlight and scratching a stray farm dog that hung around. It was just a mangy old mutt, part border collie maybe, part unknown, and with a gimpy leg, but they had named him Bonkers and lavished attention and food on him until he decided to make the Chicken Ranch his home. Bonkers limped over, wagging his tail, glad to see me. Jake seemed happy to see me too and neither of us mentioned the incident with Connie. The rolls were still warm and fresh with that newly baked cinnamon scent, and he gave one to me and one to Bonkers, and we sat there in the sun eating them, then let Bonkers lick the sticky caramel from our fingers when we were finished. Jake lit up a cigarette and took a long drag and exhaled slowly, the smoke curling upwards and drifting away.

"Hey, remember that time we went muskrat trapping," he said. "We should do that again sometime."

He fell silent. I was about to say something when the telephone rang, and he ran into the house to answer it. A few minutes later he came out smiling. "Just made a sale," he said, his cigarette now dangling in his mouth.

He was holding a large plastic garbage bag filled with pot. He sat down on the steps again. "Gotta clean this shit."

At that time I had seen pot smoked at the Chicken Ranch many times and even some of my friends smoked occasionally, but I had never seen such a large amount of it in one place.

"I had a good crop this year," he said with some pride. "Grew it out back behind the shelterbelt."

I didn't know what to say. Selling a small amount of pot in 1975, even in North Dakota, was not that big of a deal. Even I knew that. There was the danger of getting busted, but it was unlikely that they would send a Vietnam veteran to jail for selling an ounce or two. However, this looked like a huge amount to me, several pounds or more, and I knew this would be treated much more seriously.

Jake noticed my silence. He flicked his cigarette butt into the gravel by the steps where it joined the hundreds of others. "Hey, don't worry. This is all home grown. I just sell a few bags now and then. Business has been pretty good though," he chuckled.

I sat there silently and watched him as he carefully filled dozens of small clear baggies with the pot, carefully removing the stems and seeds. Some of the stems had buds on them and he pinched them off and put them in a separate bag for his own stash. He measured each baggie with four fingers so that it made a hefty lid, a generous ounce. Then he neatly rolled them up, licking the last edge to seal it. He repackaged the one ounce lids into larger plastic bags, sixteen to a bag, to make a pound. When he was done, he had seven pounds of packaged pot plus at least a pound for his own stash, which he took into the house. He came back out with a one pound bag and smiled.

"This is God's herb, man . . . seriously . . . the Rastafarians use it as a sacrament." Jake and Spencer had been into reggae music lately, listening to Bob Marley and the Wailers, Jimmy Cliff, and Toots and the Maytals.

He took a lid out of his shirt pocket and handed it to me. "Want it?" he asked, "Take it. It's yours."

I hesitated for a second. I didn't really want it, but I didn't want my brother to think I was a wimp either, so I reached for it. But he was watching my face and saw my hesitation. His voice softened, "Hey, if you don't want it, that's cool. You're a good kid. You don't need to turn out like me," he said and put it back in his pocket.

A few minutes later a gold-colored Chevy Nova with black pin-stripes drove up with two young kids in it that looked about high school age. I didn't recognize them, so I figured they were probably from Jamestown. Jake apparently knew them because he went over to the window and handed the pound of pot to the driver and came back with two hundred dollars. That was the going rate for homegrown he said, $200 a pound or fifteen dollars a lid. That was big money in North Dakota back then, compared to what my father got for a bushel of wheat.

* * *

I DID GO MUSKRAT TRAPPING with my brother later that year. He called on a Friday evening and asked me to bring his old traps over the next morning. I could only find seven of them hanging on the wall of the shed. They were a little rusty, but I dipped them in tractor oil, and they still had a vicious snap. I arrived at the Chicken Ranch at seven in the morning as we had agreed. It was still dark, and I was not surprised that there were no lights on. I knocked on the door as loudly as I could, but I didn't hear anything. Then I tried shouting up to his window on the second story. I remember that it was cold, maybe ten or fifteen degrees below zero, and the wind was blowing out of the northwest. I pulled my stocking cap lower over my ears and stood there shivering and shift-ing from foot to foot to keep warm. Finally, after the longest time, Jake came to the door and invited me in. He made a pot of coffee and sat and drank two or three cups and smoked a few cigarettes before he was ready to go.

We walked down to a slough about a half a mile away. The cold made it miserable, and Jake was quiet, seemingly caught up in his own thoughts. The wind was whipping across the ice on that slough something fierce, so we worked quickly, and in less than an hour we had set all the traps. Walking back, we had to face that wind, which made it even colder, stinging my nose and cheeks. About halfway home he said, "Colder than hell, eh," and looked at me shivering and shaking my arms to keep the circulation going. He took off his scarf and wound it around my face and ears and under my jaw and he said, "Walk behind me. I'll block the wind for you."

So I followed right behind him, following in his footsteps, just back far enough that I wouldn't step on his heels. For a minute I had a feeling like I did when I was little and I'd follow him around the ranch and it seemed like he would always be there to protect me, no matter what. By the time we returned to the house, we were both exhausted and Jake said he was going back to bed. He promised to check the traps every morning since I couldn't do it very easily with school, and I left.

The next weekend I stopped by again in the morning. Before I went to the house I checked the side of their barn, expecting to see some muskrats hanging there, but there were none in sight. I had to wait at the door for him to get up again. When he came to the door, he said, "Oh, shit, I forgot to check the traps."

That was bad news. I knew that traps should be checked every day or the muskrats were likely to chew their legs off in an effort to escape. And I didn't believe that he had forgotten. I knew they'd had a party the previous Saturday night, and I was sure Jake got wasted, as usual, and then slept in Sunday morning. He probably remembered later in the week, but figured it was too late by then or he just blew it off.

We walked down to the slough and, sure enough, he had caught four muskrats, but only one was still there. It was dead, having frozen to death, and the other three had escaped by chewing their legs off. I had a sick feeling in my stomach as I stood there looking at those chewed off legs tangled in the jaws of the cold metal traps. He said he was sorry, but I was still furious with him. We picked up all the traps and walked back without saying another word. We hung that one single muskrat on the side of the barn, but it was hardly worth driving to town to sell one muskrat, so it just hung there all winter and when warm weather arrived in the spring it thawed out and maggots ate the flesh until only the fur and bones were left.

19

OVER THOSE LAST TWO YEARS of high school, I would stop by the Chicken Ranch maybe every other week or so. Sometimes Mother would have me run some food over and I continued to go to a few of the keggers, but they were beginning to take their toll, and the house was looking more and more run down. I noticed that one of the windows was busted out, and they had nailed an old grain sack over it. The kitchen table was stacked with dirty dishes and magazines, and a rank odor of stale smoke and spoiled food permeated the air. If it was summer, flies buzzed around constantly, and dead flies piled up in the window sills. I don't think that they ever cleaned the toilet, which was crusted brown inside and disgustingly filthy. Beer cans and chunks of broken bottle glass were scattered across the yard, which went un-mowed. Jake and Spencer had turned the old chicken coop out back of the house into a greenhouse for growing pot by removing most of the roof, stripping off the old shingles and knocking out the slats, replacing it with clear plastic sheeting. They were regularly selling pot in both Jamestown and Bismarck, driving back and forth several times a week.

During this time, I began to feel more and more remote from Jake. I had my own life with Lori and the church youth group and I was becoming more and more embarrassed to be known as his brother. I heard stories from other kids about how drunk he was or how he wrecked his car. I'd laugh like this was cool and Jake was just being Jake and wasn't it great to have a brother who threw keggers and had wild parties, but I really didn't think it was so cool anymore. Jake was now in his mid-twenties and most of his friends had moved on in life and gotten married and had jobs. The people that he hung out with now were either what I considered real losers or were considerably younger and uncomfortably close to my own age.

In early April 1975, Jake got a phone call from Cathy in California saying she was pregnant. It seems that her birth control pills had run out about the time of the blizzard, and the two of them had chanced it and luck was against them. So that's how Jake first became a father, although to the best of my knowledge he never saw Cathy again or the daughter that was born of their relationship. Cathy ended up on welfare in California. Spencer later told me that Jake received a telephone call from Deputy Nordstrom regarding some child support papers he was supposed to serve on Jake, but Jake talked to him for a while and made Cathy sound like someone he barely knew. Somehow he must have garnered some sympathy, because Nordstrom told the authorities in California that he could not find anyone by the name of Jake Penner in Logan County.

Jake also got into fights in town, and I would hear about them. There were different cliques among the young people in the small towns around there just like everywhere in the world. On one end were the dopers or pot heads, like my brother. There was a lot of drug use in those rural areas, mostly because kids didn't have much to do and were utterly bored and looking for any kind of excitement, so there were more dopers than people might expect. Then there were the jocks and straight kids in the middle, and there were what we called the rednecks on the other end. The rednecks around Gackle and Napoleon wore their hair short and dressed and acted like tough cowboys. They tended to drive around in pickups, drink beer, and look for fights with people like my brother. Jake was only too happy to oblige and quick to use his fists. He liked to hit, and perhaps he liked being hit as well.

There was one guy in particular, Russell Kuntz, who was known around the community as a redneck cowboy. He was a big, beefy red-haired fellow who ranched with his dad west of town. He was one of those people who hated anyone who looked and acted a little different. He drove around in his Dodge pickup with a buddy or two, and if he saw someone he considered a doper, he'd roll down his window and yell insults at them or worse. Rumor was that the previous summer he had beaten young Joey Haskins and messed his face up pretty good simply because he had long hair.

One day Russell made the mistake of insulting Jake and a girl he was with at the time. I remember that the girl's name was Candace. She was a skinny, pale bleached blonde from Jamestown, not without her charms, but the type that some people might label a "skank," and she and Jake had a very short term relationship. I think she stayed at the Chicken Ranch a few nights, but she was only sixteen, and her parents tracked her down and drove out one day and made her come home. Anyhow, Russell pulled his pickup alongside of Jake and Candace as they were driving down Main Street in Napoleon, rolled down his window, and shouted at the girl, "Hey, do you want to fuck a real man instead of that pansy-ass hippie?"

My brother yelled back, "What the hell did you say, you dumb shit-ass."

When Russell repeated it, Jake said, "I thought that's what you said," and slammed on his brakes. When he braked, Russell did the same. He jumped out of his truck and came around to Jake's door and stood there with his fists clenched. Already cars full of kids were stopping to see the action. Jake took his time, taking a last slow drag of his cigarette and flicking the butt down towards Russell's feet.

"Fucking long-haired cocksucker," Russell said.

Jake stepped out of the car, almost reluctantly, like this was a dirty ranch chore that he had to take care of. Russell was big, maybe three inches taller than Jake, and outweighed him by twenty-five pounds, but he would prove to be slow, which is a huge liability when you're punching it out and the smaller man is able to move in close. Russell came at Jake fast and immediately threw a big roundhouse left. Jake dodged that and made one little feint and then swung, connecting and snapping Russell's head back. "Yeah, get him," Candace yelled. Russell came right back at Jake and managed to land a shot or two to Jake's ribs, but then Jake retaliated, coming over his left with a hard crossing right to Russell's jaw. Then a blur, as Jake went to work. Russell didn't go down, to his credit, until a flurry of punches broke his nose and sent blood flying. When his knees finally buckled and he did go down, Jake worked over his front and backside with well-placed kicks. Russell covered up his head and tried to crawl under his pickup to get away, but Jake grabbed him by the foot and pulled him back. He drew his foot back to kick him again but stopped mid-kick. His eyes had a perplexed look as he studied Russell cowering on the ground. Then Russell's friend waded in, and Jake swung around and knocked him flat with just three punches. By this time, a crowd of people were watching. Candace jumped out of Jake's car and screamed, "Jake, that's enough! Let's go!"

Jake backed off and lit a cigarette. "You don't look like such a big man now," he said to Russell. "Fucking redneck."

By this time, you could hear the sound of sirens in the distance screaming down the highway. Jake and Candace got in his car and "hauled ass" out of there.

* * *

JAKE HAD AN ANGER BUILT UP INSIDE, anyone could see that. I think that sometimes Spencer saved him from getting in worse trouble because Spencer never showed any anger at all. He would talk Jake down when he could, telling him to "mellow out, man." Then he would roll a joint and hand it to Jake.

They were quite the partying pair. Between the two of them, they saw countless women come and go in the years they lived at the Chicken Ranch. I guess a lot of women must have been attracted to the primitive nature of the place and the promise of wild nights and un-tethered love. "Come on in. You look beautiful. Want to hear some music? Would you like some wine? How about smoking a doobie? Ever slept in a waterbed before? Why don't we go upstairs?" There were absolutely no demands placed on any of the women, they could come and go as they pleased, and no one cared if they shaved their legs either.

For some reason, Spencer always ended up with women considered slightly different or off-beat. One summer it was a girl named

Margo, maybe nineteen or twenty, who was a student at the North Dakota School for the Deaf in Devils Lake. She seemed nice and smiled a lot, but when she wasn't watching Spencer's lips, she spent all of her time paging through old *Playboys* and other more hard-core men's magazines they had lying around the house. For some reason she really loved pornography, and Spencer claimed she was a bit of a nymphomaniac. Spencer enjoyed the frequent bedroom romps she demanded at first, but there wasn't much of a spark there, and he needed a little more slack as the summer wore on. One day he surprised Margo with a black-and-white kitten, named Starship, and that kept her occupied until she returned to school.

Another girl was a freckled redhead, kind of odd looking, but with a big friendly smile. She was not much more than four-and-a-half feet tall, skinny as a wild cat, and she was always high when I saw her and talked nonstop in a squeaky voice. Everyone knew she had a boyfriend who rode bulls on the rodeo circuit, but she'd come over and stay with Spencer whenever her boyfriend was out of town. She took to carrying a switchblade for some unknown reason, and that made Spencer nervous so he quietly ended that relationship.

Jake usually ended up with the most attractive women who showed up, although some of them had their issues, too. One woman who everyone talked about for months was a long-legged blonde that he brought back from Bismarck. She was older, in her mid-thirties, and married to an insurance salesman, but she said she wanted to have fun while she still had it. She used to lie out and suntan next to the barn where she could get out of the wind, wearing nothing but a tiny red bikini, straps down. The occasional grain truck or pickup driving by would slow to a crawl, the drivers' necks craning out the windows to get a glimpse of her. She only stayed about a month because she wanted more action than the Chicken Ranch could provide and one day she up and moved to the resort town of Detroit Lakes, Minnesota.

20

TROUBLE STARTED WHEN SPENCER got a new girlfriend. Her name was Darcy Entmacher and she was not a local girl. Darcy had moved to the area after answering an advertisement in the *Chicago Tribune* placed by a neighbor of ours, Roger Schmidt, seeking a live-in caretaker for his children.

Mr. Schmidt was desperate for help since his wife, Margaret, had passed away a year earlier and left him with the care of four children, all under the age of six, in a small ramshackle house. As the story eventually came out, Margaret had been depressed for some time after the birth of their fourth child and had lain in bed for days sobbing into her pillow, unable to even get up to feed the children. Now, they'd likely diagnose her as having postpartum depression and give her drugs to pull her through, but they didn't use that label back then where we grew up.

Mr. Schmidt had not known what to do, so he went to Bismarck and bought her a new microwave oven to cheer her up, but it didn't seem to help. He told her it was all in her head, but that didn't help either. Then he told her she was lazy and worthless and not a good Christian mother. That also didn't motivate her one bit. Like most everyone in his generation, spouses were just expected to deal with that sort of thing on their own, which was considered better than the alternative of being sent to the State Psychiatric Hospital in Jamestown for treatment. The old timers still called it the "Insane Asylum" and the rumor was that they gave you shock treatments there, and if you ever came out you were nothing but a vegetable. Even if you were released with your senses intact, word would get around, and people would never forget it, and you would be labeled a nut forever.

Mr. Schmidt thought his wife's depression would eventually pass, but she didn't get better, and one morning she got up and walked outside and two miles north and laid down on the railroad tracks and was run over by an eastbound Northern Pacific Railroad coal train. Imagine that, because one can feel the track vibrations on the plains for a good ten minutes before the train arrives.

After the death of his wife, Mr. Schmidt first hired a local farm girl by the name of Janet Kalbaus. Janet came from a large family of twelve kids and knew how to care for children, but she only lasted a month before she up and quit. It came out later that she left after an incident in which she had awaken in the middle of the night to find Mr. Schmidt in her room, kneeling by her bed and sobbing softly, while he stroked her thigh under her blanket with his rough hand.

Darcy Entmacher had been working in the Schmidt house for three months when she drove to Remboldt's Fairway in Gackle one day for groceries. The two middle kids were bawling in the grocery checkout line and she was trying to quiet them while balancing the youngest on her hip when she met Spencer standing in front of her waiting to buy cigarettes and Twizzlers. They got to talking. It seemed that Twizzlers were her favorite, too, so they hit it off, and when he was about to leave she asked him, "What's there to do for a single girl in a town like this?"

He smiled at her, "Oh, I can just think of one thing."

She was smitten and that evening she told Mr. Schmidt that she was going to town for a little while to get some ice cream. She drove straight to the Chicken Ranch instead and within an hour she and Spencer were headed upstairs. She never went back to the Schmidt's even to get her suitcase or her last paycheck.

Darcy was somewhat plump, to put it kindly, with watermelon breasts—sort of a Mama Cass type—except prettier, with rosy cheeks and long brown hair. She always wore big shapeless dresses with long sleeves around the house. It wasn't until later that we discovered that the long sleeves were to cover the small white scars on her wrists. She wore sandals all year round, putting thick socks on with them in the winter. What made her attractive was that she was funny, maybe one of the funniest people I have ever met. She had a loud voice and a loud laugh which became louder the more she drank. And she liked to drink—beer, wine, whiskey—it didn't matter. People were amazed at how much she could drink and seemingly be unaffected. The fact was that she could drink any man under the table and was proud of that. She chained smoked too, lighting one unfiltered Pall Mall off the other. With her, the party was always just starting.

Darcy became more or less the center of attention at the Chicken Ranch for a time, so, evenings, a group of people would always be sitting in a circle in the living room listening to her stories. She had a way of joking with everyone who came in the door and a lot of her jokes had a sexual innuendo, so that she made every man feel as if she was willing to do it with them, right then, right there. Spencer would mostly just sit next to her, smiling, laughing at her jokes, and rolling joints. He said no woman ever kept him warmer on cold winter nights and the word "no" was not in her vocabulary. She called him her "James Taylor love machine," although he didn't look much like James Taylor.

Darcy talked that winter about turning the Chicken Ranch into a commune. They wanted to advertise in *Rolling Stone* for like-minded people to join them. Now this was in 1977, the disco era, and the idea of communes had probably come and gone long ago with the Manson Family. North Dakota may have been behind the times compared to California, but it was about five years behind, not ten. I think she just liked having people around, the more the merrier. Anyhow, the commune plans never came to fruition.

Darcy threw a surprise birthday party for Spencer that March. It wasn't a big party, but she had Jake take Spencer to town on some excuse, and she invited about ten people over, including me, and had everyone park their cars behind the barn. When Spencer arrived, everyone jumped out and yelled "Surprise!" as one might expect. Spencer grinned so wide it looked like he would bust the seams of his face. Darcy had bought some frozen Totino's Pizzas and baked a birthday cake with fudge frosting and gave Spencer a new Cat Stevens album, which he loved. Everyone sat around and drank beer and ate pizza. It was a great time until the cake was cut and people starting eating it. Darcy was talking away as usual and when she finally got up to get some cake there was only a tiny piece left.

"What happened to all the cake?" she asked.

"Sorry, that's all that's left," someone said.

"What? You have to be fucking kidding me!" she yelled. "You guys are so damn greedy. Shit. I can't believe it. A bunch of greedy fucking pigs."

Then—and this would have been funny under normal circumstances—the dog, Bonkers, jumped up on the table and snatched that last small piece of cake and gulped it down in one bite. Darcy screamed when she saw that and went over and gave Bonkers the hardest kick I ever saw in my life. The dog literally flew through the air. It let out an excruciating yelp and slunk under the table and lay there whimpering.

Everyone thought the incident a little creepy and that was the end of the fun and festivities. I could see even Spencer was pissed off, although he cooled down when Darcy cuddled up to him and said she was going to give him his real present later that night. Fine and dandy for him, but anyone in their right mind could see that Darcy just didn't have any brakes. I was young, but even I could see a wreck coming.

Later the hard drug use started. Darcy grew up in Hammond, Indiana, and she had a source there who sold her drugs, whatever she wanted, and had them delivered via U.S. mail, hidden in a package of food. It began with her receiving a bag of speed about a month after she arrived at the Chicken Ranch. She said she used it because it helped her lose weight, but then Spencer started taking some. He was driving a milk truck that winter three days a week and on those days he got up at 4:00 a.m., and he said he needed to have something to stay awake. Pretty soon my brother was popping them too, even though he wasn't working. He claimed it just gave him a nice buzz and offset the drossiness caused by the pot. Before long, all three of them were taking a number of hits every day.

From what I observed, the speed made the three of them a little crazy. They would talk and talk, staying up all night, arguing and debating impassionedly once they got started, a perpetual flow of ideas, and they thought everything they said was absolutely brilliant. If you weren't on speed too, you couldn't begin to keep up. They might talk for hours about some musician, like Jackson Browne, who Darcy loved, or a television show—*Sanford and Son* was their favorite—or books, like *Catch-22*, *One Flew Over the Cuckoo's Nest*, and *The Dharma Bums*. A frequent topic of conversation at the time was Carlos Castaneda, the author of *The Teachings of Don Juan*, *A Separate Reality*, and *Journey to Ixtlan*. Darcy had introduced the books to Spencer, and he loved them. Castaneda's books were supposedly non-fictionalized accounts containing great spiritual truths about a Yaqui Indian shaman and a peyote-taking anthropology student he took under his wings. They are now considered pseudo-philosophical musings that the author just made up, but at the time the three of them, especially Spencer, took them seriously and read the books again and again, searching for answers to life much like their forefathers read the Bible.

Spencer got into Castaneda's books so much he decided he wanted to try "shrooming." He said it was the first step to becoming a shaman. Darcy was able to obtain some magic mushrooms from her contact, and they all ate a few buttons. Within an hour they were violently ill and took turns in the single bathroom vomiting. They said they experienced a mild high and some numbness, but that was about it. The experience made Spencer quit talking about becoming a shaman, however.

In late February of that winter Darcy obtained some LSD—blotter acid. She said she'd tried it a few times before and she talked about how fantastic tripping was. "The more people turn on, the better world it will be," she said. It was a Sunday in early March, and the three of them had been up all night speeding when they decided to take a tab. While they were waiting for it to kick in, they looked outside. The sun was coming up and it looked like a beautiful day, with the snow covered fields bathed in the morning light, and they decided to go tobogganing. They piled into Jake's car and drove west five miles to where there was a pasture with a steep hill. They each took a turn on the toboggan, but Darcy got tired immediately when she had to walk back up, so they just lay down on the side of that hill, their arms and legs stretched out, making snow angels and tripping away. Apparently, from what they related later, it started out fine. They talked about how the contrast between the blue sky and endless horizon of white snow seemed magically intense, and the very molecules of snow seemed to pulsate. They felt as if they had discovered a new dimension as they gazed over the prairie landscape.

They had an extra tab of acid left, so they split that up as well. After about two hours the tripping turned. Darcy started hallucinating heavily, taking off her sandals and her two pairs of thick socks and rubbing her feet viciously and screaming, "My feet are melting! My feet are melting!" Spencer began babbling that he had seen God on top of the hill and stumbled around its crest, talking to the sky and gesticulating wildly with his hands, like some kind of hell and brimstone preacher. At one point he thought his soul was flying through the air, and he could look down and see his body on the hill. Jake was crawling in the snow on his hands and knees, sometimes laughing, and sometimes crying, mumbling that they needed to bury the dead bodies. It took several hours for them to come down, and Darcy ended up with some slight frostbite on her toes.

You would have thought that would be the end of the LSD experimentation, but it wasn't. About a week after their tobogganing trip, I stopped over on a Saturday afternoon. As usual, I was bringing over some food—caramel rolls again—that my mother had baked for Jake. Blue Oyster Cult was blasting on the stereo as I approached the door. After I knocked and waited a few minutes, Darcy greeted me, and she was all smiles. "Peter, you cute little cherub, come on in."

I stepped in. I saw my brother and Spencer sitting on the couch smiling, and I knew immediately by the way they looked that they were truly fucked up. Both of them just nodded their heads at me and then burst into laughter. Darcy laughed too and said, "We're having fun. Funny, fun, fun." I had an uneasy feeling, as if I had just wandered into a house of primeval people by mistake.

I handed Darcy the caramel rolls. She immediately tore the biggest one out of the pan and started wolfing it down as I sat down in a lounge chair. Darcy ate that roll in about three bites and then she turned to me. "You look cute today. Maybe I should eat you too."

Spencer and Jake started laughing hysterically again.

Darcy smiled even more. "I bet you have a big German sausage in those jeans," she said. "Probably a virgin one, though."

Apparently Spencer and Jake thought this was hilarious, too, because they laughed even harder.

I was thinking about leaving, when Darcy came up close to me and whispered in my ear in a sultry voice, "Come in the kitchen. I have some special Kool-Aid for you."

I followed her and she poured me a glass of what looked like raspberry or strawberry Kool-Aid. I was young and stupid, obviously, because I drank the whole thing straight down, not suspecting what was in it.

We went back into the living room and I sat there listening to the music and looking at a *High Times* magazine. I'm not sure how much time passed, but I remember I started thinking Blue Oyster Cult was the greatest band I'd ever heard. "*(Don't Fear) the Reaper*" struck me as a tremendous relief—I no longer had to fear death!—and I started laughing with joy. It was at this point that my brother asked Darcy, "Did you give him some Kool-Aid?"

Darcy just smiled.

"Not cool," he said.

"All aboard," Spencer said.

I think I actually enjoyed the intense feeling and magical colors at first, but at some point, I remember I went into the bathroom and looked at myself in the mirror. My face was a shining, sickly gleen, I could see the blood pulsing in my veins, and then I watched in horror as my face slowly dissolved before my eyes. I was pretty scared and I had this feeling I could see inside myself and it was grotesque. I may have cried or screamed—I'm not sure—but Jake must have been coming around by then, because he came and found me in front of the mirror and took me upstairs to his room and made me lie on the bed and talked to me until I came down from the high.

When I was feeling better, Jake walked me to the door and said to Darcy in passing, "You're a fucking bitch for doing that. He's just a kid."

"Oh, fuck you," she said. "He needs to loosen up some. The little prick is such a goody-two-shoes."

I didn't go over to the Chicken Ranch for a while after that, but I heard from other kids about Jake using "angel's dust," made by dousing marijuana with horse tranquilizer. Jake, Spencer, and Darcy were in the bowling alley in Gackle one Friday night, and Jake was high on it and he started freaking out about the loud noise. Spencer tried to calm him down and told him everything was fine, but he covered up his ears crying out, "No, no . . . they'll get killed."

At that point, the owner, Mr. Pritzkau, came over and asked, "What the hell's going on here?"

Jake shook his head slightly as if to clear it. "I can't stop what's in my head sometimes," he said softly.

Spencer intervened. "We were just leaving," he said. He grabbed Jake's arm and pulled him towards the door, but when he did that, Jake dropped the bottle of beer he was holding and it fell, shattering on the floor.

"Oh, shit," Spencer said. They both stopped for a moment, starring at the mess. Then Jake reached down slowly and picked up the largest piece of broken glass and looked at it for a second and squeezed it tightly in his hand until it cut so deeply into his palm that blood began to spurt onto the floor. Jake didn't even flinch as he studied the expanding pool of blood forming at his feet.

Finally, he looked up at Spencer. "It's better now," he said.

By that time, not a single sound could be heard in that bowling alley. Mr. Pritzkau ran to the phone to call the sheriff's office. Luckily, Spencer was able to pull Jake out of there and drive away before the sheriff showed up. Darcy must have know a little first-aid because she was somehow able to wrap his hand and stem the bleeding without having to take Jake to a doctor.

Spencer and Darcy's relationship ended in a rather ugly way in late March when Darcy drove to Jamestown one afternoon for a dental appointment. She had terrible teeth that caused her endless problems, and she was in the dentist's chair for two hours. Afterwards she stopped at the Brass Rail for a quick drink to dull the pain. As she was sitting at the bar, she struck up a conversation with a farm implement salesman, whom she made laugh by reciting the dialogue, word for word, of the previous night's television episode of *Green Acres*. One drink led to another, and she ended up staying the night with him in the Best Western Motel, sharing a bottle of Southern Comfort and smoking pot and "doing freaky stuff."

"Lucky for me the Novocain hadn't worn off completely," she said.

She didn't show up back at the Chicken Ranch until the next afternoon. She immediately told Spencer where she had been and what she had done in some detail, like it was no big deal, and all part of the communal lifestyle and freedom she wanted. Spencer couldn't take it though. He got really pissed off and kicked her out the next morning and she moved back to Hammond. After she had been gone for a few days, he experienced a change of heart. He sent her flowers through FTD Florists, red and pink roses, and called her and begged her to come back, saying that he would forgive her. Jake told him that Darcy was "fucked-up in the head" and just to let her go. Spencer knew that, of course, but I guess he really loved her.

Darcy never did return. After that their only connection was that she mailed Spencer bags of white crosses, hidden in packages of chocolate chip cookies, from Hammond. Whenever Spencer received one of those packages and the speed kicked in, he would start telling stories about Darcy and how funny she was, as if she was the greatest woman in the world.

21

THE CHICKEN RANCH'S REPUTATION, along with Jake's, did not escape the world of my parents. In a rural community everyone knows what everyone else is doing eventually. I know that Mother heard things from her friends and neighbors because she would sometimes quiz me about what went on over there. I would feign ignorance and tell her not to worry. Like Mother, my father rarely drove over to the Chicken Ranch to see Jake, even though it wasn't that many miles away. I think it just pained him to see the yard overgrown and neglected. My parents were raised believing that a neat and tidy yard showed what kind of person you were. A junky yard signified that something was amiss with your character. About the only time my father went over there was if it snowed heavily. Then he would take the Oliver 88 tractor with the farmhand and drive to the Chicken Ranch and clear out the driveway for Jake, even though it took him hours driving the tractor back and forth down those gravel roads.

The stress from worrying about Jake led my parents to start arguing a lot that spring, which was something new, because they had never argued much before that. In fact, I only recall them arguing a handful of times when I was a child. Like most kids, though, I thought each argument was pretty traumatic and I still remember every instance vividly. The one time that sticks out most in my mind was when I was about six. It was the middle of July, and we were experiencing a drought that parched the wheat fields, withering them in the heat. My father came into the house with a strained look on his face and sat quietly at the kitchen table and drank his coffee. Every few minutes he would get up and look out the window to see if there were any clouds that might bring rain, but all we could see were the shimmering heat waves on the horizon. My mother said that they needed to go to town and buy a new washer and dryer. Both were worn out, and the washer had broken down completely, and it was going to take a month to get the part they needed. My father looked at her and said, "What are you thinking? You know we can't afford that right now."

"What do you expect me to do, wash clothes by hand? I'm getting a new washer and dryer and that's that," she said.

"Like hell you are," he said and he went out the front door, slamming the door behind him and heading towards the barn.

Then—and this I remember clearly—my mother stuck her head out the door and yelled after him, "Don't tell me what I can and cannot have . . . if you wanted a new pickup truck, you'd just go ahead and buy it."

My mother grabbed me by the hand and marched out to the car. She drove to Bismarck with just the two of us and went into Knutson's Appliance Store with me in tow. She said she wanted to see the washers and dryers and I remember she looked at every one and talked to the salesman for the longest time. Then I heard her tell the salesman, "I'm not paying that much. Do you think we're made out of money?" and stormed out.

She took me to the Dairy Queen and bought me an ice cream cone dipped in chocolate, which cost ten cents extra, and we didn't ordinarily get that. We sat there in the car as I ate it. She may have talked to me as we were sitting there, I'm not sure—some of the details are all gone now—but I remember that after a few minutes I looked over at her and noticed that tears were running down her cheeks. When I saw that, I lost my appetite, and I couldn't even finish that ice cream cone. She wiped off my hands with a napkin and drove home.

Later that evening, I heard them discussing the washer and dryer again. My father was calmer, but he had a weary look on his face, and he said he didn't know what we were going to do if it didn't rain. At dusk I saw my mother go outside and walk into the wheat field south of the house. I watched her from the yard and she walked a long way out into that field until I could just see her silhouette against the darkening sky. At first I thought she was just checking the crops, but then I saw her looking up at the sky and at one point she raised her hands in the air with her palms pressed together, and I knew that she was praying. She came back after some time, not saying a word. Later that night I was awakened by a clap of thunder and I ran to the window and watched the rain of a late night storm slashing the house. I don't think I ever loved my mother or God so much as at that moment. The next morning both Mother and Father went into town with the pickup, just the two of them together. They came back hours later with a new washer and dryer, and my father spent the day installing them.

Now with the problems with Jake, it was different, and no amount of praying would help. My parents were having little arguments almost every day, and my mother was often depressed. One time my mother was lying on the couch and did not make supper at the usual time. When my father came in, she told him to heat up a can of Campbell's soup and make a sandwich for himself. He was furious, but he tried to hold it in. I heard him in the kitchen, slamming cupboard doors and clattering pans. Then he went into the living room where my mother was and said, "You know the world doesn't revolve around him. There are other people in this family, and we have to eat, you know."

My mother said, "All you can think about is your stomach."

"Well, you can't run a ranch on an empty stomach. The cattle eat. I have to eat too."

He clenched his fists and stood there glaring at her, but he held it in and left the room and ate his soup.

In late March of that year, things came to a head of sorts between my brother and my parents. The incident that precipitated it was Jake getting arrested for drunk driving and possession of marijuana. As I look back at it now, it seems amazing that he had never been in trouble with the law before because he had been having wild keggers and selling pot for years, but maybe the sheriff's office had taken a tolerant view of his activities since he was a Vietnam veteran, or maybe he was just lucky.

In any event, his luck had run out. He had been tailed by a deputy coming home, swerving down the road at a high speed, and he had been pulled over. He failed the breathalyzer test with a .19 reading. A half-pint of Wild Turkey was found under the seat along with an ounce of pot. Luckily, there were no other drugs in the car, or at least none were found, because he probably would have done serious jail time for that.

Now, drinking was pretty well accepted by adults in our community, within reason. The Germans (unlike staid Norwegians) enjoyed their beer, and my parents were no exception, and they'd also have some schnapps or plum wine on holidays and family get-togethers. It was even rumored that Grandfather's brother, Raymond, had done a little bootlegging during Prohibition and brought rum and whiskey across the border from Ontario. But social drinking was one thing; seeing your son's name in the *Tri-County News*, the local newspaper, for being arrested for drunk driving and illegal possession of marijuana was something else entirely. A stigma was attached to that.

My father had to bail Jake out of jail. When he did, Deputy Nordstrom pulled him aside and told him Jake likely wouldn't do jail time for this first offense but that there were too many complaints coming from the community about Jake. Furthermore, Nordstrom told my father about the Yuba County, California, warrant out for Jake for dealing marijuana. They weren't about to extradite him back to California because it wasn't a felony charge, but veteran or not, Jake was going to get in worse trouble if he didn't, "turn things around pronto."

My father was smart enough to realize the deputy was doing him a favor and that this was a serious warning. The problem was that my parents had no understanding of how to deal with an alcohol problem, let alone a drug problem, which wasn't even in their schema. In their minds, Jake just needed to quit, something they thought could be accomplished by sheer will. In fact, to them, everything in the world could be accomplished with a teeth-clenching force of mind. You decided to do it and you did it, even if it was unpleasant, like going out in the middle of a cold winter night to pull a breach calf from a heifer.

* * *

Two days after Jake's arrest, my father went over to the Chicken Ranch to talk to him. I don't know what happened since I was at school, but it clearly wasn't a positive discussion. I heard my mother talking to my sister Marie on the phone that evening and she asked Marie to drive down from Grand Forks and talk to Jake because, "He won't listen to us." I guess Mother thought that, since Marie was a nurse, she must be good at that sort of thing.

A week later, when Marie was due down from Grand Forks, the dawn sprang bright and clear. But change happens quickly on the plains. When Mother turned on the radio and caught the weather report, she heard that a heavy snowstorm was on the way. A "blizzard" or "near blizzard" was predicted along with "hazardous driving conditions." She called Marie's house to tell her not to come, but Marie had already left.

Soon the snow started, at first coming down with just a few white flakes that drifted down slowly and covered the ground in a pristine whiteness. By late morning, however, the wind had begun to pick up out of the northwest, and it increased throughout the early afternoon. It was soon whipping across the farmyard sideways and drifts were beginning to pile up. I could barely see the barn a hundred yards away. By then, Mother was looking out the window and fingering her rosary beads, as great flakes of snow whirled against the window. Finally, at six o'clock, Mother cried out that she could see car headlights and a few minutes later Marie drove up. Marie was nonchalant about the whole thing, she had just slowed down to thirty miles per hour when the worst of the storm hit and kept opening her side window and sticking her head out to see the edge of the road. Marie was always like that in my mind, totally cool and collected.

Marie insisted on going over to the Chicken Ranch right away, so my father started up the tractor and cleared the snow out of the driveway and made sure the roads were clear the whole eight miles to the Chicken Ranch. Fortunately, he had finally bought a tractor with a cab that summer or I'm sure he would have frozen. About two in the morning I was awakened by the slamming of Marie's car door. I peered out the window and it was still snowing out, although it had let up a little. I heard my parents walk downstairs as she came through the front door. My father asked her, "How are the roads?"

"Drivable," she answered and took off her coat.

"Well, for heaven's sake, tell us what happened," my mother said.

"I'm tired, Mom, I'll tell you in the morning," she replied and went up the stairs to bed.

When I got up at seven-thirty in the morning, Marie was already sitting at the Formica-topped kitchen table, eating scrambled eggs and toast and drinking coffee with my parents. Mother was still in her bathrobe, which was unusual for her for that time of day, and she had a weary look on her face. I could tell she had been crying. Dad was standing by the kitchen window staring outside. Everyone was quiet. I could tell they had quit talking when they heard the creaking floorboards as I came down the stairs. I could see Mother was not going to make me breakfast, so I put two slices of bread in the toaster for myself.

Pretty soon Mother couldn't stand the silence and decided to ignore my presence. She asked Marie, "Why doesn't he get a job? I don't even understand how they pay the rent over there, for crying out loud."

"I don't know," she said.

If Marie knew about the pot dealing, and I suspected she did, she didn't say anything about it.

"He needs to stop drinking," my mother said. "No one wants to hire a drinker. And that marijuana. Gracious. Why did he have that in the car? I hope he's not addicted to that stuff."

"Mom, I think he is just trying to make it through the day. That's the way the world is for most people. They just try to make it through this day and if alcohol or whatever helps them make it, that's what they do. Then they get up the next day, and they try to make it through that day. It's like you and Dad trying to make it through the year. You hope you don't have a drought or it doesn't hail and the cattle prices are not too low and you don't go bankrupt. Well, it's like that, except some people have a million more problems pressing on them, so they just try to get through that one single day."

"But I don't understand what problems Jake has," my father said. "He's smart. He could get a job or go to college. Heck, he could be a terrific rancher if he wanted to."

"Times have changed, Dad. A lot of young people don't think that work and making money is the most important thing."

My father snorted when he heard this and I thought he'd choke on his coffee, but he didn't say anything.

"Besides," my sister continued. "He went through a war and you have no idea what that's like."

I thought she was treading on thin ice there because my father had always been a little sensitive that he got a deferment and did not serve in World War II. He didn't respond, but after a moment my mother said, "Our generation went through a war too, a big one, and it was hard, but people came back and got to work. We built up this country."

My father nodded in agreement.

"I don't want to debate this, Mom," Marie said, "Vietnam was just different for a lot of reasons. Let's focus on how we can help Jake."

That was what Marie was like. Other people, especially my mother, would talk things to death, but Marie would figure out a course of action and do it. That afternoon, Marie made an appointment for Jake with a social worker in Bismarck and signed him up for a Vietnam veterans support group, also in Bismarck. She went back over to the Chicken Ranch to talk to Jake about this and reported to my parents that he had agreed to attend. That was all she could do. She had her own life and kids to take care of back in Grand Forks, so she got ready to leave.

The roads had been cleared by then and the sun was out. Right before she left, she took me aside and asked me to take a short walk with her, "to see the cattle." When we got out past the barn, she said to me, "Mom and Dad are having a hard time dealing with this. Try to be as good as you can, okay? They don't need to worry about you, too."

"Yeah, I know. I will."

"Well, I remember when I was in high school. It's not so easy. You feel like you are being pulled in a lot of directions and it gets confusing and you want to try out new things and you can get into trouble. Try to help out as much as you can around here, and keep things cool."

"Sure. What about Jake?" I asked.

"He won't talk much. Doesn't think he has a problem. I think there's a reason why he has been so self-destructive, but he won't open up to me. I'm hoping he goes in and gets some help, but I don't know if he will. People sometimes need to stop falling before they can pull themselves up, and I don't know if Jake has stopped falling yet."

The next week, Marie called Jake to remind him of his appointments. He said he was going, but later Marie called the support group facilitator and found out that he never showed up.

22

AT THE END OF MY JUNIOR YEAR in high school, I heard that Jake was seeing Yvette Sheeny and a few months later she moved in with him at the Chicken Ranch. Yvette was only two years older than me, so she was about eight years younger than Jake, and all my friends knew her. Yvette had come from a tough home with a father who was an alcoholic and who left his wife and three kids when Yvette was in grade school. She was very pretty, with dirty blond hair and dark expressive lips, but she had matured early with large breasts, which can be a curse for a teenage girl. When she was in the ninth grade she began seeing a senior by the name of Matt Schmidt, and we would often see her sitting close to him in his pickup as they cruised up and down Main Street on Saturday nights. When she dropped out of school in the tenth grade, it was common knowledge that she had become pregnant and Matt, always a jerk in my mind, didn't do the right thing and marry her. She moved to Bismarck to stay with her aunt until the baby was born and gave it up for adoption. When she returned to town, she would have had to take the tenth grade over, so she never went back to school. Instead she got a job waitressing at Bender's Cafe.

I liked Yvette from the first time I met her. Liked everything about her. She had a sweet unpretending manner that made people feel at ease. The fact that she had a bad reputation didn't bother me. In fact, it made her seem slightly more exotic. Around the Chicken Ranch, she would dress in peasant blouses and short denim cut-offs when the weather was warm and walk around barefoot. She liked simple joys like baking brownies or gathering wild flowers and strange looking weeds which she would arrange and set around the house in Ball quart jars. In the winter she'd be out in the unattached garage with a propane heater for warmth, weaving plant holders out of some type of cord material. She said she was going to take them to Fargo for the street fair the next summer and sell them.

That summer, Jake and Yvette took Lori and me to the North Dakota State Fair at Minot. Waylon Jennings and Willie Nelson were headlining the show at the grandstand. Jake called me up unexpectedly and asked if Lori and I wanted to go with the two of them. It was a lucky break for me because it was late July and we had already started combining the early wheat, but we'd had a thunderstorm and it rained over an inch. We had to quit combining for two or three days until it dried out, so my father couldn't object. Jake's invitation was the first and only time since Jake had been home from California that he ever took me anyplace.

Getting permission from Lori's parents was going to be a problem, but she begged, and we promised to bring her back right after the show. It was about a three-hour drive to Minot and we figured the show would be over by 10:00 p.m. and we could have her home by her curfew.

We hit the road about eleven in the morning. Jake was driving his big Ford LTD, and we were tooling along fast like he always drove, bugs splattering the windshield at such a rate that we had to stop twice to clean them off. He had just installed an eight-track player beneath the dashboard, and he put in Waylon and Willie's new tape, *Wanted! The Outlaws*, and cranked it up. We listened to it the whole way. Most people would probably remember the hits, "My Heroes Have Always Been Cowboys," and "Good Hearted Woman".

My brother was in the best mood I had ever seen him in. He started singing the lyrics to "Good Hearted Woman." Then Yvette started, and Lori and I joined in, and we sang all the way to Minot. At one point Jake pulled a joint out of his shirt pocket and put it in his mouth. He was about to light it when Yvette said, "Not now. You're driving." To my surprise he looked over at her and smiled and put the joint back in his pocket without a word.

When we got to the fair the first thing Jake wanted to see was the animal barns. Jake knew a lot about what made a good steer and he had done some livestock judging in 4-H. We went through the cattle barn, and Jake commented on the attributes of every steer, imitating a livestock judge: "This steer's thick and full through the hindquarter, wide chested, deep ribbed, trim through the brisket, and long from hooks to pins."

Yvette was impressed. I remember we spent hours going through the barns looking at the cattle and horses and hogs and chickens. Jake held onto Yvette's hand, and Lori and I following them hand-in-hand. Yvette had on a tight clingy T-shirt with no bra and her nipples showed through the thin cotton fabric. I saw more than one man follow her with their eyes. She was a heart-stopper, no doubt about it. I thought Lori looked attractive too, wearing a cropped blouse and a pair of jeans with the patched look that was popular then.

Jake had a wad of twenty-dollar bills, and he kept peeling them off and paid for everything. I figured they were from his pot sales, but I wasn't going to object. I remember we ate blue cotton candy and foot-long hotdogs. Jake took his foot-long out of the bun and held it up by his crotch and wagged it. Both Yvette and Lori laughed like it was the most hilarious thing in the world. The soda pop Yvette was drinking came out of her nose, she was laughing so hard. We went on all the carnival rides too—the Ferris wheel, the Tilt-A-Whirl, the Zipper, the Roller Coaster, and the Himalaya. We saw the freak show with the Siamese twins, Ronnie and Donnie, a sword swallower, a bearded lady, and the rubber-necked man. Yvette and Lori made spin-art pictures, and we played games on the Midway. Jake won Yvette an enormous pink panda by knocking down wooden milk bottles throwing baseballs. The carnival worker kept bugging me, "You wanna play, mista? Come on in. Win one for the lady." So I tried too, but I wasn't a baseball pitcher like Jake—I never could hit a thing. I lost ten dollars before he offered to try for me. He won one for Lori too, but that was fine with me.

Waylon and Willie started late and we had terrible seats way up at the top of the grandstand, but it was a great concert. It was a beautiful, warm summer evening and the sun was just going down as they began playing. The whole sky turned a bright pink and orange. Jake pulled out his joint again and this time I saw Yvette look at him, and with one finger she signaled, "Just one." Jake nodded and he lit the joint with his big brass Army lighter. When the band swung into their second set, Yvette stood up and started swaying and dancing with the music. Jake stood up right behind her and Yvette pressed back against him, grinding her hips against his crotch and they couldn't have looked more in love.

Waylon and Willie played two encores. By the time the concert was over, it was close to twelve o'clock, so we knew we would never get Lori back home by her one o'clock curfew. Anyway Jake was hungry, so we stopped at Homesteaders Restaurant, and we all ordered breakfast steaks with scrambled eggs and enormous plates of greasy hashbrowns. Jake took out his cigarette lighter and lit the grease on the plate and we watched as flames shot up. We all got a huge kick out of that, and we sat in the booth and talked and laughed for an hour and a half.

It was one of the most fun days I remember, and I only wish we could have had more days like that. The only thing that marred the whole day was that Lori's parents screamed at her when she got home so late and she got grounded for a month.

23

THAT FALL I STOPPED by to retrieve a battery charger Jake had borrowed from my father. Jake wasn't home, but Yvette met me at the door, dressed in a pink terrycloth bathrobe with a towel wrapped around her wet hair. She invited me in for cocoa and as she waited for the water to heat she told me about her plans for fixing up the house. "I want to get some red curtains for the kitchen and paint the living room sunshine yellow to brighten it up and maybe get some new carpeting. It's pretty gross, don't you think?"

"Yeah, I guess it's seen better days," I replied as I glanced around. The carpet was worn thin and covered with stains and cigarette burns from all the parties, so that it was impossible to tell what color it was supposed to be, except at the corners or under the chairs, although I did notice that the house was a lot cleaner since she had moved in and the broken window was fixed. She stirred some cocoa mix into the hot water, added some pink and white miniature marshmallows, handed me a mug, and sat down.

"There is so much to do it's mind-boggling," she said.

"Maybe I could help you out and paint or something."

"Oh . . . thanks. But the big problem is that I don't have any money saved up right now to buy anything. Jake said he'd give me some, but I don't know where he's going to get it either. Everything costs so darn much money these days."

She could talk a blue streak once she got started. She sat across from me and rambled on and on, lighting one Virginia Slims cigarette from another as she talked, and occasionally sipping her cocoa. She got started on her work at the cafe and all the regular customers and how the fry cook was always brushing up against her and commenting on how pretty she looked. "He wanted me to help him close up one night, but I don't trust that old perv as far as I can spit. Do you know he has a daughter almost the same age as I am?" she said.

I just sat there and listened for a long time and watched her face. I liked how her face was so expressive and how animated she got. At one point her robe fell open slightly at the top, and she saw my eyes wander there. She blushed slightly and pulled it together at the throat.

When she had finished telling me about the cafe, she paused and looked into my eyes, "Do you know you're a lot like your brother?"

"What do you mean?"

"You both hide a lot inside . . . not the same things, though. With Jake, it's as if he's hiding something he doesn't want to think about. With you, it's more like you're hiding what you *are* thinking about."

I thought she was probably right, but I didn't say anything. She took a deep drag from her cigarette and blew a long thin stream of smoke across the room. "I'm trying to help Jake, but it's hard. He doesn't want to share his true feelings . . . they're buried so deep you couldn't pry them out with a wrecking bar."

She looked at me again closely, and for a second I wanted badly to hold her, but I didn't make a move. Then she said, "Sometimes I wonder what's going on inside that head of yours. You always look like you are thinking and worrying."

"I'll have to think about that," I said, and I furrowed my brow in a worried look, and she laughed. She began to comb out her wet hair and I sat there for a long time and watched her.

A few weeks later, I stopped by again to pick up a pan my mom had sent over earlier in the week with Jake's favorite apple strudel. It was a morning of sharp autumn frost, clear and cool. When I drove up, Yvette was outside of the house stuffing tin foil into a crack just above the foundation by the front door. She was wearing faded jeans and a big gray sweatshirt jacket and she squinted into the morning light as I approached the door.

"We got mice," she said, "This is supposed to stop them from coming in. They won't eat through tin foil."

"I didn't know that."

"Yeah, I read it in the *Ladies Home Journal*. This place is a dump though . . . they probably got a hundred places to get in."

She sat down on the steps. She had a weary look on her face. "You know, when I was a kid I wanted to be a stewardess. I used to practice, 'coffee, tea, cigarettes.' I thought I'd fly to all these exotic places like Hawaii and Acapulco. Now look at me. I'm nineteen, and I already had a baby, and I'm living out here in the country in this crappy house. I don't think I'll ever go anyplace."

I said, "Maybe you will," as cheerily as I could, but it was to make her feel good. I don't think I really believed it at the time.

There was an uncomfortable silence. Then I asked, "Is Jake home?"

"No, he went to Bismarck again," she said.

"What's he doing in Bismarck all the time?"

"You're not too swift, are you?" she said, wiping her face with the back of her hand. "Where do you think he gets all those eight-track stereos and speakers?"

I knew Jake has been selling used car stereos and speakers out of the Chicken Ranch, but I just assumed he bought them someplace and resold them. In hindsight, I guess that it was stupid of me not to put two and two together.

"Is he stealing them?"

"Duh," she responded, and looked at me, raising her eyebrows.

"What if he gets caught?"

"I don't think he cares," she said.

She went into the house and came out with a pack of cigarettes. She lit one, took a long drag, and said, "He doesn't do it for the money, you know. And it's not like he doesn't know it's wrong. He says he just needs a little thrill once in a while. He and Spencer just treat it like it's a big joke."

I stared at the ground a moment thinking about that. Then she said, "Don't get bent out of shape about it. I'll try to look after him and keep him out of trouble."

That is when I first realized she really cared for him, loved him even. But I also could sense that she ached for something, ached for Jake to be more responsible, ached for a better house to live in, ached for a career, ached for a fuller life, and I didn't know if she could get that with Jake. I clung to hope for my brother just as she did, but I didn't see him changing. Not anytime soon anyway.

* * *

ONE DAY IN EARLY DECEMBER, I stopped by and Jake was outside grilling steaks on an old Weber grill in the front yard. Jake did not have a jacket on, even though it was about twenty degrees out and windy, and he was shuffling from one foot to the other and moving about to keep warm. We chatted for a few minutes until the steaks were done and he brought them inside. Four of his friends were over besides Yvette and Spencer. Jake offered me a beer, but I refused because it was a school night, and I still had studying to do. I did accept half of Jake's steak, and I ate it with ketchup and toast, listening to the Allman Brothers album playing on the stereo.

"Where did you get the steaks?" I asked. Yvette gave Jake a dirty look, but he just ignored it, and explained that he got them at Bender's Cafe. It seems that he had started going into the cafe, sitting down and ordering a cup of coffee. Then he'd linger and wait until Mr. Bender was talking to a customer up front. He'd get up like he was going to the restroom and duck into the back storage room, enter the food locker, and grab some steaks, usually whole tenderloins, and stuff them into his jacket and walk out.

Yvette snapped, "Don't do that again. I could lose my job."

Jake said, "Hey, don't worry. They have boxes of them back there. They won't even notice."

Yvette gave him the look again. She didn't say anything with all those people there, but I could see that she was seething.

About halfway through *Whipping Post* Yvette turned off the stereo and turned on the television. "I need to see the weather forecast on the six o'clock news," she explained.

"Nooooo!" my brother cried out. "Leave the music on. What's the fucking difference what the weather's going to be? We can't change it."

Yvette yelled back at him, "The difference is I have to drive in to work tomorrow. I need to see what the weather will be. I don't sit on my ass all day like some people."

"Then quit your damn job or call in sick," he said. "You don't have to work."

"Yeah, maybe I can just steal stuff like you do."

There was an awkward pause. Then, as if he had just noticed a half-dozen people were in the room besides himself and Yvette, Jake said more quietly, "Besides, I am working. This is a chicken ranch, isn't it? I'm a rancher." He looked at Yvette when he said that and smiled. But she was not taking this as a joke. She stubbed her cigarette out in the ash tray hard.

"You have four damn chickens," she said. She turned her head as if she was looking out the window. I could see the beginnings of tears in her eyes, but she brushed them aside and didn't say anything further.

Jake jumped up. "Come in the kitchen . . . now!"

She gave him another look, but followed him. They were gone quite a few minutes. No one in the room said a word and we all pretended to be fascinated with the laundry detergent advertisement on the TV. When they came out of the kitchen, Yvette had a pert little smile on her face and she sat on Jake's lap in the big orange lounge chair and ran her fingers through his hair. Jake always had that.

24

ORRYING ABOUT JAKE TOOK a lot out of my mother. Her kids were her life and she felt that she had done a pretty good job raising them, but now there were all these problems with Jake and it was doubly hard because Jake had shown so much promise when he was young. It aged her. When I look at old photos of my mother when she was young, I am amazed how different she looked as a young woman compared to how I remember her from those days. She seemed to get a lot of winkles around her eyes and mouth almost overnight. Of course, by the time I was in my teens, she was in her mid-fifties, so her hair had turned gray, too. The only thing that hadn't changed was that she had kept her trim figure, maybe because she never ate much, taking joy in the preparation of food rather than its consumption.

In those early photos she has wavy dark hair, dark-brown eyes, and she's always smiling with a touch of red lipstick perfectly lined on her lips. She had grown up as the youngest of four daughters and dressed very fashionably for someone from a family with little money, although I think she probably sewed most of her clothes herself. Mother was half German and half Irish. Her mother was a German farm girl, and her father was an Irish railroad station master. She was a very good singer all her life. When she was just out of high school, she had worked at the Gladstone Hotel coffee shop in Jamestown and spent time with a girl named Norma Egstrom, who also worked there. They weren't best friends—Norma ran around with a rowdier crowd—but they would occasionally go ice skating together or to see a movie at the Grand Theater. Norma was already well known for her singing talent and appeared on the local radio station accompanied by a piano. My mother wanted to sing on the radio like Norma, but her mother, my Grandmother Edna, forbid it. She thought singing should be reserved for church lest a singing career led to association with the wrong types. Norma soon moved to Fargo, changed her name to Peggy Lee and later became world famous as a singer with Benny Goodman's band. She had a string of failed relationships and marriages with musicians and movie stars, so maybe Grandma Edna was right, although I don't know what my mother thought. I like to think she was happy with her choice to be a mother and homemaker, but I really don't know for sure.

Mother met my father one day at the coffee shop when he drove to Jamestown to buy salt blocks for the cattle. My father remembered every detail of their first meeting and told us about it more than a few times. He often said it was his lucky day. It was a bitterly cold March afternoon and he took a stool at the counter and ordered a cup of coffee and a ham sandwich. He sat for a long time to warm up, and that gave him a chance to talk to her between waiting on customers. Mother was wearing a blue skirt and a white apron and had her hair tied back with a ribbon. He sat there for almost two hours, and she kept refilling his cup. He got to the point where he couldn't drink any more coffee because he was so jittery, so he ordered a malted milk because he didn't want to leave. The cup of coffee cost a nickel, the ham sandwich cost twenty cents, the malted milk cost nine cents, and he left a dime tip, which was very generous at the time.

My mother had sworn to herself as a teenager that she would never marry a farmer or rancher, but my father had recently graduated from the Agricultural College in Fargo, and he looked rather jaunty in a felt hat driving his 1932 Nash Lafayette Coup. Father spent almost two years courting her, driving some forty miles each way every weekend. He used to take her to polka dances, which were popular in the small towns around Gackle and Napoleon. I know they must have been good dancers because when I was young and a polka came on during the Lawrence Welk show on television, they'd get up and take a few swings around the living room. "The Village Tavern Polka," the "Champagne Polka," and, of course, the "Beer Barrel Polka," were the ones I remember.

My mother's parents weren't too keen on Father marrying their daughter. They liked him well enough at first, but sometime during the second year they were dating, my father and mother were driving back from a dance in Napoleon late at night and hit an icy patch on the road during an early November sleet storm and slid into the ditch. They had enough warm clothes on and some extra blankets in the trunk of the car so they were all right, but they had to spend the night in that car until someone drove by the next morning and pulled them out. My mother still lived with her parents at that time. They were up all night, of course, worrying about whether she would come home. Grandfather Mel took a dislike to my father after that and didn't favor a marriage, so they eloped one night, driving down to Aberdeen, South Dakota, and getting married there. They had to go to South Dakota because North Dakota law at that time required a pre-marital Wassermann blood test for venereal disease, and they didn't want to have to wait for the test results.

When Father began courting Mother, he promised her he would build her a new house and get her an upright piano for the parlor when they got married. The trouble was, he was courting her at the end of the Depression. Then the war started, so money was a problem, as well as rationing of building materials. My father said the house and piano would have to wait. After they got married, they lived in a tiny four-room house in Gackle for three years and the new house and piano were put on hold until cattle and grain prices rose towards the end of the war and they got ahead a little and could eventually afford to build that new house on the ranch and buy a piano.

Mother used to play that piano at Christmas, and the whole family would gather around and sing Christmas carols. Those Christmases were a magical time—the Christmas tree decorated with colored lights and strung with tinsel and strands of popcorn, and the presents under the tree that were opened one at a time while everyone oohed and ahhed at each one. Mother would cook for days and make all the German food my father loved as a child, especially dumplings, endless dumplings—potato dumplings, cheese dumplings, and kraut dumplings. Then she would bake *kuchen*, with prune filling, and make plates of cookies, Russian tea cakes with walnuts and powdered sugar, which my sisters loved, and *lebkuchen*, a German spice cookie. My sister Marie would come home for Christmas and always bring me the best presents, nothing "useful," and perfectly wrapped in new paper with a bow. No one else did that, it was considered extravagant, but Marie did as she pleased.

My father used to tell us stories about his Christmases as a child. In those days the German Christmas celebrations used to include people dressed up as characters, including the *Belznickel* and *Krist Kindle*, as well as Santa Claus. The *Belznickel* was always portrayed as a mean male, a monster really, who carried a willow whip and dragged a chain. He came to the house about six weeks before Christmas in the evening (by prearrangement of the parents) to identify which children had been naughty and which had been nice. He would stand at the door and ask, "Have all the children in this house been good?" The parents then talked about each child and their good behavior and bad behavior for the year, whereupon the *Belznickel* would warn them, "If you do not be good, you will receive nothing for Christmas." My father said they lived in fear of the *Belznickel* as a child, and that was why they behaved better than our generation. (Mother called that idea "poppycock.")

Krist Kindle arrived a night or so before *Heilige Nacht* (Holy Night). She was portrayed as a kind woman and talked to the parents about their children's good behavior. She gave the children candy and small gifts. The children adored her. Then on Christmas Day, his father, my grandfather Josef, dressed up as Santa Claus and brought each of the children a few gifts. Often they were wooden toys he'd made himself.

Since I had an older brother and sisters, I wised up and quit believing in Santa Claus when I was about five, but Christmases were still a time of wonder for me. I loved the ritual of the Christmas Eve church service with the church decorated with greens and aglow in candles. We always brought a large evergreen tree into the church that would be decorated with strings of red berries and colored lights twinkling like stars. The church also had a wooden nativity scene that an old German farmer had carved and as a child it seemed to come alive for me in that church. When the lights were switched off, so only the candles lit the room, and everyone sang "Silent Night," it was if everyone in the church was touched and could feel the very presence of God.

I would try the rest of my life to recapture the magical and spiritual feeling I had as a child at Christmas. Years later, as a monk at St. John's Abbey Church, I would close my eyes and try to summon up the melodious melting voices of the congregation at home and occasionally felt a hint of it, but the pure innocence and joy that made it so remarkable as a child was lost forever.

That last Christmas before I went off to college, there was a big clash in the family over whether Yvette would be coming. Jake had told mother rather nonchalantly over the telephone that he had invited her over for our Christmas day dinner. My mother didn't say anything at first, but the more she thought about it, the more opposed she became. Mother had never even met Yvette, but she knew about her past and had heard that she was living over at the Chicken Ranch—"living in sin"—as she put it. She acted as if Yvette was somehow solely responsible for that sinful living, not Jake. My mother could be like that sometimes, quick to get on her high horse about others.

One day I was coming down the stairs, and I heard my parents talking and stopped on the stairway. My mother was saying, "What kind of lesson does that send to Marie's kids, and Peter, for that matter? That it's okay to sleep around with whomever you want to? We're just supposed to sit there at dinner and pretend they're not living together?"

My father tried to calm her, "No one has to say anything, and Marie is no innocent in that department, anyhow."

My ears perked up. This was the first I'd heard anything about Marie.

"Marie was living with a doctor . . . that was different. Anyhow, they got married, didn't they? You of all people should know something about that," Mother said.

"Maybe Jake and Yvette will get married someday, too," Father said. "You never know about these things."

"Oh, God forbid! Don't even say that!" Mother huffed. "That girl is nothing but trouble."

Somehow my father won out because Yvette did come over on Christmas Day. She looked beautiful in a green dress, which set off her hair, and she had put on lipstick and perfume. She was perfectly behaved, and she brought presents for everyone, including a scarf for my mother, chocolate-covered cherries for my father, and a J. Giels Band album for me. Mother seemed polite, but aloof at first, until Yvette offered to make the gravy and set the table. Then mother warmed up to her, and we all had a very pleasant time. After dinner, Yvette helped clear the plates and complemented my mother on her cooking, "Mrs. Penner, that was the most wonderful dinner I ever had. You'll have to give me the recipe for the sweet potato casserole."

I don't know if Yvette was just trying to get in Mother's good graces or not. If she was, it worked. Mother commented later that she was surprised Yvette was not like she expected. "I think she has gumption," she said. "It's not easy coming back here after you had a baby out-of-wedlock and everyone knows about it." My mother could be a source of surprise to me sometimes, as well.

Marie took to Yvette instantly. When Yvette and Jake played with Marie's children after dinner and helped them make cupcakes in their new Easy Bake Oven, I saw Marie smile at the two of them. Late in the afternoon Jake went out behind the barn and smoked a joint. When he came back in, we could smell it on him, and Marie and Yvette exchanged glances. Marie furrowed her brow, and Yvette shrugged her shoulders and shook her head slightly as if to say, "What can I do?"

Jake lay down on the floor under the Christmas tree, staring up at the colored lights. He soon fell asleep, but at some point he must have awoken and tried to light a cigarette while still lying on his back, and the lighter flame got too close to the tree. I was in the kitchen with Yvette and Marie and my parents. We heard Marie's eldest daughter yell, "Fire!" We all rushed into the living room just as there was a loud whoosh and the flames raced up the dried branches of the tree. My father grabbed the fire extinguisher and quickly put it out, but my mother and father later had to repaint the entire room and repair some fire damage to the ceiling.

A week later, Yvette announced that she was moving to Fargo to attend Don's Hairstyling Academy. She wanted Jake to move with her, but he kept making up excuses why he couldn't. To everyone's surprise, she up and moved by herself. Jake went to visit her a few times, but she shared an efficiency apartment with a roommate, so it wasn't the best arrangement. She took the three month course in hairstyling, but she couldn't get a job afterwards, and anyhow, she missed Jake, so in late April she was back at the Chicken Ranch. Jake was glad to have her back, too, and he even bought her a new couch, dumping the old one which was covered in coffee and other unidentifiable stains on the back porch, where the weather eventually took its toll and mice chewed up the covering until the springs showed.

25

SHORTLY AFTER YVETTE CAME BACK from beauty school, I told my mother I was driving over to see Jake. My mother sent over some food as usual, a still warm coffee cake that smelled of apples and cinnamon. A cold drizzle mixed with sleet was coming down as I arrived. Jake came to the door, and his face brightened when he smelled the cake and invited me in. Yvette and Spencer were both there. It was about eleven o'clock in the morning, and they were sitting around watching cartoons. Yvette got some plates, and we watched *Tom and Jerry* while we ate the coffee cake. I thought something looked different about Jake and Spencer. "Hey, did you guys get haircuts?"

"Yvette cut it," Jake said, and smiled at her.

She looked pleased, "You guys owe me big time for that."

Jake said, "I'll cut your hair for you."

"Yeah, right. That'll be the day." She turned to me. "I'm doing some hair styling around here for a few people now. Besides Jake and Spencer, I cut the hair of three women. I even gave Freda Bartz a perm."

"Hey, that's cool," I said.

She looked over towards Jake, "I'll have to move to Bismarck or Jamestown, if I want to make more money though. Most of the ladies around here do their own perms, and that's where the real money is."

Jake looked up and said, "I told you that it'll happen someday . . . I mean . . . in a year or two."

This was the first I had ever heard about that. Just then the phone rang in the kitchen, and Jake took it and talked for a while. When he came back, he said to Spencer, "That was Jay Knutson. He's buying a pound. We need to meet him in Jamestown."

I looked over at Yvette when he said this and saw her clench her lips. A short time later, Jake and Spencer left, and Yvette and I stayed watching cartoons. I could tell she had something on her mind. Eventually she said, "Jake's going to get caught someday if he doesn't watch out. I hope not, but everyone knows he's dealing the stuff." She looked out the window. "Maybe not. I don't know. He promised me that this year would be his last crop. He says he wants to grow a lot of pot and make a bundle of money and then get out of the dealing. Anyhow, what can I do? Jake is Jake." Then she brightened, "Do you want me to give you a haircut?"

My hair had gotten stylishly long over the last year and was over my collar, but I liked it that way. I said, "That'd be great, but just a trim."

Yvette sat me down on a kitchen stool and put an old sheet around my shoulders and took out a professional-looking leather scissor case. She talked nonstop as she snipped my hair, telling me about all the students at the hairstyling academy. I couldn't help but enjoy the tingling touch of her hands on my head, her closeness, and the clean fresh smell about her that was attractive. She wore a pair of jeans and a blouse that maybe had one too many buttons unbuttoned. It was impossible not to notice.

"You need to keep your head still," she said.

I tried, but when she stood in front of me to cut my bangs, I had to avert my gaze in order to avoid starring at the swells of her breasts. When she was finished, she had me stand up so she could brush the hair off with a towel. She said, "You look pretty cute now."

She was standing about three feet away, and I thanked her. I stepped forward to give her a hug, but somehow a hidden corner of my brain seemed to take over, and I tried to kiss her on the lips. For a fraction of a second I thought she was going to return my kiss until she stepped back, smiled, and shook her head no. I think my face flushed, but I just pretended like it was no big deal. I left shortly after that, but I remember feeling that she was a very special girl and Jake didn't really deserve her. And for the first time, I begrudged my brother. I don't know where the feeling came from—someplace out in the dark or somewhere inside. All I know is that I badly coveted what he had.

26

I N LATE APRIL, JAKE'S ARMY BUDDY, Nate Swenson, came to stay at the Chicken Ranch for a few weeks. He had served in the same platoon as Jake, and they'd seen plenty of action together. He was now working as a Forest Service smokejumper in Montana. He was athletic and good looking, with a strong jaw and long blond hair that he wore in a ponytail. I liked him because he was smart and thoughtful, not what I had been taught to expect from a Norwegian.

He and Jake spent evenings in the living room, passing a bong back and forth, drinking beer, and shooting the breeze about people they knew in the Army. Nate would fall asleep on the couch, but unlike Jake, he got up every morning at the crack of dawn. He'd fix himself a big breakfast of bacon and eggs and then go for a long walk. Like me, he loved wandering in the outdoors and spent hours walking around the countryside, scanning the sky for migrating sandhill cranes and snow geese, or sitting by the slough and watching the ducks mating and nesting.

One Saturday morning I was driving to Jamestown for tractor parts my father needed and saw a solitary figure walking in the field just southeast of the Chicken Ranch. He was about a quarter of a mile away. As I got closer I recognized Nate from his ponytail and fatigue jacket. I wasn't in a hurry, so I stopped the car and walked out to meet him. It was one of those rare and glorious early spring days on the prairie. The sun was shining, and I could feel the warm southern breeze thawing the ground and smell the earth freeing itself from the grip of winter. New buds, the size of wheat kernels, were just beginning to appear on the weeping willows along the coulee floor. The snow was almost all melted, except where it could hide from the sun behind some tall grass or a fence post, and there were small puddles of water everywhere, which had frozen overnight, waiting for the day's sun to soften them up. I stomped on these as I was walking. I liked to jump on the pearly white spots where I could see the air bubbles trapped beneath the surface, just to hear the ice crackle under my weight, or see the water spurt up when the ice cracked. When Nate saw me doing this he ran over to meet me, and we were soon running around from one frozen puddle to another, seeing who could stomp on the most white spots, laughing like little kids.

When we tired of this, he led me to a spot behind a draw over-looking a slough where we could sit out of the wind and watch the rau-cous waterfowl fly in and out: pintails, mallards, blue-winged teal, scaup, gadwalls, widgeon, and shovelers. The ducks appeared out of the sky as if by magic, soaring down with wings set, then dipped their wings and plummeted downward like falling leaves, before flapping and using their wings like parachutes for the final splashdown. We sat there for a while talking about smokejumping and fires. As I listened intently, he told of deadly "blowups," explosions of flame that could outrun a man and trap a smokejumper in a gulch or ravine, and "crown fires," a hun-dred feet in the air that sounded like a freight train coming and were so powerful they created their own wind.

He talked too of the science of fighting fires and about the fact that they just let some fires burn, because controllable forest fires were beneficial sometimes. He said it was necessary to burn out the old trees to replenish the forest with new growth. Then he looked at me and said, "Sometimes that applies to what's inside a man as well as forests." I thought about that for some time as we studied the sky for more wa-terfowl. It was odd for someone to speak to me like that. I grew up in a community where people were uncomfortable with metaphors. Every-thing was either said directly or left unsaid.

After a while, I asked him about people who work as fire look-outs. It was something I was interested in because, at the time, I thought there would be no better life than sitting in a fire lookout tower in some remote western forest all summer long, alone, and way up there above the trees, with nothing but binoculars and books and my own thoughts. Nate knew a lot of fire lookouts from his work in Montana, but he said that job did not hold enough excitement for him. He preferred jumping out of a plane with a parachute and fighting fires on the ground.

A commotion on the slough attracted our attention. Three drake mallards were wildly chasing after a single hen with a fierce urgency. *Quack, quack, quack.* Then, only the sound of rustling weeds and grass. I summoned up the courage to raise something else that was on my mind. "What was it like in Vietnam?" I asked.

He looked down and seemed to gather his thoughts. "It's hard to explain. Every day was different . . . except when they were the same," and he laughed weirdly to himself.

He paused. "Most days were just sitting around on your ass waiting for something to happen, pure drudgery . . . or doing shit work, like cleaning equipment and hauling stuff around. Most people don't understand just how much shit needs to be hauled around to fight a war. At least the way we did it in 'Nam. The gooks were different. Give them a rifle and a small bag of rice and they could fight for months."

He pulled out a pack of Marlboros, tapped it down, and lit one. "Other times though it was pure adrenaline—the most fun and excitement you'll have in your life. Well, fun isn't the right word. It's more like the purest rush . . . but a fearful rush. Like when the chopper settles down and you jump out and don't know what to expect, or when you're being shot at and shooting back. Your senses are awakened, and it's like a thousand scary thrills hitting you at once. Or maybe you're walking through the jungle on patrol and your senses are so acute that your ability to smell and hear and see is heightened . . . like an animal . . . you become an animal really, a predatory animal. And the thing is, once you've awakened the dark animal inside you, it doesn't go away for a long time. For some people it never goes away."

He took a long drag on his cigarette. "You don't ever want to be in a war, man. If you ever get drafted, run to Canada, run anywhere."

"You seemed to have come out all right."

He laughed lightly, "Yeah, I just jump out of planes into fires."

Then his mood changed again and he was quiet for a minute. "I guess I am looking for that rush again. I know I'm addicted to adrenaline. But, I'm luckier than some. I only have a few demons to deal with."

I knew that he was thinking about my brother, even though he had not mentioned him. "Did something bad happen to my brother over there?" I asked.

He looked at me as if he was about to say something and then stopped. After a moment he said, "Lots of bad shit happened to him . . . and other people . . . but you better ask him about that."

That was the end of it. He got up slowly and motioned for me to follow. We headed east and walked up and down the gently rolling hills for hours. I had left my gloves in the car and my hands got numb, so I stuck them in my jean pockets, and we just kept walking.

27

AS MY BROTHER CONTINUED to slide in the eyes of my parents, my mother began to pin more and more of her hopes on me. I could see how much pain Jake had caused her, and I tried desperately to please her. I began to help her clear and wash the dishes, something men on ranches ordinarily never did, and I would talk to her about things she was interested in—her television shows and garden and flowers. I studied harder in school and almost every evening I would sit at the kitchen table and do my homework. I had always been a good student. School was pretty easy for me, but because of my lack of concentration I would usually get a B or two every marking period. In my last two years of high school, though, I got straight As. Granted, that wasn't too hard at little Gackle High School in the 1970s. The teachers didn't have the highest expectations for students, but it made my mother happy.

It was in Father Ryan's youth group I really excelled, becoming the youth leader my senior year. Being the youth leader meant that I helped plan the activities, and I was often called upon to lead prayers. When I was with the youth group, I often felt like a different person: more confident, more talkative, and sometimes even funny. I really liked most of the kids in the group, it gave me a sense of belonging, and it seemed sometimes as if we were separated from the rest of the world. We had the fervent belief of youth, and, oh, how we would sing, sitting around in a circle, our faces shining and our voices thundering with the spirit. We ached to be good Christians, as only the young can ache for something beyond themselves.

In March of my senior year, I came home from school one day and noticed strange overshoes sitting in a puddle of water in the hallway.

I recognized Father Ryan's voice along with my mother's coming from the living room. I hung up my jacket and went in, glad to see Father Ryan, although somewhat mystified as to why he would be at our house. I was afraid it had something to do with Jake's behavior or Mother's depression.

Mother was serving coffee and sugar cookies to him on a tray. I saw that she was smiling, so I relaxed. She was wearing her blue-and-white dress, and her hair was pulled back in a bun. She looked like she had applied a touch of make-up. Father Ryan stood up when I entered and stuck out his hand, "How are you, Pete?"

I said I was fine and took a handful of cookies and sat down. My mother was looking at me in a strange way, as if she was about to burst with something, and then she looked at Father Ryan, and he tipped his head slightly up and down. Mother said, "Father Ryan and I were talking, and he tells me you might have a calling to the priesthood." I could detect a distinct echo of hope in her voice.

I looked at Father Ryan and he was smiling now too. I wasn't sure how to respond. I had thought about it, yes, especially after Father Ryan had complimented me about the prayer I had given, but every time I thought about it, I also thought about girls, and Lori, in particular, and I was at that age when a guy is plagued by spontaneous hard-ons. I didn't think a life of celibacy was for me. But seeing my mother's face that day and how she looked truly happy for the first time in years, I didn't express any reservations. I simply said, "I might . . . if that's what God intends."

"Well, good! The church needs people like you," Father Ryan said. "We'll talk about it more later, but I think you're on the right track."

My mother smiled again. "Would you care for some peach schnapps, Father?" she asked.

"I don't mind if I do."

Mother retrieved the bottle of peach schnapps she always kept for guests behind the molasses in the top cupboard. She poured a small glass for each of them, and I sat there happy with myself and happy my mother was happy.

28

THAT WINTER AND SPRING LORI and I had begun to spend more and more time together and we developed a certain routine. On Friday and Saturday nights, we'd go to a basketball game or a dance. Afterwards we'd drive out into the country. About three miles from town, we'd drive off onto a rutted dirt trail that led to a small grove of trees where I could park the car out of sight of the main road. We might drink and talk for a short while, but it wouldn't be long before we would be kissing and I would "feel her up." There was, of course, a natural progression to this over a few months—first touching her breasts outside her blouse, then under her blouse but outside her brassiere, then inside her brassiere, and then clumsily unsnapping her brassiere, and occasionally even kissing her breasts if she let me. I remember her breasts were creamy soft and smooth, and her nipples hardened under my touch. That was heady stuff, but, I wanted more. I'd reach down lower to caress her, but she'd always grab my hand and move it back to her breasts. I resorted to begging, but that also got me nowhere. Lori still had a strict 1:00 a.m. curfew, which meant that these sessions would be ended by her promptly at 12:45, and I would have to drive her home.

Of my four best friends in high school at that time, I was the only one who had not gone all the way, and I was feeling some pressure, but I wasn't quite sure how to get Lori to the point of having sex. One night in early June, right after graduation, I asked my brother to buy me two bottles of Boones Farm Strawberry Hill Wine. Lori and I had drunk wine a few times before, but we always shared a bottle. I thought that if Lori drank a whole bottle herself it might help loosen her up. To be frank, it seems shameful now, but that was the conventional wisdom among boys of high school age at that time—getting a girl drunk was always a necessary prelude to sex.

My brother had no problem buying me liquor and suggested I meet him outside the bar at nine. I was a little concerned this was risky because it would be right in the open under the street lights. A deputy sheriff could see him and arrest him for providing alcohol to a minor. Jake dismissed that and told me not to worry.

At nine o'clock Lori and I were waiting as planned across the street from the bar. I can remember every detail. We had David Bowie cranked up high on my car stereo and I kept looking up and down Main Street for my brother to show up. Even though it was early June, it was cold and windy and raining, but I had the car heater on high, and it was putting out so much heat my shins were getting hot, and the heat was radiating up my legs to my waist. Lori was talking a mile a minute and singing along to the songs when she knew the words. I loved to see her like that—it was just the greatest feeling in the world to be with her. She was pretty and laughing and smiling and her jacket was off because the car was warm and she had on a tight blue sweater that showed off her rounded breasts. I liked the smell of her fruity perfume that smelled like strawberries.

Eventually I began to worry that my brother would not show up, but I had no back-up plan, so we stayed and waited. He finally drove up forty-five minutes late and pulled alongside of me. He got out, yelled something to me I couldn't hear, and stumbled on the curb as he walked into the bar. I was embarrassed to have Lori see him like that. A short time later he came out with the two bottles of wine in brown paper bags and a twelve pack of Pabst Blue Ribbon for himself. He handed the wine to me through the car window and only said, "Have fun, kiddos."

Lori and I drove out to our spot in the country and parked. We listened to music and drank the cold sweet wine and we moved to the backseat where there was more room. Lori was in a good mood that night and we were both getting pretty drunk. Our lips were soon locked together and every few minutes I came up for air. I slowly moved my hands below her waist. She gently, but firmly, moved my hands back up. Then it was getting late, and I was getting frustrated with just making out. The alcohol was beginning to make me a little woozy. I had a low tolerance for alcohol and still do.

I know I shouldn't have pressured her, but I did. "Please, just this one time. I really want to."

"Can't you just love me for me," she said. "You know I love you, but I don't want you to go out with me just for sex."

"You don't know what it's like for me," I said.

"Oh, I think you'll survive."

"It's not good for men to get excited and nothing happens."

I took out my wallet, reached into the inner fold, and pulled out a condom I had been carrying for the past year. (We called them rubbers back then.) Holding it in front of her, I pled again, "Look, I have this. You won't get pregnant, and I won't tell anyone, I promise." And again, "Please, please, just this once."

She hesitated for a moment and then asked, "What time is it?"

I looked at my watch. "12:30."

Without a word she suddenly unsnapped and unzipped her jeans, lifted her butt up, and slid her jeans and panties down in a single motion, raising her legs up and pulling them off. "Okay," she sighed, "Do it quick, I have to leave in fifteen minutes."

Oh, my God, I thought. *This is it.*

I shed my jeans and underwear in a flash. I ripped open the condom package. It felt dry and stiff and was difficult to unroll. I was only semi-hard by the time I figured it out and it took me a long time to roll it on, but eventually I did. We were sitting side-by-side at this point, and I awkwardly, half crouching, lifted and moved her legs so that she could lie down the length of the backseat. I maneuvered on top of her.

"Careful, you're crushing me," she said.

I tried to hold myself up on one elbow as I tried to guide myself with the other hand, but I was not fully hard yet. I started to kiss her, but after a second she moved her head to the side.

"Hurry up," she said, as if she just wanted to get it over with.

When I look back on the incident now, I realize that alcohol probably played a role, along with my awkwardness, and not knowing what I was doing. But I didn't have the experience then to understand that. Anyhow, I panicked and absolutely nothing happened. It was one of the worst and most humiliating moments of my life.

I drove her home in silence. As I dropped her off, I told her I was sorry, even though I was seething inside, and I wanted to yell at her and tell her that it was all her fault. Of course, she knew me well enough to know I was angry at her.

"I guess it was just not meant to be," she said, as she got out of the car and slammed the door.

Lori and I never went out again. I was too ashamed to call her and she didn't call me either. A few weeks later, I saw her with Dan Hoefsta in his souped-up blue Camaro. That tore at me. He was a town kid and had the hottest car in Gackle. He would rev the engine and pop the clutch, tires squealing, right on Main Street, while all the kids watched in admiration. In November, I heard that Lori had gotten pregnant. That winter she and Dan got married and moved to Wishek where Dan got a job at the John Deer Implement dealership until it closed two years later. Then they moved to Bismarck where he got a job selling used cars.

It amazes me how we remember the tiniest details of certain events but are unable to remember others entirely. That night with Lori was one of the events I can recall in the tiniest detail and many nights I have wondered, "What if." What if I hadn't been rushed? What if I hadn't drunk so much? What if I had been more agile? What if I had bought a new condom that unrolled more easily, or no condom? My life could be different in a thousand ways. Of course, what happened did happen, and my failure with Lori shattered my teenage confidence and I thought that maybe God did not intend for me to get married and have children. Shortly after that, when Father Ryan asked me if I'd thought more about the church as a vocation, I told him I was definitely interested. He was thrilled and suggested I attend Cardinal Meunch Seminary in Fargo, where I could prepare for the priesthood. I probably would have gone there except for what happened later that summer.

29

WHILE NORTH DAKOTA WINTERS are renowned for their fierce winds and bitter cold, the summers are the opposite extreme. North Dakota has one of the highest temperature differentials anywhere, with a record high of 121 degrees Fahrenheit just north of where I grew up at Steele, and a low of minus sixty degrees at Parshall. That August saw a week of record-breaking high temperatures, and I suffered in the blistering heat. We had no sooner finished putting up the last of the hay when my father put me on the windrower to start cutting the wheat. I was looking forward to moving to Fargo, a big town in my mind, and starting at the seminary, and I chafed under my father's ceaseless persistence to work.

Once you're used to it, driving a windrower requires only minimal attention. All you need to do is keep the rows straight for the combine and adjust the height of the cutter depending upon the height of the grain. On the hills, the grain is usually short, and you need to get the sickle down to the ground, so as not to miss any short grain stems, and to make sure there is enough of the stalk for the combine header to pick up. In the low areas around the sloughs, you cut the grain higher, so not as much straw runs through the combine and potentially clogs up the feeder. Those adjustments became automatic for me after a time. As I drove 'round and 'round the field, I would look to the sky and pray for thunderclouds and rain. If it rained, I could stop windrowing and drive to town and have some fun. While I was praying for thunderclouds, I knew my mother, at that same exact moment, was standing at the kitchen window fingering her rosary beads and praying for the thunderclouds that might bring hail and ruin the crops, to stay away.

It was very hot, the sun was beating down fiercely, and the sweat was making my shirt stick to the skin between my shoulder blades. The rotating reel of the windrower kicked up dust that settled on my perspiring skin, making me uncomfortably itchy. Grasshoppers flew up and struck me in the face. At the end of each row I stopped and took a drink from a half-gallon Thermos of cherry Kool-Aid Mother had sent with me. Before I even got around the field finishing the next row, I was thirsty again and thinking about the next drink and how cool and delicious it would taste when I gulped it.

On this day, the Lord may have heard my prayers and not Mothers. I could see thunderheads rising up to the west. Hour after hour they rose, slowly building up, and then churning more and more rapidly, until they towered into the sky and slowly swallowed the western sun, casting a gray shadow upon the earth. At six o'clock my father drove up in the pickup. He said that it looked like it was going to storm. I should just do a few more rows and then come in. Hurray!

I finished three more rows. By then I could hear thunder rumbling and saw lightning like photoflashes in the distant clouds. I called it quits and drove the windrower home and parked it in the Quonset. Mom had dinner ready for me—pork chops and gravy, mashed potatoes, green beans from the garden, Jell-O salad, and her special rhubarb supreme cake for dessert—the usual country fare. I shoveled the food down, showered, and in a short time I was ready to head into town to see what was going on. In a small town in the summer that was typically driving around and stopping to see friends also driving around and then driving around some more, but it beat sitting on the windrower all day. I was about to leave when Mother gave me some of the rhubarb cake and told me to drop it off at Jake's.

As I drove over, I noticed the storm was approaching quickly now, the temperature had dropped, and the wind had suddenly gone still. The air had that eerie feeling it gets before a storm and smelled of electricity. In the west, the sky was turning a greenish-gray luminance that looked menacing. I drove up to Jake's house just as the wind picked up and sheets of rain began to strike down in torrents. I raced for the house. I didn't wait for anyone to come to the door, but dashed into the entryway and called out, "Is anybody home?"

Yvette shouted from upstairs, "Hi, Peter. I'll be down in a minute."

When she bounded downstairs a moment later, she said, "I'm so glad you came over. I've been home by myself all day."

She had on a pair of jean cutoffs and a print blouse tied at the waist. I couldn't help but compliment her. "You look really good Yvette."

She did a little pirouette and laughed, "I lost some weight this summer. I never eat much when it's hot."

I gave her the cake, and she thanked me and went to the kitchen and dished herself a piece. "Do you want some?" she yelled.

"No thanks. I just ate."

"Well, tell your mom thanks too. She is always so nice."

She came back into the living room with a large piece on the plate and sat on the couch and wolfed it down. "This is so good!" she said, licking her lips.

The storm was now hitting with a fury, it was almost dark, thunder was crashing, lightning was flashing all around, and you could hear the rain slashing the house. I should have left anyhow, but I didn't, and that was my mistake. We sat and talked, facing each other on opposite ends of the couch, and she put her feet up and leaned back on a pillow.

"I heard you and Lori broke up," she said.

I wasn't surprised she knew that. It was a small town, and she probably had seen Lori riding around town with Dan in his Camaro. "Yeah, I'm going to move to Fargo this fall anyhow, so I thought I might as well end it now."

That was mostly a lie, of course. I also didn't say I was headed for the seminary. I think she thought I was going to North Dakota State University in Fargo to attend college like many of the local kids did.

"She was a sweet girl, but I bet you'll have lots of other girlfriends in college," she said.

"I doubt it," I said, trying to be self-effacing, but still not being fully honest again at the same time.

"Oh, you will. Trust me. Lots of girls will want to go out with you."

She told me she was thinking about getting her GED and possibly going to college herself for a degree in elementary education. "I want a real career," she said. "They always need teachers, and I like kids. What do you think?"

I told her she should definitely do it. I could honestly see her as a teacher, and I thought the kids would love her.

The problem, she explained, was that she didn't have any money, and she wasn't saving any waitressing at the cafe. I sympathized, "Yeah, I can understand that." I knew the people in Gackle were frugal with their money (some would say cheap), and they didn't tip much at all—maybe a dime if they had coffee and a piece of pie.

We talked about various possibilities for her, like moving to Bismark and getting a higher paying job, but that cost money for an apartment deposit and first month's rent. I was not sure what to say, but I tried to be as encouraging as possible.

A lightning bolt struck close and a terrific explosion of thunder shook the house. She was momentarily startled and as she looked out the window, I couldn't help but steal a glance at her smooth summer-brown legs, which ran right up to the crotch of her cut-offs and exposed the tiniest sliver of white flesh that had never seen the sun. I lost track of what she was saying, but I don't think she noticed, and she kept on talking.

A loud metallic crash came from just outside the house, and she jumped up to look out the window. I followed her and stood right behind her as she bent down and peered out. A steel garbage barrel had blown over in the wind and had rolled across the yard until it hit the side of the house. She turned back around and was only inches from me. I didn't move. I was looking at her face and her half-parted lips and at that moment I forgot everything in the world and I bent down and kissed her. I pressed my body against hers and placed my hands on her buttocks and drew her close. As I was doing this, I knew she could feel me, and she pressed into me. For a moment she returned my kiss, fervently engulfing her lips on mine as we embraced. Then she pulled her head back.

"I probably shouldn't do this," she whispered.

I pulled her even closer. "It's okay," I said, and I kissed her once more.

She pulled back again, but only very slightly, and her lips were still almost touching mine. "I don't know," she whispered, "I don't think this is a good idea."

"Please."

We both took a deep slow breath at the same time, hesitated for a mere fraction of a second, and then we kissed again, and this time she relented fully. Our bodies followed, and I pulled her back on to the couch. This time it was not like when I was with Lori, I was not awkward, our clothes seemed to fly off, she knew exactly what to do, and we madly made love until we both collapsed in each other's arms, exhausted and breathing heavily.

Afterwards she lay still a minute, and then got up naked. She took out a cigarette from a pack on the coffee table and lit it, inhaling deeply, and blowing the smoke across the room. I took one too and lit it, even though I didn't smoke at the time, and we sat there silently for a moment until I got slightly dizzy and the couch seemed to sway and I coughed from the smoke. She looked away out the window. "It's stopped storming," she said. "You better leave."

I put my clothes back on and noticed a spot on the couch and asked her to make sure she wiped it off. Then I leaned down to kiss her goodbye, but she pulled back. "Don't get any ideas about this," she said. "You're a sweet kid, but this doesn't mean anything." As I walked to the car, she stuck her head out of the doorway and yelled, "Just so you understand, it's not going to happen again. Don't even think about it. I love Jake, you know."

I was giddy with happiness as I drove off. I guess I was like every male the first time he has sex. I thought it was the absolute, number one, without a doubt, most fantastic, incredible thing in the world. *So this is what it's all about*, I thought. *It really is as good as they say.* I craned my neck so I could see myself in the rear view mirror. *Who is that guy?*

I was about a mile away from the Chicken Ranch when I saw my brother approaching from the other direction, his blue car barreling down the road like he always drove, about eighty miles per hour. He raised his index finger from the steering wheel to say hello as we passed, and I thought I was very lucky I'd left when I did.

* * *

THE NEXT DAY my conscience started to bother me. I had been taught like all Catholics that our conscience comes from our souls instinctually reaching out towards God. We were to listen to its insistence with rapt attention, and the price of our failing to do so was guilt. At first, my conscience was just a whisper I could ignore. I was still giddy from having sex for the first time, and giddiness trumps your conscience speaking every time. Over the day, however, I felt more and more uneasy as my conscience spoke up louder and louder. Then guilt flooded in, not about having sex so much as betraying my brother. I thought about going to confession. I knew it could be a release, but our only confessor was Father Ryan. The idea of confessing to him was just too much. I valued his opinion of me terribly and couldn't jeopardize that. This was a deception that I would repeat later in life.

Somehow that evening I found myself driving by the church and saw the light on in Father Ryan's office. I needed desperately to talk to someone, and he was the only one I could turn to. I wasn't about to mention Yvette, but the whole idea of becoming a priest was now bothering me. The gist of the problem was that I wanted to be holy and good, I wanted it desperately, but I couldn't imagine myself being a priest. I couldn't imagine I could be truly virtuous and I thought I would fall short as a priest. At the same time, I could not imagine disappointing my mother and telling her I would not become a priest.

If Father Ryan was surprised to see me, and I guess he probably was, he didn't show it. He didn't ask me a lot of questions or pry into my reasoning when I expressed my doubts. He just said it was important for me to take my time to make a decision. He suggested I attend St. John's University in Minnesota, instead of Cardinal Meunch Seminary. This would give me a broad-based liberal education and, after a few years of study, I could make a decision and choose whatever career was right for me. I would still have option of studying for the priesthood if God called me to do that. He also mentioned for the first time that I could also consider entering St. John's Abbey, the affiliated monastery of St. John's University. This was the first time he had brought up the idea of a monastic life, and it immediately struck me as something more plausible for me. I had no idea what being a monk involved, but suddenly I could see myself in a habit and fasting and praying on my knees for hours, striving to be good. At the time, in my ignorance, it seemed to me like a halfway measure for people who wanted to be holy like I did, but would never be able to attain true holiness.

Father Ryan later wrote a letter of recommendation for me to St. John's University and made some telephone calls because it was late in the year to get admitted, but with his help I was accepted immediately. I felt better as I left his office. I had a plan of sorts, which would still please my mother.

30

LATER THAT EVENING, I saw my brother for the last time before he robbed the bank and was sentenced to prison. It was very late, and I was about to go to bed. I turned off the television and all the lights in the house and stood for a minute looking out the kitchen window. It was pitch dark except for the yellow yard light, which looked like a strange halo swarmed by a cloud of insects. I saw car lights coming down the road. As the car pulled into the yard, I recognized it as Spencer's car. He came up to the steps, and I opened the inside door and looked at him through the screen door.

"You need to get over there right away!" he said.

"Where?"

"The Chicken Ranch. Come on. Quick."

"Why? What's going on?"

"Your brother flipped out. He's shooting up everything."

"What? What do you mean shooting up everything?"

"He shot out the windows on Yvette's car and the tires and everything else in the barn."

"Oh, my God. Why would he do that?"

"Don't ask me. Just hurry up."

"Why didn't you call?"

"Phone's disconnected . . . we didn't pay the bill again."

I followed him, closed the door behind me, and I didn't bother to tell my parents, even though I knew my father had been woken by the car door slamming. He was probably peering out his bedroom window, wondering what the hell was going on.

As we walked to the cars, I asked Spencer to tell me everything.

"Jake and Yvette must have had a fight last night," he said. "I got home late and I saw Yvette sleeping out in her car. For some weird reason, the couch was sitting out in the yard, tipped on its side. I couldn't figure that out, so I checked on Jake. He was passed out drunk. Then he was up in his room all day today. I could hear him pacing back and forth, but he wouldn't answer when I knocked on his door. Yvette came home from work about an hour ago. She headed upstairs just as Jake came flying down. He didn't say a word, just took your grandpa's old shotgun out of the closet and started putting shells in his pocket. I asked him what the fuck he was doing and told him to mellow out. He headed outside and the next thing I knew, I heard these shots. I looked out and he was shooting the front window out of Yvette's car. Yvette screamed at him from the upstairs window, asking him to stop, but Jake just yelled back, 'I ought to shoot you, too.' He shot all the windows and tires out of her car, and then went in the barn and started shooting up at the rafters and yelling, 'Call in the fucking air strike. Light 'em up.' Crazy shit like that. That's when I told Yvette to lock herself in the house, and I came over here. Maybe he'll listen to you."

"What were Jake and Yvette fighting about?" I asked, although deep down inside I already thought I knew.

"I don't know. I didn't hear what started it. Come on. We're wasting time."

I followed him in my car, driving fast. The drive must have taken less than ten minutes, but it seemed like an eternity. My heart was pounding when we pulled into the farmyard. Yvette came out of the house. "He's still acting crazy," she said, and just then a loud boom came from the barn, followed by another a few seconds later, and the window on the west side crashed to bits and glass flew. I could hear my brother yelling something, although I couldn't make out the words.

"I'm worried he might hurt himself," Yvette said.

I started walking towards the barn. "I don't think you should be the one to go in there," Yvette said.

When I was about twenty feet away I yelled, "Jake, it's me, Peter, I'm coming in." He didn't respond, and I walked closer and peered through the barn door. I could see him at the far end of the barn, and he was putting another shell in the shotgun and muttering something. I walked into the barn and the air was thick with the smell of burnt gunpowder. He looked up at me and he had an empty look in his eyes, and for a second I was scared because he seemed as if he was looking right through me.

"Get out of here," he yelled.

"Jake, put the shotgun down. Calm down."

"No, get the fuck out!"

"Please, Jake. Someone could get hurt."

"Like you?" he said in a low, mean voice. He pointed the shotgun at my chest. I was so scared all I could do was take short, gulping breaths. I thought he was going to kill me.

He didn't say anything for a minute, just stood there staring at me. Finally he blinked slightly. "You little asshole . . . you had to do it, didn't you?"

I wanted to lie, but I couldn't. "I'm so sorry, Jake," I said.

"I thought you were somehow different," Jake said, "being the big church youth-group leader and all . . . but no . . . you're just like everyone else. Shit. I can't even trust my own brother. Quit pretending you're so damn holy. Get the fuck out of here."

He slowly lowered the shotgun and dropped it to the ground. He took a step backwards and looked down and shook his head and began to sob quietly. Yvette came in at this point and tried to put her arms around Jake, but he shrugged her off, and she started crying. I just left and walked out to my car. I slumped in the front seat for a minute, my head resting on the steering wheel. I felt there was something more I should say or do, but I didn't know what. I started the car and drove home.

Yvette moved out later that night. She called her mother, bawling on the phone, and her mother drove out to the Chicken Ranch and picked her up.

31

TWENTY-THREE YEARS LATER, I sat on that herbicide pail on our old porch and looked at my watch. I needed to leave in order to meet Sheriff Nordstrom at two o'clock. I wanted to talk to him to find out what happened at Jake's accident. I headed out of the driveway of our ranch and drove slowly north and then east, the ever-present trail of dust billowing up behind me. When I saw the marked spot next to the road, I pulled over and stopped the car. A raw northwest wind coming down from Canada thrashed the dried grass in a frenzy and a strand of yellow police tape used to mark the accident spot snapped with the wind. I took a deep breath and reached in the backseat for my coat. Nordstrom had not arrived yet, so I rested a minute, listening to the wind buffet the car and staring across the prairie fields. The area immediately to my right was a slough bottom. To the east was nothing but brown stubble running up at least four miles to the hills and the horizon. The wheat had been harvested months ago, and the farmer had already dug the ground in preparation for next year. Across the road to the north was another stubble field, with the nearest farm just below the crest of a hill, perhaps two miles away. *What a Godforsaken place to die.*

When Sheriff Nordstrom finally pulled up, I was dozing but awoke at the sound of his car door slamming. Nordstrom hadn't changed much in twenty plus years, except he was thicker, with fat folds on his upper neck, and his belly now hung over his belt. We shook hands. He said, "I'm sorry for your loss. You know, I knew your brother when he lived at that old place . . . the Chicken Ranch, it was called, wasn't it? Seems pretty innocent now, but the things that went on over there gave us a few headaches at the time. Nothing like the meth houses these days, though."

He stopped and used one finger to block a nostril while he blew snot out of the other onto the ground. "Excuse me," he said. "Anyhow, we had a few run-ins at the time, but nothing since he got out of prison. I hated to hear that he died. He was a decorated vet, you know. I always respected that."

He paused, momentarily, then looked around and zipped his jacket all the way up. "It's effing cold, eh?"

I shook my head. "What happened here, Allen?"

"Well . . . Jake was riding his motorcycle . . . you already know that . . . ah, anyhow . . . he was coming from the west, driving fast, we estimate about seventy-five miles per hour. Now that's tooling along for a gravel road, but with a big Harley like that, usually not a problem. It was a nice day, not like today, about sixty degrees, sunny. Then something happened. I'm not sure exactly, but I have a good theory."

He walked over to the shoulder of the road. "Come over here. See this ridge in the road. Last summer we had a lot of rain and the water washed out a gulley across the road. Now the road's been graded since then, but you still have this unevenness and the bad bump. I think when he hit that bump he probably touched the brake. It would be the natural thing to do."

"Okay, now look up here," Nordstrom continued, pointing about a hundred feet up the road. "Here you have loose gravel. Braking, loose gravel, and seventy-five miles per hour don't mix, if you know what I mean." Walking up further on the road he pointed down. "He left the road here, hit the ditch about sixty miles per hour or so and flew into the slough. The impact threw him from the bike about forty feet. The coroner said he likely broke his neck when he hit the ground."

He looked at the ground, paused, and wiped his nose with the back of his hand. "The coroner wasn't exactly sure about the time of death, he may not have died on impact. But he didn't live long in any event. A day or so at most. There was no sign that he moved or anything."

I looked toward the slough bottom, but tall grass and, further on, cattails, hid any sign of an accident. We stood there for a moment and a small flock of the last of the migrating blackbirds rose from the slough and left with the wind.

Nordstrom walked into the slough. I followed. Now I could see tracks from the emergency vehicles, which must have come from an approach further east. On the perimeter of the slough the tall grass was beaten down and the ground scorched from the exhaust of the motorcycle. It must have continued running some time after Jake was thrown off.

"No one found his body for six days," Nordstrom said. "This road used to be a school bus route, but since the Schulte girls graduated from high school, the bus doesn't come up here anymore. There are only three farms between here and Highway 56, and the Werners are old so they hardly ever drive to town. Old Mr. Hankinson finally saw the sunlight catch the motorcycle mirror sticking up out of the grass. He found the body but said he drove past here a half dozen times before he noticed it."

"What was Jake doing riding way out here in the middle of nowhere?"

"I don't know. Like I said, it was a beautiful day. Probably just enjoying the country."

"Did anyone even know he was missing?" I asked.

"Sure, his fiancée, Jill, filed a missing person report the first day."

"Who?" I didn't know anything about her, but then it had been years since I had spoken to my brother.

"Jill Johnson. She and the kid were in the sheriff's office in Bismarck every day bugging the sheriff."

"What kid?"

Nordstrom stared at me, searching my face, and this time, I looked at the ground. "I guess you didn't know," he said. "Your brother and Jill had a daughter."

I didn't feel anything at that moment. Sometimes you think you should feel something, but there is just nothing there. *Maybe I'll feel something later*, I thought.

After Nordstrom left, I stayed, sitting in the car. I started the car to warm up and then tried to pray, but what once came so easily for me was now very difficult. Outside, the wind blew and blew. Soon the snow would come and cover the fields so that only the tops of the stubble would remain. It was still gray and overcast and it felt as if nothing ever changes in this country. But I was wrong about that, and wrong about a lot of things, including my brother. I turned the car around and headed towards Bismarck.

Part 2

32

I WAS SCHEDULED TO BE at the funeral home the next morning at ten to make arrangements for Jake's funeral. As I drove west on I-94, it looked like the sky was brightening a bit, the grayness giving way to blue. As I got closer to Bismarck, the clouds cleared just as the sun started to fall towards the horizon, creating a vista of color in the western sky. As melancholy as I felt, this lifted my spirits. Surely, the sky is the saving grace of this country. Stretching from horizon to horizon, blue by day, and often a soft orange in the morning and evening light, it is the one thing that people who grow up on the prairie commonly come to cherish. When I first moved to Minnesota, everyone talked about the beauty of the woods, but I hated the trees. They made me feel trapped, claustrophobic. I wanted to take a chain saw and cut down every last one of them so I could see the sky. It was only later in the fall, when the woods around St. John's University exploded into color with blood-red oaks and maples and scatterings of golden birch, that I could begin to see its splendor and understand why people could cherish it as well.

When I arrived at St. John's University in the fall of 1977, my intention, following Father Ryan's counsel, was to take a broad range of studies with a concentration in theology. Later, he advised, through prayer, God would reveal his plans for me. If the church did not appear to be my vocation, I would still have a Bachelor of Arts degree, and I could do something else with my life. He didn't say it directly, but I knew any other course in life other than the priesthood or the monastery would be a disappointment to him, as well as to my mother.

As I began my studies at St. John's University, I found that student life was not exactly what I expected. I had this image that the students would all be serious scholars. We would sit around the dormitory lounge or the Commons and have eloquent debates about religion and philosophy and the meaning of life. That's one problem growing up on a ranch in North Dakota. You have this vision of the outside world based on very little real information, so you make up a romantic vision to conform to the way you think it ought to be. You either face disappointment in the real world as a result, or you struggle to try to make the world conform to your expectations.

Upon my arrival, I found out that, yes, the university was officially run by the Benedictine brothers and the president of the university was a Benedictine priest, but, in many ways, the university was very much like any other small Midwestern college or university. A few classes were taught by Benedictine brothers and priests, but most were taught by professors with academic credentials similar to those on any other campus. Although women did not attend St. John's University per se, the affiliated women's college, St. Benedict, was just down the road and the sexes mixed freely both academically and otherwise. (The women students are called "Bennies" and took "the Link," the shuttle bus, between the two campuses.) The intention of the university was that the Catholic, Benedictine spirituality be manifested in the classroom and all facets of student life, but it seemed to me that it too often got lost in the daily grind.

The university student body (the male students at St. John's are called "Johnnies") had a reputation in Minnesota for drinking and, indeed, that seemed to be the major social activity. "AITs" some people called us, "Alcoholics in Training." Many of the students at St. John's were from well-off families from Minneapolis or other large cities in the Midwest, and they knew how to party hard. Athletics, particularly football, were the other preeminent focus of the university, much more so than scholarship. The football team won many conference championships under Coach John Gagliardi, "The Winningest Coach in College Football History," and the football players were the privileged elite of the campus. I know now that it is the same in colleges everywhere, but it was a real revelation to me at the time. I was a naïve country boy when I arrived.

I initially fell into student life like most other students. I moved into the freshman dorm, Saint Thomas Aquinas Hall (Tommy Hall), and my first roommate was Randy Rieker. Randy was a computer science major, and he had a friendly, easy-going manner, always the jokester. He had grown up on a dairy farm near New Prague, Minnesota, so he didn't have a wealthy background like a lot of the students, but his parents wanted him to have a "Catholic education," so they somehow found a way to foot the high cost, as did my parents.

I remember the first day when I met him in our dorm room. After we introduced ourselves and he helped me carry my things up to the room, he tacked a pin-up of Miss September to the bulletin board above his desk.

He stepped back and looked at her. "Wouldn't you like to eat that?" he asked.

"I guess so."

"Guess so? I'd eat through a mile of shit just to take a bite of her ass."

He leaned over and pressed his lips against the pin-up and kissed her between her legs. "She is the most edible playmate ever," he said. "I worship her."

He stared at her a minute and then handed me a can of Hamms beer. "Come on. Let's go find a party," he said.

I was to find out that a "party" was usually a few guys sitting in a dorm room, often ours, drinking warm beer. Hamms was Randy's favorite. It was cheap, and he bought it by the case. Carrying it into the room, he would do a shuffling Indian dance while loudly singing the advertising jingle, "From the Land of Sky Blue Waters, comes the beer refreshing. Hamm's the beer refreshing. Hamm's the beer refreshing."

He soon started a pyramid of empty beer cans in our room that he added to every weekend. By the end of the first semester it reached the ceiling and the room reeked of stale beer. I don't remember having any discussions with him about religion or philosophy. Sports, beer, and pursuing women ("chasing poon-tang," he called it) were his major interests.

At the time, I thought he was a pretty fun guy. Now that I'm older and a monk, his behavior seems less amusing, even somewhat disturbing at times. *How do we get our students to have loftier aspirations?* I wonder.

After the first semester, Randy moved into a house he rented with some other students so he could throw bigger parties. I saw him on campus now and then over the next three-and-a-half years and he always took time to stop and chat and invite me to his parties. We remained friends for a long time, although we had our moments.

The second semester my roommate was Keith Peterson, the son of a physician at Mayo Clinic in Rochester, Minnesota. Keith was a pre-med student and a hard core partier too, a drinker, of course, but also a dedicated pot head. He was religious about rolling a joint every night before he went to bed and placing it, along with matches, at his bedside, so that he could light it the minute he woke up. That way, he said, he could always be stoned.

Keith was very popular with the preppy-type students. Our room soon became the place for their parties and smoking pot. Smoking pot in the dorm room was forbidden, of course, but Keith set a huge fan facing out at the open window to blow the smoke out and put towels around the crack at the bottom of the door to keep the pot smell out of the hallway. Although I tried pot a few times, I wasn't much of a pot smoker—mostly it just made me tired. I'd sit in the room, usually on my top bunk, and listen to the boisterous banter of Keith and his buddies, hoping they would mostly ignore me. At times I envied the way they could talk so coolly about their expensive sound systems, the concerts they'd attended, their skiing weekends, and the babes at St. Benedict they said they had fucked, or wanted to fuck. At other times, I loathed them for the very same things. Life was a game for them and it was as if they'd all started out with a lot of points on the board. Deep down I knew that, coming from a ranch, I was starting with zero points and would never catch up. In fact, I wasn't even sure I wanted to play their game. Fortunately for me probably, Keith ended up quitting after his first year of college when he received Ds in algebra and chemistry.

I drifted academically that first year of college, taking English, German, history, psychology, theology—whatever I thought was interesting or would be an easy grade. Like most students, I was trying to figure out who I was and where I was going, but it was all confusion. I studied diligently, went to classes and took notes, but the classes weren't that difficult for me. I could get decent grades by studying a day or two a week. To be honest, I wasted a lot of time those first years sitting in the dorm lounge watching television or playing ping pong.

One reason I never fit in well with the student life at St. John's was because I wasn't a big drinker, at least that first year. I would have one or two to be social, but that was about it. I'd seen a lot of drunken partiers at the Chicken Ranch and had seen my brother drunk many times. Drinking was bound up in my head with people acting stupid and doing things they'd be sorry for later.

With few exceptions, I also never had any long-term relationships with women in college. I'd sometimes meet girls at parties and talk to them, but that usually was the extent of it. It wasn't that I was ugly or couldn't be social. I had matured and I was tall, fairly good looking, and I could even be funny with effort. It was just that a lot of the women bored the heck out of me. Maybe I was just too serious, but I couldn't listen to their endless chatter about parties and what they did on spring break.

The first woman I spent any significant time with was Andrea, a Bennie I met in psychology class (Psychology 111: Introductory Psychology). I guess you could call Andrea an outdoor enthusiast, the kind one might meet in Colorado or Montana who wear jeans and flannel shirts and hiking boots and thrive on granola bars and cocoa they carry in a Thermos in their backpack. She wasn't particularly pretty, although she had a wholesome look that was appealing. I recall she was from Chicago, but she had spent the past two summers working at a camp near the Boundary Waters Canoe Area. We kind of hung out for a while, meeting at the Commons or library and studying together. Once I saw her at a party, and we talked for quite a long time and had a beer together. She thought it was cool that I grew up on a ranch. She insisted she wanted to visit there and ride horses some day. I thought she was full of life and fun to talk to and I guess I also admired her trim athletic figure and the way she looked in jeans. The thing was, she had a boyfriend, which was no secret, and she often talked about camping trips they'd been on together. For a while I thought I wanted to be her boyfriend. I pictured us on romantic camping trips where we would sit before the campfire at night and look up at the stars before we went inside the tent and climbed into our down-filled sleeping bags, two singles zipped together in my imagination.

I had been spending time with her occasionally for a few weeks when I called her up and asked her to hop on the Link and meet me at the Fireplace Lounge in the Commons to study, although I really didn't have studying on my mind. Mostly I just wanted to see her. To my disappointment, she showed up with her boyfriend, a tall, lanky senior with a touch of a dark beard, giving him that swarthy look I always distrusted in men. She introduced me as if we would all become great friends, but I could tell instantly the guy didn't trust me, either. I thought he was obnoxious and full of himself. He spent the whole time talking about rock climbing in the Rocky Mountains and canoeing in the Boundary Waters and how he planned to hike the Appalachian Trail. She watched him and listened with rapt attention to his every word. The whole thing was very awkward for me. I felt like a third wheel, and when I saw her with him like that, I suddenly had a strong feeling I didn't really like her at all. I rarely saw her after that. She kind of just disappeared. I imagine her now, camping out in the rain and slapping mosquitoes, black flies, and no-see-ums somewhere in the North Woods with her boyfriend. I hope she's happy.

The second woman I went out with was a sweet girl named Rene and in a lot of ways she was the opposite of Andrea. I met her at a campus ministry one-day retreat I attended towards the end of my freshman year. I wasn't keen on attending, but a friend from my dorm, Nick, was going and talked me into it. The retreat was supposedly a chance to enrich our spiritual lives, but Nick had gone to one previously and said it was a great place to meet women. It was a joint event with St. Benedict, and about thirty students were at the retreat, with only eight of them guys, but every one of them was ogling Rene. She was drop-dead gorgeous, way out of my league as far as looks, but I summoned up all my courage and talked to her during the lunch break and got her phone number. I was usually too shy to do something like that, so I felt proud of myself, and Nick was very impressed.

When I say Rene was drop-dead gorgeous, I'm not exaggerating or being boastful. She looked like a Miss America—perfect body and long, thick, naturally blonde hair that she could flick back perfectly. She often wore tight white slacks and a short pink quilted jacket with a white fur-lined hood. When she walked down the street, everyone, and I mean everyone, would turn their heads to watch her go by.

A day after the retreat, I called her up and asked her if she wanted to get some pizza. She said sure, so we drove into St. Cloud and went to Sammy's Pizza. I remember we shared a large sausage and mushroom pizza. She told me she had just broken up with her boyfriend with whom she had gone steady since she was a sophomore in high school. He was a hockey player at the University of North Dakota. Distance had made their relationship difficult and she split with him after she found out he'd been seeing another girl at UND. I figured that was fortunate for me because I doubt she would have gone out with me if not on the rebound. When she wasn't talking about her ex-boyfriend, she talked about her sisters. She came from a large Catholic family of twelve kids, eight of whom were girls, and grew up on a farm near Crookston, Minnesota. She must have been close to her sisters the way she talked about them all the time.

People might describe Rene as "pure as the driven snow." She was that kind of woman, religious in an unquestioning, sincere manner. She never missed Holy Mass or confession and would never consider dating outside her faith. It was just the way she was brought up. She told me straight up, "I'm saving myself for marriage." To be honest, I was hoping that wasn't true at the time, at least for me, although the whole idea of her being wholesome and chaste was enticing.

A week or so later I took her to a movie, *The Day of the Locust*, the campus was showing as part of its student film series. After we left the theater I immediately blurted, "Wow, that was great, wasn't it?"

She looked at me strangely, "Ooooh, I didn't like it. It was way too violent for me. I had to close my eyes when that mob was beating the man to death, and I hated the ending."

"Why?"

"I like happy endings. I want everything to end happily."

I said, "Yeah, I guess you're right," and I felt stupid. I wanted to impress her badly. I was mad at myself for opening my mouth too soon.

It was apparent from the start that other than our religion and the retreat we had gone on, we didn't have much in common or to talk about. She was a huge hockey fan. I didn't know a thing about it. She loved clothes. I paid almost no attention to them. She liked country music and, despite growing up on a ranch, I found it formulaic and boring (with some exceptions, like Waylon and Willie!). She wasn't completely dumb, but she had no interest in academics at all that I could see. Mostly she just talked about her sisters.

Even though we didn't have much in common, I still wanted to go out with her, partly, I suppose, because of my ego. I enjoyed the way people looked at me when we were together. I felt they saw me differently too—much cooler. I was trying to be someone I wasn't.

One of Rene's sisters was a dental hygienist in Minneapolis. Rene asked me to give her a ride there one Saturday because her sister was out of town for the weekend and she wanted someone to feed her cat. I quickly agreed, of course. I was hoping Rene had an ulterior motive in mind. I remember I bought a new shirt and aftershave just for the trip. I also remember I made a mental list of things to talk to her about on the drive down. I don't remember exactly what that included, but probably things like books she liked, classes she was taking next semester, what she wanted to do after college, where she wanted to travel—that sort of thing. She wasn't much of a talker though, except when she was talking about her sisters, and she responded to everything

I brought up with a sentence or two reply. I had run out of things to ask her about forty-five minutes down the road. At that point, I had no choice but to ask about her sisters to keep the conversation going and she became animated with excitement and told me about each of them. Four of them were married and had children of their own, so I also had to hear about her baby nieces and nephews and how cute they were and how it was so funny when they threw peas on the floor and on and on.

When we got to her sister's apartment in Minneapolis, we fed and petted the cat for a while. We had cats on the ranch to keep the mice down, so I was fine with that. Her sister had a trundle bed in the apartment and one doesn't see those very often anymore, so she showed me how it came down out of the wall and that got my mental neurons firing for a second, but she put it right back up.

We sat down on the couch to watch her favorite show, *Laverne and Shirley*, on television. I remember glancing at her and feeling that this couldn't be real. She was almost too perfect, like a giant chocolate Easter bunny in your basket Easter morning that looks too good to eat and you save it, until one day, overcome by desire, you bite its ear off. I waited until almost the end of the show and then slowly eased my arm around her and kissed her full red lips. She kissed me back for a moment, but just when I thought something more might happen, she abruptly broke it off. She took my arm off her shoulder, smiled prettily, and gently tapped the tip of my nose with her index finger. "We better not," she said, "one thing leads to another."

Exactly, I thought, but I behaved myself. After *Laverne and Shirley* was over, she said we had to go, so we drove back to college. She talked about her sisters nonstop the whole way home. I asked her out again one more time about two weeks later, but she said she was busy that night shampooing her hair, and I never asked her out again. Two years after I graduated, I heard the sad news that she died in a car rollover south of East Grand Forks, Minnesota.

I had exactly one sexual experience, or should I say, near sexual experience, with a woman in college. I met Jan in March of my sophomore year at a party my first roommate, Randy, threw at his house. When I got there, there were already quite a few Bennies milling about and surrounded by all the testosterone-fueled men. Loud disco music blared from gigantic speakers, a few people were dancing, doing the bump to "Give Up the Funk," and they were already on their way to emptying their fourth keg of beer. There was a game of "Indian" going on in the middle of the room, and although I had never played before, Randy cajoled me into trying.

Indian was a college drinking game, popular at that time, where the players would sit in chairs around a circle drumming on their knees and making an Indian war whoop sound. Each player had their own Indian sign, like, "snake in the grass," which was made by the player making a snake motion with the hand or "buffalo shit," which was made by placing a loose fist on the other hand. The first player made their sign, followed by the sign of another player. That player then repeated their own sign, followed by that of someone else, and play continued until someone made a mistake. The game was fast and furious, and if a person hesitated for a second and made a mistake, he or she lost and had to chug a beer. While chugging, everyone in the circle would make an Indian, "whoop, whoop, whoop," sound using their hands against their months.

I ended up sitting next to Jan and I could tell she had not played this game before, either. About the only thing I remember about her was that I thought she was cute and she had dark frizzy hair with the big hair look that was becoming very popular then. As the game progressed, I started to lose a few times, and after I had chugged a few beers my reflexes and thinking got slower. I started to lose more often. By the time I had chugged my sixth or seventh beer I had to pee badly, which was probably fortunate for me. It got me away from the game or I might have been one of the ones puking later. When I got up to use the bathroom, Jan apparently had the same need, because she followed me. It took a long time because there was a long line of women waiting to go, so we started talking. When I was done, I waited for her and when she came out we fell to talking again. The music was very loud, and I couldn't hear half of what she was saying so after a while I suggested we go outside to get some fresh air.

We talked outside for a minute, but it was cold, so I pulled her into my car, which was parked in the alley behind the house, and turned on the heat. We were both pretty drunk, and she had the spins so we sat there for a while until they went away, and then we talked some more, although I have no memory of what we said. I do remember she moved in close and started kissing me. I returned her kiss, and we made out for a while. She was a good kisser, with a hard, urgent tongue that did marvelous things I had not experienced before. I slowly moved my hands under her sweater and began feeling her breasts over her bra. To my surprise she said, "I'll take it off," and removed her bra. She did this without taking off her sweater—I have no idea how. That kind of thing is still a mystery to me. I remember too that she had long erect nipples. After caressing them for the longest period of time, we jumped in the backseat where there was more room. As soon as we did, she reached down and unbuckled my belt and unzipped my pants. I shed them quickly and then helped her remove her jeans and panties. I maneuvered on top of her between her soft white thighs, and I don't remember any awkwardness. All I remember is that she had just grabbed me to guide me in and I was a milli-second from entering her when I was startled by a loud banging on the window. I looked up. It was Randy, his face pressed against the frosted glass of the car window. He was making faces and laughing and yelling, "Oh, yeah. Oh, yeah. Oh, yeah." Jan screamed. Then when she saw who it was, she swore, calling him a "fucking asshole" about ten times. She threw her clothes back on and headed back in the house to find her girlfriends. I didn't even follow her. I figured there was no point. I never saw her again, and I didn't even know her last name so I couldn't have called her even if I had wanted to.

33

I N THE SPRING OF 1978 I received the call from my father. I remember that it was about eight o'clock in the evening, and the phone call came in my dorm room. My roommate, Keith, answered and handed the receiver to me. "It's your dad," he said. I hesitated a minute before I took the phone from him. It was a Thursday, and my parents only called on Sundays, every other week, so I had a feeling immediately that something was wrong.

After my hello, my father said at once, "I have some bad news."

"What is it?"

"It's Jake. He's been arrested for bank robbery."

"What? What are you talking about?" I thought for a second I had misheard what he was saying.

"We don't understand it either, but that's what they're saying."

"That's what who is saying, Dad?"

"The Barnes County Sheriff called us."

"It's some mistake. Jake would never do anything like that."

"Peter, they're saying he had the money, eight thousand dollars, in the car."

I could hear my mother bawling in the background as he said this. Then he said, "That's not all. They say Spencer was shot during the arrest. He's dead."

"Oh, my God. No. It can't be."

When one first hears something like that, the mind struggles to comprehend it because part of the mind desperately wants to deny it. At the same time I was aware that I could hardly take a breath, my stomach clenching, and my whole body tightening as if it wanted to flee my mind.

"Can you come home?" he asked.

I left immediately, driving straight through without stopping. It seemed like the drive took days, even though it was less than six hours. As I drove, I kept hoping that this was a dream and I'd wake up, but I knew that wasn't going to happen. I wish I had more strength to endure when bad things like that happen, but I didn't then, anymore than now, and I felt sick and weak.

I arrived at the ranch about two o'clock in the morning. Even as I approached the steps of the house I could hear my mother crying, a loud wail really, and when I went in, she grabbed me and cried hysterically. "Oh, Peter, how could this happen? How could this happen?"

I was speechless and I just hugged her. My father looked haggard, pacing back and forth, and every once in a while he would try to comfort my mother. She would be quiet a minute, and then she would start sobbing again, her shoulders hitching, until he would put his arms around her and pull her tight. She kept crying, "Why? Why? Dear God, please don't let it be true. Please don't let it be true."

My sister Marie arrived a short time later, having driven from Grand Forks. Needless to say, we were up all night trying to comfort my mother and father. I stayed four days, as did Marie, and we never left the house except that my father and I went out a few times to feed the cattle. Marie was better at handling this sort of thing than I was and she made some phone calls to try to find the best criminal defense attorney they could get in North Dakota. Other than that, there wasn't much anyone could do. Jake was being held in the Barnes County jail, and they wouldn't even let him have visitors yet.

The last day we were at the ranch, Marie was trying to console my father in the kitchen. I was in the living room with my mother, who was lying on the couch, but I heard Marie say, "I don't think Jake is a bad person. He's had a tough time, and he just wasn't able to handle it well, but he's a good person, Dad. You have to know that."

My father said, "He was never the same after he came back from Vietnam . . . we never should have been in that God-forsaken war in the first place. I can see that now . . . that damn LBJ . . . and Nixon and Kissinger too. It was all for nothing."

"You're probably right about that," Marie said. "I don't know what happened to him over there . . . but I think the drinking and drugs made things worse, too. I just wish I could have gotten him help. I should have tried harder. If we could have just got him into some type of counseling, maybe this wouldn't have happened."

I thought it was unfair for Marie to blame herself. I knew she had tried her utmost to help him. Then Marie said, "The other thing is, I don't think he has ever recovered from Yvette leaving him."

Hearing those words was like a stabbing thrust to my chest. I knew it was true the instant she said it, and I knew it would forever be my cross to bear.

My mother heard what Marie said too, and she got up off the couch and walked into the kitchen. "I knew she was a tramp from the beginning," she said. "She was no good for him."

Of course, I didn't have the guts to say anything.

I returned to college and, for quite a while, I was adrift, living as if nothing mattered. I tried to attend classes and study some in the afternoons, but in the evenings my mind wandered, and I would think about my brother and Spencer and Yvette. I'd sit in my room and drink beer until the alcohol kicked in, and I became sedated and eventually fell asleep. When I woke up in the morning I felt terrible, of course, and nothing had changed.

That summer I went home to work on the ranch, and it was the most miserable three months of my life. Jake was still in jail, awaiting trial, and every evening my mother talked endlessly about the cause of Jake robbing the bank, speculating on everything from Jake having brain damage from exposure to Agent Orange in the war, to it all being Spencer's fault, or to some defect in parenting on their part. Maybe they were too strict or not strict enough. Maybe he worked too much on the ranch or not enough. Or maybe it was the permissive culture he had experienced in California. She could think of dozens of possible reasons, but she would always mention Yvette, as if she undoubtedly bore a share of the blame. She couldn't accept that Jake had done anything wrong, and I guess I couldn't blame her for that as a mother. She kept going to Mass and confession, however, and she talked to the priest. Father Ryan had moved on to another diocese, but we had a new priest, Father Henne, who was of German heritage, originally from Kulm, North Dakota. He told her we sometimes cannot understand the ways of God, but that God would surely forgive Jake. That seemed to give her some hope. She had been worried that Jake was destined for hell, and when she came back from seeing the priest at least she was no longer clenching her lips so tightly.

My father continued to work and expected me to do the same, but now he always had a pained look in his face, his eyes racked with sorrow. I would sometimes see him staring off into space, lost in his own thoughts, for long periods of time. On top of the immediate worry about what would happen to Jake, I think at this point he gave up any hope of passing the ranch on to one of his sons. I was obviously not interested in ranching, and now Jake, who he had still held out hope for, was facing years in prison. That must have cut him deeply because he had worked his whole life to pass that ranch on to his children. Keeping the land in the family was almost a sacred obligation in our community.

That summer my father got badly injured by one of our Angus bulls. I think all the distractions caused it, because my father wasn't stupid when it came to animals. Angus bulls can be mean, everyone who worked around them knew that, and my father knew it, too. A lot of people are probably familiar with them from rodeos where their big shoulder humps and nasty natures wow the crowd during the bull riding. The bull we had was a mean SOB named Happy Jack, obviously misnamed. He would be calm most of the time, but when he got in a foul mood, we had to watch out, as he would come at us head down, intending to do serious damage. My father had been around bulls all his life, of course, and knew how to handle them. He never showed fear, which was half the trick, and he kept one eye on them when he was working around them just in case. He also had a long black bullwhip like most ranchers did, but he rarely used it, preferring to use a good cutting horse if he had to drive the bull into a pasture or corral. If he had to work up close with a bull, he used a nose tong.

On this particular day, my father was repairing a wooden gate between the feedlot and the pasture where the bull was grazing. He had just finished hammering, and he stepped back. Although he didn't admit it, I suspect his mind was on other things, because he said the next thing he knew he heard a sound behind him and saw the bull charging. Before he could take two steps towards the gate, Happy Jack struck him low, behind his thighs, flinging Dad into the air, his body gyrating and spinning, and he came down hard on his right arm and side. The bull spun around and came after him again, but my father somehow jumped up and flung himself over the gate to safety. He trudged slowly up to the house holding his arm. My mother saw him out the kitchen window and immediately knew something was wrong. "My God, Albert, what's the matter?"

He acted like it was nothing serious, just a bad sprain he thought, and a few bruises, but after two days and nights in which my mother heard him moaning every time he moved in his sleep, she insisted he see a doctor, which he did, and he found out the arm was broken.

His arm was in a cast the rest of the summer, and while Dad continued to ranch with one good arm, certain things on the ranch required the use of two hands, so he was always calling me to help him with this or that. I felt like I spent half the summer at his beck and call. By the end of the summer I was itching to get away.

34

THAT FALL I GOT A SINGLE ROOM at the university so I didn't have to deal with a roommate. I felt like I was always tired, and I often skipped classes, lying on my bed and sleeping or just thinking. Since I often napped during the day, I slept fitfully at night, often waking up at 3:00 a.m. with my mind racing, and I would be unable to get back to sleep. My grades were bad that semester, too. I wasn't flunking, but I was receiving mostly Cs, just barely getting by.

I returned home again in late October when Jake's trial came up. My father had hired the best criminal defense attorney in North Dakota, Kenneth Singer, out of Fargo. He was quite renowned in the state because he had gotten a high school student off for shooting another student in the back on the steps of Fargo North High School. The perpetrator was the son of a state senator, and Singer somehow managed to convince the jury it was self defense. Murder trials are rare in North Dakota, and not-guilty verdicts for a murder charge almost unheard of. As a result of the acquittal, Singer's reputation soared, and he could command just about any fee he wanted. He charged my father a $50,000 retainer up front.

Singer couldn't do much for Jake, though, no matter how good a lawyer he was. Since Spencer had died in the course of committing a felony, Jake was facing a second-degree murder charge as well as the charge of armed robbery. Singer's major strategy was to make Jake out as a patriotic hero with a Bronze Star, but Jake wasn't in favor of that. He told Singer he was no hero. "That medal was tarnished the day I got it," he said.

Jake wasn't much help in his own defense actually, ceaselessly arguing that the young Highway Patrol officer who shot Spencer should be prosecuted. Singer told us flat out that Jake's attitude wouldn't sit well with the judge. It also didn't help that Jake had a previous conviction for possession of marijuana and there was the issue of the outstanding California warrant.

My father wanted Singer to argue that the shotgun used in the robbery wasn't loaded and that Jake and Spencer had no intention of harming anyone. Of course, that wasn't the way it worked. Singer told him the fact that the gun wasn't loaded didn't make any difference under the law. They talked, too, about a temporary insanity defense, but there wasn't much to base that on besides the drug use, and Singer didn't think that would fly. Singer finally struck a deal on the courthouse steps with the States Attorney. Jake pled guilty to manslaughter and armed robbery and received a twelve- to eighteen-year sentence.

That winter was the roughest time for me. I got drunk almost every weekend, mostly in my own room, but occasionally sitting in someone else's dorm room drinking beer and listening to music. It wasn't like I was having fun, I was just behaving badly, and I would look back at that period of time with some degree of shame. I also got in the first, and only, fight in my life that winter.

I had been drinking in someone's dorm room, and I must have got pretty drunk because some of the details I've forgotten, but I do remember it was one of those nasty cold Minnesota nights when everything was coated with snow and ice, and the wind was blowing. I was in the dark mood that men get into sometimes when they just feel they want to punch someone. I had just left to walk back to my dorm when I brushed against some guy coming in, and I slipped and fell down. I don't even know what caused me to slip, whether it was my drunken state, or the ice, or the guy brushing me, probably all three. I got up and said to the guy, "Watch where the fuck you're going."

"Sorry," he said.

But that wasn't good enough for me. I recognized him as a football player, and I was itching for a confrontation. I called him a "dumb asshole"—typical student hothead talk.

That made him angry. He said, "You're the asshole," and he shoved me. I slipped on the ice again, lost my balance and fell. This time I came up intending to fight. I came at him, and he decked me with one punch. I must have lain there for a few minutes because the next thing I remember was that the same guy was helping me up (to their credit, Johnnies are like that). He asked me if I was okay and told me to go home and sober up. I was dizzy and stood there for a minute and then got back down on my hands and knees and threw up all over the sidewalk. The guy picked me up and helped me back to my dorm room.

That wasn't even the low point. That came when I went Christmas shopping in downtown St. Cloud before I drove home to spend Christmas with my family. I was in the Ben Franklin Store looking for something for my mother. I found a necklace with a silver cross on it that I thought she would like and I picked it up to purchase it for her. I think it cost about eight dollars. Before I went up to the cashier, I decided to go back to the toy section to find something for Marie's daughters. I remember I was looking at the Barbies. I had the necklace in my hand, and I don't know what I was thinking, but I looked around and saw I was the only person in the aisle. I didn't see any mirrors to spot shoplifters, so I thrust it down the front of my pants into my underwear. Then I just walked out of the store.

I might have dropped out of college that year and who knows what would have become of me, but I think God must have taken mercy on my wretched soul because he led me into a theology class that spring taught by Brother Michael (Theology 310: Forms of Christian Community). Brother Michael was a Benedictine monk and a well regarded theology professor at St. John's. He was a thick, portly man, with a ruddy disheveled look, his black hair sticking up at odd angles. He always wore brown corduroy pants and the same two turtleneck sweaters all winter long, one dark-green and one red, alternating every other day.

Brother Michael always started each class with a few jokes, so he was well regarded by the students, and his classes were always filled. But he was not only funny—he was a good teacher too. He had a way of making theology seem relevant in the modern world. He spent summers working at a homeless shelter in Minneapolis and wasn't afraid to draw on real-life examples—stories of death and loss, but also love and compassion. He always contended we must act in the world if we want God to manifest in us. Brother Michael changed the image of what a monk could be for me, that within the Benedictine Order there was room for modernity and humor and a worldliness that extended beyond the abbey or campus walls.

That spring I went to see him during his office hours to discuss a paper I was writing for his class on the Catholic Worker Movement. After he had given me some leads on sources, he inquired as to what I was doing that summer. I didn't have a job yet, but I told him that a friend and I wanted to get an apartment in St. Cloud for the summer and maybe obtain work on a road crew or doing construction. (There was no way I was going home to work on the ranch again!)

"Physical labor is good for your soul," he said, "but I know another opportunity that might offer something more, if you're interested."

"What is it?"

"We could use someone at the homeless shelter in Minneapolis. We're doing fix-up work this summer and need all the help we can get. A lot of it might be using a hammer or paintbrush, but I can also try to find you some opportunities to work with the homeless men and women."

My initial reaction was less than enthusiastic. We didn't have homeless people out in the country where I grew up, although I had seen a few homeless Indians in Bismarck under the bridge or staggering around town drunk. Working with drunk people seemed like the last thing I wanted to do, but the idea of spending the summer in Minneapolis appealed to me since I had never lived in a big city before.

"Would I make much?" I asked.

Brother Michael smiled, "If you want to make money, take a construction job. You could make good money, go out drinking after work, and have a great summer doing that. This is a volunteer position. About the best we could do is find you a place to flop down on the floor and you would get one meal a day. The only thing it offers is that it may change the way you see the world. Those chances are rare in life."

35

IN EARLY JUNE I FOUND myself driving to Minneapolis with Brother
Michael. The Guiding Light Homeless Shelter was in an old
church basement just off Franklin Avenue. The place was empty
when we arrived because it was a nighttime facility only, and the shelter
residents had to be out by 7:00 a.m. Michael showed me around,
which didn't take long, pointing out the large main room utilized as a
sleeping area for the men and packed with thirty blue plastic-covered
mats in two long rows, not more than three feet apart. Besides the
sleeping area for men, there was a smaller room for women with ten
beds, a small recreation room with two couches and a TV, a kitchen,
and a large communal dining area where one meal a day was served,
in the evening at six o'clock.

A coatroom off the entrance had been made into a small sleeping quarters for the overnight female staff person, who that summer
was a wonderful elderly nun named Sister Edith. She had to be in her
seventies, but there was something in her being that instantly exuded
vitality and energy. Michael would later teasingly call her "Va-Voom,"
a nickname that she did not object to.

When he introduced me to her she said, "So you're here to do
God's work," and she smiled with sparkling eyes as she grasped my hand
in both of hers.

"I guess so."

"Well, you might think you're working for the Devil himself,"
she said and she looked at Brother Michael and they both chuckled.

"Now, now," he said. And then to me, "As you can see, we've
worked together before."

Off to the side of the dining area was a small office with a single cot for the overnight male staff. That was where Brother Michael dropped his small green suitcase.

"Where do I sleep?" I asked hesitantly, because I feared what the answer would be.

"You sleep out with the men in the main sleeping area. It's not so bad once you get used to the smell." He told me that with a smile, and when I think about it, I can hardly remember a time that summer when he wasn't smiling. He went on to explain that the shelter did not fill up in the summer like it did in the winter, when people came in to get out of the cold and they'd have to turn people away because they didn't have enough beds. Those turned away were in danger of getting frostbitten fingers and toes or, as it happened to a few every year, freezing to death. In the summer, it was quieter because a lot of the homeless preferred to sleep out on the streets—one reason being that the shelter had a "no alcohol" rule.

The shelter averaged twelve to fifteen men per night and maybe a half dozen women in the summer, but even with that limited number of people, the stench could be almost overwhelming sometimes. People came in who hadn't bathed in who knows how long and reeked of urine and some of them wore the same dirt-stained clothes year round, including parkas and jackets. I thought living in a dorm with a roommate was bad, but I was to find out that this was like living with a dozen roommates who rarely, if ever, showered.

The first night I nearly gagged from the smell, and I hardly slept because of the noise of incessant coughing, farting and snoring. On the third night, I was awakened by a homeless man two pads down loudly mumbling, "Shit, piss, fuck, cunt . . . shit, piss, fuck, cunt . . . shit, piss, fuck, cunt," over and over, for a least an hour. After a week of this, I was seriously thinking of telling Brother Michael I was going home, but he was a step ahead of me and came in one day with a large fan. He put me on a mat by the far wall with the fan blowing into the rest of the room. The steady drone of the fan helped me sleep and cut down on the smell.

It still stunk at times, but I got used to it over the summer and, to be honest, I had cleaned out cattle barns on the ranch that smelled worse.

People started lining up outside at five o'clock for the six o'clock meal. For many of them it was their only meal of the day, and some would stay the night and some would leave after they ate. We served forty to fifty meals a day. It was simple food: macaroni and cheese, sloppy-joe's, fried Spam, potatoes, fruit cocktail—that sort of fare. A lot of it was donated, so the shelter made do with what it could get. The homeless people always seemed grateful for it, however, and I don't ever remember any complaints, even when it was pork and beans heated out of a size-ten can.

The shelter residents seemed faceless at first. They arrived ragged and usually filthy, faces ravaged by alcohol, fights, and outdoor living. Many had missing teeth and open ulcers and sores, and they were often loud, cursing, yelling, and talking to the voices they heard in their heads. Most of them suffered from mental illness, substance abuse, and physical health problems and that was apparent immediately. After a few days though, I began to put faces on the people and recognize the regulars by name. Then I could see the smile of the man who limped in with a deformed foot, or the quiet humor of the gap-toothed woman whose face looked like it went through a meat grinder, and I began to see them as people. After a few weeks I learned some of their stories and that was when they became fellow human beings to me, and I could feel real compassion. I found out that they had virtually all been beaten down sometime in their past—victims of broken families, sexual and physical abuse, the atrocities of war, and mental illness. They had fallen through the cracks and many of them suffered from depression, schizophrenia, paranoid delusions, or psychotic episodes.

My day began after the shelter residents left at 7:00 a.m., mopping the floors and scrubbing the toilets with disinfectant. To say that they were filthy would be an understatement. Many mornings I scrubbed off diarrhea, vomited blood, and worse. I think Brother Michael was testing me by giving me the foulest and most disgusting work. "Somebody has to do it," he said, "and none of us are better than our fellow man." When I was done with the cleaning, I'd do fix-up work, repairing holes punched in the walls, replacing ceiling tile, and painting the worst of the walls where the paint and plaster were falling off.

After a few weeks, Brother Michael occasionally had me accompany him to learn about his advocacy work, much of which involved trying to assist residents to access needed social services. He'd spend the day trudging from agency to agency, with the homeless in tow, negotiating red tape and trying to secure housing, disability, or veteran's benefits for them.

During the evening meal, after everyone had been served, Brother Michael would sit and talk with the shelter residents. He encouraged me to do the same. A few of them really stuck out in my mind. One of them who came in that summer was a man named John Kapinsky. John had a red, hardened face and oily, slicked-back hair. He hobbled in off the street looking for a meal in late June. Initially he was scowling and angry about having to wait in line for the meal. He didn't sleep in the shelter and left after eating, but he came back the next evening to eat and most evenings after that. I sat with him one day and asked him where he was sleeping.

His eyes were cast down and to the side, but he answered, "I was sleeping in a stairwell, but I got a place under the bridge now that it's warmer."

"You can sleep here if you would like. We have room."

"Nope. I'm an alcoholic, so I got to have a drink. I get the shakes bad if I don't."

"How did you hurt your leg?"

"I don't know . . . down by the river. Big rocks there. I fell. Broke my bottle of vodka, too. That was the shits. I tried to suck it off the rocks but most of it flowed off." He smiled at himself when he said that, and then he rolled down his stinky sock and showed me his ankle. I couldn't believe how swollen and blue it was.

John was a Vietnam veteran who claimed to have a metal plate in his head. He was eligible for treatment at the VA Hospital, so that gave us a better option than the county hospital. I spoke to Brother

Michael about John that evening. He suggested we accompany him to the VA Hospital to see if we could get his ankle checked. It turned out that the ankle wasn't broken, but they were able to give him a wrap for it and a pair of crutches. John spent most of the time in the hospital begging the physician and nurses for some Vicodin, but they refused. He thanked us profusely for taking him anyhow and left in a hurry, clopping along on those crutches and heading towards downtown.

About a week later John showed up at the shelter, still limping and without his crutches. When I asked him what happened to his crutches, he looked down, seemingly ashamed, and said he'd lost them. The next day we took him back to the VA, but they said that he was limited to one pair in twelve months, so Brother Michael took him to the pharmacy down the street and paid for a pair of crutches with his own money.

A few days later John came back and said those crutches were stolen, so Brother Michael bought him his third pair. A week later he came in yet again, claiming that the crutches had been stolen once more. This time Brother Michael sat and talked to him for a long time. He finally admitted that he had sold all three pairs for a few dollars at a downtown medical supply store to buy some booze. Brother Michael bought him a fourth pair on his promise that he would keep them. We saw John again at the shelter about two weeks later. He didn't have his crutches again, but swore he "lost them." When Brother Michael refused to spring for another pair, John glanced down and muttered, "Suck-a-duck, I never have any luck." Brother Michael just smiled and shook his head.

Another person I remember vividly from that summer was a woman named Faith, who came in that July. She had a disheveled look, with thin, wispy hair under an old baseball cap, and several missing teeth. She must have been pretty at one time, but now her face only looked wasted. Looking at her, I guessed she was in her late fifties or early sixties, but later I found out she was only forty-two. I don't think she weighed more than ninety pounds and she had on a black ski jacket that was too big for her and what looked like a pair of men's stained brown trousers.

I watched her for a few days first before I said anything to her. She was very guarded and suspicious. She would come in, line up for her food, and then sit as far away from other people as she could. After eating, she headed outside again. She refused to stay in the shelter overnight and no one knew where she went or where she slept after she left.

One day I saw Faith pocket a knife from the kitchen. I didn't want to confront her directly, but we couldn't allow that kind of theft for a lot of reasons, so I sat down with her and tried to talk with her. She didn't want to talk, although she did give me the knife back when I asked, without apologizing.

Over the next few weeks I sat with Faith and talked to her almost every day. She was often nonresponsive at first, answering all my questions with a yes or no or silence. The most I could get out of her was that she grew up in Brainerd, Minnesota, and had been living in Minneapolis since she left home when she was fourteen. Eventually, as she came to trust me, she told me more of her story. Sometimes it was hard for me to even sit and listen. She told of her mother, an alcoholic, who brought a series of boyfriends, stepfathers, and strangers into her life. She told of beatings with electrical cords, belts, and broom handles, of pushing her dresser up against her bedroom door and sleeping next to it to keep her mother's boyfriend out, of her second stepfather, standing at the top of the stairs, ordering her to come up, and then kicking her in the face as she reached the top, and laughing as she tumbled down. She talked of gang bangs and gang rapes and of giving head in bar restroom stalls to strangers for money to buy drinks or drugs, and an endless series of men who had abused her ever since she could remember. Sometimes when she was finished talking, I had to get up and go into the next room to take a deep breath and steady my trembling guts. It made me realize what a stable, sheltered world I grew up in on the ranch. It also troubled me, because I thought I should help her, but I wasn't sure how. What did I know of the life of a homeless person? I only knew life on a ranch—castrating calves, fixing broken mower sickles and tending sick cattle. Saving a human being was something else entirely.

* * *

FAITH FINALLY DIVULGED TO ME that she was sleeping in an abandoned car behind an old warehouse, but she still had no desire to come into the shelter. "I found an old car. It's hid good behind a building. It don't run, but I got through the window, so I sleep in there. I don't want anyone to know, 'cuz if the men find out, they'll be comin' round there."

"You could freeze to death there in the winter," I said.

She just shrugged.

I talked to Brother Michael and Sister Edith about her. They told me she needed some type of permanent housing as a first step, but no place was available at that time that would take an alcoholic. One day, at wit's end about how to help her, I urged her to go into a residential alcohol treatment program.

"I tried that once and just start drinkin' again when I get out," she said.

"You need to try again. Sometimes it takes more than one try. I'll take you there myself. We can go first thing tomorrow."

I could see that she got visibly upset when I said that. She spit out her words angrily. "I ain't going I tell you. I ain't. Leave me the hell alone." She turned her head and looked down, and I knew I had lost her. She never came back to the shelter again.

John and Faith were the tough cases, the kind that gave me a sick feeling in my stomach and left me immensely discouraged. But we had some successes, too: getting people disability or veteran's benefits or into a treatment program or permanent housing, and Brother Michael just kept at it day after day. It was more interesting and rewarding than I had imagined, because every day was something different and a challenge. For the first time in my life I felt something approaching purpose and grace.

At the end of the day, Brother Michael and Sister Edith and I would sit together in his small room and talk. Brother Michael would take out a gallon jug of Mogan David Concord Wine from under his bed and pour it into three paper cups. We weren't supposed to have it in the shelter, but he said, "Don't worry about it. Wine is the only thing that keeps the Catholic Church going. That and bingo." Sister Edith always brought some crackers or bread and maybe a little cheese to share. We would sit there and sip our wine and have our little snack and hash over the day's events. No matter how dismal the day had been, the two of them would soon be chuckling and cracking jokes. I can't explain in words what those times meant to me, other than that I had a feeling of being enveloped in a deep joyous warmth, and they stay with me always.

At the end of the summer, Brother Michael took me out for pizza. I remember that we went to the Green Mill Restaurant and had a huge deep-dish pizza, with pepperoni, sausage, ground beef, and extra cheese. Halfway through the meal, Brother Michael told me that he thought I might have a vocation to be a monk. I said I wasn't so sure. I would need to think about it. "Don't worry about certainty in your decision at this point," he said. "It's a long process, and you will often have doubts, but just let the idea rest in you for a time. When you feel like it, pray, and God will reveal to you if you have the calling."

"How will I know?" I asked.

"When you feel that you want to give yourself to God," he said simply. "And by doing that you will find God within yourself."

I wasn't so sure that would happen, but at that moment, I deeply aspired to try to be more like Brother Michael.

36

I WORKED AT THE GUIDING LIGHT SHELTER again with Brother Michael the summer after my junior year. I did better in my studies those last two years of college and graduated from St. John's University in the spring of 1981, with a major in social work and a minor in theology and entered the affiliated monastery, St. John's Abbey.

At this point I should probably explain some things about monks and monasteries. People often have an image about monks from television and movies, typically an image of a monk in some isolated monastery on a mountain, living an austere life of fasting and silence, sleeping on woven mats, and practicing corporal mortification, such as flogging themselves or wearing hair shirts. (Hair shirts are garments of rough cloth made from goat hair, worn for mortification and penance.) Of course, that image is mostly a Hollywood concoction. While it is true that fasting and silence are part of the life of many monastic orders, the extent to which it is practiced varies widely. Personally, I fast occasionally, during Lent and on some holy days, but I know many people who are not monks who do so as well. I have never personally seen any monks flog themselves (I will say more about that later) or wear a hair shirt for that matter, and it's not a part of the ordinary practice of our order. Only the Carthusian and Carmelite Orders wear hair shirts by rule.

The hugely popular book and movie, *The Da Vinci Code*, presented Opus Dei members as monks. In that movie, a monk uses both the cilice (a metal chain with sharp prongs worn around the thigh) and the discipline (self flogging). The blood flies in those scenes and splatters the walls. It goes without saying that *The Da Vinci Code* was a highly fictionalized depiction of monks. In reality, Opus Dei is not a monastic order, rather a Catholic institution for lay people and diocesan priests. Opus Dei does not have monks at all. While some members may use the cilice and the discipline, the depiction in the movie is grossly exaggerated from what I have been told.

Monasteries date back to the earliest days of Christianity, the third century A.D., when St. Antony, a semi-literate Egyptian farmer, rejected the violent sexuality and materialism he had found in Alexandria and set off for the desert to live as a hermit in a cave. He later organized his followers, who venerated him for his asceticism and power over demons, into a loose-knit community that became the first monastery. Within the Catholic faith, there are now many different Catholic monastic orders: Cluniacs, Cistercians, Carthusians, Premonstratensians, and the Camaldolese, among others. I entered the Benedictine Order, meaning we take our rule from St. Benedict.

Monastic life is part of the spiritual tradition in many religions. Most people are probably aware of Buddhist monasteries, in part, because of the fame and writing of the Dalai Lama of Tibet. Interestingly, across religions, time, and cultures, the essentials of monastic life—the silence, the simple clothing, the solitude and withdrawal from everyday life, and the discipline in day-to-day activities and prayer—are remarkably similar. People have universally found these practices are necessary if one is to lead a contemplative life and feel closer to God—an interesting concept in an age when life for most people is trending in the opposite direction.

Thomas Merton, a well-known American Trappist (Cistercian) monk and author, proclaimed, "The spiritual life is the life of man's real self, the life of the interior self whose flame is often allowed to be smothered under the ashes of anxiety and futile concern." At St. John's Abbey we strove for simplicity of life and believed that silence and fasting could help us better understand our true selves and what God called us to do. Quiet space and prayer are part of the life we try to create within the cloistered walls. I found that aspect greatly appealing because the solitude one could find in the monastery reminded me of the solitude of the Great Plains, where I could be the only person for miles around. I believe, as do my Brothers, that in solitude and silence we can better hear God's voice talking to us. Think about two friends—when they want to have a deep conversation, they do not do so in the middle of a crowd of people; they find a quiet secluded place to speak and be alone.

We are not overly strict at St. John's, and we are not ascetics, living a life of abstinence from all worldly pleasures. Many people might be surprised to find that our work often requires us to be engaged with the world just like people outside the cloister walls. We have televisions and most of us are active Internet users. Some traditionalist monks in other orders would not view us as monks at all because of our lack of strictness, but we believe we have struck a balance that is right for us.

St. John's Abbey was established in 1856, so we have a long history in Minnesota. The first Benedictine monks at St. John's were all European-born and German-speaking. Immigrants from Germany were moving to Minnesota in the thousands, and they founded small, heavily German towns where they always built a saloon first, and a Catholic Church with its tall spires, second. The abbey was established to educate, minister, and serve this mostly German group of immigrants in central Minnesota, and the Benedictine monks went on to establish St. John's University, and St. John's Preparatory School all in the same area, near St. Cloud, Minnesota.

At St. John's Abbey, we now have close to two hundred monks, making us the largest monastery in the Western world. Work is central to what we do, and we have monks who are professors and teachers, physicians, social workers, counselors, librarians, woodworkers, potters, painters, sculptors, groundskeepers, bakers, cooks, and a number of abbey and university administrators, like me. In addition, some monks are also priests and serve the Catholic parishes in the surrounding communities. I should explain that when I first came to the monastery a certain amount of anti-clericalism existed among the brothers who were not priests. This came out of a history of special privileges for the priests that dated back hundreds of years, when "the lay brothers" were the peasants of the Benedictine Order and did the menial work, like the baking and the winemaking and tending the monastery cattle ("Clean those barns!"). Even in the early years at St. John's Abbey, the brothers and "the fathers" prayed separately and had separate living quarters and recreational rooms. That was mostly ended with Vatican II, but remnants of that division still remain today.

What binds us at the monastery is that we are a family, in a sense. And we have a common purpose: to serve God through our worship as well as work, *Ora et Labore*. Saint Ignatius of Loyola understood the need for this balance, admonishing us, "Work as if everything depended on you, but pray as if everything depended on God."

Benedictine monks practice *lectio contina*, reading through whole books of the Bible at morning and evening prayer. We read or chant the psalms daily with long periods of silences between them. The Bible is often thought of as God speaking to man, but in the psalms it is clearly man speaking to God, and that is part of the tradition of the Benedictine order, to speak to, and please God.

Oh, I wish everyone could hear the liturgical chanting to understand how truly beautiful it is. The monks on one side of the altar chant, followed by the monks on the opposite side. *Gloria in excelsis Deo. Et in terra pax hominibus.* Sometimes when I close my eyes, I feel as if it is no longer chanting, but the wind I hear blowing across the prairie. This mystery is magnified because the Abbey Church was architecturally designed to act as an echo chamber, so that the echoing sound has the softness of the wind. At Sunday worship we have a liturgical procession where all the monks walk in two-by-two, chanting. We learn to treasure this physical participation in the liturgy. There is something about singing together that can be an aesthetic experience that touches one at the deepest level of one's being and provides a profound sense of God's presence that cannot be articulated.

Togetherness is maintained by this sharing of time, the (endless) community meetings, and the sharing of food and serving each other in our dining. Sometimes the communal dining is the most difficult part of being a monk. Consider one's own extended family, or better yet, co-workers, as much as we love them, we need a certain amount of space and might not want to dine with them every single day, three times a day. To be honest, when you are constantly living in such close proximity, little idiosyncrasies of some of the brothers can drive you crazy after a while. It might be the way someone slurps soup during a meal or a rasping cough during the liturgy. Even monks have the feeling they want to strangle people sometimes.

Undoubtedly, we are a motley crew of monks and we do have some eccentric members. One monk was frequently seen walking in the woods near St. John's talking to the squirrels and feeding flour to the ants. That might be considered a little crazy to outsiders, but after all, St. Francis of Assisi preached to the birds, and a lot of lay people talk to animals as well, particularly their pets. My grandfather Josef had two matched Percheron horses, Sam and Leo, that he talked to all the time while he was plowing. Feeding flour to ants is a little strange, I admit, but again, not that big of a deal. People feed birds and other wild animals all the time. Like any large extended family that has a loony aunt or uncle, you try to overlook it or excuse it.

37

RIVING TO BISMARCK to make funeral arrangements for my brother, I took the first exit into Bismarck, which passed the North Dakota State Penitentiary, the prison where Jake spent twelve years of his life. The penitentiary sat on a flat area southeast of town, almost next to the highway. Concrete guard towers with gimbal lights looked over the open yard and it was surrounded by high fences, topped by razor wire.

It was a shameful but inescapable fact that I only visited Jake one time in prison, in 1981, when I was in my first year at the monastery. I had been hesitant to visit him. It was easier to push him out of my mind and not face the guilt I felt about Yvette. I relented only because my mother was still alive and urged me to see him. She and my father made the trip from the ranch every other week, even if there was a severe snowstorm, always bringing a homemade apple pie that mother left for the guards.

It was very cold the day I visited him, maybe ten degrees below zero, with a nasty wind out of the northwest. The visitors' parking lot was a long distance from the main gate, so I ran to the door to keep from freezing. I had arrived early to check in, and a guard told me to take a seat until I was called. I sat for what seemed like the longest time, making it impossible to escape my thoughts.

The waiting room was lit too brightly with rows of florescent lights and furnished with blue plastic chairs and a few green plastic plants. It smelled of piney disinfectant. Old magazines rested on a corner table, and a picture of President Ford hung on one wall, even though Reagan was president at that time. As I looked around the room, I noticed I was the only male present, except for one old fellow chewing tobacco who would get up every once in a while and spit into a pot that held one of the plastic plants. The rest of the visitors were women: mothers, wives, and girlfriends. Two women had babies, both with coughs and runny noses. A coffee maker in the corner had a coffee can for donations. I put two quarters in and took a cardboard cup and helped myself. It had that dark, oily, burnt taste coffee gets after sitting on the warmer a long time. I sipped it slowly.

When the time for my visit finally arrived, I was searched and then led into a large visiting room that looked comfortable enough with tables and chairs, but the gate clanging shut behind me was still somewhat unsettling. The place was all concrete and steel and the echoes seemed to reverberate forever. I sat trying to think how to react and what to say to Jake. Nothing seemed right. "How are you?" didn't seem particularly appropriate when a person was in prison and things couldn't get much worse. Finally, I settled on the topics of weather and food.

A few minutes later, the gate buzzed, and Jake entered the room. I was shocked at his appearance—his hair was cut short and he looked older and hardened from when I had last seen him at his sentencing. He was wearing a bright-orange prison uniform with the shirt sleeves precisely rolled up and I could see the bottom of a prison tattoo peeking out from underneath. His biceps looked larger than I remembered and rock hard.

He grinned and gave me a hug, and I choked up a little. We stood there for a minute before either of us said anything. Then he said, "I bet it's colder than shit out, isn't it?"

I acknowledged that it was and we were on to a safe topic of discussion. Jake told me he only got one hour a day, five days a week, in the exercise yard, so he liked to pay attention to the weather. When the sun was out, he would walk around the yard or sit in a certain spot on the south side of the building out of the wind and just "soak up the rays." Unfortunately, there had been only eight days that month (it was December 27) when there was any sun at all during his time outside. He knew the number exactly. The only exercise he got besides that was lifting weights.

"I pump iron every day until my arms burn," he said. A lot of the inmates were into pumping iron. They all wanted to look like "bad asses."

He looked at my coffee cup and asked, "How's the coffee?"

"Terrible."

"Figures."

I asked him how the food was in prison. He said it was mostly bad and overcooked, although they had some kind of meat every day, even if he couldn't always tell what kind, and the cooks made a delicious apple strudel in the fall when they could get cheap apples. Then he described what they had to eat every day of the week over the past few weeks, like it was the most important happening in his life, which I suspect it was. As he described the food, it occurred to me he ate much of the same simple fare we served at the monastery, although certainly not as well prepared, and he ate communally like we did. "The problem is we only have about fifteen minutes to get our food, find a place to sit that's not next to the wrong people and eat it," he said.

Next we discussed his work making license plates, which he said made the day go faster and paid enough so that he could buy cigarettes. "That's pretty much it," he said, "I work, eat, lift weights, go outside when I can. The rest of the time I sit in my cell and usually read or take naps."

He asked about our parents. I told them they were fine. I didn't say anything about the Christmas we had just spent together. I thought it would make him too sad that he'd missed it. We had run out of safe topics to talk about so there was an awkward silence for a moment. Finally, he said, "Mom told me you're going to be a monk."

"Yes, I am."

"Really?"

"Yes, really. I have to prepare and study some first, but I'm becoming a monk."

I suppose you think that'll make you some kind of holy man," he said, and I detected a slight edge of hostility.

"I wouldn't put it that way, but I do think I have a calling for it . . . why? Do you think there is something wrong with that?"

"I didn't say anything was wrong with it . . . it just sounds like a stupid thing to do, that's all. Why do you want to waste your life like that?"

I was taken aback and maybe a little irritated at this sudden confrontation, but I tried not to show it. "I don't think serving God and dedicating myself to prayer and good works is a waste of my life," I said.

He took a deep breath, as if trying hard to keep something in, and then he exploded. "For Christ's sake, Peter, there is no God! The sooner you figure that out, the better off you'll be. If there was a God, would Spencer's head have been blown off by that idiot highway patrolman? Spencer . . . shit . . . he was one of the nicest guys in the world. I still get so pissed off thinking about it I want to kill the fucker who shot him."

He paused, staring off into space. I could see his veins swell up on his forehead just like my father's did when he was mad. Then he continued angrily, "The whole concept of God is just something that humans made up so they don't go crazy realizing they have one fucking short life to live and no fucking control over it. We're just made up of atoms and molecules and cells. Just another form of life, no better than any other. Worse really, because we destroy things for every other creature on the planet."

"How can you not believe in God?"

"Oh, I don't know, maybe because I don't see him around here. Do you? Where is he? Where was he when Grandma got run over by the cattle truck? Or during all the wars when people killed each other without a thought, like 'Nam? Nowhere to be found I guess . . . maybe he was on vacation . . . or maybe he was just taking a cigarette break."

I thought of a dozen stock answers from my theology classes, but somehow none of them seemed like the right thing to say.

He continued, "Remember your biology. You had that, right? Think about it. Our genes form who we are, our selfish genes, and if we are rational, we spend our lives trying to pass on our genes, so that a part of us continues. That's all there is. Sometimes when I sit in my cell at night I think about my daughter with Cathy in California, or wherever, and I think, you know, at least I have that. Even though I wouldn't know her if I passed her on the street, I know she is out there, carrying my genes, sure as shit. I might die tomorrow in this place but my genes will be passed on for generations so my body has done its part . . . it's done its part . . . I could die tomorrow . . . at least I have that . . . not that anyone would give a flying fuck."

He was on a roll now and talking fast. I wondered if he had somehow got a hold of some speed in prison, because that was some-times how he used to talk when the speed kicked in and no one could shut him up. "You know what I'm going to do if I ever get out of here? I'm gonna fuck every girl in sight, and if they make me wear a rubber, I'm going to poke holes in it. I'm just going to spread my genes around the world. Then I'm going to get some booze and dope and sit back and sedate myself until the day I croak. And you know what you're going to do? You're going to be kneeling and chanting and suffering and die without any kids. And you know who wins, Peter? I do, because my genes live on and you won't ever have children if you are a monk. You'll just get eaten up by the worms and turn to dust."

I felt as if I had been sucker-punched. *What an asshole*, I thought, but all I could say was, "I don't believe that, Jake . . . in fact, I know it's not true." I took a deep breath and gathered my thoughts. "There is a God. I see God every day. I see Him working through the church. I see Him in people I know. When I see people doing kind acts for each other, I know it's God working through us. I believe that. You have to see that before it's too late. If you pray enough and God wills it, He can work through you as well. That work will live on just as surely as your genes."

I went on, "Yes, you're right. Our genes are selfish. That's part of the natural order God's made, but that's not the end of it. When the love of God shines in us, we can become much more than our genes. We can become transformed."

"Don't give me your religious bullshit. You like to be nice to people and play the holy game because it makes you feel good inside, but that's just more selfishness on your part," Jake replied.

I was upset now, "So anything kind we do for other people is just selfishness to make ourselves feel good? I don't believe you really think that, Jake. What about all the things Mother's done for you? She used to spend hours making hotdishes and pies and cakes for you and pickled beets because you liked them. Remember the caramel rolls she made for you? She did it out of love, not selfishness."

"Maybe she did it out of guilt. Catholics are good at that."

I pounded my fist down hard on the table. "What does she have to feel guilty about?"

Jake didn't answer and I suddenly realized the visiting room had grown quiet. I looked up. Everyone was staring at us. The guard in the corner of the room glared at me and then raised his eyebrow as a warning.

But now my mind was rolling. More quietly I said, "What about Grandpa Josef and the Texas horse breakers? Did he get the crap beat out of him out of selfishness? Do you think a gene made him do that? Do you?"

Jake looked down at the table. He was quiet for a moment and then he said, "Maybe it was just stupid of him to get beat up like that."

After another pause, he said, "Plus we both know you're not as pure as you make out." I knew he was referring to the incident with Yvette, and I didn't have a response to that. It hurt and I felt deeply ashamed.

He continued, "I guess you'd say that was God shining through you that day . . . shining, shining, shining . . . yup, God was shining right through you all right."

I had to take a deep breath and clench my face to keep control. Neither of us said anything for a few minutes, just staring off into space.

We tried to talk about other subjects after that—our sisters, sports, television—but I knew he had a storm raging in his mind, as I did. I was thinking he was the one who drove up to that bank window with Grandpa's shotgun. He could blame everyone else for what a crappy world it was, but he was the idiot who'd done that, no matter what he had been through and what he was on at the time. He did that on his own. And he had got caught red-handed. Maybe he didn't believe in God, but maybe God didn't believe in him, either.

I realize now I was as angry at him as he was at me and his anger was probably more deserved than mine, but it's too late for that now.

That was the last time I saw my brother. I'm sure it sounds hardhearted, but even after I became a monk and prayed to be a forgiving person like Jesus, a thousand times, I couldn't bring myself to reconcile with him. That's the way it is with family wounds. Somehow you find it the hardest to forgive the people you should be closest to, and I was certainly not saintly enough to be an exception.

Five years later my father passed away, and Jake was not even released from prison to attend the funeral. Dad dropped dead of a heart attack at the age of sixty-seven, still working like a draft horse. It had snowed heavily the night before, and he had gone out with the tractor loader to feed the cattle. He must have jumped off to cut the twine on a bail and spread the hay out, when he was hit by a massive coronary. He fell straight down and never moved an inch. The cows paid him no attention, clamoring and climbing on each other's backs to get at the hay, and several of them must have stepped right on top of him, because he was covered with dirt and straw, and there was a perfect cow pie splattered on his chest. My mother found him like that when she went out to check on him after he failed to show up at lunch time. She said she had a feeling that something was wrong the minute she stepped out of the house, so she ran out to the feedlot. The tractor was still running. Then she saw him lying on the ground, covered in straw and manure.

Not only did my sisters and I face the grief of losing a parent, but the whole aftermath was a nightmare. We were at a loss as to what to do with Mother. She wanted to stay on the ranch, but we could hardly leave her out there in the middle of nowhere by herself. She had aged very rapidly after Jake had been sent to prison, and she broke her hip slipping on the ice the winter before and still used a cane, so there was really no question in our minds of her staying. She couldn't begin to shovel the walk and driveway if it snowed, and she needed to get to town. Marie intervened and found her a small house in Gackle on Fourth Street. We helped her move and boarded up the ranch house.

On top of that, Father passed away in the middle of the farm crisis. Like a lot of farmers and ranchers, he had borrowed money from the bank, first to pay for Jake's lawyer, and then to expand his feedlot operation. Plus, he was still paying the mortgage on the last 480 acres he had purchased. Then interest rates went up, and cattle and grain prices plummeted. He'd had some dry years and had to borrow more money to put in the crops. Why he borrowed so much from the bank after what happened to farmers in the Great Depression, I'll never know. Maybe he was convinced by a fast-talking banker or maybe he just wasn't thinking straight. The bottom line was that he wasn't as well off as we thought, and owed over $600,000 to the bank. After we had an auction to get rid of the machinery and equipment and sold the cattle, some of the land had to be sold to pay off the loan. Mother still had enough to live on, but it wasn't what one would think after a lifetime of work and struggle by the two of them.

Three years later, in 1989, my mother passed away. She had a heart attack too, just like my father, except that she survived the first one. After several weeks she was released from the hospital, and Marie cared for her in her home. She never seemed to regain her strength, however, and died of heart failure in her sleep about six months later. We all suffered tremendous grief over that. We laid her down to eternal rest in the Gackle Cemetery beside my father and grandparents.

My parents' relatively early demise was not particularly unusual for ranchers in the Dakotas. They often died young from too much worry or too much work or both. It was the nature of ranching. Still, I couldn't help but think that the stress and worrying about my brother may have played a role in shortening their lives, and I couldn't shake that thought.

After my mother passed away, we had a household auction sale and sold what was left in her house. There wasn't much of value. Some of the old furniture didn't even sell at the auction, and we ended up paying someone to haul it to the county dump. My sisters and I went through the remaining personal belongings and divided up what was of value and threw the rest out—tons of junk that no one wanted anymore, including home-made crafts, remnant material from sewing projects neatly arranged in plastic storage tubs, and stacks of old magazines and animal husbandry books from the 1940s. We kept all of the old photos, of course, and we found some things of interest, like a letter mother had received from the singer Peggy Lee, dated 1946, inviting her to come to Los Angeles to visit her, and some old music records that might have some value, if we could ever find a collector who wanted them. We found a bundle of letters my father had sent her when they were courting, and I never would have guessed he could be so romantic, calling her "My Dearest Luscious Lois," and, in one place, "Sugar Jugs." Marie kept those.

The biggest surprise for me was when we found my sister Annette's birth certificate. It showed her weight as eight pounds seven ounces. Annette was born six-and-a-half months after my mother and father were married, and we had always been told that she was born "premature." Eight-and-a-half pounds was obviously not premature. But if it was a surprise to me, it wasn't for my sisters. They told me before they went off to college mother had talked to them all about birth control and even took Marie, the youngest, to a doctor in Bismarck to get her birth control pills. Of course, mother knew this was against church teaching, but she dismissed that, saying, "Popes don't have babies. What do they know?" and not to tell their father.

38

WHEN I SAY I GRADUATED from St. John's University and entered the monastery in 1981, what I really did was move a few personal belongings from my dorm room across campus to the novitiate at the abbey adjacent to the university. The novitiate is the living facility where the novices, or prospective monks, live prior to taking vows. I spent a year there, praying with the monks and studying monastic spirituality, history, and the Rule of Saint Benedict. The Rule of St. Benedict was written in the sixth century and is a practical description of how we can best live in a community. Remarkably relevant even in today's world, it consists of seventy-three chapters setting forth the main principles of the religious life.

The journey to becoming a brother also means that one does the humble work of the abbey: preparing and serving meals, housekeeping, and gardening. Saint Benedict wrote that Benedictine brothers must truly seek God and show eagerness for the work of God through community, prayer, obedience, and humble tasks of service. If one decided to continue, as I did, and are accepted by the community, that person continued to study and live a monastic life for a minimum of three years as a "junior monk" before make a final, lifetime commitment of solemn vows to God and this monastery.

The day I finally took my vows and became a monk was one of the most joyous days of my life, albeit, also somewhat nervewracking. My mother and father were still alive then, and they drove down from North Dakota to attend. The initiation was held in the Abbey Church and when it commenced, I walked down the aisle with Brother Michael and Brother Anthony, the novice master, at my side. The smell of incense filled the air and the brothers' voices rose and fell with song. I saw my mother and father turn in their pew and smile at me, but I remained solemn, my lips pressed tight. I approached the altar and the abbot greeted me and then spoke at length of the teachings of St. Benedict and the rules of obedience. He said, "Shun the satisfaction of this age, so as to be happy in the age to come."

After reciting my vows, a black habit with a hood was placed upon me. Then I lay down, prostrate on the floor, and a large black cloth was placed over me, completely covering my body. I remember that the touch of the floor felt cold, but strangely, I somehow felt safe and warm under that cloth. Finally, after more words, the abbot waved the smoking incense vessel over me and the black cloth was lifted, signifying my re-birth. I stood up. We take on a new name at the initiation to signify our new life and I took the name Philip. Now, I could smile.

As I walked back up the aisle, I looked over at my parents. My mother had tears in her eyes. In the narthex, as I exited, my father shook my hand. "We're proud of you," he said. That was the first time in my life he had said anything like that to me.

After the service, the whole monastic community gathered out-side the church for the traditional Corona, the circle of conferees. A sharp wind snapped the brothers' black habits in unison, making them appear like a flock of crows encircling carrion. Each brother greeted me in turn with a hug and their own words of blessing. It was especially poignant when Brother Michael gave me his blessing, and then whis-pered in my ear, "I always knew you had it in you, Philip." I was sub-merged in the moment, my tears testifying to my heartfelt emotions.

On that day I truly believed, maybe for the first time, that I had been called by God. When I took my vows, I fully intended to be faith-ful to them. It was only later in life I understood how little we know ourselves sometimes.

* * *

AFTER I BECAME A MONK, I began full-time work at the Guiding Light Homeless Shelter and moved to Minneapolis. I lived there for three years, this time residing in an old house on Franklin Avenue in south Minneapolis with four other brothers. It was a spartan existence, as befits the monastic life, but hardly one of silence and solitude—I could never get used to the nightly ambulance and police sirens. When I was awakened in the night, I would sometimes slip out and sit on the stoop. I could often feel the cool northwest wind sweeping down from the Dakota plains and I'd gulp it like sweet wine, longing for something beyond.

During those years I took over more and more of the administrative duties of the shelter as well as doing advocacy work. I also set up the shelter's first computerized records using a donated Apple computer and constructed an area where we posted job openings for the homeless who might be searching for jobs. I loved the work for the most part, even though I often worked fourteen-hour days, but after three years I felt my energy slowly being sapped. When I snapped and kicked out a homeless person for throwing up on the dining table, I knew it was time to leave. I was no Brother Michael with infinite patience.

In 1984, I moved back to St. John's Abbey and began my work as an administrator at the university. I started as an assistant to the provost, Brother Andrew Karajuan, the academic head of the college. I worked on a number of key issues during that time, including the contentious task of creating a common core curriculum with the College of St. Benedict. Brother Karajuan developed a fair amount of esteem for me because I was capable of interacting with the faculty without upsetting their immense egos. He told me (privately) that in academia, the amount of attention paid to an issue by the faculty is inversely proportional to its real importance. The trick, he said, was to manage the small issues by giving them an open airing and making sure that everyone had an ample chance to vent their opinions, while personally focusing on the big issues and moving them forward under the radar.

In addition, outside my normal academic administrative duties, I worked on organizing the United States Conference of Bishops meetings held at St. John's University in 1985, 1986, and 1988. I was proud to be involved in that, although it was somewhat disconcerting at times to see the hierarchy of the Catholic Church in action and how petty and political the infighting could get behind the scenes. I came to the realization that many of the bishops, along with their entourage, had a mothball smell that seemed to permeate their very beings.

In 1994, I became an assistant to the president, Father Blanda. We got along superbly until his retirement two years later. Then Father McLaughlin became president of the university. I had not known Father McLaughlin well prior to his becoming president. He had lived at the monastery and dined with the brothers for years, but the monastery is like a high school in a way. Despite our best efforts and intentions, there are cliques, and Father McLaughlin tended to socialize with the brothers who were higher up in status: the abbot, the former president, and a few of the older established priests. That group didn't include me, obviously.

Father McLaughlin had only been with the Benedictine Order fifteen years. He was one of the newer monks indicative of the change in the monastery. Prior to and through the 1960s, most of the monks were young, having recently come out of theology school or college. But that began to change in the seventies and eighties, so that many of the new monks had already been established in some type of outside career work. They were older, usually in their thirties, but some in their forties and fifties as well. Father McLaughlin certainly had an out-of-the-ordinary background, having once been a corporate executive and rising star at the 3M Corporation in Minneapolis. Word was that he had left abruptly, in somewhat of a mid-life crisis, divorced his wife, and subsequently entered St. John's School of Theology. He was ordained as a priest in 1988, and rose quickly because of his personality and executive skills. Previous to becoming president, he had been the head of St. John's Preparatory School, just down the road from the abbey, where he was apparently well regarded. He was a model of moral rectitude and egregious self-confidence.

Anyone could see Father McLaughlin as a successful corporate executive. He was a physically imposing man, with peppered silver hair and an engaging manner. To be honest, I had a very high opinion of him initially, but it soon diminished when I saw he had little interest in the day-to-day work of the university, which he left to the vice-presidents and the provost. He was a bit of a self-promoter and enjoyed hosting dinners and receptions where he would work the room, taking the time to greet everyone with a handshake and a smile. He could be very entertaining and had a dozen jokes for every occasion. As one might expect, he was superb at alumni relations and soon increased the alumni donations to the university. The Board of Regents was delighted.

There is not that much to say about my life after I started my administrative work at St. John's University. My life seemed full, and as I look back on it now, the years seemed to have skidded by. Day to day, it seemed like I was always busy. I rose early to attend morning prayers, eat breakfast, rush over to the administration building and work until noon. I'd rush back for prayers and lunch, then head back to work until Mass and dinner and, finally, Evening Vespers. During the Christmas season I was even busier, as I additionally took on the responsibility of decorating the Abbey Church. I no longer had time to visit my sister Marie at Christmas, and we slowly lost touch, other than to exchange holiday and birthday cards. It sometimes seemed to me I was always working, although I received a certain amount of satisfaction from my work and seeing the university expand and improve.

Of course, there were tough days both in my administrative work and my relationship with God. I'll be honest about that. Brother Michael advised me that being a monk was a journey—ascending glorious peaks and descending into the darkest valleys, over and over again. And always, the constant struggle: to liberate the spirit from the flesh.

Sometimes I think monks spend too much time working in occupations and not enough time in solitude, silence, and reading. It seems we are always hurrying from work to prayer and back again. Part of the reason I didn't want to ranch was, like Jake, I didn't want a life of work from morning to night. But when I became a monk, my schedule wound up being almost as grueling as my father's or grandfather's. It's strange how life turns out. But like everyone else, it often seems like we take one day at a time and grow older and set aside the questions.

I had little time for any sort of personal life, the one exception being that I began to make time for regular exercise. I started with running when it became a mass cultural phenomenon in the 1980s and 1990s. Why everyone started to run at the same time was a mystery, but, like a lot of people, the running bug bit me. And it was true that, for me, as for many other runners, I experienced a sort of "runner's high" from the release of endorphins in the brain.

A group of five monks at St. John's Abbey had all taken up running about the same time. The "running monks," as we were called, would rise at 5:00 a.m. and do a four-mile run before morning prayers. Mostly I think we enjoyed the exercise and companionship, although there was an ascetic dimension as well. According to St. Paul, the Christian life is like a race, in that it requires discipline and training if we are to do it well. I think the discipline in running can help us better understand the discipline necessary in the rest of our lives.

In 1989, our little running group drove to Minneapolis and ran the Grand Avenue Five Mile Race. We enjoyed that so much we began to train for a longer race, a half marathon in New Prague. Unfortunately, once my mileage increased, I developed a torn meniscus in my left knee, so I had to rest it. To keep in shape I started swimming instead.

Like my brother, I never learned to swim growing up on the ranch. We were usually working on the ranch in the summer, so there was little time for fun activities like swimming. Our only swimming experience was at Hehn Schaffer Lake, located about five miles north of Gackle. It was a typical North Dakota lake, clear and frigid cold in the early summer, and then turning pea green with algae by July after it warmed up. We always used a big tractor inner tube to float on, and my mother watched us like a hawk to make sure it didn't drift out too deep. I remember her calling out to us, "Don't go out so far now. Make sure you can touch the bottom."

She was funny that way. We rode horses almost from the time we could walk, and drove tractors when we were ten or eleven years old and just big enough to reach the pedals, but swimming was something to be feared, in her mind. Both my brother and I learned to dog-paddle a little, but that was about it.

During my freshman year at St. John's, I took a swimming class for my physical education requirement. I remember when I started the class I was the only student who didn't know how to swim. I was embarrassed because I had to get special instruction on the basics, literally starting out with turning my head and bubble blowing. It was humiliating, but that made me work harder at it. After a while I caught on and actually became a first-rate swimmer by the end of the semester. I had big hands and feet and a long torso, so I guess it just came naturally for me.

When I started to swim regularly after my running injury, it was a bit of a struggle, but after a few months I became more efficient. It seemed effortless to do thirty or forty laps every morning. When I was swimming, I was totally in my own world and I enjoyed the solitude and opportunity to let my mind wander.

Swimming after my running injury led to some totally new and unexpected directions in my life. For one thing, I came to know the swimming coach at St. John's, Larry Summers, because he was at the pool every day, and I would stop to chat with him. One time he needed some assistance with timing his relay team, so I volunteered, and I was soon helping him on a regular basis. Eventually I attended some seminars on coaching techniques, and he made me the third assistant coach. I knew that, as someone who had never swum competitively in college and without any real credentials for coaching, I would never be any more than an assistant, but that was fine with me. We had some excellent swim teams, in those early years especially. I enjoyed it and felt I got a lot out of coaching. It was only in hindsight that I wondered if perhaps my mother had a premonition about the dangers of swimming and getting in over your head.

39

A FTER I DROVE BY THE PRISON the day I saw Sheriff Nordstrom and the site of my brother's fatal motorcycle accident, I checked into the Bismarck Motel 8. It dawned on to me to call Jake's fiancée, Jill Johnson. It would only be considerate to meet and talk with her before the funeral. She answered on the first ring and it took her a minute to realize who I was and why I was calling but she did want to meet me. We arranged to meet at Perkins Restaurant at 8:30 a.m., prior to the meeting with the funeral director.

The next morning, I asked the hostess for a booth by the window, and I sat and sipped my coffee while I waited for her. I had quit smoking almost twenty years ago (having smoked while working at the homeless shelter), but I suddenly wanted a cigarette in the worst way. I was a little bit nervous, not knowing what to say to her. I suspected the whole thing would be awkward. I watched who came through the door, and I expected her to look like someone willing to marry an ex-con, but no one fitting my preconceived notion came in. Eventually, a strikingly attractive woman came through the door. She looked to be in her early thirties and was holding the hand of a young girl. She looked around just once and then walked straight over to me, and put out her hand.

"Hi. You must be Brother Philip. You look just like your brother. I'm Jill, and this is Courtney."

"It's good to meet you," I said. "Thank you for coming. And you too, Courtney."

Courtney put her delicate little hand out and said very politely, as if she had been practicing, "It's nice to meet you, Brother Philip."

Jill looked at her daughter proudly. I had to admit that Jill was not at all what I expected. She was pretty, with porcelain white skin and black hair, which she wore in a simple, short style with one side tucked behind her ear. She was dressed in a subdued black suit. She had beautiful brown eyes, although she looked tired and weary, with dark semicircles under her eyes, as might be expected under the circumstances. After we exchanged condolences, she thanked me for calling her.

"I already called the funeral director, Mr. White, yesterday. He said he preferred to deal with the immediate family members, even though I told him Jake and I were to be married next year. I thought he was pretty rude to me, considering."

"I'm so sorry," I said. "I didn't tell Mr. White about you . . . I didn't know Jake was engaged until yesterday . . . or that he had a daughter." I glanced at Courtney, who was now busy coloring the placemat. "Of course, we'll want you involved in making the arrangements."

The waitress came to take our orders, and Jill took a quick look at the menu. She suggested I go ahead and order. I was hungry and ordered a big breakfast with pancakes, hash browns, bacon, and two eggs, over easy. Since we ate communally in the monastery, I wasn't used to having my eggs any way I chose. They were almost always scrambled, so it was a treat for me to have them soft and runny, the way I liked. Jill paged through the menu without really looking at it and then just ordered coffee for herself and pancakes with chocolate chips for Courtney.

"How did your meeting with Sheriff Nordstrom go?" she asked.

I was surprised she even knew about it. "It wasn't much of anything. Not a meeting really. I just felt a need to see where it happened."

"And what did he say?"

"Not much. Jake was going too fast, he hit a bump and flew into the ditch. I guess it's not surprising he'd do something like that. Jake was always doing crazy things."

She glared at me, her eyes flashing, "Listen, I don't know what you think you know about your brother. But he wasn't always doing 'crazy things,' as you put it. I understand there was a washout of some sort, so it was purely an accident . . . or an act of God . . . if you prefer that way of putting it . . . but don't say it happened because he was doing something crazy. You don't even know him."

"I'm sorry. I shouldn't have said that," I said, "but I think I do know my own brother."

"Well, maybe he changed. You haven't bothered to see him for years," she said and stared out of the window, lips pursed.

There was an awkward silence and then, fortunately, the waitress came with more coffee. I regained my composure, and we started talking about the weather and other safer topics of conversation. I could have left it at that, but my curiosity got the better of me. I inquired as delicately as I could how long she had known Jake. I was surprised to find out that they had known each other for six years. Jill was thirty-six, seven years younger than I was, making her seventeen years younger than Jake. Quite an age difference, I thought.

The food arrived, but as she began to tell me about the two of them, I just picked at it. I was no longer so hungry. She recounted that she and Jake met at St. Mary's University in Bismarck, where she worked as a career counselor in the student job placement office. After prison, Jake had worked for a time at a gas station, and then enrolled in a four-year program in social work and addiction counseling at St. Mary's. "He wasn't your typical student," she said. "Obviously he was older, but it wasn't just that. I guess you could say he knew himself, which not many students do."

This was news to me. I wasn't sure what to make of it. Marie had told me she'd helped Jake get the job at the gas station, but that was the last I'd heard. I had not seen my brother since my visit at the prison some twenty years ago. It didn't sound like the Jake I knew.

Jill went on to tell me that after graduating from college, Jake worked as a substance abuse counselor at the Standing Rock Indian Reservation in Fort Yates, North Dakota, for four years, driving eighty miles back and forth every day from Bismarck. About a year ago, he got a counseling job in Bismarck for the Farmer's Aid Program, which offered counseling and an 800 phone number for farmers caught up in the farm crisis. Substance abuse was just one of the problems he dealt with in that job—many farmers facing the loss of their farms and way of life suffered from depression and related ailments, and domestic abuse had grown as well.

"Your brother had a way about him. People trusted him, and he was good at that sort of thing," she said.

I had a hard time imagining that, but I didn't say anything.

"He asked me to marry him when I became pregnant with Courtney," she continued, and I noticed that Courtney looked up when she heard her name mentioned, but Jill went on. "I was the one who put him off. I had reservations about making a life with an ex-con with a history of substance abuse. All my training told me it was a big risk, but I told him if he was clean for five years and still wanted to marry me, I would. When we hit that five-year anniversary, two months ago, he gave me an engagement ring." She held out her hand and showed me. Her eyes welled up with tears as she finished talking.

How does one react to something like that? I wanted to comfort her, but my thoughts were wheeling and couldn't settle. For the first time, I began to realize that the truth about Jake might be different than the narrative I had in my head.

Her attitude seemed to have softened. She said, "I wish you could have spent some time with him in the last few years. Jake talked about you a lot, and we talked about contacting you, but Jake always said that he wanted to get his life together first. He waited too long, I guess." She started sobbing. When she did this, Courtney looked at her mother and burst into tears also. I was speechless and just sat quietly as Jill comforted her daughter, and then excused herself to the ladies' room. Courtney eventually went back to coloring. I sat there, trying to get my head around this new information.

When Jill returned she seemed more composed. She looked directly at me and said, "Jake was so proud of you, you know. Whenever he'd mention you, he'd talk about the fact that you were a monk. I guess he thought that was pretty awesome."

I was feeling more and more like a lout, and I said the simplest, but most essential silent prayer—God, please forgive me. Out loud, I said, "I'm so glad that he had you. You must have helped him a lot."

She smiled. "I tried to. But he helped me, too. We helped each other."

It was time to go, so she followed me in her car to the funeral home. We talked to the funeral director and then I picked out a simple wooden casket while Jill waited in the parlor area because she didn't think that Courtney was up for that. I wasn't either, frankly, but it had to be done. As we left, I asked Jill if she wanted to have dinner, but she said she was exhausted and needed some time alone. We agreed to meet again for a late breakfast at Perkins in the morning.

The next morning she arrived right on time, and she did not have Courtney with her, but explained that her mother was staying with her. This time I just ordered a muffin and Jill had coffee again. As she sipped her coffee, she looked at me as if she had met me just that instant. "I've never met a monk before," she said.

"Maybe you have and just don't know it," I replied. "Most monks don't wear habits outside the abbey and even the fathers don't always wear a collar. It's just easier to fit into the outside world and, to be honest, one reason we don't is that people leave you alone and don't ask you prying questions all the time and you don't have drunks coming up to you and making impromptu confessions."

"I suppose," she said. I could tell that she was wondering how much she should ask, but her curiosity got the better of her. "I don't know how you can live in a monastery. It seems so far removed from rest of the world."

"A lot of people might wonder how you can live in Bismarck, North Dakota. It seems so far removed from the rest of the world," I replied.

She smiled for the first time since I met her, and I noticed that her face came alive at that moment.

"What's it like?" she asked.

I explained that it was like living with two hundred family members. "We're all different, and we have problems like everyone else, but what binds us, our dedication to the service of the Lord, is stronger than our differences."

"What about being celibate? I'd think that would be difficult."

I hesitated before responding. I wanted to divulge the truth to her, but I knew I couldn't do that. Even in confession, I had failed to be honest, so I gave the rote answer, "There are practical reasons for it. Being celibate allows us to lead the type of community life that is important to us and we can better devote ourselves to God's will. Our primary relationship is to God. By being celibate, we can be faithful to that relationship."

I continued, "But yes, the vow of celibacy is challenging. The hardest thing for me is not having children. And, to be honest, I have seen brothers have a difficult time with it. Sometimes they project their sexual energy into food or alcohol or occasionally even disdain of women. But most brothers learn to deal with it through prayer and eventually see it as a gift."

"It must take enormous strength. I could never do it, but I'm glad that there are virtuous people in the world who can, like you."

As she said that, I knew to the bottom of my soul that it was not true, and I felt a deep shame.

40

M OST OF MY EXPERIENCES with women since becoming a monk had been in fantasy only. Once I joined the monastery, I saw and interacted with few women at all. Much of my life was spent solely in the company of men and the less I saw women, the less I thought about them. Of course, we had women working in university administration and as professors. But my encounters with them were generally brief and professional. I rarely went to bars or any place of that nature, so that limited interactions with women as well. Occasionally I'd go to K-Mart or Target like any other person and if it was summer and I saw an attractive woman in a pair of skimpy shorts or a mini-skirt—especially a mini-skirt—I might have an initial reaction like any other male and I would wonder what it would be like to no longer be a monk. I tried my best to put such thoughts out of my head, but I'd be lying if I said it wasn't tremendously difficult for me at times. There were many nights I had sharp pangs, longing for the warmth of a woman, and I'd curl up in a fetal position and feel a deep loneliness that seemed to sink to my bones.

One of the most challenging times in my monastic life was when I was sorely attracted to a woman I worked with by the name of Edie Mayer. Edie was hired by the provost as a part-time assistant in the fall of 1996 and worked just outside my office, down the hall in the cubicle area. She was strikingly beautiful, with thick brown hair, streaked very lightly with blonde highlights, a clear complexion, and languorous blue eyes (although I later found out that she wore colored contacts). She dressed conservatively, always in fashionable pantsuits or skirts. Although she had curves, she never wore clothes that were in the least bit provocative. It was as if she was so confident in her beauty she didn't have to and the conservative clothes sent a message that there was more here than beauty.

I remember the very first time I saw her. She was sitting in her cubicle at her computer. I went by and did a double-take, and I thought she was simply gorgeous. I introduced myself and we talked a bit about her work, and she proudly showed me photos of her two daughters. From the first time I met Edie, however, there was something about her I found tremendously attractive besides her beauty. For the longest time I couldn't put my finger on it until I finally realized it was her scent. This might sound strange, but for some reason I found it absolutely intoxicating. Whenever she got close to me, I could detect this subtle fragrance about her and it did something weird and wonderful to me. At first I thought it was some kind of soap or lotion she used, or maybe perfume, although it was not a flowery scent, more of a warm, pleasing ambrosial fragrance—like ginger, and licorice, and vanilla all mixed together, with a dusky animal undertone. After a time, I realized it was her own natural scent, and I was unquestionably attracted to it, like a stallion to a mare in heat. That might not be completely crazy. Some scientists think that males and females have an attraction to certain potential mates based on their odors and pheromones. Maybe that had something to do with it, maybe not. All I know is that when she would stand close to me, I would clearly detect this breathtaking aroma, inhale deeply, and want terribly to press my face into the back of her neck.

As weeks went by, I found out that Edie was not only beautiful, but also very bright. Even though she had a lower level assistant job at the university—tracking schedules, typing meeting agendas and that sort of thing—I found out that she had graduated from the Carlson School of Management at the University of Minnesota with top honors. She could have undoubtedly been hired for a higher position somewhere, but she only wanted to work three days a week so she could spend more time at home with her children. She was very organized and efficient in her work, and I soon began to rely on her for my interactions with the provost.

Over the two years Edie worked in the office, we spent more and more time together, albeit, always office-related. (In fact, we never spent time together outside of the office, other than when I took her to lunch for her birthday.) We talked for long periods of time, not only about work, but also about books, and art, and music, and her two little girls, who she loved dearly and were always a source of amazement to her. For me these conversations were generally platonic, although I have to admit that occasionally my thoughts would wander if she was sitting in such a way as to provide me with a glimpse of her crossed legs. They were shapely and beautiful, with just the tiniest trace of cellulite on her thighs, which I somehow found to be extremely sexy.

Edie sometimes came coasting into my office unexpectedly, excited and with a big smile on her face, and would close the door behind her. I knew that she just wanted to tell me the latest university gossip. We both came from a rural community, and gossip was fuel for our minds (she had grown up in Eveleth, Minnesota). Despite the difference in our ages, she was twenty-nine and I was nearly eight years older, it felt as if we had everything in common and that we thought totally alike. The only thing we disagreed on to any extent was President McLaughlin. She disliked him intensely, although I never knew why. I knew he had faults, of course, but I couldn't understand the depth of her dislike. I thought they must have had some type of interaction that was unpleasant or he corrected or criticized her work, which he was prone to do, but this was just speculation on my part. On one occasion she called him, "a pompous sexist ass that can't be trusted," which I thought was not only a bit harsh, but also somewhat daring on her part. He was a priest after all, and she was Catholic, but her spunkiness just made her more endearing to me.

Edie seemed to like to be with me as much as I liked to be with her, but she never expressed a word to me about how she felt. I often wondered if she was attracted to me or just thought of me as an older monk who could be useful to her in her work. I had not had a lot of experience with women, especially since becoming a monk, so I was in the dark.

Women are a mystery to men and a double mystery to monks. At times, it seemed she intentionally tried to be close to me. On one occasion, we were talking about the university budget, and she was sitting across from me at my desk and pointing to some figures, which I was trying to read upside down. She said, "Let me show you," and came around to my side of the desk and stood very close to me, pointing to the figures. She was standing so close that her hip rubbed against me. When she leaned down over the desk, our heads were only inches apart and a few fine strands of her hair brushed my cheek. I wondered if she was doing that on purpose. I could smell her intoxicating scent, and I had an enormous desire to touch her or more than that, to hold her in my arms. I resisted. I still had the strength and will then to be faithful to my monastic vows. On top of that, we had recently received extensive training on sexual harassment, so that entered my mind as well. Still, that didn't stop me from fantasizing, and I certainly committed the sin of having lust in my heart.

Besides the sexual fantasies, I had fantasies of another nature. I would sometimes let my imagination run and invent scenarios that usually involved her husband dying or she and her husband getting divorced. Then I would leave the monastery, and we would get married. I would take care of her and her two daughters. I even pictured where we would live and what our house would look like. We would go to see choral concerts and the theater and movies together. I imagined I would love her better, and make her happier than her husband ever did. In reality, I had never met her husband and didn't know anything about him, other than what I gathered from a few conversations with Edie. I just assumed they were not well-suited for each other, but that may have just been wishful thinking on my part.

As time went by, this period of time became an increasingly difficult one for me in my monastic life. I often woke up at night in a panic, thinking I would face this loneliness and longing the rest of my life. I desperately needed something in my life I was not receiving in my monastic existence, the closeness and intimacy to be had in a physical relationship with someone I loved.

I tried to comprehend these feelings within the framework of monastic teaching. We had been taught as Benedictines that falling in love was natural and a normal human reaction that could not be denied. It was part of celibate life, but we were also taught that with prayer and penance, we could resist sexual intimacy and regain an undivided heart. For a while I tried to return my faithfulness to God, and I spent hours kneeling in prayer or reciting the psalms, but it did not change what was in my heart for her. On weekends when I could not see her, I would find myself longing for Monday when I would be able to see her glide into the office with that sweet smile on her face.

One day in the fall of 1998, she came into my office and we chatted for some time about work, but I could tell something else was on her mind. I thought she was about to leave when she said, "I have something important to tell you."

"What?"

"I gave my two-week notice today. My husband got a better job offer in Minneapolis, and we're moving at the end of the month."

My heart sank when she told me that. Inside I wanted to beg her to stay, but I remained cool. I reached out and took her hand and held it for a second and simply told her it sounded like a great opportunity. There was a sense of inevitability about it, as if we were fated never to be together, at least not in this life.

On her last day of work, the office threw her a small going-away party. I remember I came into the room and saw her in the far corner talking to some other women. She had a blue dress on and she looked absolutely luminous. For me she was the only person in the room. Even as I worked the room greeting everyone, I couldn't keep my eyes off her and kept looking over to where she was standing.

I stayed as late as possible at the party until everyone had left and offered to help her take a few going-away gifts to her car. We didn't say much. I remember it was raining, and I held her umbrella for her as she put the gifts in the rear seat. Then she turned and faced me and she said, "I guess this is it. I'll miss our talks," and we hugged very properly, and then we both took a step back and looked at each other. What happened that next moment made me question everything, because she stepped forward and kissed me lightly on the lips and whispered, "I love you." Then she turned, got in her car and drove away. It was the last time I ever saw her.

I thought about that "I love you" a thousand times afterwards. Did she mean "I love you," as someone would say to a dear friend or relative, or did she mean, "I love you" in a romantic way? Eventually I convinced myself that it was the latter and that was what really hurt. I knew that a person only had a chance for true love a few times in life, if ever, and I wondered if I had missed mine. I think it left me vulnerable because I wanted that feeling again.

41

I N THE FALL OF 1999 I met Jackie Conway at a reception for the
university regents and their spouses prior to the annual homecom-
ing game. Jackie was the wife of businessman David Conway, who
was from a very well-known and wealthy family in central Minnesota.
David Conway's grandfather had started with a small family-run sign
business in St. Cloud and his son, Rupert, turned that into a statewide,
and then regional, outdoor advertising company now worth several
hundred million dollars.

Rupert was a major supporter of the university and gave millions
of dollars to St. John's over the years. All three of his sons were educated
there. After he passed away in 1996, the three sons inherited the family
business. John, the oldest, lived in south Florida and spent most of his
time on his sixty-five foot luxury fishing boat. That left David and
younger brother, Scott, in Minnesota to run the business. David, in particular, continued the family tradition of supporting the university financially, and he was named a regent in 1999. Both David and Scott
continued to live in St. Cloud. Scott lived relatively modestly, but David
was known for his flamboyant lifestyle, and he had reportedly built a
huge monstrosity of a house in a new development south of the city.

Jackie was actually David's second wife, often referred to as his
"trophy wife." While he must have been in his mid-fifties, she was only
thirty-four. Jackie was very attractive, although not what one would
consider knock-out gorgeous. She was petite, with blonde hair (not natural), an aquiline nose, and an impertinent little mouth with thin red
lips. Her most striking features were her beautiful dark piercing eyes
and her charming smile. Men were known to watch her other features

in passing, as she had an attractive rear end and alluring cleavage (also not natural) which was always prominently displayed in low-cut blouses or sweaters. Frankly, some people considered her on the trashy side, but she had a vivacious personality, was flirtatious with men, and she had the gift of being able to talk to anyone and make them laugh. Most people took to her instantly.

I was getting a Jameson whiskey at the reception bar when I heard a voice behind me, "That looks good to me."

I turned around. She was smiling at me. That day she was wearing a white blouse with a string of black pearls, a black leather skirt with a slit up the side, and black spiked heels, and she looked absolutely stunning. I paused and looked at her and then looked behind me, because for a second I wasn't sure if she was talking to me, but I finally realized she was. I asked her, "Can I get you one?"

"I'd love one . . . make that a double. I need something to get me through this."

"That bad, huh?"

"I guess it comes with the territory . . . I'm Jackie Conway, by the way."

"I know who you are. We're very happy you and your husband could attend. I'm Brother Philip."

"A brother?" she said, almost mockingly. "You don't look like one. Aren't you supposed to be wearing a collar or something?"

"We brothers come in all shapes and sizes and only priests wear collars."

"You need one to keep the ladies away," she said. She was looking directly at me with her dark eyes when she said that, and they seemed to lock onto mine. I knew then for sure she was flirting with me. I thought it was inappropriate under the circumstances, but I liked it anyhow. The saying goes, "Vanity is the quicksand of reason," and that applies to monks as well.

I got her a whiskey from the bar, and we found a quiet corner to converse. To my surprise, she had once lived in Minot, North

Dakota. Her father had been in the military and was stationed at the Minot Air Force Base for four years. She was no snob about it, however, like some wealthy ex-residents embarrassed to admit their roots. She thought it was a great place to be from and spoke with pride about working at the local A&W Drive-In when she was in high school. "It kept me in beer, cigarette, and make-up money." I found her unpretentiousness a sheer delight.

She inquired about my work, and I told her about my administrative position and my part-time coaching of the swim team. When she found that out she told me that she was an avid swimmer. Then she went into some long story about how she had met David Conway at a hotel bar in Miami Beach and how he had taken her and some girl-friends out on a yacht. They got drunk, and she and one of her girl-friends had taken their clothes off and gone skinny-dipping in the ocean. I just smiled at her and shook my head like I'd heard this kind of thing every day, but, in truth, I had absolutely no idea how to respond to a story like that.

We talked for most of an hour before she excused herself. Later, I couldn't help watching her across the room. At one point I heard her loud laugh, and I looked up and saw that she was talking with the provost and surrounded by a group of men. To be honest, I found her very attractive from the start, but I thought she was just being sociable with me, and it would have been ridiculous for me to think more than that.

I didn't see her for another year, but when the regents had the annual pre-homecoming game reception the following fall, I found myself hoping she would be there. An hour into the reception, she showed up on David Conway's arm, and she and President McLaughlin talked at length. I could see her across the room, and the president was laughing at something she said as her husband looked proudly at her. I felt like a fool for caring so much whether she recognized me.

Later I heard her voice from behind me, "Hi, Brother Philip. Remember me?" I turned around, and there she was.

"Of course," I said, pleasantly surprised. She smiled, the corners of her mouth turning up halfway between a grin and a flirtatious smirk. We were soon talking away again about Minot, and she asked me about the swim team. She had a good memory. As she was about to leave, she asked me if I would give her a swimming lesson sometime so that she could improve her breaststroke. At the time I thought it an odd request, but I said I'd be happy to, and she excused herself to mingle with other people. As I thought about it later, I assumed she was just making polite conversation.

I met David Conway that day for the first time. He looked every bit the successful businessman: tall, good looking, with wavy hair, graying slightly at the temples, and a slight paunch. He spoke loudly in an overly gregarious manner. Maybe I was prepared to dislike him, but I thought he was a bit of an egocentric. He was holding court with a circle of men when I approached, talking about investments in high tech start-up companies, and I heard him boast about how he had invested in one company and saw the value of his stock rise three hundred percent in a few months. He said this with an air of superiority, as if he was the smartest person in the world.

To my surprise, Jackie called the next week and asked when I could give her a swimming lesson. "Let me think about the schedule," I said, and I was momentarily speechless as I tried to recall the pool schedule. I knew there was an open swim time for students, and I guessed she could come then. She wasn't a student, but as the wife of a regent we could hardly say no. I wondered how it would look if I gave her a private lesson and who I would need to notify. I couldn't sort it all out in my head but, somewhat flabbergasted, I said, "I guess you could come Wednesday at four."

She laughed, "No, I'm not coming to St. John's. We have a private pool in our house. Can you come here and give me a lesson?"

I was somewhat taken aback, but I quickly agreed. After she hung up, my first thought was that it was a strange request, but then I figured that was how wealthy people lived. They expected you to come to them. I was probably considered hired help to her. Since she was the wife of a regent, she obviously thought she was entitled to request anything she wanted from the university, including free swimming lessons from the assistant swim coach. I thought about telling her it was inappropriate and I couldn't do it, and I thought I should tell a fellow brother or the abbot or the president or someone, but I didn't. Afterwards I would think about how God puts forks in the road as a way to test us and that maybe this was a fork for me. The problem is that at the time it never appeared that I was facing a fork. I simply got caught up and took the wrong way, and I didn't realize it until it was too late.

The following Wednesday I drove out to her house, which was located in Plum Creek Estates, an exclusive area south of the city with which I was unfamiliar. As soon as I entered the development, I could see it reeked of new money—full of oversized homes sitting on oversized lots. I arrived a little early, so I passed by the house and waited by the side of the road for ten minutes before I finally drove up the long concrete driveway. She greeted me at the door dressed in casual clothes, jeans and a cream-colored sweater with a plunging neckline. She smiled as only she could, and said teasingly, "Come on in, Mr. Monk."

She gave me a quick tour of the lower level of the house. I was a little intimidated by it all. A spacious foyer hung with silver sconces led into the living room that had two-story windows overlooking a perfectly landscaped backyard. An imposing stone fireplace dominated the room, which had a teak floor and white area rugs. A massive kitchen was connected off to the side, as well as a dining room table with seating for twenty. Toward the back of the house was a recreational room with a fully stocked bar and two pool tables. Everything was ostentatious and marble fountains spouted water throughout the house.

Adjacent to the recreational room was the pool area extending out towards the patio in the rear of the house with a 100-foot pool, exercise machines, lounge chairs, and changing rooms. She offered me a drink, but I declined, as it was a bit early in the day for me, and then she excused herself to change. I had brought my swim trunks but did not change into them, thinking it might be more appropriate to give her some swimming tips without getting into the water with her. I waited, sitting on one of the pool lounges. It seemed like she was gone a long time, but she finally appeared and said, "Sorry, I didn't know which swim suit to wear." She had on a white one-piece swimsuit cut high on her hips and tantalizingly low in front. She smiled, and it took my breath away just to look at her. *Oh, those holy hills!*

"Aren't you getting in the water?" she asked.

"I already swam this morning."

"Oh, come on. Don't be a wuss," she laughed. "The water's warm."

I went to the changing room. When I came out with my swimming trunks on, she was already doing laps, cutting the water in an easy front-to-back motion, and turning her head sharply to breathe. She was definitely not a novice, but I saw some elements we could work on. I reached down to feel the temperature of the water and it was indeed very warm. I couldn't help but wonder how much it cost to heat the pool in the winter. I dived in and swam a few laps to warm up and quickly fell into a rhythm. The swimming felt good and I felt strong, like I was riding the very top of the water. I rolled over on my back and did a few laps of the back crawl. I watched her swimming next to me, our eyes met for a second as we passed, and I could hear the air going in and out of my mouth as I inhaled and exhaled.

After we warmed up, we spent almost an hour working on her kick and proper arm movement. I would demonstrate the proper technique, and she would pick it up very quickly. She was receptive to instruction and a quick learner. It was all very businesslike, and I was focused on her swimming technique, so it kept my mind off other things. When she had enough swimming for the day, we talked for a few minutes about what she needed to work on. As I walked to the changing room, I could feel her eyes on me. She said, "You know, Brother Phil, you have nice buns for a monk."

I didn't respond, but I was sure my face reddened. It did not seem like something she should be saying but, again, it did stroke my ego. At the door as I was leaving, she insisted I come back the following week, and she gave me a quick hug and thanked me for coming.

That week was very difficult for me. We were taught that lust was one of the seven deadly sins and I was in danger of damnation and I knew it. During our morning, afternoon, and evening prayers, I would pray for God to give me strength so as not to have lustful thoughts, but all day my mind would wander, and I would see her in that swim suit and wish I wasn't a monk. I went back to my cell and held the Benedictine Medal I was given when I first became a monk. The medal was engraved with fourteen letters around the Cross, making its border: V.R.S.N.S.M.V.; S.M.Q.L.I.V.B. The initials stand for the verses:

Vade retro Satana;
Nunquam suade mihi vana.
Sunt mala quae libas;
Ipse venana bibas!

In English: "Begone Satan! Suggest not to me vain things. The cup you offer me is evil; drink the poison yourself!" It gave me little consolation, because I knew my own will was the demon I was fighting.

The following Wednesday when I went to Jackie's house, I brought an instructional video. The video was professionally shot, with underwater scenes to demonstrate the proper technique, and I had used it a few times for freshman swimmers. This time Jackie greeted me in her swim suit—black this time—covered by a short sheer robe. She offered me a drink, whiskey. I told her I'd have a short one and she poured one for me and a taller one for herself. We talked for a time, and then she led me into the recreation room, which had a very large plasma television. I sat down on the couch while she put the video in. She came back to sit very close to me, her body touching mine. We began to watch the video and after a short time I felt her hand lightly on my lower back. She massaged it ever so slightly.

As we continued to watch the video, Jackie put her hand on my inner thigh and began to rub up and down my leg very slowly. As I became aroused, she began caressing me. We turned to each other and began a long smoldering kiss I thought lasted forever before she said, "Help me out of this swimsuit."

We made love quickly and fervently, and then lay on the couch together in each other's arms, catching our breath.

I think I fell in love with her at that very instant. I had been a monk and celibate for so long I had forgotten the joy the touch of a woman could bring. I felt ecstatically happy, as if I had been in a fog that suddenly lifted, and a whole new exquisite world had opened up to me. I wondered why I had denied myself this feeling for so long. It was as if my past and future were erased and there was only the present.

As we lay there, I thought Jackie was feeling the same way I was, but she was quiet, not saying a word. I wondered for a moment whether she had fallen asleep, so I looked at her eyes. She wasn't. She just seemed deep in thought. I wanted to hear her talk, so I started asking her about her life, and she livened up. She loved to talk about herself and tell stories. I just let her go on and on, fascinated by every word she said.

If I had known anything about women and was in my right mind, I might have thought twice about some of the things she told me. At one point, she was describing her wild single life before she got married and said, "I think if I had kept up with that, I'd be dead by now." At another point she was talking about a friend of hers, Mimi from South Miami. "Once we tried to make a list of all the men we'd slept with. I had the longest list, including a football player with the Miami Dolphins . . . he was huge by the way . . . and my high school science teacher." Still later she said, "My husband is so nice to me. Sometimes I don't think I have a conscience." Even while she was telling me these things it seemed as if she was talking about someone else. I remember thinking as I lay there, enjoying the warmth of her body next to mine, that her past did not matter anymore than mine did, and for me, the monastery was already in my past.

Eventually she told me I needed to leave, and I hugged her at the door and tried to kiss her, but she turned her head, saying softly; "Not now. You need to go."

As I drove away, I was about as elated as a person can be and my Benedictine vows seemed very far removed. And for the next three weeks, maybe for the first time in my life, I was to have a deep sense of peace and quiet and love. Surprisingly, I felt no guilt whatsoever in those first few weeks, as if our relationship was ordained by heaven itself.

We made love again the following Wednesday. This time we made no pretense of swimming lessons. As soon as she opened the door she flung her arms around my neck, pulled me inside, and whispered in my ear, "Are you going to give it to me, Mr. Monk? I need it soooo bad."

She led me to the recreation room. She had a little black dress on which she threw off in an instant and she was naked underneath. I flung my clothes off, and she pulled me down to the floor on the thick white carpet, and we immediately made love, almost violently hard and with total abandon, and she screamed loudly as she came, "Oh, God, yes, yes, yes!" Later we made love again on the couch, this time more deliberately and tenderly, her legs wrapped around me and her hands clinging to my neck and back, and it seemed to last forever.

Afterwards we lay with our bodies entwined, limp, exhausted, and wet with perspiration. At that point it occurred to me I was forty-three years old and had made love exactly four times in my life, and that doing it on the floor was the first time I had done it somewhere besides a couch. I must have smiled, thinking a new life was starting for me and that I would make love with Jackie a thousand times in a thousand different places. After we lay quietly for several minutes, she turned toward me and draped her slender arm across my chest and looked into my face. "What are you so happy about?" she asked.

"Isn't it obvious?"

She laughed loudly, and then asked teasingly, "Will I go to hell for this?"

I laughed and said no. I didn't even think at the time about her being married and that she was committing adultery and that I was committing a form of adultery against my own Benedictine vows, a mortal sin. I told her, "I don't think this could be wrong. It feels so natural, like it was meant to be."

Later I reached over and held her small warm hand, squeezing it tightly, "I want to make you happy," I said. She did not remove her hand but she didn't respond either. It was as if she was thinking about this, or something, for a long time. The quiet made me uneasy. I said, "I know I can't give you what your husband can, but we could be so happy together."

She twisted her hand out of my grip. "Oh, it's getting late. You better go."

I returned to the abbey, but at this point in my life I was absent in all but my physical body and thinking about her day and night, living in a state of perpetual expectancy. I'm ashamed to admit it now, but I would be thinking about her even in the midst of the liturgy and during prayers where memories of her beckoning flesh would rise up in my head. At mealtime I could hardly eat. I simply had no appetite. At night I'd lie awake for hours thinking about her, actually preferring that to sleep.

I had read enough to understand there was a secular scientific explanation for the feelings coursing through my body. My adrenaline levels were boosted, prompting the release of the chemical dopamine, which in turn ran down the neuronal pathways, thereby diluting and canceling out the chemical serotonin, which controls impulses like unruly passions and obsessive behavior. Testosterones were released, as well as endorphins—powerful drugs we want to experience again and again.

Under this explanation, my mind and body were already irreversibly out of control. But I also knew that this explanation, the biological one, could be just the devil's game to weaken my will to resist. We were taught that all of humanity was weakened by what St. Augustine (who spoke from experience) called "concupiscence," a strong irrational desire, often sexual. This was a natural part of human nature, and the battle between the desire of the lower appetite for sexual gratification and reason was a consequence of the fall of Adam. "The flesh lusteth against the spirit, and the spirit against the flesh." But we were also taught that God gave us a free will and we were called to resist this rebellion within us through our will. Thus, the same story really, the secular, scientific one, and the spiritual one, but with different languages, and one critical difference. The spiritual story damned me for my failure to resist through my will.

On the third Wednesday, I was excited and tingling with anticipation even before I got to the door. As she opened it, I drew her into my arms, carried her to the sofa, and we quickly shed our clothes. "Are you happy to see me or what?" she asked giddily, right before I entered her. We ended up in the missionary position, and I tried to make it last as long as possible.

Afterwards we lay together, her head on my shoulder, and I asked, "Was it good for you?"

"Yes, of course."

"Just good or great?"

"Men . . . you're all the same," she said. "Don't worry, it was fine."

Later, as we had a drink, I said to her, "I'm thinking about leaving the monastery. I can't keep up this pretense much longer."

She didn't respond and a moment later she said, "Shit, I broke a nail."

"Are you even listening to what I am saying?"

"What?"

"I said I'm thinking about leaving the monastery."

She frowned and said icily, "Don't leave on account of me."

I felt my insides go hollow because, of course, she was the only reason I would leave. There was nothing else for me. But I quickly dismissed every negative signal from her. There is nothing more sad or exhilarating than a doomed love.

Even now, with hindsight, I don't know what she wanted from me. Women are as mysterious as God to me sometimes. Maybe I was just a conquest for her, a challenge, and as a celibate monk I might have been the ultimate challenge for her. Maybe it was just kicks. I still don't know, but at the time I thought we had a special connection. I told myself she loved me because I was kind to her and she enjoyed talking to me and I amused her and made her laugh. I thought somehow we could be together. This was against any rational thinking, of course, and one part of me knew it. I would try to tell myself how stupid this all was. She was married and supported by a wealthy husband, and I was a monk, who, even if I left the Benedictine order, would have no immediate means of support. She had a flamboyant personality and liked to be the center of attention; I liked quiet and solitude. She was a materialist; I was a spiritualist. In short, it was absurd for a million reasons, but still that absurdity was all my mind could entertain.

Two days before the next Wednesday, I received an e-mail from her: "Philip, I can't meet this week. I'll contact you when I have time for another lesson." It was a cold, impersonal e-mail and for me this was like getting stabbed in the chest with a frozen knife. It was a small thing, but I feared for the first time that the whole thing wasn't real.

For several weeks after that I sent her e-mails daily, but she either didn't respond or she made a curt remark like, "Got your message. Very busy. Will write later." That kind of response drove me further into despair.

Thinking that the sex might be the problem, I wrote her, "I just want to see you. We don't have to do it." She didn't respond, so then I thought maybe that was the wrong thing to say, and I wrote again, "Of course, we can do it if you want. I can accept a relationship on any terms you want. I just want to see you!" When I think back on it now, my behavior seems so juvenile and pathetic, like a teenager in love.

Finally she responded positively to an e-mail request I sent her asking if she wanted to have lunch the following week. We made a date for the following Tuesday, and I spent that week feeling like I was in heaven again. Maybe she did care for me!

We met at Anton's, a log cabin restaurant in Waite Park. She was sitting at a far table when I arrived and talking on her cell phone. She stood up and gave me a half-hug, but she continued to talk on her phone for a good five minutes. That was annoying, and she acted a little subdued at first, but she ordered a Bloody Mary and by her second, she was in a good mood and I thought we had a marvelous time. We talked about university life and the regents, particularly about how conceited and full of themselves they were. I did an imitation of one man who was particularly obnoxious, and she laughed loudly, which delighted me. We talked about living in Minnesota, and the long winters, and the Minnesota Vikings football team, and the music that she loved: pop, disco, and country. In my mind, we were back where we started and in love again.

Later as we lingered over coffee I asked her, "Do you want to have children someday?"

"I don't think I would be the best mother."

"Sure you would," I said, even though I had a hard time imagining her in that role.

She got a little quieter and said, "I didn't have the best role models growing up. My dad was gone somewhere most of the time and when he was home he was one of those military fathers who acted like a drill sergeant. Everything had to be done exactly the way he wanted. My sister Cheryl and I were expected to be perfect. He was that way with my mom, too. Yelling at her and slapping her around if the house wasn't perfectly clean or one thing was out of order. And my mom was a nutcase about the whole thing, always worried about trying to please him. Then on Sunday he would make us all go to this Pentecostal Church, and it would be all 'Hallelujah' and 'Praise the Lord' and pretending that everything was perfectly hunky-dory."

"That's too bad. It sounds like it was rough."

"Yeah, well, we survived, I guess . . . that's one thing I have going for me. I'm a survivor . . . a bitch sometimes, but a survivor bitch," and she laughed. "What about you? I don't think they will let you have kids in the monastery," she said.

"No, I guess I'd have to leave if I wanted kids," I responded, and suddenly I wanted nothing more.

I switched the subject to North Dakota, safer territory, and suggested that we could find a reason to travel together there. I had this fantasy of driving through North Dakota and visiting her former home in Minot. We would listen to a Peggy Lee CD while driving, "Fever," for sure, and maybe, "I Get a Kick Out of You," and we would stop at a motel after a few hours of driving and make love. She just laughed when I suggested visiting North Dakota, like it was ridiculous, but just the fact that she did not say a definite no, in my twisted deluded state of mind, gave me hope.

That day at Anton's Restaurant was the last time I had any extended conversation with her. Just when I thought there was hope for us again, it all melted away. I continued to e-mail her, but she rarely responded. When she did it was very curt. So I started calling her on her cell phone instead. She never answered—no matter what time I called—and I just got her voicemail. Finally after two weeks of this, I was surprised when she answered one of my calls. "Hi, it's me," I said.

"Oh, hi," she said, and there was an awkward pause. I could hear her typing on a keyboard, so I knew she was at her computer, and she kept typing as we talked. "What do you want?" Her voice sounded mechanical and cold.

"I just need to see you," I said, and I knew my voice sounded embarrassingly weak and pitiable, but it was as if I couldn't control what was coming out.

"I don't know. I'm really busy right now. It's not a good time."

"Just for a short time. Maybe we could have lunch again . . . we had fun last time," I reminded her.

"That was nice . . . but I just can't right now," she said.

"I miss you," I said, and I realized again how feeble I sounded.

There was another pause, "We did have some fun, but I gotta go right now . . . I'll call you back soon. Bye," and she hung up.

I didn't really expect her to call me back soon and she didn't, but I kept thinking she had said we'd had fun together, clinging to any thread of hope. Of course, she never answered when I tried to call her again.

About a week later, I was surprised when I saw her going into the entrance of Old Main Hall, which held the office of the president and where I worked. It was windy and cold and her hair was blowing across her face, but to me she looked as entrancing as ever. She greeted me with a formal politeness, "Hi, Brother Phil. It's good to see you."

"What are you doing here?" I said, hoping she came to see me.

"Oh, my husband just wanted me to drop something off at the president's office," she replied

We ducked into the foyer out of the cold. We chatted a few minutes but she said she was in a hurry and excused herself. She was ushered into President McLaughlin's office. I hovered outside my own office two doors down so as to catch her when she left. I went through some files, made copies, and went through files again. At one point I heard her distinct laugh coming through the closed door. Finally I had to take a telephone call. At that exact minute I saw her leave the president's office and I ended the conversation as quickly as I could and frantically ran out the building. I caught her just as she was leaving the parking lot in her car. I knocked on her window and she slowly rolled it down. I wanted to kiss her although I knew I couldn't do that in public. I blurted out, "I love you."

"No you don't," she said, like I was a fool. "Don't be ridiculous. Whatever we had is over," and she drove off. I watched her and I noticed that she didn't even look at me in the rearview mirror.

At that point I could no longer pretend I had any hope, and I fell into a deep despair. I called into work and told them I was sick. How could I work? What did that matter anymore? I would not, could not move from my cell. It was late March, the sky was gray, and it began to snow. I lay on my bed facing my small window for three days and watched as icicles slowly formed like daggers, drip after drip of water coming off the roof, and then freezing in the bitter cold.

After a few days I returned to my schedule, but I wasn't the same. Experiences that once gave me a sense of inner peace, like listening to the liturgy of the hours, now seemed crushingly boring, and the hours dragged by. I would kneel for prayer and pray dozens of Our Fathers and Hail Marys but it only seemed like hocus pocus to me. Occasionally I heard things in the Psalms reading that would speak to me, but it was only the despair I heard; "the very light has gone from my eyes" (Psalms 38:10) and "my pain is always before me" (Psalms 38:17). I had descended into a state of blackness utterly without light.

42

EVEN THOUGH I KNEW in my rational mind it was over, some part of me deep inside could not accept it. I began to send Jackie e-mails again every few days, none of which she acknowledged. I had an uncontrollable urge to see her, if for no other reason than to tell her how I felt and that she had hurt me deeply. Eventually, I decided I had to see her in person. I wasn't sure how I would explain my appearance, so I concocted the excuse that I needed to drop off some materials at her house from the University Development Office regarding revocable trusts. It was a poor excuse, and not especially clever, but it was all I could think of in my desperate state of mind.

I just assumed she would be home. I had not called in advance, but it was mid-morning, and I figured the chances of catching her would be good. I was surprised when David Conway answered the door. He looked tired and unshaven, although he invited me in when I told him I was dropping off some materials. I detected a whiff of booze on his breath and it was obvious he'd had more than one. He tossed the materials I brought him on the coffee table and sat down.

"Are you home alone?" I inquired.

"Yes, Jackie is staying in Minneapolis a few days. She needed some time. Maybe she's shopping at the Mall of America. How women can shop for days is beyond me," he said.

I tried to talk to him about university news, issues coming up for the Board of Regents and so forth, but he seemed totally disinterested. He just sat there, obviously preoccupied.

I was about to leave when he asked, "Can I talk to you about something? I'm having a hard time. I don't know where to turn."

I said, "Sure, anything," though I hoped what he had to say was not in the nature of a confession.

"You know, life's a funny thing," he said. "Sometimes you think you have it all, and then one day you realize you really have nothing. I wish I would've had the guts to do what you did and take a simpler route."

"I don't know that it's necessarily a simpler route."

He looked at me questionably, but did not say anything. Then he got up and poured himself another drink, sat down and rolled the ice around in his glass. "I'm not sure about anything anymore," he said. "You think you know certain things, but you find out too late you don't know shit and the world crashes around you."

I wasn't sure at first what he was talking about, but I listened. After a few minutes I realized he was referring to the recent stock market crash. Apparently he had made some substantial investments in some new start-up tech companies and lost very heavily.

"I lost more in a year than my father and grandfather accumulated in two lifetimes of work. I'm going to lose all of this," he said, looking around the house.

I didn't like the guy, but I almost felt sorry for him, he was so obviously crestfallen. He talked for an hour or more. I just sat there and listened. I didn't understand all the details, but apparently he had given a large interest in the family business as equity to cover other investments, and it was now all threatened.

Then, out of the blue, he looked at me and said, "That isn't the worst of it, Brother Philip. The worst part is that I think Jackie's having an affair."

I looked at his eyes when he said that, hoping that my own eyes wouldn't betray my emotions. I wondered if he knew about Jackie and me, and I half expected him to pull out a gun and shoot me. A long silence followed, the only sound the ice clinking in his glass. I tried to concentrate on taking even breaths. Finally, as calmly as I could, I asked, "How do you know that?"

"She told me as much. She was drinking, and I told her we would be facing a serious financial setback, and she called me a fucking idiot for making such stupid investments. Then she started drinking doubles and ragging on me with that foul mouth of hers. 'God damn this and God damn that.' I was pretty teed off by then, and I yelled back at her and told her it was obvious she had married me for my money. I said some things I shouldn't have and I called her a gold-digger and a cunt. That was stupid of me, because then she got angrier and called me a lousy lover and said she didn't need me and that she was getting it elsewhere anyhow."

He stopped and looked out the window.

"I had suspected it before then anyhow," he finally continued. "I think it's someone connected to the university. I just don't know who the bastard is. She is, and always has been, a sneaking, conniving liar."

He was quiet for a minute and then he said, "You know . . . I knew that when I married her. I knew she'd drop her dress whenever she felt the itch. The thing is, I loved her anyhow. We had some good times . . . some great times." He paused again, "Pathetic, isn't it?" He gulped down his drink, and then began to sob—not a quiet sob—and he didn't try to hide it. His whole body shook as if in deep pain.

As I watching him, I knew I should console him and say something to give him hope, but I was too weak. My soul was poisoned, and I couldn't do the right thing. It was as if the devil was whispering in my ear and it occurred to me that, if they split up, maybe Jackie would come to me. It was a totally ludicrous thought, but in my state of mind, it didn't seem ludicrous at all.

Instead of consoling him, I said, "I don't know much about marriages, but it sounds like yours is over. Maybe you'll just have to move on."

He looked at me with a shocked, perplexed expression. "You don't understand. Despite everything, I still love her. I don't think I can live without her."

"You may have to," I said.

"I can't," he cried. "You don't understand . . . I can't."

I was suddenly feeling very uncomfortable, as if I was about to retch. I told him I had to go and I left him there, weeping on the couch. As I drove back to the abbey, I knew I had not done the right thing. I almost turned around, but I was drained and weak, and I drove on. I was never blessed with my grandfather's strength and fortitude.

The day after my visit with David Conway, I managed to go into work. I had somehow put the previous day's incident behind me, telling myself there was nothing I could do. It's funny how you can always justify your own conduct in a thousand ways. Later in the afternoon, I saw the provost and Father McLaughlin talking in hushed tones. Father McLaughlin called me over and asked me if I had heard the news. Regent David Conway had been found dead that morning. He had apparently committed suicide through carbon monoxide poisoning. He was discovered in his garage, slumped over the wheel of his Mercedes, with the engine running and the garage doors closed.

I was stunned, and the thoughts in my head tumbled. I was barely able to mumble a feeble, "I'm sorry to hear that."

"Has anyone talked to the wife?" the provost asked.

"I talked to her on the phone already," Father McLaughlin answered. "As you can imagine, she's very upset. I'm going to go see her later."

I excused myself and went back to my cell and did not leave for dinner or evening prayers. I fell into a deep sleep, which was only disturbed when I woke early in the morning, chills coursing through my body, as if I had walked through a door from my dreams. I had been dreaming that I was in horrific blizzard, wandering hopelessly, and everything was white. I looked down and saw that I was naked, and my body was caked with ice. I fell to the ground and tried to get back up, but the snow had already drifted over me, and it held me under.

43

THE MORNING AFTER I FOUND OUT about David Conway's suicide, I entered the church and knelt in a pew for a long time and prayed for forgiveness. I wanted it to hurt, but my knees had grown callous over the years, and the sweet pain I sought was not forthcoming. I could have sought relief in the confessional, but after going regularly for the past twenty years I could no longer go. I knew confessing would mean I had to face the true consequences of my actions.

For days I was lost in a deep despair. I could not go to the funeral because I knew I would see Jackie, and I was far too weak for that. The guilt now came flooding into my mind with a vengeance—guilt for my affair with Jackie, guilt for causing pain to Jackie's husband, guilt for my failure to reach out to him in his despair, guilt for his very death. The guilt was so heavy that it literally felt like it was crushing my chest, and I took long walks alone in the woods or simply sat in my cell because I could not face my brothers.

On the fifth day after David Conway's death and the day after his funeral, I managed to go to the pool. I thought perhaps in strenuous physical exercise I could dispel the torment that had taken hold of my mind. The pool was busy because it was open swim, but after a short wait I was able to secure a lane. I swam laps for an hour, but it was to no avail. My mind was still swirling.

As I walked back to the locker room along the side of the pool, I passed an attractive redhead. Even though I knew I should use my utmost willpower to resist, I could not help but turn my head to watch her pass, and her ass jiggled like two bouncing volleyballs. For a second I had that "I wish I was not a monk" feeling. Then I regained my senses and thought, *Damn me, when will I ever get control over my sexual desire? Why am I so sinful, Lord?* I wanted to strike myself down.

I think that was the moment the idea of corporal mortification entered my head, piercing me to the core, and I could not shake it. In my mind it was the only form of penance harsh enough for a sinner like me.

As I said, corporal mortification was not something ordinarily practiced by Benedictines in modern times, at least certainly not at St. John's Abbey. I had never seen or heard of it practiced there, but I knew something of it from my Catholic theology studies. The term mortification meant literally, "putting the flesh to death." It actually originated with St. Paul: "If you live after the flesh, you shall die, but if through the spirit you mortify the deeds of the flesh, you shall live." (Romans 8:13) Mortification is thus a means to repress our passions and sexual urges and conform our desire to the rule of reason and faith. It can also serve as a form of penance and, if we were earnest in our self-discipline, God will be pleased and reward us with divine grace.

I also knew from my theology that St. Benedict himself was not averse to corporal mortification. St. Gregory, writing of the life of St. Benedict, told of how he overcame a temptation of the flesh:

> *For the remembrance of a woman which sometimes he had seen was so lively presented to his fancy by the wicked spirit, and so vehemently did her image inflame his breast with lustful desires, that almost overcome by pleasure, he was determined to leave the wilderness. But, suddenly assisted by divine grace, he came to himself, and seeing near him a thicket of nettles and briars, he threw off his garments and cast himself naked into the midst of those sharp thorns and nettles, where he rolled himself so long, that when he rose up, his body was pitifully rent. Thus, by the wounds of his flesh he cured those of his soul.*

Once the idea of corporal mortification entered my head I thought incessantly about the various forms it could take. Cold showers could be a form, but that did not seem nearly harsh enough for me. Living in Minnesota, a cold shower didn't seem any harsher than going outside on a cold January day. The idea of the cilice was not appealing. I couldn't see myself at work with a device pinching into my flesh. What if I bled and it showed through my trousers? Furthermore, I had no idea of where to get a cilice or how to make one. A hair shirt posed the same problem. I could hardly weave a shirt out of goat's hair, and while it might be itchy, it didn't seem harsh enough either. I did not know where I could find a thicket of nettles and briars, and besides, those wounds would show. Sleeping on a hard mat was out of the question as I was prone to back problems. I couldn't wear a heavy iron chain, for obvious reasons. Flagellation, sometimes called the discipline, seemed to me to be the only thing severe enough for me, and the idea of it vaguely excited me. In my head I thought it would produce the pain I needed to truly repent.

If this all sounds crazy, and it probably does, think about the pain that some athletes go through in training. The idea of "no pain, no gain" in weight lifting is not all that different. Or think of taking a very hot sauna and diving into a hole cut into the ice of a Minnesota lake. Or think of young people, most often women, indulging in "cutting," lightly cutting their wrists or other parts of the body to become more self-aware. Those aren't the same, but they share the desire for shock or pain as a means to restore and invigorate our souls. We all do things in our life that appear stupid upon reflection, but at the time, and given a desperate state of mind, they seem the only means to get relief.

I was determined, desperate actually, to do it, but not sure exactly how. I knew that the use of the discipline most often entailed the use of a rope of sorts made of cotton cords, sometimes knotted, used for self-flagellation upon one's back. But cotton cords seemed too light for what I needed. That evening I drove to Walmart and purchased a square of chamois leather cloth, some duct tape, a broom, and an Exacto knife. I returned to my cell at the abbey and wedged the broom between two slates on my bed and broke off a piece about a foot long. I cut up the chamois with the knife to get a dozen thin leather strips about eighteen inches long—tying knots at the ends—and I attached them to the short broom handle with the duct tape, winding it around many times to secure it.

I tried out my self-made whip by smacking it against my pillow and it made a pleasing sound. I removed my habit and T-shirt and turned up the radio in my room to drown out any more noise. I struck myself and I could hear the smack on my back and feel a sting, but it hardly felt painful, so I sat there for a minute contemplating the wretchedness of my soul and the damage I had done to others in my life, and let the guilt build within my mind. Then I dipped the chamois strips in a glass of water and I whipped myself harder—fifteen or twenty times—not enough to draw blood, but I do remember it brought tears to my eyes.

That night as I lay in my cell, I prayed God would see my penance and grant me relief from the torments in my mind, but I slept fitfully. I was awakened several times from the pain when I rolled over onto my back. The next evening I whipped myself again. This time I gave myself forty lashes, and I thought I felt some exhilaration, but maybe I just wanted to feel something so badly I imagined it. And it did not provide any relief whatsoever. It was more like the temporary exhilaration I felt when I had gone on a long run or swum a hundred laps.

The next morning, as we were walking to morning prayers, Brother Michael came over to me and we fell into conversation. I suspect he sensed something was bothering me, but I wasn't ready to tell anyone. As we parted, he lightly touched my back in friendship, and I winced slightly. When I did this, he looked in my eyes, but didn't say anything.

That evening as I was preparing for bed and intending to whip myself again, I heard a knock on the door. It was Brother Michael. He asked if he could enter. After some light conversation, he looked at me and said softly, "Philip, I have had a feeling for some time that something's troubling you. Sometimes it helps to confide in someone."

"No," I said, "Nothing's bothering me. I just have a lot of issues to deal with at work."

He didn't respond, just looked me in the eye with that calm, serene look of his. Of course, we both knew it was a lie, and after a moment of silence it was too much for me. I could not deceive him. "Please sit down," I said. He sat quietly, and I confessed the whole sordid affair with Jackie and my failure to help her husband, pacing back and forth across my small cell as I poured it out.

He listened quietly. When I was through, he told me I would find relief in time, that getting over these things often takes a very long time. He said I should pray and when I was in the right state of mind and contrite I should go to confession and I would receive absolution, that God would forgive me, indeed, that God was generous with forgiveness for those who repent of a great passion, but that God also calls upon us to forgive ourselves. Then he motioned to my back and said, "You don't have to do that. You'll find the grace of God without it."

I was silent a moment. Then I took a breath and said quietly, "Sometimes I'm not sure I even believe in God anymore."

He searched my eyes with some sympathy, hesitated, and then said, "We all have our doubts sometimes. But even in times of doubt, we all must choose to act like a devil or a Christ. Only a devil wields a whip."

44

I DIDN'T TELL JILL ANYTHING ABOUT JACKIE that day prior to my brother's wake and funeral. People have little sympathy for that kind of thing because it only appears sleazy and perverse when told to someone else. Plus, it was obviously the wrong time. But I wanted to. She seemed like the kind of person I could tell anything to, even though we had just met.

The morning of the wake my sister Marie arrived at my motel in Bismarck. I had not seen her in eight years, but she looked beautiful to me, with the loveliness some women seem to acquire as they age and their features soften and their smiles and sparkling eyes are the only things you notice. After lunch, we drove to the airport to pick up Annette and Eva, who I hadn't seen since our mother passed away. It was a sad occasion to get together, but it was good to see my sisters again, especially Marie, who I had adored as a child. I felt sorry I had not kept in closer touch, but after we started talking, it seemed as if time vanished.

We drove together to the funeral home for the wake, and the four of us walked up to the casket and stood silently for a minute. A lot of people sent wreaths, and the casket was surrounded by floral sprays. The casket was closed because some birds, probably crows, had found Jake's body before he was discovered and pecked his face and eyes up badly. I wanted terribly to look at him one last time. The closed coffin looked so cold.

Jill came early. When she entered, she slowly approached the casket and reached out and put her two hands on the gleaming wood and stood there for the longest time. Once other people eventually started to arrive, I was surprised at the number of people who showed up. It seemed like they just kept coming and coming. People lined up to speak with my sisters and me and say their sorry-for-your-loss in soft voices and shake our hands or give us hugs, although I knew very few of them. Many of them had tears in their eyes, and they all had kind words to say about Jake. There must have been thirty people from the Indian Reservation, which says a lot, and one of them, a fairly young Native American woman, came up to me and told me she was a physician at the Indian Health Clinic and that Jake helped the clinic secure a grant for an alcoholic treatment program. "Everyone loved your brother so much," she said. There were ex-cons who had known him in prison, fellow students from St. Mary's University, neighbors, co-workers, and friends whom he'd met along the long road of his life.

A man walked toward me who looked familiar, but it wasn't until he began to offer his hand that I recognized him—Nate Swenson, Jake's Army buddy. He was still a handsome man, although he had gotten quite bald, and his ponytail was gone. I was glad to see him. He was one of those rare persons one meets in life with whom there is an everlasting bond. He asked me if I'd like to meet for a drink after the wake, and even though I felt very tired, I agreed.

We met later that evening at the Peacock Alley Bar, and Nate had obviously had a few when I got there, but he ordered another for himself and one for me. I could tell he was pretty broken up about Jake. "I still can't believe he's dead," he kept saying, over and over.

Nate was no longer a smokejumper. He said he'd broken too many bones and quit. He now worked selling real estate in Missoula, Montana, so I asked him about that. He didn't say a lot, although from what little he related, he must have been doing very well. I was astounded when he mentioned some of the prices of ranch properties he was selling to wealthy people from California and the East Coast. Mostly he wanted to talk about Jake, and we reminisced about the Chicken Ranch for a long time.

"That was the greatest place in the world," he said. "No one around for miles, just wide open spaces and total freedom. Life doesn't get any better than that. You ever go back there?"

"Not really."

"You should, man. Start a monastery there. That would be cool. Trust me. In another ten or twenty years, people will be flocking to North Dakota, just like they are now to Montana, buying up all the beautiful scenic property."

I laughed. "I don't know how much scenic property we have. We don't have mountains like Montana."

"Doesn't matter, you have that healthy rural living and empty spaces, and there's not much of that left in the world. And how about the North Dakota Badlands? That's some of the most beautiful country anywhere. It'll be prime real estate some day."

"Maybe." It took me a minute to realize he wasn't joking.

"Jake loved it, you know," he said in a more subdued tone. "When I visited him in prison, he said that was what he missed most of all, the wide open spaces."

"I didn't know you visited him in prison."

He looked at me incredulously. "I visited him two or three times a year . . . Jake never told you?"

I felt embarrassed. "I didn't see him as much as I should have."

Nate studied the foam of his beer for a minute. "Yeah, I guess I can understand that. Your brother was a bitter man when he first went in, and he could be a horse's ass at times. He still had a lot of anger inside him. He changed, though. Not many men in prison do that. It took time, but people came to trust him and look up to him, even in prison. He became a cell block leader and advisor. He had those leadership qualities in Vietnam too. He could have been an officer if all that bad shit wouldn't have happened to him."

I was embarrassed a second time, but I asked anyhow, "What bad shit?"

Nate looked at me. "I guess he didn't talk to many people about it."

He finished his beer and ordered two shots of bourbon with beer chasers for the two of us. Then he took a deep breath, as if he was steadying himself. "I was in the same platoon with Jake . . . you know that . . . anyhow, we hit it off right from the start. In fact, almost everyone liked Jake. Your brother started out as the model soldier. He was tough as nails, we could all see that, even in boot camp, and then when he was in advanced infantry training, he really excelled. If the drill sergeant told us to give him fifty push-ups, Jake would do a hundred. If we were asked to run two miles with a fifty-pound pack, Jake would wear a hundred-pound pack. He was just the best—strong, determined, sure of himself.

"When he didn't pass the Army Ranger test, it surprised the hell out of all of us. He wanted to be a Green Beret eventually. Could have done it too, if he had known how to swim better. I remember him taking the swimming test. It would have been funny if he wasn't so damn serious about it. He made it about halfway using a dog-paddle, but the boots and clothing you have to wear for the test dragged him down, and he was struggling to keep his head up. Then he took some water in his lungs and started choking, but he just kept his arms and legs churning even when he was going under, trying to somehow make it, until the sergeant had to dive in and grab him by the collar and pull him out. The whole platoon joked about it afterwards and called him 'Sinker,' and the name stuck."

Our shots came, and Nate tossed his back in one swift motion, tilting his head back as he swallowed. I did the same, and the burn felt good as it went down my throat. Nate took a sip of his beer, shook out a cigarette from a crumbled pack, lit it, and continued. "When we got our orders to ship out to 'Nam, Jake was primed for it. He was gung ho, ready to save the world. The problem was that 'Nam had a way of fucking with people like that. It's not the black-and-white world you think it's going to be, and the people brought up to see the world that way are the ones who have the hardest time. They keep trying to sort things out, to fit everything into their black-and-white construct. When they can't, they get beat down by it all.

"It takes time, though. When we first got there, we were all primed and thought we were invincible. We were initially stationed near the air field at Saigon for six months. Basically our job was to patrol the perimeter of the airfield and the surrounding countryside. We were all young and dumb, and for the first few weeks we would get stoked every time we went out, expecting to see Viet Cong behind every tree and bush. But we didn't see any action. None. Zip.

"After those first few weeks, we loosened up and going out on patrol was just a walk in the park for us. The days were sunny and warm and after our patrol, we'd spend the evenings sitting in lawn chairs, playing blackjack, reading comic books, drinking beer, smoking dope, and a few guys smuggled some Vietnamese girls in. We thought we had it made.

"Del Amundsen was our second lieutenant and platoon leader. He was a big, husky red-headed guy, the type of person who looked like he'd only be comfortable wearing a buzz cut his entire life. His right earlobe was partly missing, partly mangled from some shrapnel. He could be an arrogant SOB, thought he knew everything, and he would bust your ass for little shit, like not keeping your equipment clean. He was career all the way and sucking up to all the higher ups, hoping to get a promotion, but he could loosen up and throw the book away and let things slide if he thought no one was looking. You had to do that in 'Nam to survive, and this was his second tour, so he knew that.

"The easy work ended after those first six months, though, and we were told to get ready to deploy elsewhere. One day, with only a few hours' notice, we received new orders and were loaded onto choppers. We were supposed to be part of an effort to pacify the Hau Nghia Province, although it was never exactly clear what they meant by 'pacify.' Hau Nghia was an area of mostly peasant hamlets and farms with sugar cane and rice paddies located between Saigon and the Cambodian border. It looked peaceful enough as you flew over, but at times it was thick with VC, hiding in the stands of wild reeds and elephant grass or melting into the civilian population.

"We would be sent out on patrol, sometimes to a particular destination, although most of the time it seemed that we were just out patrolling without any rhyme or reason, at least not that we were told. Those first few weeks were mostly calm. We took a few shots from stray sniper fire, but when we did, we hunkered down and we never took any casualties. It was basic shit grunt work, every fucking day, nothing but sun and heat and humidity. We would spend our days crossing paddy after paddy, watching out for snipers and snakes and slapping mosquitoes.

"At night we would dig our foxholes, clean our M-16s, eat our C-rations, and smoke our cigarettes or marijuana. We would bend down to light them up with our Zippo lighters and then cup them in our hands. It was against the rules to light up at night because the VC might smell the smoke or see the flame and shoot at it, but after a few days when we didn't see any action and wanted a smoke or a high in the worst way, we said fuck it to the rules.

"In the second month we moved further northwest, closer to the jungle. The country there was full of booby traps and land mines, Bouncing Betties we called them, and they'd blow your leg off if they didn't kill you. We got so we'd walk around like robots, our eyes glued to the ground, walking in single file, and trying to step in the footsteps of the soldier in front of us. No one wanted to walk point, but your brother volunteered and after a while some of the men became superstitious, like he had some type of aura around him. They thought if they followed in his footsteps, they'd be lucky. There was one guy in particular, a small, skinny, fresh-faced kid from San Diego, we called him Wavy Davey, who followed your brother around religiously and wouldn't take a step unless your brother had stepped there first. He was one of those young dipshits who didn't know anything about life yet, but he could be funny at times, and your brother liked him and kind of took him under his wing and watched out for him. The kid tried to be a good soldier, I'd give him credit for that—not like some of the fucking shirker draftees who just ducked their heads until they could get back home.

"Andy Donaldson was the first to step on a mine. We heard the explosion and the sound of the dirt spraying all around, and Donaldson screamed out, 'I can't feel my legs! I can't feel my legs.' We all stood there rock still, not daring to move, and listening to his agonizing screams for a good ten minutes before the medic could tiptoe in and shoot him up with enough morphine to quiet him. He wasn't following your brother when he stepped on the mine, so that just increased your brother's aura for some of us.

"We had been told that sometimes the Viet Cong slept in safe houses they built in the hamlets. They were hard to spot because they looked just like peasant huts, but we were instructed to look for huts that didn't have cultivation around them or didn't have animals. That was supposed to be a sign. The problem was, we couldn't really ever tell for sure. Some of the peasants only had a few pigs, anyhow. As I said, nothing was black and white. We were just guessing most of the time, and if we weren't sure, Lieutenant Amundsen would label it a 'Viet Cong hamlet' anyhow, and it was fair game. He'd say, 'We're going in to surprise Charlie and kick some ass.'

"We'd enter the villages before dawn and bust down the doors and rouse everyone out of bed. If anyone ran or showed any resistance, we were ordered to 'waste 'em,' but that rarely happened, and when it did, it'd turn out to be some old man or woman who just panicked or didn't understand our yelling to 'halt.' Then we'd round everyone up and go through the houses and blow up any underground bunkers. A lot of the peasants had bunkers to protect themselves from our shelling, but we were told these could be used for Viet Cong hiding places, so they all had to be blown up.

"We took our first sniper casualty about three weeks into it. He was a tall, skinny white kid from Tennessee who everyone liked, no more than nineteen, by the name of Jimmy Petters. He walked out to the edge of a rice paddy one day and squatted down on his haunches to take a shit, and he was hit by sniper fire in the ass and then, even before he fell to the ground, a second shot tore through his back and lungs. It scared the hell out of us all for a while. He was such a skinny kid. We figured the sniper must be a damn good shot to hit him. No one dared take a crap, and we all walked around constipated for days.

"One day we got word from headquarters that the guerrillas had shot down an American helicopter with six men aboard. They told us an American-manufactured .50 caliber machine gun, which had been captured by the VC, brought it down. A lot of times they were just guessing, but we were sent into the area to search the hamlets, flush out the guerillas, and recapture the machine gun. The area was about thirty klicks away, so we were transported by choppers. I remember that four or five of them came in low for us, the rotors thudding so loudly that you couldn't hear a damn thing, and we tried to shield our faces from the stones and dirt whirled up, but we got shit in our eyes anyhow. We jumped in, and those choppers shook like crazy. Once we took off we had to hang on to the webbing so we weren't flung out. When we landed it was in a flooded rice paddy, and we jumped out, knee deep in muck, and there was a low fog hugging the ground. We couldn't even see where we were. We just had a feeling that we were in for some real shit.

"Not an hour later, as we were walking down an old ox-cart path, we took some fire. We hit the ground and tried to figure out where the shots came from. It was all a blank green canvas to us. After a few moments of silence, we heard some moans and realized that Danny Gilman had taken a bullet. By the time the medic reached him, it was too late, and you could already see a patch of blooming blood beneath him. He muttered something about his mama, and his head rolled to the side, and he was dead.

"The days were a blur after that. We just kept patrolling from here to there, back to here, and it didn't make any sense, but we just did what we were told. We all became pretty jumpy, and we'd just pray to get through the day, especially if we took fire or thought we were in an area where we might. It's funny how it's so easy to pray when you are scared shitless like that, 'God, please just let me get through this.' At other times, when you feel safe and secure, you think you have no need for God.

"Soon we were taking fire almost daily. The thing is, there were never any battles . . . you never actually saw the enemy . . . you just saw the dirt kick up around you, and then heard the shots in the distance. Now we were firing back in the general direction we thought the shots came from, thousands of rounds, but we were just trimming trees. The

VC were like ghosts. They'd just disappear into the mist or tunnels somewhere. The more we got shot at, and the more we didn't see the enemy, the more pissed off we got. We were fueled by adrenaline and wanted to kill someone by that point.

"Lieutenant Amundsen was convinced they were all around us, just moving ahead of us by night, so he asked for volunteers for night patrols. Most of us were afraid of the dark. It seemed like we were always peering into it and seeing strange shapes and shadows filtering past. Your brother volunteered, though. He'd been made a squad leader, and at first he went out with a five-man patrol. After a few nights, though, he volunteered to go alone, saying the other soldiers made too much noise.

"Some thought he was crazy, but he liked the calmness and solitude of the night when it'd be eerily quiet, except once in a while you could hear the sound of wild animals scurrying around in the dark. We thought they could be tigers, but Jake just shrugged that off. 'Hell, there just small jungle animals. No bigger than the raccoons we have at home,' he said.

"Jake reported some nighttime VC movement, but when we checked it out the next day they'd be gone, always one step ahead of us. We humped around for another week, but we still hadn't seen anything, and the lieutenant wanted some action, so he could report a body count, so we were moved even further west towards the jungle where intelligence reported some suspicious activity around several rural hamlets. As we got close to the first one, Jake and a soldier by the name of Bobby Sanders—an ass-kissing, gung ho dumb fuck from South Carolina— were sent on foot to do reconnaissance.

"The hamlet was your typical delta hamlet sitting on a large irrigation ditch that fed the rice fields. Jake took four troops and wound around to the south side and up a narrow paddy dike where he could approach the village close enough to glass it. Sanders and his group came up from the east and were just approaching the hamlet when they took some automatic rifle fire. It was hard to tell whether it was one rifle or several, but Sanders was the jumpy type. He came back excited and reported that there were a large number of VC in the village.

"Amundsen was raring to go, but he had to wait for Jake to get back. When he finally did, Jake reported there were Vietnamese peasants in the field west of the hamlet and he had spotted a number of women and children in the hamlet itself. 'Nothing suspicious,' he said.

"Amundsen got in his face. 'Nothing suspicious? Are you fucking deaf? Didn't you hear the shots?'

"'Yeah, I heard shots,' Jake said, 'but they came from the hedgerows to the north. Probably a lone sniper. They didn't come from the hamlet.'

"'You can't be fucking sure,' Amundsen said.

"I heard the three of them arguing and one of the sergeants joined in for a while, but the lieutenant believed Sanders, or wanted to believe him. It was a rare clear day and he was just gung ho to call in an air strike. 'Soften 'em up first,' he said. Jake argued against it, but the lieutenant looked at him and shouted, 'I'm the one who's responsible here. I'm not marching in there and taking casualties if I don't need to.'

"Your brother seemed pretty pissed. He yelled back, 'Jesus Christ, the civilians will get slaughtered.'

"Amundsen stared at him for the longest time and said, 'There are no civilians here. Gooks are gooks.'

"Jake muttered something I didn't hear, but it must have set Amundsen off, because he grabbed Jake by the front of his shirt and shouted in his face, 'Listen, you stupid moron. They sent us over here to kill commies, and that's what were gonna do. You got that!'

"The next thing I knew, Amundsen was talking to one of the sergeants. They had a map spread out on the ground, and they were kneeling down trying to figure out their exact coordinates so that we wouldn't get anything dropped on us. I heard the field radio operator, J.J., yell, 'Hey, give that the fuck back.'

"I looked over and saw that Jake was holding the battery pack of the radio. J.J. was a big black dude from Alabama—you had to be big to carry those radios on top of all your other gear. We called the radios 'Prick Twenty-Fives' or just 'Pricks' for short. They came in two metal boxes, one holding the radio and one holding the battery. Jake had taken the battery and was holding it and he had his bayonet out like he was going to cut the wires or cut someone if they tried to take the battery back.

"Amundsen noticed the commotion and yelled, 'What the fuck is going on here?'

"Jake looked him straight in the eye and said, 'Sir, I don't think we should call in an air strike yet. I think we need to think about this more, maybe do some more reconnaissance.'

"Amundsen went ballistic. 'Who the fuck do you think you are? I'm in charge here. You'll drop that battery, or I'll have you court-mar-shaled. They'll crucify you! You'll spend the rest of your life in a shit-hole stockade. You hear me, you stupid fucking moron?'

"Jake looked down and fingered the wire on the radio with one hand while still holding his bayonet in the other. At that point you couldn't hear a single sound. We all just gazed at the two of them, wondering what was going to happen.

"'I said drop that, you fucking moron!' Amundsen said.

"Jake looked up, and he could see by the faces of the rest of us that he was alone on this. Most of us had some doubts about VC being in that hamlet, but we weren't about to side against the lieutenant, not after what we had been through and the frame of mind he was in. So Jake sat there for the longest time with the radio battery and bayonet in his hand, and the two of them stared at each other. I knew that Jake was trying to decide what to do. I remember thinking that Amundsen was so pissed off that he just might take out his pistol and shoot him, and Jake suddenly tossed the battery down and said, 'To hell with you fuckheads,' and walked away.

"Amundsen got on the radio and called in the coordinates and I heard him say, 'Light 'em up.'

"We sat there for about forty minutes before we saw two fighter-bombers come in, shrieking and screaming low over the drop zone, and strike with rockets, bombs, and napalm. We were about two klicks away at that point, on a small knob of a hill. We had a good view, and we just watched. At first you could just see white puffs of smoke, but the heat of the napalm was so intense it incinerated the thatched roofs, and soon you could see flames leaping up in the air. We watched the hamlet burn, and you could smell the burning from as far away as we were. Then three helicopter gunships came in just over the tree line and laid down a barrage and everything was lit up by red-orange tracers and fire.

"The lieutenant waited an hour after the choppers had hit and the fires had died down and ordered us to march in, saying, 'Anything moves, let's give 'em hell, boys.'

"Shit, we never gave 'em hell. They were already in their own hell. We broke up into teams of two and walked into that hamlet, or what was left of it, and I'll never get that scene out of my mind as long as I live. I can still remember every detail, like some sick horror film you're forced to watch over and over again.

"The air was thick with this blackish smoke and everything was covered with a gray dust, so that the place had this darkened surreal appearance, and as soon as we got to the edge of the hamlet we saw the first dead, an old man, lying face down. I remember his body was already covered with flies. When we got up close to the burnt huts, we could see the ground was littered with dead villagers. The stench was so bad we had to put handkerchiefs over our noses. Some of the women and children were burned so badly by the napalm that their skin was literally scorched off their bodies. There were dead dogs, dead pigs, dead ducks, dead chickens.

"Ones that weren't dead probably wished they were. Children were standing around whimpering and crying, and old people were in shock, their faces blank to any emotion. I remember an old women lying on a pile of straw, her skinny leg half gone. She turned her head in my direction, but her eyes looked completely dead, as if she didn't have a clue where she was. We saw two brothers dead, one about six and the other no more than two, and the older one lay on top of the younger one as if he had tried to cover him up. They were just black and shriveled up like burnt marshmallows.

"It didn't seem real, like we were not participating, just watching. The only shots I heard fired were when a water buffalo stumbled across the hamlet and its hind quarters were so badly burnt it stunk of burnt flesh. Someone shot it to bring it down, but it just let out a low bellow and kept stumbling along. Then several soldiers shot about twenty rounds into it, globs of bloody flesh flew off, and it finally staggered and fell with a loud groan.

"We didn't find any VC or any weapons, but Amundsen said we couldn't stay to attend to the dead and dying because some of the guerrillas might be sitting in their foxholes, probably hidden in the shrubbery along the ridge to the north, and even now preparing to attack us. He radioed in and said that the ARVN, South Vietnamese troops, would send in some medics for the civilians, but I doubt that ever happened.

"We spent the next week humping around in circles again. It was the beginning of the monsoon season, and it seemed to rain endlessly, a relentless fucking downpour, and the sound of it beating on the leaves drowned out everything except the thoughts in your head. It's funny how people react differently to the same thing. Some of the soldiers were spooked by the carnage from the bombing and were quiet. You could tell it was playing on their minds. Wavy Davey was one. He looked white and ashen, as if the life had been sucked out of him. Other soldiers just joked about it, as if it was nothing, talking about how the slant-eyed *papa-sans* and *mama-sans* got what they deserved. 'Crispy critters now,' they laughed.

"Amundsen never said a word to Jake about his actions before the air strike. I think he knew your brother had been right about the hamlet not having any VC. Your brother was just dead silent, never said a single word, not even to me, like there was his own little war going on inside his mind.

"We didn't see any action for some time, although one guy lost his legs when he got hit by a Bouncing Betty. He had been following behind your brother, too, maybe fifty yards behind him, when we heard the explosion. The medic got to him right away, he was screaming in agony, and we could see there was nothing left of his legs, they were nothing but mush, but the medic stabilized him enough so that he was medevaced out of there and somehow he lived. After that, we never took our eyes off the ground, and it rained so hard the water would run right off your helmet and down your back. We were soaking wet everywhere, and we never got dry. All day long we would slosh through mud and water up to our knees and every night we'd pick off thumb-size leeches from our legs and step on them and watch our own blood spurt out.

"Eventually we arrived outside a second hamlet that intelligence reported had looked suspicious. Jake volunteered again to go on reconnaissance, and the lieutenant thought about it for a minute, and he looked around and everyone else looked down to the ground. Finally he said to Jake, 'Go . . . but don't be a goddamned pussy about this now, you hear me, Sinker? We're not taking any fucking chances with these gooks.'

"The hamlet was boxed by hedgerows and bamboo thickets and it was raining hard. Jake was gone for a long time, and the whole time the lieutenant was impatiently pacing. After a few hours, Jake came back and said he didn't see any active sign of VC in the area.

"'What about the huts?' Amundsen asked.

"'Negative, sir.'

"'Are you sure? You're making the call, soldier.'

"'I didn't see anything, sir.'

"We were ordered to march in, and as we came up the last canal dike about four hundred yards from the hamlet, we saw a few men and women running from the hamlet in panic. We figured they must have heard what had happened at the last hamlet.

"We entered the hamlet and started going hut to hut. It was eerily quiet, except for a few chickens squawking. I guess that should have tipped us off, but we didn't see anyone except an old man who was too sickly to flee. Then, as we were approaching the far side, all hell broke loose. We had walked into an ambush, and we heard a series of shots and then a kid named Connors fell dead with a shot to his throat. He never made a sound or moved an inch. Just flat went down.

"A few seconds later, Wavy Davy took a shot in the chest. Your brother had stopped and kneeled down, looking to shoot, and he hadn't noticed that Wavy Davey had kept advancing and gotten out ahead of him. I remember when he got hit, he seemed confused, as if this couldn't be happening to him, and he looked down in disbelief at his shirt, which was turning red with blood. 'Oh shit, oh shit,' he said. 'I'm hit. God dammit,' and he sat down. He was still in the open and being shot at, you could see the dirt fly all around him where the bullets hit.

"At that point Jake crawled out on his hands and knees, all the time bullets whining and the dirt flying up around him, and pulled him to safety behind a bamboo fence. That was the action that later earned him the Bronze Star. Your brother held Wavy Davey and pressed down on the wound to try to stop the bleeding, and he kept saying, 'Don't die. Don't die. God, please don't let him die,' and then the medic crawled up and cut off his shirt and applied a compress to his chest and gave Wavy Davey a shot of morphine, but you could see the compress seeping red, and then his eyes rolled back in his head.

"We took some more heavy fire for maybe five minutes and returned it with everything we had. Two more of our platoon got hit, though they would both live—a guy named Russell got hit in the knee and thigh and later lost his leg, and Jackson, took a hit in the shoulder. Then it was completely quiet. The shooting had quit, and not a sound, except those damn chickens, and now a few pigs grunting and squealing. We figured the VC must have slipped out the back, so we slowly scoured the hamlet, going from hut to hut.

"We were almost finished when we heard a *pop, pop, pop*, from a VC rifle, and Vince went down with a shot to his side. When we heard the shots, your brother and three or four other guys fired back, and the shooting stopped. It was impossible to know for sure who nailed the shooter, although we all thought it was your brother. He didn't miss often. We eventually entered the hut where the shooting had come from and found a dead VC, lying partially behind a bag of rice. He was skinny and small, barely more than a kid really, and he had wet himself, and his eyes were closed. You couldn't even see where he had been shot. He looked like he was sleeping except for a thin thread of blood trickling out of his nose. One of the guys walked up to him and was about to cut off one of his ears for a souvenir until your brother yelled at him, 'Leave him the fuck alone.' The guy stood there for a minute, fingering his knife, but Jake had a wild, crazed look in his eyes, and eventually the guy just sheaved his knife, spit on the dead gook, and walked away.

"We were out for three more weeks but didn't see much action. Your brother was scarily quiet and withdrawn most of that time. I don't think he was ever the same, actually. It wasn't until a few months later when we were in Saigon waiting to be shipped home, spending our time in whorehouses and getting ripped in bars and smoking dope, when Jake and I got stinking drunk, and he admitted to me that he had lied to the lieutenant the day Connors and Wavy Davy got killed. He confessed that a hut in that hamlet had raised his suspicion—not a soul entering or exiting it, and no garden or animals around it—but he wasn't sure, so he hadn't said anything to Amundsen. He figured if he did, Amundsen would call in an air strike, and he didn't want to see a scene like we had at the previous hamlet. But that lie cost us casualties, with two dead and three wounded, including Russell, who would spend the rest of his sorry life limping around with an artificial leg. Jake said to me, 'I walked right into a storm and didn't even know it. I fucked up everything.'

"I argued with him, told him it wasn't his fault, but he believed what he believed. I never saw anyone beat themselves up more over the war than Jake did. The problem was that your brother wanted to do the right thing, but when you are immersed in that mire, you don't know what the right thing to do is. You want clarity, but it's all confusion. Jake couldn't accept that, he thought he had fucked up twice, and both times people were dead as a result, and it's not easy lugging that guilt around all your life."

45

UNERALS ARE DIFFICULT FOR ME because, at a funeral, you really
have to confront your faith. On the one hand, it makes you want
to believe more deeply, because where would we be as humans if
we did not entertain the thought of something after death? Our minds
are not designed to deal with nothingness, and we're hoping it is heaven
for us and not hell. I think that even people who profess to be atheist
or agnostic hold out an unexpressed hope for a hereafter. On the other
hand, there is the coldness of the death, with the body laid out in the
casket or the urn full of ashes. There is such a finality to it. So these two
thoughts clash in your mind and you feel uncomfortable as a result.

The funeral for my brother sticks in my head, probably even
more so than that of my mother and father. It was just such a beautiful
way to remember him. My sister Annette read some Bible passages, Eva
gave a prayer, and little Courtney did the presentation of gifts, walking
down the aisle while bringing up a bouquet of flowers. Every few steps
she would wipe away tears from the corner of her eye with her free hand.
We celebrated Mass, and I assisted the priest with the Holy Commun-
ion, standing by his side as he distributed the host, and giving a drink
of the blood of Christ to all who approached.

Marie gave the eulogy and, as befits a funeral, she spoke of the
goodness in my brother, his childhood and teenage years when he was an
athletic star, his service in the Army and winning the Bronze Star, and his
work as a counselor after prison, something I had known nothing about
other than what Jill had told me. She did not mention the bank robbery
directly, but she said this at the end: "Jake went through a lot of difficult
and trying times in life, seeing friends die in Vietnam, seeing his best friend
Spencer shot dead before his eyes, spending twelve years in prison. It was

the natural thing to retreat into bitterness and regret, and he did that from time to time, but somehow he had the courage, resilience, and gumption to pull himself up from the very bottom and become a loving and caring man, concerned with the plight of others who tried to do good in the world. So at this moment when we are about to lay his body to rest, let's all think back and remember the good things he did and how he touched our lives. This is not the moment for us to shed our tears, but we should all be thankful we were given the chance to have known Jake and have his life as an example of how, with God's grace, we can overcome any obstacle."

When she finished there wasn't a dry eye among the mourners, and for the first time since learning about my brother's death, tears gathered in my own eyes.

After the funeral, we drove out to St. Mary's Cemetery in a long procession of cars behind the hearse for the burial. The cemetery sits on a hill overlooking Bismarck and the Missouri River and it was windy and cold on that hill but everyone stood around the green-draped platform concealing the grave. The crowd blocked the wind slightly, and the sun peeked out between the clouds just as the burial service commenced. The service was brief and then there was a three volley salute and the playing of Taps by members of the American Legion Honor Guard, and the folding of the American flag into the traditional triangle and the presentation of the flag to Jill, all of which Marie had arranged.

Afterwards a lunch was served in the church basement: ham, roast beef, baked beans, potato salad, cole slaw, rolls, vegetable trays, and chocolate cake. A ten-gallon Thermos of fruit punch and an urn of coffee provided beverages. Lunches are the best part of funerals, not because of the food, but because one finally has time to take a breath and look around at all the people who have come and realize that the deceased really did touch others. People came up to me and my sisters and expressed their condolences, and they all had memories to share. It made me realize Jake had a much fuller life than I had known and touched people in a good way.

One of the last people I saw was, to my surprise, Yvette. I hadn't seen her at the funeral or burial, although I expect she was there. She came up to me towards the very end as the women from the church were putting away the leftovers in the Tupperware. Even though it had been twenty years since I had seen her, I knew who she was immediately. She was a little heavier, but still very pretty, and as pleasant and talkative as ever.

"Hi, Peter. You haven't changed a bit," she said. (I didn't bother to tell her my name was now Philip.)

"Neither have you," I said, "You're just as beautiful as ever."

"Well, I'm not as slim as I used to be. The cold weather always makes me want to eat. Plus, I quit smoking too, which doesn't help."

"No, you look . . . healthy . . . healthy good . . . really good . . . really, really good," I said.

She knew that I was a monk, I suppose through things she had heard from her family back home, and we talked very briefly about my work at St. John's. I knew nothing about what she had been doing in the last twenty years, however, so I asked her about that.

It turned out she had gotten an education as she had talked about doing so many years before, first her GED, then graduating from Valley City State College in elementary education. Since then she had been a second-grade teacher for fifteen years in Bismarck. She was married to a fellow teacher and had three beautiful children of her own. She told me they had recently taken vacations to Hawaii and Disneyworld with their kids, and they had been to Las Vegas twice. It sounded like a good life, and I was happy for her. I would have loved to talk to her more, but people were still coming up to me to express their condolences, so it was difficult. Just as she was about to leave, she said, "You know I loved him once. He had some tough times back then, but I could see he had so much love and kindness inside. I'm just happy he seems to have found peace in the last few years of his life."

"Thank you for saying that," I said. Then as she began to walk away, I grabbed her arm. She turned. I said, "I'm sorry for what I did that day. Please forgive me."

"I forgave you a long time ago," she said. "I hope you haven't been carrying around the guilt all these years."

She looked at me, searching my eyes, "Oh, Peter, it was something that happened a long time ago. Besides, I share the blame too. Just let it go."

46

I STAYED ANOTHER DAY TO SPEND TIME with my sisters and then began the drive home early the next morning. The sun was just coming up and there was almost no traffic and I had plenty of time to think. I contemplated all the mistakes I had made in my life and the things undone and unsaid and I thought I should make amends and should start with apologizing to Jackie. I hadn't spoken with her since her husband's death. I had my cell phone, so I called her while I was driving. To my surprise, she answered on the second ring.

"Hi, this is Philip."

"Hey, Phil, how's it going?"

"Good, but how are you? I should have called you much earlier. I'm so sorry about the loss of your husband." As I said that, I thought about telling her about my own loss, but I was never able to get a chance.

"Oh, thank you," she said. "It's been so hard on me. Do you realize how difficult it is to plan a funeral? You have to make a million decisions. There's picking out the casket, planning the service, the tombstone, the burial. It's endless. Thank God that's over. Now I have to deal with all the estate lawyers. Lawyers can be such assholes."

She went on and on, and I listened but couldn't help thinking how incredibly self-centered she was. That's not a nice thing to think, and maybe it's harsh, but I couldn't help it at that moment. She didn't say a word about her husband or that she loved him or missed him. The thing was, her reaction wasn't a surprise to me. I had known that she was like that from the beginning. I had been so intrigued by her that I had deceived myself. I had wanted her to be someone else. That was my fault, not hers.

After a while I had to steer the conversation back. "Jackie, if my behavior played any role in his death, I'm so sorry."

"No . . . why would you think that?"

I swallowed hard. "I think he knew about our affair."

She made no response.

"Are you still there?" I asked.

"Yeah, I was just thinking. I'm pretty sure he didn't know about us."

"How do you know that?"

"He would've said something. It was something else."

"What do you mean, something else?"

"I mean someone else . . . he found out about someone else."

My heart started beating faster when she said that. "You were having an affair with someone besides me?"

"Yeah, well, it was no big deal, just a little fling."

"What do you mean, it was no big deal? Your husband committed suicide! I think that's a pretty big deal."

She was quiet again. "I know it probably sounds like I don't care, but I do. There was more involved than that. He was sinking financially. That was a part of it, too."

I was starting to seethe. "Who were you having this so-called fling with?"

"You don't want to know."

"No, I do actually. Was it someone connected to the university? Just tell me that."

"Yeah, but I don't want to get him in trouble. It would be a big scandal."

When she said that, it was as if a bolt of lightning was flung down from above. It was Father McLaughlin! She'd had an affair with Father McLaughlin. I instantly knew it to the depth of my bones, but I still had to ask. "You didn't have an affair with Father McLaughlin did you? Tell me you didn't."

She hesitated for a second, then said, "If you tell anyone, I'll kill you. Don't act so fucking holy," and she hung up.

47

Februrary 2002

I ROSE EARLY AND LEFT ST. JOHN'S ABBEY at 6:00 a.m. for Bismarck. After Jake's funeral, I had asked Jill if she wanted to help me dispose of the possessions in Jake's apartment, and I thought it best to let some time pass before we attempted this, but now I had to make the trip and get it over with.

The weather forecast predicted hazardous driving conditions, so the abbot allowed me to take one of the two larger Toyota Camrys in the monastery fleet, not the Corollas that the brothers usually drove. I was grateful to him for that. As I left, there were just a few small snowflakes dancing into the headlights, but by the time I hit the North Dakota border, it was snowing hard and the wind blowing, not a full-blown blizzard, but enough to get your attention while driving. The wet swirling snow turned the highway into an ice-glazed surface. Near Casselton I saw several cars spun out into the ditch, and I slowed down and hunched over, gripping the wheel and trying to see the center line. Another monk had hung a St. Christopher's medal from the rear view mirror, but I wasn't sure even St. Christopher protects reckless drivers. He likely gets out of the car and walks when the snow starts flying.

Growing up in North Dakota, we learned to take bad weather in stride, but we were always taught to respect it, because it could turn at any minute. As I drove, I remembered a blizzard story I'd heard as a child and passed down since my grandfather's generation.

The story goes that in 1909, William Zenker, a dray worker in Gackle, was asked to take a rural teacher, Elizabeth Borth, to her school about nine miles southeast of Gackle. He hitched two horses to a home-made sled and put Elizabeth next to him on the single wooden driver's seat. It was mostly calm when they left, so they had no reason to suspect trouble, but, of course, there were no weather reports back then. They had only traveled a couple of miles when the wind suddenly came up, and it began to snow heavily. They were soon caught in a severe blizzard. After a few miles, they lost the road, and the horses panicked, plunging in the snow. They broke their eveners and refused to budge, and the two were left to the elements.

William gave Elizabeth his coat and a blanket he had with them, and they sought refuge in a haystack nearby. They dug into the hay the best they could and waited the storm out until the next morning when William crawled out. His feet and hands were frozen stiff, and the horses and sled were nowhere in sight. It was very cold, but he somehow stumbled and crawled to the August Stolnake farm, about a mile away. August took the two of them to town in his wagon to seek medical attention. Miss Borth recovered after a few weeks with nothing but minor frostbite, but William nearly died from exposure. At first they put oil of spermaceti on the frostbitten areas in an attempt to save them, but they were too far gone. A few weeks later, his legs had to be amputated below the knee, and he lost most of his fingers as well. He was considered a hero for saving the young woman's life, and the community took up a subscription to buy him wooden "peg legs." Eventually he took up farming and could even handle a plow. Three years later, he married Miss Borth, and they went on to have eleven children.

I think about that story every time the winter weather turns bad. I still wonder how William managed to walk behind a plow with two artificial legs. Something gave him an inner strength. Some of his descendants still live near Gackle, and I've heard that they keep those wooden legs hung on the kitchen wall as a reminder.

Once I got past Jamestown, the wind died down some, and the road mostly got better. I arrived in Bismarck safely, thankfully, after a tense seven-hour drive. The next morning Jill met me at Jake's apartment. She looked lovely, even in the bulky down coat she wore, and she gave me a warm hug. She'd rented a U-Haul trailer, as we planned to haul most of the clothing and other small items to the Salvation Army, and she'd already arranged for an abused women's shelter to come by and pick up the furniture. While we waited for the landlord to let us in, I asked her how Courtney was doing.

"Oh, I don't know what I would do without her right now. She's a godsend. She loves kindergarten, and she just started taking riding lessons. She's only riding small ponies so far, but she has absolutely no fear. She must get that from Jake's side of the family."

She was quiet for a minute, then said, "You know, sometimes I still can't believe he's gone."

"Do you think you can handle this?" I asked her.

"I think so. We'll see."

I was just hoping we didn't find something in the apartment that would shake her up. I didn't know what, but I envisioned finding drugs or evidence of another woman or something of that nature. I guess I still couldn't totally accept the idea that Jake had turned his life around, despite everything I'd heard at the funeral.

The landlord arrived, right on time, and let us in. He told us to take our time and lock the door behind us. The apartment was a typical one-bedroom unit in a faceless cinder-block complex. I was surprised how small it was, but Jill told me Jake had been saving his money because he wanted to buy a house with a few acres in the country. Then he and Jill and Courtney could have some horses of their own.

It didn't take us long to do our work. We cleaned out the kitchen first, throwing out most everything except canned goods, which Jill would take to a food pantry. The refrigerator stank, with strange molds growing on some of the food, so we spent some time washing that out. The living room and bath needed little attention, so we tackled the bedroom next. There was a stationary bicycle and a computer on his desk, but it was old, so we tossed it. Two bookshelves were full of books, and I told Jill to take those. We hauled them down to her car and put them in the trunk.

Other than that, we found nothing much except a box in the closet with some old photos. We sat in the living room and looked through those together. A few were taken in the Army, and I could identify Nate Swenson in a group of about eight soldiers, including Jake. It must have been taken in boot camp because it was posed in front of what looks like barracks. They were all smiling for the camera, John Wayning it and giving big thumbs up.

Four photos were of me, one of which was taken of the two of us on horseback. I must have been about six at the time and I was sitting in front of Jake on his horse holding onto the saddle horn. When I saw it, I remembered he had taken me out to the north pasture that day to show me a new foal that had just been born. When we got there, the foal was already trying out wobbly legs, although it stuck close to its mother's side. We sat on his horse for half an hour or so, just watching.

Memory can be a mercurial mirror. I'd had absolutely no memory of that day until I saw the photo thirty-eight years later. Then it seemed so real I could remember every detail of that afternoon as if it had been yesterday and I could almost smell the fresh grass of the pasture and see the mare flare her nostrils and hear her snort when we got too close.

On Jake's desk he had a photo of our entire family, which must have been taken at Christmas when I was just a baby. I looked about a year old in my mother's arms. He also had a photo of himself and Jill, taken overlooking the Missouri River with the slanting sunlight playing on the hills in the background. Jake looked handsome, smiling like I remembered from when we were kids, and Jill was pretty, of course, and squinting into the camera with a peaceful, contented look.

I couldn't help wonder what Jill was thinking. It must have been hard for her because she must have slept in that bedroom on occasion only a few months ago. She was pretty quiet and didn't say much, although once I saw her sniff one of Jake's shirts and hold it to her cheek.

We found nothing unsettling in the apartment—no drug paraphernalia, no porn, not even a beer in the fridge. After we finished, Jill asked me if I'd take her out to the spot where Jake died in the motorcycle accident. I told her there wasn't much to see out in the middle of nowhere on a gravel road, but she wanted to go anyhow and place some flowers there, so I agreed to take her.

The next morning I picked her up early. She lived in a small rambler on the north side of the city and I could see the North Dakota capital building from the street in front of her house, the tallest building in North Dakota. I was a few minutes early and her babysitter hadn't arrived, so I talked to Courtney while her mother finished getting ready.

Courtney was indeed a darling little girl, with her dark hair tied back with mini butterfly clips, and I noticed for the first time that she has my brother's dark eyes and long lashes. She wanted to show me her goldfish named "Cinco," and her dolls, and her games, and her sticker books, and her stuffed animals. At one point she turned to me and asked, "Do you have any kids?"

"No, I'm a monk."

"I know that . . . but can't monks have kids?"

"No, monks don't have kids."

"Why not?"

"It's hard to explain, we spend all our time praising and serving God, so we don't have much time for other things."

"Oh, that's too bad . . . well, if you ever do have time and have some kids, you can bring them here to visit."

I wasn't sure what to say to that, but then she wanted to show me a picture she drew in kindergarten and we looked at it and she explained what all the stick figures in the picture were— her mommy, a zebra, a dog, a cat, a bird, a house. Jill had to drag her away when the babysitter came, saying that she was quite a talker once she got started.

Jill filled a Thermos with coffee and we hit the road. The Dixie Chicks' "Wide Open Spaces" came on the radio, and she sang along. Even I joined in on the chorus. As we drove east, the sun was just coming up, the wind had eased the night before, and we were treated to a brilliant sunrise of intense orange as it peaked over the horizon, the early morning light then softening as it met the clouds and glowing a brushed pink and rose before turning to a watered purple. The sunlight reflected-off the vast winter landscape, rendering it a shimmering gold and blue.

There are some occasions in life when the briefest moment in time is like a small glimpse of eternity and you remember it forever. Such moments are almost always shared moments, and this was one of them.

48

THE DRIVE GAVE US SOME uninterrupted time, and Jill began to tell me more about herself. She'd grown up in a large Catholic family in Bismarck, her father owned a hardware store, and she attended St. Mary's Catholic High School. They lived in a two-story colonial in town, right next to the park. The way she talked, it sounded like she had an idyllic childhood, the kind I always dreamed about when I was a kid and pitching hay or cleaning the barn in the summer on the ranch.

At sixteen, she began dating a local boy, Troy Johnson, two years older. His dad had a Cadillac and Chevrolet dealership. She and Troy were married when she was nineteen. "He was the life of the party, rich and handsome," she said. "We bought a house overlooking the Missouri River, just west of town, and Troy had a Donzi speedboat that we took out on weekends and cruised up and down the river. I thought I had everything."

She looked out the window and shook her head. "Was I ever stupid. We had only been married a couple of months when I found out that he was snorting cocaine. Before long that was the number one thing in his life. He went through fifty thousand dollars in one year—gone, poof, up his nose—and that is real money in Bismarck."

"What about you?" I asked.

"What about me, what?"

"Did you use cocaine, too?"

She shrugged. "Occasionally. I wasn't an angel. I was young and crazy once, too, just like everyone else. He would cut me a little line . . . and then cut one four times as big for himself. But I could take it or leave it. He would totally freak if he ran out."

"What happened then?"

"The age-old story. I found out he was cheating on me with the receptionist at the dealership. She was a little blond bimbo without a brain in her head, but she had big boobs and didn't seem to care that he was a married man. Some nights he wouldn't even bother to come home."

She described filing for divorce and that drawn-out affair. "In the end the judge gave me nothing," she said. "Not a penny! Troy worked with his dad at the dealership and everything we had was in his dad's name. The judge knew the family, so it was a foregone conclusion. I had a good lawyer, too, but she told me that's the way it works sometimes in North Dakota. You probably know that from growing up here. There's still an old boys' network among the people who run this state, mostly the Norwegians." She said this matter-of-factly, without bitterness.

Damn Norwegian Lutherans, I thought, even though I realized this was an old sinful prejudice from when I was growing up.

She continued. "I did fine on my own. I was twenty-four years old, but I went to college at the University of North Dakota, graduated in three years, and then got my Master's in guidance counseling. I learned I could stand on my own two feet."

We turned at the Cleveland exit. As the sun rose higher, the snow dazzled with a brilliant whiteness. I put my Ray-Bans on. "Tell me more about Jake," I said, "I kind of lost track of him after prison."

"I know," she said. "He changed a lot . . . well, maybe that's not true . . . maybe I should say something different came out of him as he got older. It didn't happen overnight, though. He still had some bitterness inside him when he came out of prison, I guess anybody would. The first thing he did was to buy a half gallon of Windsor Canadian whiskey and go on a wild drunk. Your sister Marie drove down from Grand Forks and found him at an old hotel in downtown Bismarck lying in his own puke. She cleaned him up and took him to her home.

"That was the last time he drank, though. He swore he'd never touch another drop of alcohol or drugs, and he stuck to it. He knew if he didn't quit he could end up in prison again and he didn't want to do that. Marie got him in a veterans' support group. That helped him, too.

He found out it wasn't just him, other vets had gone through the same thing, and he learned some therapeutic techniques to deal with the flashbacks he was having about the war."

"I wish I'd known years ago. Maybe I could've done something."

"Maybe, but Jake had to find his own time. And it wasn't just the veterans' group. Your sister gave him a lot of support and Nate Swenson stayed with him for a while. Your brother had a good upbringing, so he had something to build on. That's important. Somehow he turned it around. Then we met in the cafeteria at the university. He was ahead of me in line and took the longest time to pick out a dessert. There were too many choices he'd said, he wasn't used to that in prison. I was floored he'd admit to being in prison. To be honest, I was a little scared of him because of that, but I found out he was actually very sweet. Pretty soon we were having lunch almost every day and I found he had a real sense of humor. We would talk and talk and totally lose track of the time. We both liked to talk about people and life and what was really important. And we both liked books. He'd read every book in the prison library. Did you know that?"

I shook my head. Obviously I hadn't known a lot about him.

"I was cautious at first because of his past," she said, "but we fell in love and one thing led to another and we weren't as careful as we should have been with birth control, and the next thing I knew I was pregnant with Courtney. I think that changed him more than anything. He even went to Lamaze classes with me and he rushed to the hospital when Courtney was born. You should have seen the look on his face when he first held Courtney."

"Was he a good father?"

"Oh, yeah, he doted on Courtney like she was a little princess . . . which she is."

Then I asked something that was bothering me. "Did he believe in God? I mean, at the end."

"Probably not. I don't know. Who the hell knows what goes on in someone else's head? He did say he was glad to wake up every day. He felt he'd been reborn. That's something, right?"

49

J ILL WANTED TO SEE OUR HOME TOWN, Gackle. It was close to where we were going anyhow, so we drove into town. I hadn't been back since my mother passed away in 1989. Admittedly, this was not the best time of year to show her the town. In the summer, when the trees and lawns are green, everything looked quite different. Now with piles of dirty snow lining the streets, it only looked drab, dour, and dull.

I could see more businesses were boarded then ten years ago, although a three-block-long business district still had a few businesses holding on: Dee's Café, Tastee Freez, a hair salon, a bank, the Co-op Oil Company, a grain elevator, an insurance company, Syde Street Ceramics, a post office, two trucking companies, Dani's Bar, a senior citizens center, a nursing home, and a funeral home. Miraculously, the movie theater survived, although it only showed previously released movies May through September. For recreation Gackle had a nine-hole pubic golf course, the Alfred Lehr Park, tennis courts, and the Gackle Pool, open summers only, of course. The city could be proud it preserved at least a remnant of an active community. Many small North Dakota towns had less or were boarded up entirely. People drove to larger cities to shop at Walmart or the Dollar Store, or bought online. The small towns that remained just wait to blow away.

The public school I attended for twelve years was still open, now with 106 students in grades seven through twelve, about half of the enrollment when I went there, and that likely would decline in the years to come. Fewer kids came up through the elementary school every year and the high school had already consolidated with the Streeter, North Dakota, High School and was called the Gackle-Streeter High School.

Jill and I stopped at Dee's Café. Two dirt-streaked pickups and one car were parked outside, the only vehicles on the street in the entire town. When we entered, the eight or so customers turned to look at us, all senior citizens. The café only had seven tables, but one corner had a few crafts and knick-knacks for sale. We took a table by the wall and the waitress brought us coffee without asking. I ordered eggs over-easy with bacon, sausage, and toast, and Jill ordered an omelet and bacon.

After maybe ten minutes, an old fellow, wearing a Weist Trucking hat, and pulling a green oxygen tank on two small wheels behind him, came over to our table and stood there scrutinizing me.

"Aren't you one of the Penner boys?" he finally asked.

I recognized him as a rancher who used to live about five miles north of us and it took me a moment, but his name came to me. "Hello, Mr. Muller, it's good to see you."

"Yah, I thought that was you. You look just like your dad. Come back to see the town, eh?" he said in a low wheezing voice.

"Just driving through. We thought we'd stop for a bite to eat. This is Jill Johnson, a friend . . . well . . . fiancée . . . Jake's fiancée."

He looked at her as if he was trying to place her and said in German, "*Aye, aber du bist a shoenes maedle*," (Oh, but you are a pretty girl) and then in English, "You're not from around here, are you? I always remember the girls."

"I'm from Bismarck, but it's nice to meet you," Jill said.

"Bismarck, eh. That's a big city now. I can't drive there anymore. Too many cars. Whoosh, whoosh, everybody in a hurry."

He took a suck on his oxygen hose. "Yah, I was sorry to hear about Jake. He was a good basketball player. I remember when he played in that championship game against Medina. Scored a lot of points. He had a good jump shot."

It didn't surprise me he remembered, even though that game was over thirty years ago.

"How are you doing?" I asked. "Still ranching?"

"Nah, I quit that ten years ago. Weren't no money in it anymore, and I got the emphysema. Cigarettes you know . . . still sneak a few now and then. Figure it don't make much difference now. Damage been done, so I might was well enjoy myself," he chuckled.

I was not sure how to respond to that. "How's Alpha?" I asked.

"Oh . . . she passed a few years back. After that I moved to town. Now I just chase the young ladies around here," he said, loud enough for the table of elderly women, all in their seventies and eighties, to hear, and one of them looked up and he winked at her.

We chatted for a few more minutes, then he said it was good to see me and shuffled back to his seat dragging his oxygen tank.

"The last of the Marlboro cowboys," Jill said quietly.

"You got that right."

We tore into our breakfasts and then lingered over coffee. I was still curious for more missing pieces of Jake's story. "Did Jake ever say anything to you about the bank robbery?" I asked.

"It took years for that to come out but, yeah, eventually he talked about it. I think it was complicated for him to understand, let alone explain to someone else. Life is like that, you know. There's not just one reason that people do the things they do. There are a lot of reasons. I call it the rule of seven. I like to think that there are at least seven reasons for any explanation of human behavior."

"Umm . . . okay . . . but what were Jake's seven reasons?"

"Well, I don't know all of them, but one was that he and Spencer were just living day to day, with no idea for the future. That can lead to trouble. Another reason was they needed some money, and a bank seemed like the logical place to get it. That's pretty basic. Let's see . . . a third reason is that they were high, which impaired their judgment . . . obviously. Another was that they were bored and needed some excitement."

She thought for a minute. "Oh, yeah, they thought it would be cool to tell their friends some day that they had robbed a bank. Sounds stupid, but Jake said the speed made him think things like that. So that's five reasons. Hmm, I'm not sure what the sixth reason was, but the seventh was that Jake said that he and Spencer had both lost their girlfriends, and they just didn't give a damn about anything."

When she said this, I thought of Yvette and my role in all that. I took a deep breath. "Can I tell you something I've never told anyone else?"

"Sure, you can tell me anything."

I confessed everything to her about how I had sex with Yvette and that led to their breakup. I talked for a long time and told her the whole sordid history. When I finished, the last thing I said was, "I don't think I can ever get over that. I mean, think about it . . . you said it yourself, that was one of the reasons for the bank robbery."

She looked at me and was quiet a minute and I could tell she was thinking about how to respond. "First of all, you were just a kid with your hormones raging. What you did was wrong, but don't make it out to be a moral Armageddon. Second, you need to forgive yourself. It was almost twenty-five years ago, for God's sake."

"It doesn't seem that long ago to me."

"Well, it was. You know, I have another rule of seven, the second rule of seven, I call it. It says that people shouldn't blame themselves for stuff they did more than seven years ago. I read one time that every cell in your body is replaced and renewed every seven years. So if you think about it, your physical body is really never more than seven years old. It looks identical, except for aging, and you have the same DNA, but it's really new. In essence, you're a new person. So I made up the second rule of seven thinking that if you're a new person every seven years, it'd be stupid to blame yourself for something your old self did." She looked into my eyes and smiled. "What do you think?"

"You're full of rules of seven," I said.

"You mean, as in full of shit?" she asked. But she smiled again. I loved it when she did that.

"No, that's not what I mean," I said. "But you are obviously a more forgiving person than I am."

"I don't know about that. But try it sometime."

We got up. I paid for our breakfast. Then I noticed the sour cream raisin pie in the display case. I loved sour cream raisin pie. I bought the entire pie to go.

50

WE TURNED EAST ONTO THE ROAD where Jake had his fatal accident. The yellow police tape was gone, but I knew the exact spot. It was one of those rare windless days in North Dakota as we got out of the car, the sky was a depthless diamond blue, the air was clear and cool, and perhaps because of that, it felt as if time had stopped. Jill followed as I walked out to the slough and showed her where it happened. There was no longer any sign of the accident, and it seemed serene, the landscape quiet and cloaked in a whispery white. Even the snow-covered muskrat huts on the slough appeared frozen in time.

We stood there for some time and looked around. I felt happy I'd came back here on this day. As we walked back to the car, Jill said, "I guess if he had chosen how to die, it would have been quick like that and on his motorcycle. He was crazy about that motorcycle, you know. He said it was the opposite of prison. He would ride for hours sometimes on old back country roads to clear his mind. He used to ride down to the motorcycle rally in Sturgis, South Dakota, every year, too. He loved that."

"Really?" I said.

"Oh, yeah, despite what I've been telling you about what a great guy your brother was, and he really was, he still had a little bit of the wild streak in him and he liked to play the bad boy sometimes. He wasn't an angel all the time either. Let me put it that way."

Then she went to the car and took out the small white cross and some fresh flowers she had brought. I didn't see any way we were going to stick that cross in the frozen ground and told her so, but she wanted me to try. It seemed hopeless and I looked in the trunk for a shovel, but there was nothing. *Damn, I should have checked before I left.* Finally, I took out the tire iron and used my boot to scrape away the snow and began to hack at the ground with the tire iron. I spent a half-hour hacking away until I got down about ten inches. I set the cross in the hole and used a few rocks from the side of the road to prop it up. She laid down the flowers next to the cross, and we both stood quietly for a few minutes. I prayed for Jake, and I expect she did, as well. After a moment, she gently took my hand, interlocking her fingers in mine, and gave it a slight squeeze, and we walked back to the car.

Afterwards she asked me to show her where the Chicken Ranch was. It was about fifteen miles from the site of the accident. I hadn't seen it for over twenty years, but I was not surprised that the house and barn were now abandoned. The barn had blown partly down on one side, but the house was still standing, the windows and doors boarded up. We walked around it and I told her stories about Jake's life there, the good stories, because those are the ones that matter in the end.

Epilogue
June 2005

I WOKE UP EARLY. The alarm clock read 6:00 a.m. I couldn't sleep so I just lay there. The sun rose early in the morning in the North Dakota summer and the room was already bathed in a soft light.

I'd left the Order of St. Benedict ten months after Jake's funeral and I was no longer a monk. I lived in Bismarck where I worked in administration at St. Mary's University, not as high a position as I used to have, but I still enjoyed the work, most of the time. At least my life did not seem as hectic since I no longer needed to rush between work and prayer services. I had time, like this Saturday morning, to let my mind wander, and as I watched the light filter through the blinds, I thought about the evening before my brother left for the army. I distinctly remember that I had a tan bedspread with Conestoga Wagons pulled by teams of horses. Indians swarmed the wagons, and the driver and someone in the rear of the wagons were shooting at the Indians. I had been lying on top of that bed cover reading, my book propped open on my chest, and my eyes were just starting to droop when my brother came in. He had a large stack of comics and *Mad Magazines,* which he set on my dresser. He said, "Here. I want you to have these. You can read them while I'm gone."

I thought that was cool. I loved comics and was just getting to the age where I also liked to read *Mad Magazine* although my mother wouldn't let me buy them because she considered them too mature.

"Wow, thanks!"

"You take care of yourself now, Buckaroo."

"I will. You take care of yourself too . . . are you scared?"

"Nah, it's those commies who should be scared."

"What if you get shot?"

"That's not going to happen, little guy . . . but if I did die . . . well, you'd need to hold down the fort around here."

"Okay . . . don't worry . . . nothing's going to happen to you . . . bye . . . you're a good brother, Jake."

"So are you, Buckaroo, so are you."

Now, so many years later, I thought about the narratives of our lives and the lives of others and how sometimes those narratives are false, mere fiction, and we don't have the time, or don't take the time, or don't have the strength or the courage to correct them. I know now there are two narratives about every person's life. If we choose to focus on the good, we have one story to tell, and if we choose to focus on the bad, we have another. I've learned, too, that there are many things that determine our narratives, some known and some unknown, and that we should not be so quick to judge others in our ignorance.

I heard a train whistle in the distance, the Northern Pacific train crossing the state in a hurry to get somewhere else. I was about to get up when Jill rolled over and placed her thin arm across my chest. "Good morning," she said and kissed me lightly on the lips. I looked at her face in the soft light and thought I was the luckiest man in the world to have married her. *Thank you, God.*

"I feel the baby kicking," she said.

"Where?"

She pulled up her nightgown and took my hand and placed it on her stomach.

"There. Do you feel it?"

I don't feel a thing, but I waited. Then, there it was. A tiny little kick. Unmistakable.

"Yes, I felt it that time!"

"Our little Jacob is kicking up a storm."

"Well, it could be a girl."

"I suppose so. We still need to decide on a girl's name."

"If it's a girl, she'll be a nun, so we should name her Sister Agnes or Sister Bertha or something."

"Yeah right, Bozo."

We got up and dressed and walked out to the kitchen. Soon Courtney would wake up. She was an early riser, too, and we'd pour her cereal and watch her eat and take her to riding class.

Peace.